Dreams Can Come True

Born on the Wirral just after the Second World War, Vivienne Dockerty has always been a great storyteller. Her sagas are based on the amazing lives of her Irish ancestors and continue through each generation until her own autobiography in the 1960s.

Also by Vivienne Dockerty

Song for Ireland

A Woman Undefeated
Dreams Can Come True

VIVIENNE DOCKERTY

Dreams Can Come True

CANELO

First published in the United Kingdom in 2011 by Matador UK, an imprint
of Troubador Publishing Ltd

This edition published in the United Kingdom in 2021 by

Canelo
31 Helen Road
Oxford OX2 0DF
United Kingdom

A CIP catalogue record for this book is available from the British Library.

Print ISBN 978 1 80032 273 8
Ebook ISBN 978 1 80032 066 6

Look for more great books at www.canelo.co

Printed and bound in Great Britain by Clays Ltd, Elcograf S.p.A.

Chapter 1

Katie tried in vain to get her very large mother off the mattress. She was quite a big girl herself, but her mother's bulk defeated her.

"I'm going ter have to get a doctor to yer," Katie gasped. "That leg is getting worse now. It seems to be growing bigger by the day and I don't like the look of those running sores at all."

Ruthie slapped at her daughter's hand in frustration and fell back, grumbling in annoyance.

"Yer know we can't afford no doctors, Katie. Just go and get some bilberries from that bush down the lane. They seem to ease me. You'll have to get me up, girl, I need ter piss. Unless yer want me to do it in the bed. Can't see how they made yer a nurse, when yer can't even lift yer own mother. Oh, give me a minute, will yer? I'll get there me bloomin' self."

Ruthie rocked from side to side until she eventually rolled off onto the cold flagged floor. She crawled on her hands and knees, swearing and muttering painfully, while Katie tried to keep her mother's dirty, floor-length nightdress from catching on the uneven flags, or winding round her swollen legs.

It was a long and pitiful process, made worse by the distance involved in getting Ruthie to the lavvy anyway.

It was housed in a shed attached to the cottage, a replacement for the midden that they had been used to before.

Life had not got any better for Ruthie Tibbs since the days that she was Maggie Haines, the Irish immigrant's, neighbour. Ruthie was still allowed to live in Farmer Briggs' tied cottage, even though Solly, her husband, had died two years before. He'd been found dead in a ditch on a cold winter's night on his way back from his favourite hostelry, but Ernie, Ruthie's grown-up son, was able to step into his father's shoes. Ernie had never had a regular job, preferring to make his living as a wild fowler, paddling the punt he had carved himself along the coast of the Dee estuary. He was five feet ten, big framed, muscle-bound and just the person to fill the vacancy at the farm.

Ruthie spent most of her days lying on the mattress in the living room-cum-kitchen of Thistledown Cottage, counting the injustices that had visited her poverty-stricken life. Solly, her husband, had gone, and her elder son had joined the army and hadn't even bothered to visit in nearly ten years. Her disabled boy, Lenny, God bless him, had been taken from her. Died in his sleep with no bother to anyone. Then there was Annie, a mouthy girl who'd got married to Sam Piper a few years before. She only came to visit on high days and holidays, too busy with those kids of hers to come along to see her Mam.

Out of all her family, Katie seemed to have made something of herself. Though her attendance had been poor, she had managed to learn to read and write at the local infant school and had been rewarded with a job as a probationer nurse, at the newly-built cottage hospital. She had found it hard going, working long hours and studying to the level needed to pass the staff nurse examination, especially as her mother's illness left her relying on Katie more.

"Didn't yer say yer were goin' to ask one of them doctors at the hospital what could be wrong with me?" asked Ruthie, when she inched her way back from the privy.

"Mam, they're like gods up there. Someone like me would never dream of even lookin' in their direction, never mind askin' them a question. No, I think I'm goin' to ask the local doctor to call. You can't go on like this, you know."

"I told yer, doctors cost money and we got none. I've had legs like tree trunks fer years, though now I'm older they don't seem to hold me up like they used to do. Will yer get more money when yer pass this examination? Maybe we could wait 'til then or ask Ernie fer some."

"I'll get more money, Mam, but I don't know how much it'll be. I know me uniform will change though. From a grey dress with a white belt to a striped grey dress and a blue belt. I'll still have me starched cuffs and apron with me lacy bonnet and warm woollen cloak."

Katie puffed her chest out proudly as she explained the changes to her mother.

"Are yer legs worse than usual today? Perhaps I could ask the chemist if they have some kind of salve. If not, I could borrow a little money from the Sheldon Loan Company to pay fer a doctor. They don't charge much interest, I could repay it in a couple of weeks or so."

Ruthie tried to pull herself up again in her agitation. "Yer'll not go anywhere near that place, our Katie! That woman has made her money off the backs of people like me. When yer dad was alive and he had spent all the wages up at the Wheatsheaf, I had ter go and see that Mr.

3

'Arrinton. I didn't know she owned that loan place then, I thought 'Arrinton did, until yer dad told me what she'd bin up to. It was talk of the village fer weeks, yer know."

Katie pushed her mother back down gently and told her not to get so excited, just to take a good deep breath, relax and start again.

"This Maggie. Maggie Haines, her name is. She came over from Ireland with a load of other immigrants and her and her husband got a job with Farmer Briggs. Yer dad helped Jack, her husband, by setting up fighting matches fer him, 'cos Jack was a pugilist. Anyway, we used to be good friends, me and Maggie. She lived at Lilac Cottage just up the way. We were always poppin' in and out of each other's cottages havin' cups of tea. I was even the one who told her she was expectin', that's how close we were. Then, one night at a fightin' match, yer dad got accused of stealin' some money that belonged ter Jack and he got banged up in Neston Jail. Not one of them lifted a finger ter get him out and he sat in that stinkin' prison fer two days. He was never right after, didn't like being closed in, yer see. Then before we knew it they'd gone. Dumped all her unwanted things on me and went to live with the mother-in-law. Well, I never saw her fer months after, 'til one day she came lookin' fer our Annie. Wanted yer sister to be a nursemaid, fer this babby I said she was expectin', but this time she was livin' at Selwyn Lodge! That big place on Burton Road. Yer know where Ernie said they've built that thingy fer horses? Well, the house belonged to the dressmaker, Miss Rosemary, and that left-footer got herself in with her. Then our Annie told me the rest, though they never took her on as a nursemaid. It seems that this Maggie told everyone that her husband Jack had died and she started seein' this man. He was a

4

sea captain, who lodged at the Brown Horse Pub. Then it turns out, so that woman Madeline who lives at the pub as well said, that the husband wasn't dead at all. The family had pretended he was dead, because he'd got some woman up the duff and he and her had gone ter America. Seems he's back now and they've got even more money, 'cos he came back a rich man as well! So, if I was dying of these legs tomorrer, yer not ter go to the Sheldon Loan Company. 'Cos I'd rather be buried in a pauper's grave like yer dad was then go cap in hand ter them."

"I know who yer mean now," said Katie. "There's a son called Mikey and a daughter called Hannah. I've seen them together in the family's carriage, or sometimes walking their great big dogs. I used to see them when I was comin' home from school. In those days the nursemaid walked them down to the promenade, 'cos they went to a private school down there."

"Yeah, the local school wasn't good enough fer them. When I think how I put meself out makin' sure yer got a good education, takin' yer up ter Lily's barrow on the market and findin' yer good clothes ter wear. I said ter meself, Ruthie, I got a clever child here. Don't know where she gets it from, but it's not from Solly's side."

Katie smiled to herself. Strange how older people could look back and everything was rosy in their memories. As soon as Annie, her sister, had got a job as an alter-ation hand, it was herself who had taken over helping out her mother. She had been six at the time, but Ruthie had made full use of her. She looked after Lenny, her poor, now dead, brother; she went to the grocer's for messages when she couldn't even see over the counter to pay the man. Then, there was the school that Katie had demanded that she went to. She had seen the children playing through the railings and had asked a girl, what they did in there all day? Sums and reading, was the reply. For weeks she had nagged to be allowed to go, took the cuffs and blows from Ruthie and the nasty remarks from her dad, but eventually she wore them down. Though it had been very difficult, with Ruthie finding all sorts of reasons why she shouldn't go, it had become a necessity to her. An urge to learn, to find out more about the world beyond the cottage. Her mother had never been out of Neston and she didn't want to end up being the same.

"You got any interestin' cases up there, our Katie? What 'appened ter that old woman that kept failin' on the floor?"

"Oh, yer mean poor Dolly? She should be up at Clatterbridge hospital really. She's cloggin' up a bed that could be used fer a sick person. Someone like yerself, aye Mam, if yer don't get yer legs sorted out. Well, there is a new patient. His name is Joe Collins. He works as a labourer over at Haven Farm. Seems he was workin' in a marl pit, yer know digging out the sea shells fer spreadin' on the fields and his fork went through his boot. His foot ballooned up so much that he had to hop all the way ter the hospital on one leg. That's nearly a mile or so. He couldn't speak fer the pain of it, but I felt so sorry, because that was the farm where they had the rinderpest last year. Not only that, but I remember some of his family, when they came to stay at the hospital to get over the cholera. His dad died of it and his younger brother, but his mother and Tilly, his sister, came and stayed a few weeks. They say that where our hospital stands, it benefits from the gusting wind that comes over the salt marshes. Not like the fever ward at Clatterbridge. It used ter be a workhouse yer know, but they closed it down a few years ago."

Ruthie shuddered. "Yer don't have ter remind me. Many a time I thought we'd end up in there, especially when yer dad went on the piss, so I didn't get no wages to spend. When I was younger I used ter fight him fer it. I'd get him under me arm and squeeze him 'til the pips popped, but sometimes he was cunnin' and he wouldn't come home fer his tea. But one thing I'll say in defence of yer dad, he always said it was best to live down here near the estuary. Down here we've got the spring water, up in the village they've got open sewers. They might have piped water, but the sewage gets into it, even if the authorities said the infection was carried in the air. No, that's why you'll never see me in any hurry to mix with the villagers. It carried me folks off in '44."

"Well, they're settin' up a waterworks now, seems they've learnt their lesson. I remember Tilly tellin' me that all their beddin' had ter be burnt and they had to apply ter the Board of Guardians fer compensation. Said they got a voucher, which the authorities paid fer and they went ter Frogerty's in Chester and got a new bed!"

"That's her again. Got her hand in everythin'. Bounty vouchers, property, loans and rest of it. I heard tell she made a fortune, sellin' the land she'd bought to the railway company, so that they could bring the train ter Neston. What do they say our Katie, money makes money? All I can say is that one day the mighty will fall and I hope I'll still be here, ter see the day."

"I can hear our Ernie, Mam, comin' down the path. It'll be time fer me ter get up te the hospital. I'll call in the chemists in the mornin' on me way back."

Katie went to put her cloak on. She was so proud to be seen in her distinctive cloak and bonnet; folk always nodded and smiled as she passed them by. She had put her light brown wavy hair into a bun at the nape of her neck and glanced down at her large plump hands to check that there was no dirt under her fingernails. Matron was a stickler for cleanliness and Katie hadn't realised what a slattern her mother was until she had been shown round the hospital near Neston Green.

"Hello there, Sis'. Not made yer Matron yet?"

"Get away with yer, our Ernie. I'm still waitin' te hear if I'm ter become a staff nurse, never mind a Matron. But I'll get there, I promise, one day."

"I'm just hoping I'm never struck down with an illness, our Katie. The first thing yer'll do if I come to yer place, is ter stick one of them tubes up me bum. Ter pay me back fer all the ragging yer've had off me."

Katie smiled with affection at her brother. He had turned out to be a really special man. He used to be very withdrawn when his father was around, going off for days on end, never saying where he had been. Once Solly was buried, Ernie seemed to thrive on the responsibility of keeping hearth and home together, happy to take his father's place as a farm hand and to look after his mother, when Katie wasn't home. He was a fine-looking man, with kind eyes, a neat, thin nose and with a moustache and short beard that suited him. Katie couldn't understand why none of the village girls had thrown their cap at him. Maybe there was a girl, but Ernie wouldn't say. As for herself, she was not looking for a lifetime partner. She wanted to dedicate herself to caring for the sick for the rest of her days. She did not rule out a chance romance with a tall and handsome doctor, but for the moment she was satisfied. Doing things for other people brought its own rewards.

"Can yer help me off with these boots before yer go, Katie? Mother hasn't got the strength in her fingers any more. They're that tight today. I've bin' workin' in six inches of water over Cock's Hill. Farmer wants the field ploughin' tomorrer, though I think we'll all be sinkin' in the mud. Oh, I must tell yer before yer go. Briggs is puttin' up some of his land fer sale, Lower Rake Meadow, Claypool and Daisy Croft. Says he's gettin' on now and wants to have some money fer his retirement, especially as he has no sons to carry the farmin' on. I think he'll keep me, 'cos I'm the youngest and fittest, but I think they'll be building houses all along there soon."

"Well, I think it'll be good fer the village. There's too many young couples havin' to live with their parents. Yer only have ter look at our Annie and Sam," Katie said.

"Yeah, and where would they get the money from to buy these fine new houses?" Ruthie, who had been listening, piped up from where she lay.

Katie laughed and replied to her mother. "The Sheldon Loan Company?"

–

The proprietor of the Sheldon Loan Company was at that moment sitting in the place she called her office, in the smallest bedroom of Sclwyn Lodge. It had been raining most of the day, so she had taken the opportunity to spend some time scrutinising her bank accounts.

She had chosen this room to work from, because of the panoramic views from the window, which overlooked the Dee estuary to her beloved Welsh hills, six miles away – not that she had ever travelled across the water to visit this wondrous place, as Maggie was a home bird and disliked being far away.

Her eyes were tired and she felt a certain lethargy. She had been feeling like this for a while now, ever since her good friend and companion, Miss Rosemary, had died early the year before. Nothing had seemed the same since then. No more sitting comfortably together in the evenings, sipping sherry before they had their meal, no more discussions on the businesses they owned or chuckling over a happening in their day. That was what their relationship was all about. Maggie and Betty, as she called Miss Rosemary, Maggie and Betty against the world. There had been a forty-year age gap between them, but they had been soul mates, caring for each other as good friends should. Now there was no one to fill that gap. She had her husband and there were the children, but they all got on with whatever interested them and only met up in the evenings for meals.

Jack, her husband, had become involved in the horse racing business. Mikey, her son, was the front man for the company they ran. Hannah, her stepdaughter, attended college in nearby Chester. It was a sort of finishing school for young ladies, but they learnt to do household accounts as well.

Maggie toyed with the silver ink well that Betty had given her one time as a present. Such a long time ago now – nearly twenty years. The dressmaker had been the only one in the village of Neston to give the raggedy Irish immigrant girl a chance. Without her, Maggie would never have risen to the status she was enjoying now. She would probably still be a farm labourer's wife, giving birth to a child each year.

Poor Betty. The harsh winter had brought down the young and the elderly. Though Selwyn Lodge was quite a warm place, Betty would still insist on venturing out in her dog cart to play canasta with her elderly friends from the church. She had caught a chill and too weak to throw it off and she had died. Maggie had felt like a wounded animal; she had felt her friend's death more than she had mourned when her own dear mother had gone. She still looked at the chair that Betty had sat in, expecting her to be sat in it, still thought she heard Betty's tread on the stairway, still expected to greet her friend at breakfast each morning and still looked out into the garden to see if she was pottering there.

It had been the company that Maggie and Betty had started, that had kept her sane over that following year: that and the inheritance that her friend had left her. So much to sort through and so much to gain. Selwyn Lodge had been given to Maggie, with a request that it be loved as much as Betty had loved it. A thousand pounds from the good lady's bank account and every thing that was Betty's share, in all that they owned together. Thus, Maggie became the outright owner of the Sheldon Loan and Property Company. She couldn't believe how her initial investment had grown.

At seventeen, she had entrusted Miss Rosemary with the secret contents of the feather mattress that she had brought with her from her old home. Little did she know that the mattress held her ex-employer's Granddad Filbey's savings, until she came across the money while stitching up a loosened seam. The dressmaker had started a small company for Maggie which had gone from strength to strength, giving her protégé's money out as loans. Then she had merged it with her own rental interests and the Sheldon Loan and Property Company had been born.

"Mrs. Haines," Olive, her maid, knocked urgently on the door.

"Cook wants ter know if the Master will be in for supper. Do yer know if he's coming back tonight?"

Maggie opened the door to her maid, glad of the interruption. Maybe she should go and wallow in a hot bath, then lay herself down for an hour.

"I think so, Olive, I didn't ask him this morning. But he probably will be, he's only gone to Chester today."

The maid bobbed a curtsey and ran off down the stairs to the kitchen. She had only been working at Selwyn Lodge for a week or so and Maggie felt she had a lot to learn. Mary, the maid before Olive, had been a faithful servant from the start, but had gone back home to nurse her mother. Things had changed so much since Betty had died. She felt bereft now that her friend wasn't there.

Maggie lay in her comforting bath and thought back to when her husband had made his reappearance. It had been a few years after she had said goodbye to Johnny, the sea-going son of her friend from Killala, who had marriage to her on his mind. He hadn't known that her husband, Jack was still alive and living in America, so had set his sights on Maggie. The house, the businesses and easy living were what attracted him. Neither of them were sure that it was love they felt for each other.

Johnny only really loved his mother and when she had died, he had looked for a comfortable berth. Maggie was drawn to his handsome looks and became confused with his attention, thinking that perhaps one day she may fall in love. Throughout it all was Betty, the voice of Maggie's conscience.

"You must tell him that you're not free to marry. It isn't fair for you to lead him on."

So, the next time Johnny came back to Neston, Maggie had told him her story. How Jack had got a young woman into trouble and the pair had gone to America to start a new life. To save a scandal, she'd had to keep a secret — that his disappearance had been because of his untimely death.

Talk about a woman scorned! Johnny had exploded, angry that he had discharged himself from the shipping company, just to be with her! The next thing she knew, the tale was all round the village, spread by Johnny's sister-in-law, Madeline. Of course that was the end of the relationship with Maddy, as Betty sacked her from her job as a designer at the dressmaker's shop.

Sadly things started going down hill at 'Anne Rose-mary's'. Nobody in the village wanted to associate with the two women, who they had been told were a pair of liars. The older woman must have become inveigled; look how she had taken the Irish one to live in that grand house of hers. But though it was heartbreaking for Betty to close her business down, they had the loan company to give them an income and no one knew that Maggie had a share.

Then one day Alice, Jack's mother, received a letter. Since the story of Jack's disappearance had got around the village, things hadn't gone well between her and her daughter-in-law. Though Alice still went to St. Winefred's Church on a Sunday and was involved in some of the activities there, she had quickly let it be known that they had been told Jack was dead by his landlady and they had only just found out that he was still alive! He had sent her a letter to say that all was well and he was living in America. That story seemed to satisfy her friends amongst the congregation, but Alice let rip at Maggie, saying that it was all her fault that this uproar had occurred. The relationship cooled, not that it bothered either of them as they didn't have a lot of love for one another, until the day that the letter came to Seagull Cottage and everything began to change.

"I've had enough of the fighting game," the scribe had written on Jack's behalf. "I've made enough money to live comfortably, so I'll be settling my affairs and be coming home."

That had put the cat amongst the pigeons. Alice was overjoyed at her son's homecoming, but Maggie was dreading her husband's return.

"He'll be able to move in with you all at the big house," Alice had said. "Mikey will get his father back and you your husband as well. He'll be able to take over that company you make such a fuss about. Change its name ter Haines!"

No mention of Hannah; surely Jack would be a father to her as well. And the thought of Jack interfering with the business gave Maggie palpitations. It was Betty's company too! She walked round in dread for days on end, though Betty said there was nothing that Jack could do. The business had been started with Maggie's own money. He had gone away hadn't he, leaving her and Mikey to fend for themselves?

Maggie smiled to herself as she wrapped a towel around her body and then walked into the bedroom that the pair of them shared. Jack had been delighted with her good fortune, pleased as punch that she accepted him back again and spent all his waking moments showing her how much she was loved. She wished she could get rid of this listless feeling, because life at the moment should be very good. She had just received the statement from the bank, showing the amount lodged by the railway company for the land they had bought. With what she had in the account already, becoming a millionairess got nearer every day!

Maggie put on her loose-flowing gown that she liked to wear when she was relaxing. She had made it herself on the treadle machine that they had brought to Selwyn Lodge from the dressmaker's shop. It was a pretty shade of blue and she had matching slippers on her feet. She brushed her hair until it shone, then tied it up with ribbons on the back of her head.

She glanced at the clock on the bedroom mantelpiece. Still another hour before Mikey or Hannah would make an appearance. Mikey only had to walk from the village, while Hannah came from Chester on the train.

She had given the responsibility of overseeing the Sheldon Loan and Property Company to Mikey. His private education had equipped him to give orders and to be her front man. Maggie still had problems being accepted as a business woman, men still thinking that a woman's place was in the home. Mr. Arlington, Betty's right hand man still worked for them, though he was getting on in years. Mr. Peel, who was younger went out to get the business. Mikey was the man at the company's helm. They had moved into premises across the High Street, when Betty had closed the shop and rented out the original to a woman who sold handmade baby clothes.

Maggie took a peek into her cheval mirror. She didn't look so bad for a woman of nearly thirty seven. A slim figure still and not too many facial lines – though she didn't like the look of those smudges that sat drearily under her eyes. Maybe she should take a holiday, somewhere distant, somewhere warm. Jack was always saying the family should go on holiday together, but he was talking of foreign lands like France or Italy. Maggie was thinking of somewhere nearer; she had heard that the south of England could be very warm.

"The master's here," shouted Olive, her voice floating up from the bottom of the stairs. Maggie's heart skipped a beat. Jack had come home earlier than she had thought he would. She walked demurely down to greet him.

"Thought I would surprise yer me darlin' girl. P'raps we could sit together in the conservatory and have our afternoon tea. See to it Olive, if yer would. Now, tell me, Maggie, what yer've been doing with yer day?"

Jack smiled at her happily. His wife was looking a picture and sure that colour suited her. Maggie had a lot of style. He mourned the time that he had been away from her, thinking only of his selfish needs. He had been a proper eejit leaving her to go in pursuit of his dreams. Though they wouldn't have their Hannah if he hadn't have done so. She was the spit of her mother, Kitty May and pretty and bubbly with it and the kindest heart for a girl so young. Maggie had been a princess taking another woman's child on like she had. Not that Hannah knew that Maggie wasn't her mother. What was the point of dragging up the past?

Jack had changed since he had come home to Maggie. Facially he was still the same, with the crooked nose and the pale blue eyes, though his skin wasn't weather-beaten any more. And, underneath his fine clothes lurked a roll of fat around his waist, where before he had been hard with muscle. He wore his fair hair in the fashion of the day, parted in the middle with long bushy side burns and a pencil thin moustache. But his personality had mellowed. He had been so grateful that Maggie had given him a second chance that he would have moved heaven and earth for her. And when she had said he could move in with her at Selwyn Lodge — well, what more could he have had? He had even been welcomed by the lady who was known as Miss Rosemary. Not a trace of bitterness was shown by her, even though she must have felt he was an intruder in her home.

Jack smiled to himself as he thought back to when he had arrived at Seagull Cottage. He had stared in disbelief at Alice, when she had told him that Maggie and Mikey didn't live there any more.

His mother had been triumphant, telling him that they had gone to live with the dressmaker at a grand place on Burton Road, but he was welcome to stay with his parents for as long as he chose. What had he expected, she asked him? That his wife was sitting waiting, nursing his two children, everything going to be as it was before. Then when she told him of what had gone on to cover his disappearance, he felt mortified. What purgatory his wife must have gone through, to shield scandal from the family name. He was determined to make things up to her. His promoter days had brought him wealth that now they both could share. She wouldn't have to work again, they'd buy a pleasant house on the sea front and Maggie could sit on the window seat and dream like she had before.

Jack had been unprepared for the shock he felt when he found the place where she was living. It was the same house he had coveted when they had walked passed it all those years ago. He had felt glad he had donned the best clothes in his wardrobe; his long tan double breasted jacket, matching tie and light brown trousers, which brought out the fairness of his hair.

He had hung around on the corner waiting for some courage to appear. Then there Maggie was, walking up the road towards him, with two darling children linked into her arms. A solemn-looking boy of twelve or thirteen and a pert and pretty doll of a girl.

Jack's heart had been awash with the sentimentality of the occasion and he could only stand and stare.

Maggie had just smiled when she noticed him, saying softly that she knew he would come back one day. Not an ounce of censure, not a trace of bitterness; she just introduced the children and said it was their father who had returned from overseas. What a wonderful person, to be so forgiving after the way she had been treated. Though he found out later, the reconciliation didn't come without strings!

Jack turned to look upon Maggie as she showed him a letter that had come from the Bank Manager. He still couldn't read, but saw that the letter looked official. She told him that a meeting had been requested, at any time convenient to her.

That had been one of Maggie's conditions before she agreed to take him back again. She had managed without a husband and without his input for many years, employing Mr. Arlington who had taken her businesses into serious growth. There was no room for another boss; he would have to like it or lump it. Jack chose to like it, as financially he didn't care. He had plans of his own that involved the training of race horses. He already knew a man called Paddy Fearon, who he had met on the fighting circuit in Chicago. The man had agreed to use his contacts back home in Ireland, to make Jack an even wealthier man!

"So, what I was thinkin', Jack," Maggie's voice chimed into his thoughts. "I was thinkin' of starting up a building company. It could be incorporated into Sheldon Property. What do you think? Would it work? I'll need a foreman and his gang of men, something similar to when they were building the railway. I need another sort of investment, rather than leave it all in the bank account. Betty was always saying that money made money and it's true. This statement says I'm on me way ter becomin' a millionaire. When I think that I found seventeen pounds in that dirty old mattress and that was just the start of it. And don't go saying it was your money. I made six little sacks fer your money to go in!"

It was said with pride, because Jack was always teasing her. If he hadn't got the mattress off Alice for her when they'd all come over in the boat, she'd still be a tatty young woman working hard for her bread.

"Let's forget about you and yer millions, why don't we go upstairs and do what a loving couple should be doing?" Jack dropped a kiss on the side of Maggie's neck, then leaned his head toward hers. She moved away, pretending to swat a fly that was passing overhead. He laughed at her as she began to look a bit self-conscious.

"You weren't turning away from me in bed last night, when I tickled yer tummy and other places I could name. Come on now, me sweet colleen, an afternoon of passion will do us both good and put a bit of sparkle in those eyes of yours."

"Jack, will ye give over. Mikey will be here in half an hour and Hannah will be on her way too. What will Olive and Joan be thinkin' if we disappear off ter bed in the middle of the afternoon?"

"Yer an old misery, woman. All yer think of is countin' yer money. Well, wait 'til I get yer alone tonight, I'll be makin' up fer all our lost time!"

That had been another condition of their proposed reconciliation. There had been no question of him taking his place in her bed. It was a proper courtship that Maggie had wanted and he had to stay at Alice's house, until she was ready to have him back again. She'd been adamant, there was no way that she could be sweet-talked out of it and because Jack loved her, he took on the role of a gallant swain.

They had taken the train to Chester, a place he hadn't been to before. Maggie had shown him around the cathedral, they had walked the city walls and had tea at a little cafe at the side of the River Dee. He had bought her a pretty ring, a cluster of garnets and diamonds, with a necklace and earrings to match. She had never before been given jewellery. "You deserve them," Jack had said, "for continuing to be my wife."

Finally, she succumbed to his advances, but one further deed was to be done, before he could claim her as his own. They had to spend a weekend at the newly opened Grosvenor Hotel. It bit quite a lot into Jack's hard-earned savings, but it would be worth it in the end.

Or so Jack thought.

The last condition was voiced as they had prepared for bed in the sumptuous marital suite and Maggie announced there were to be no more babies. To give birth again after thirteen years was too much to ask of her. If he wasn't happy about it, then she would go back to Selwyn Lodge.

But Jack had been speaking to his friend Paddy, thinking that this situation might arise. Paddy knew about these things or so he had said and gave Jack a tip for this first night with his reclaimed bride.

"Maggie, me darlin', light of me life," Jack had whispered, planting little kisses on to her sweet-smelling hair. "I know *exactly* how to stop yer from expectin' a wee one. Have yer got a handkerchief in yer bag?"

Chapter 2

At exactly five o'clock, the train pulled into Neston Station and a young attractive girl alighted. She was slimly built, average height, with tawny kitten eyes in a pale oval face. She wore a dark blue travelling coat over a floor length gown of the same hue and on her brown glossy head of soft curls was a blue bonnet trimmed with matching ribbon. She glanced from left to right as she stood on the platform, as if she was looking for someone she knew. This done, she walked slowly out of the station gate on to Raby Road.

"Hannah, wait!" she heard someone shouting and looked behind to see a young man running up the hill.

Hannah looked over impatiently, then continued walking. The young man caught up with her, out of breath for a moment, but trying unsuccessfully to take hold of her arm. "What are you doing, Eddie? You know my train comes in at five o'clock. I cannot hang about waiting for you. My mother will be expecting me in the next ten minutes. Now, do get out of my way. Do."

"I'm sorry, Hannah. I had to shift some barrels into the cellar and I just forgot the time. Can I walk with you up the road a little way? Please, Hannah, I've not seen yer to speak to fer a few days."

"You cannot. Surely you heard the train as it was pulling up at the station. It makes enough noise to wake the dead. If you can't meet me on the station as we agreed you would do, then what is the use of us having snatched moments? Just make sure you are here at five o'clock tomorrow, then you can meet me in the waiting room as planned."

With that, Hannah walked up the high street and onto Burton Road, leaving the poor man wishing he hadn't promised to give his father a hand. Eddie loved every inch of Hannah Victoria Haines and guessed he had done since he was a small child. Mikey, Hannah and Eddie had been in the Selwyn Lodge nursery together – that is until his mother, Madeline had been given the sack for speaking out of turn. Eddie had been only three at the time, but for months he had felt that something was missing and life didn't get any better when his mother gave birth to another child. He was apt to wander off when she gave birth to each successive one. At seven he could be seen hanging around the promenade, or playing in the sea, or helping the fishermen load their carts from the Middle Slip or pestering the donkey man to let him have a ride. His mother didn't even notice some days that her son had gone, so busy was she with the others.

Eddie found that if he slipped out of the side door of the Brown Horse tavern where he lived, by the time the postman had made his deliveries, he could see Mikey Haines and Hannah being taken to their school on the promenade; sometimes by their mother, sometimes by the maid. He would watch, feeling jealous that he wasn't allowed to go with them. But when he had asked his mother why he couldn't go to the Halkyn School, she had said the place was for rich children and he wasn't one!

If he wanted to go to a school, she'd let him go to the Catholic one on Burton Road, but he'd have to get himself ready in the mornings, as she had no time now she was expecting another child.

Eddie hated all these babies that kept appearing in his world. He wished he belonged to the Haines family. They only had one boy and one girl.

He started wandering further afield each morning, as soon as his vigil was over at quarter past nine. Along the coast to Gayton, making friends with the wild fowlers who rowed in their punts along the shallow gullies, whilst searching for targets with their gun. Onto Gayton Cottage where lived a pleasant man, then through the abundant bracken growing twice as high as Eddie, to watch the ponies and traps on the Heswall shore, loaded up with the fishermen's catch.

Then his freedom came to an end when one day his father insisted he was running wild and he had to be taught his letters. Eddie had felt he was wearing a ball and chain – though, not for long. A few months later he began to play truant and his teacher didn't seem concerned, as Eddie was a disruptive boy and came and went as he pleased. Eventually though even she lost patience and Eddie was expelled. Ted took him on as his pot boy and he didn't go to school again.

Throughout it all the lovelorn lad still watched out for Hannah, who hardly ever glanced his way. He grew tall and strong with the heavy lifting and became more and more handsome each day.

–

Hannah walked along the road, thinking about the feelings she had for Eddie. It seemed as though he had always been there in her life. On the perimeter of course, as they both came from two very different worlds. Hers had been one of feather bedding; her parents had given her every advantage in her life. There had been piano lessons at the Halkyn School, singing lessons with Madame Dupre and her very own horse called Simba, when Jack had built stabling at the bottom of the lawn. Her friends had been from the gentry. Two girls named Cecelia and Florence Adshead had been encouraged to call. They were classmates for most of her time at the private school and Hannah had visited their home on the Chester Road, a turreted dwelling called Causey Hall. She went with them to the dances, the ones that were held monthly at the Assembly Rooms, always chaperoned by an elderly matron, who looked over the young ladies' fellow dancer's first.

One evening at the Assembly Rooms, when Hannah had recently turned seventeen, a young man presented himself and asked could he claim one of the waltzes on her dancing card? Hannah had been puzzled; the young man looked familiar, but she couldn't quite put a name to him. He was dressed very splendidly in a blue tailcoat, his fitted waistcoat was of a silver figured hue and his trousers were narrow and black. Upon his feet were patent leather shoes and his dark brown hair was pomaded into a front quiff. As he bowed low over Hannah's hand, she noticed he was wearing short white gloves. She paused and looked in the direction of the chaperone, who nodded her permission back to her. Hannah remembered that her card at the time was staring blankly up at her, because she had foolishly come without a pen. So she had agreed to dance with him quite eagerly, rather than suffering the other girls' pity for being a wallflower.

The young man had taken her in his arms and had whisked her away competently. From the start, she was enchanted by his footwork and the intricate movements that he introduced as they glided around the floor. Little did she know that it was the work of Eddie's mother, who had always been willing to practice dance steps at home with him.

Hannah had come to rest later, breathless, and glad that the young man had brought her back in one piece. Some of her peers could be heavy-footed and were a danger to a young girl's tender toes. The young man had asked if he could get her some refreshment. Again the chaperone nodded and the pair had walked to a table situated at the back of the hall. While they had sipped a refreshing glass of lemonade each, he had introduced himself as Edward Cornelius Dockerty.

"At your service, Hannah Victoria Haines," he had said in a mocking tone.

"Eddie? Oh, you were the little boy who shared our nursery! Well, you have changed, I didn't recognise you."

"And so have you changed, Hannah and may I say, delightfully so. I wonder, could I intrude upon your generosity and invite you for a stroll along the promenade one afternoon? We could catch up on where the years have taken us and perhaps get to know each other again."

"I think I should like that," Hannah had replied, overjoyed that she was planning a tryst with such an attractive young man. This would be the first time that she had ever been alone with a male, other than her father and brother and she felt she was in for an exciting time!

Had she known what an uproar that meeting would bring, she would not have readily agreed to it. They were seen walking together by Hannah's grandmama, but that was only the start of things! What had annoyed Hannah more was her parents' attitude, after they had asked who the boy's family was, then their fury when they found who they were!

"What was the son of a pub landlord doing at the Assembly Rooms? We thought it was only the better class of people who went there." This had been from Maggie, who desperately wanted Hannah to meet the right type of man acceptable to the circles that she was now engaged in. She was on the Board of Governors at the hospital, the school and the workhouse, helping to raise funds for charities. She had been under the impression that only the sons of suitable people would be allowed to dance at the Assembly Rooms.

"Yer mother has spent a lot of money on yer education," Jack had put in. "Yer a cut above these lads from the village. Why do yer think we've never allowed yer to play with the children from down there?"

"I thought it was because you didn't want me to catch anything from the locals. That was what Mother said when there was the cholera epidemic."

"Go to your room, Hannah. Young ladies do not answer back to their elders. In future yer ter be banned from attending any social occasions that involve the company of young men, unless yer mother and I have approved of it first. Understand? Yer can come down later, when yer feel yer can apologize."

"I can apologize now, Father. I am truly sorry if I have offended you or Mother."

Hannah had gone over to Jack and given him a big hug. Then she had smiled at her mother, blowing them both a kiss, and fled from the drawing room while she could.

But it hadn't ended there, thought Hannah, as she knocked on the door of Selwyn Lodge for Olive, the new maid, to come and let her in. She might be an obedient young daughter and not walk along the promenade with an unsuitable partner, but that hadn't stopped her from seeing Eddie. Where else would she find a young man who adored every bone in her body? She wasn't ready for marriage yet, so she would have some excitement while she could!

–

Next day, Eddie was there on the dot of five as the train steamed into the station. He had waited until the outgoing passengers had come from the waiting room, then had dashed inside. Eddie was no longer dressed fashionably in the clothes that his Uncle Johnny had left in the wardrobe, while he was away at sea, but in a dark grey cut-away jacket over a white collarless shirt, black fustian trousers and a small bowler hat. But he was nonetheless dashing in Hannah's eyes, as he peeped around the corner of the door while she alighted from the train. With her eyes sparkling at their daringness, she took one minute to be at his side.

"Shut the door properly, stupid," she giggled at him. Then Eddie took her in his arms. Stolen kisses seemed to be the best ones, because they both felt a thrill course through them as they abandoned all senses to each other's charms.

"Oh, that was wonderful." Hannah purred and stretched upwards as if she had just woken up from a dream. Eddie could see the outline of her bosom as she had abandoned her cloak on a nearby bench. His knees went all wobbly and he took her in his arms again.

"No, I'll have to be going," she squeaked, as his lips sought her luscious lips again. "I've been thinking. Could we have some time together in Chester? Could you manage to meet me next Wednesday afternoon? I've only got a tennis lesson then. I could say I have the cramps and have to go home to lie down in my bedroom. Could you do that, get away to Chester I mean, not come and lie down in my bedroom?"

"If only," Eddie replied. "Yes, I'll make some excuse up for me dad. I'll meet yer outside the cathedral at half past one. I can catch the one o'clock train."

So, with another hurried kiss, the couple then parted for home, to dream of what delights the following Wednesday would bring.

–

Eddie stepped down from the train at the General Railway station, wondering which way the cathedral lay. He had never been on the train to Chester before, only once ever to the city and that was when he had travelled on the stagecoach, at age seven with his dad.

Ted had given him a day out then, thinking that it would help the boy to settle down. Perhaps bond a bit with his eldest lad, now that Madeline had all the children to rear.

Eddie was directed to the cathedral by a porter and soon found himself outside the imposing place opposite St Werburgh Street. It was a fine sunny day for the time of the year; what you could call an Indian summer. Hannah arrived a few minutes after, explaining breathlessly that their lunch at the college had been served quite late.

"Where would you like to go, Eddie? Around the cathedral, or a tour of the walls? Or would you like to go to the new department store? It's just opened on Eastgate Street. All the gentry seem to be patronising it. You should see the carriages all in a line in front of the doors! Or we could have a look around the market hall. There's a cheese fair on at the moment, if you want to sample lots of different sorts of cheese. And the buildings here are quite the finest, all black and white timber and there are lots of shops on what are called The Rows. Oh, there's so much to do and so much to see in Chester, Eddie. Tell me what you would like to do."

"Whitherest you go, then I will follow," quoted Eddie, the only line he could remember from the hour he had once spent in Sunday School. He had been cajoled into going, because his mother had said you got to go on trips or attend the Field Days that they had every year. But Eddie couldn't bear to be closeted, having to learn words so you could join in the singing, but strangely enough that line from the Bible had stayed in his mind.

"Then we'll walk along Eastgate Street and have a look in all the shop windows, the cathedral can wait for another day. It's too nice an afternoon to spend it in there. Then we'll go to the gardens by the amphitheatre. It's lovely there on a sunny day and perhaps later we'll walk by the River Dee. Are you sure you don't want to go to the market hall, we could go in there for a cup of tea?"

Eddie shook his head and held out his arm for Hannah to link it. He'd had to borrow the train fare from his father, who had grumbled at him when Eddie had told him that he was meeting a girl. He had warned him to keep his baby maker in his trousers, that they had enough of them already at the tavern and he wasn't ready to become a granddad for a while.

In fact Eddie was feeling rather hungry, but was glad that Hannah had said she'd had a meal at her school. He hoped his stomach wouldn't start rumbling. He should have thought to have more breakfast, knowing he didn't have money to buy a sausage or pie. He was a fool. But not such a fool when he thought about it. He was living a dream that he had thought about for many, many years. Just to be in Hannah's company was all Eddie had ever wished for and now he could feel her closeness on his arm. Just how lucky could he be?

Hannah was dressed plainly in what she would call her day dress. The crinoline was becoming the fashion of yester year. The hoop had gone, but a skirt could still be worn with several underskirts. She had on a plain grey skirt, high necked blouse and a bolero with long narrow sleeves. On her head was an oval shaped boater, trimmed with tiny pink flowers. She smelled of rose water and Eddie thought that he was in heaven, given that she had even considered meeting him!

"Did yer have any problems getting out of yer tennis practice?" he asked politely, as they wandered down the street.

"No, there's at least one young lady every week who goes down with the cramps, so they're used to us coming up with that one. Oh, look, Eddie. There's the Town Crier. Doesn't he look fine in his wig and tricorn hat? It must be nearly two o'clock already, it appears he's going to ring his bell!"

"Perhaps we should go straight to the gardens then, Hannah, or we won't have much time together if we go into the department store."

"You're right, I can go into Browns at any time. Let's find a place to sit and enjoy the sun and there's always a few pretty flowers lingering at this time of the year."

They sat on a park bench together while Hannah regaled Eddie with stories of various members of her group at school. Especially of her teacher, Miss Edmondson, who had a hairy chin and buck teeth and spat out saliva when she was talking to them!

Hannah was an animated speaker and kept Eddie amused with all she had to tell him. If he hadn't been in love with her before today, he was now; he was very, very sure.

It was warm sitting in the sunshine and Eddie wished he could take his jacket off. He was wearing his uncle's suit again with a different shirt more suitable for daytime wear. Eventually Hannah suggested that they walk on the banks of the river.

It was cooler as they strolled along 'The Groves', watching people enjoying themselves in the pleasure boats, or feeding the many swans that swam along the river. Hannah kept glancing towards the refreshment stand, watching people purchase the dessert named ice cream. Eddie had one penny in his pocket and was worried sick that if she asked for one, it might cost more.

"Would you like to try one of those ice creams, Eddie?" Hannah suddenly asked him. His heart sank into his shoes. It was going to sound as if he was a miser, when he said he'd not enough money for one. "My treat. I bought one a few weeks ago just to try, and it's really delicious. Made from ice, milk and cream and some ingredient I know not what. I have a little money left over from my allowance, so I'll get us two, shall I?"

Oh, to get an allowance, Eddie thought. He was lucky to be getting his bed and board from his father, though he felt he did his share at the Brown Horse. Occasionally, if Ted was feeling generous, Eddie was given a little money to jingle in his pocket. It spurred his intention to find some paid employment – though doing what he didn't know.

"Shall we walk back after we've eaten these?" asked Hannah, as she came back bearing the creamy-looking mixture in two little pots. "I've had to pay a deposit on these bowls, so we'll sit over on that bench and eat them there. See, isn't that the best taste ever?"

She looked at Eddie to see if he was enjoying his. Eddie agreed that he was. He could have stayed forever, watching her delicately spooning the ice cream onto her pink dainty tongue, longing to kiss those delectable lips of hers, to lick her cheek and the bottom of her chin, where like a child she had let the ice cream dribble. In fact if they had not been in public, he would have crushed her to him. The thought of which started a stirring in his loins. He had to see her, somewhere they could be alone together, but after her grandma had seen them on the promenade, he knew it was difficult for her to get away.

They didn't sit together on the train journey back to Neston. She had a first class ticket in the carriage with the plush seats. Eddie sat on a bench in the third class coach, crowded with shoppers as it had been market day. They both dashed into the waiting room as they got down from the train, there to do a spot of canoodling before they went their separate ways.

"Do you think yer could get away for a few hours next Sunday afternoon, Hannah?" Eddie managed to gasp, as they both came up for air. "Say yer going for a walk with the dogs down to the shore."

"I'll try, but someone might want to come with me and it could only be a short walk because it goes dark at half past four. Why, where do you want us to meet if I can manage it?"

"I know of this derelict cottage on Brigg's land. I used to take shelter there sometimes, if I was out walking and it came on to rain. If yer go down the lane at the side of Selwyn Lodge, you come to a gap in the hedge. Over that field takes yer to the lane where the farmhouse is. Past the gate and onto another field, where there's a stream. You can hear it babble as yer walking. Then cross the footbridge which takes you through another field, then you'll see a cottage on the lane. It's called Lilac Cottage. You'll know it by the bushes in the garden, though they've got very overgrown."

"I think I know where you're talking about. I used to ride my pony down there, but I used to start at the coastal path and ride along up that lane. There are three cottages, I didn't know that one was empty. I'd better go now, Eddie, or my father will be sending the dogs out to look for me. What time will you get there?"

"Around two, I think, as long as dinner is put on the table early. I'll stay until four and if yer don't turn up, I'll be there at the same time the following Sunday."

They kissed goodbye and Hannah made her way out sedately, as if she had been spending time in the Ladies' rest room. Eddie sighed. He had to find a job that would pay enough for him to rent a cottage. Then he could ask Hannah if she would marry him.

–

It was easy enough to find the cottage. With Fang and Rufus, her wolfhounds, it had taken no more than ten minutes of brisk walking to get them there. The garden was overgrown, as Eddie had said it would be, and the hinge on the front door wanted fixing, as the door was swinging about drunkenly in the wind.

It was freezing cold inside the living room, not helped by the flagged floor with no rugs upon it and the burnt-out range that they dared not light in case someone knew there were intruders there. Hannah was as warm as toast in her walking outfit; a heavy dark green bombazine skirt, long sleeved bodice and lots of underskirts. She wore a thick woollen travelling coat and a pretty velour bonnet in a russet shade that seemed to match the colour of the falling leaves. Eddie was enchanted, though he couldn't help his poorly-clad body from shivering, so they shared an old blanket as they sat on the dusty settee.

The conversation was desultory, mostly with Eddie moaning about his boring life at the pub. The family's two wolfhounds sat like bookends at each end of the sofa and from time to time got up to wander, stretch, then sit down again. They both spoke again of playing together in Selwyn Lodge's nursery and how Hannah had been upset when Sarah the nursemaid had married Ezra and gone to live with him.

"Not that I knew she had married the grocer, it was what my mother told me. It was sad when Ezra died and Sarah moved away."

"It must have been sad for you that your mother died," commented Eddie, in between placing little kisses on Hannah's lips and eyes. "As much as I loathe my younger brothers and sister, I still love me mam."

"What do you mean, Eddie, about my mother dying?" asked Hannah, alert now, as she had felt very languorous lying with him on the sofa.

"As far as I know, she's alive and well. At least she was when I saw her at luncheon today."

Eddie grew pale and started back-peddling. His chances of doing more than giving Hannah little kisses were beginning to drain away! "Oh, forget I said it. Come here, lie back where it's warm, you're letting all the cold air in. We've this place all to ourselves and you're wasting it."

Hannah's cat like eyes began to glitter dangerously. If Eddie had something to impart of an earth-shattering nature, she really wanted to know. She poked him hard on his shoulder and he yelped.

"All right, all right. It was just something me mother said when I was about nine or ten. I asked why I wasn't allowed ter play with you and Mikey and she said there had been a falling out. She said that you were being passed off as a legitimate child of the Haines family, when everyone knew that yer mother had died and your grandma didn't want yer living with her."

Eddie tapped his head. "I could be confusing it with something else she said."

"Like what? What else could your mother be saying?"

"She just said it seemed strange that with your father not being around at the time, your mother had still given birth!"

Hannah jumped up from the sofa then, throwing the blanket over Eddie, where he trembled beneath because of what he had said. He'd blown his chances. Wasn't there a saying about shooting the messenger? Well, he was truly wounded, as Hannah and her dogs rushed out of the cottage without a backward glance at him.

–

Mikey Haines, or Michael as he liked people to call him now he was grown up, was lying on his bed, staring at the ceiling. He had been trying hard to read a book called *Gulliver's Travels*, but he couldn't get interested. He had a lot on his mind instead. Michael had been working at the Sheldon Loan and Property Company for five years now from when his mother had considered it time to put his private education to use in running her firm. It had been hard working under Mr. Arlington, a precise and diligent employee, whose only wish was for the company to flourish. Which it did, with his assistant Mr. Peel. Michael was treated as the 'go for'. He had no serious input other than running errands and making the tea, but Mr. Arlington liked to wheel him out if the occasion arose, as the proprietor's son to whom all decisions were deferred.

Michael would have liked to spend his days with Mr. Peel, who had the more interesting job of overseeing the Bounty vouchers. He got to visit all the stores that had been recruited to carry out the borrowing scheme and went as far as Staffordshire, sometimes on the train. The only time Michael made his escape from the office was on a Wednesday. It was his job to take the banking to Chester, getting to know the city quite well.

Occasionally he arranged to meet his sister and had asked her last week if they could meet this Wednesday in her lunch hour? To this she had replied that she was far too busy, perhaps they could meet on another Wednesday instead.

Michael had two problems to ponder over. First, he was sure he'd seen that Eddie fellow hanging around the cathedral, when he had passed by to walk down to the Rows. Then he thought that he had seen Hannah and

Eddie together, as he sat in Cottles having a cake and a cup of tea. They were walking quite briskly so he couldn't be sure it was them, but if it was true his parents would be furious, because Eddie was an undesirable to them.

Michael's other problem was – to where was his life leading? Perhaps he should ask his mother to buy him a commission in the Army, which was what a lot of his friends were going to do. They had plans to join the Cheshire Regiment as his pals, Jeremy Adshead and Monty Renfrew, were both from families that had a military background. Michael, when he got to thinking, thought this would be a lot of fun.

Suddenly, he heard someone at the door knocking furiously. It could only be Hannah, Michael thought. Why didn't the folks just give her a key? Then pandemonium seemed to erupt. He could hear the shouting from below. Whatever the matter was, he hoped the servants were not around to hear it, as servants were apt to carry gossip to their friends.

He got his tall frame off the bed, stretched languidly and walked to the top of the landing. The noise seemed to be coming from the conservatory now. He would go down and see what the row was all about, then hopefully come back to lie on his bed.

The scene that met his eyes as he walked in was shocking. Hannah was bent double in a low cane chair crying uncontrollably. His mother was standing, white-faced, watching as his father was trying to console his sister, patting her shoulder ineffectively.

"Whatever is the matter, Mother?" Michael began, his boyish face creased with concern for her, but Maggie just flapped him away silently. He sat down on another chair nearby and listened to what was being said.

Hannah's outburst started to give way to a hiccoughing weeping, so Michael seized his chance to ask what was going on.

"Some lout has told Hannah that she doesn't belong to the Haines family. I'm trying to find out who it was, because I'll give him a good thrashing when I get to the bottom of this." But his father looked scared as he said it and Michael wondered what was really bothering him.

"Is it true, Mother?" Hannah seemed at last to be getting hold of herself. "Is it true you're not really my mother? I was born to somebody else?"

Both Jack and Maggie were in a turmoil. This was the moment they had dreaded. Had Hannah been told the real truth, the one that told of Kitty May and Jack's adultery? Or the version that Alice would prefer them to tell? That she was the granddaughter of her sister, sent over from Ireland when Alice's sister couldn't cope? For Maggie's part, the latter story was the least painful, but that meant that Jack could not claim Hannah as his daughter, only a distant cousin.

She looked at Jack for guidance, but he was of no help at all. He was staring at her now. Was it pleading that she saw in his eyes, or one of resignation? She couldn't be sure.

"Tell me again, exactly what this person told yer," Maggie said to Hannah gently. "He said I wasn't yer mother. What did he say about yer father as well?"

"He said that Father couldn't possibly be my father, because he wasn't here when you were expecting me."

"I'll tell her, Maggie," Jack said, when he saw that his wife was now being painted as a loose woman. "I'll tell them the truth, the both of them, but I know neither of them will ever forgive me."

He sat heavily into another chair, then drew an ornate table closer, so that he could rest his now trembling hands upon it.

"What is it, Papa?" said Hannah in a quiet, almost inaudible voice, using the childish name she had called her father when she used to sit on his knee.

"I am yer father, Hannah, but Maggie is not yer real mother."

He went on to tell Hannah and Mikey of how his youthful ambition was to be great pugilist. No matter what it cost him, he wanted fame and fortune at that time.

Maggie had been content being mother to Mikey, with no ambition other than being a faithful wife. He had wanted her to follow him to Liverpool, where he was the protégé of a lord who had an interest in fighting, but Maggie preferred to live in Neston, with her wonderful view of the Welsh Hills. He had been lonely and Kitty May had been kind to him, nursing him through the resulting injuries from his last fight.

"She made me happy, Hannah. Gave me comfort while I was away from me family. But before I knew it, Kitty May was going to expect my child."

"The child being Hannah," remarked Michael dryly, his eyes narrowing. "So you were unfaithful to my mother, while she stayed at home looking after me."

"It wasn't quite like that, Mikey…" Maggie began.

"The fact is, Mother, your husband here committed adultery and you obviously condoned it because here we have the result. Kitty May's child." Michael waved in Hannah's direction, who had now started crying hysterically after hearing his words.

"I didn't condone it, Mikey. As yer know I built a new life fer the pair of us. That's why we have the Sheldon companies, because I was able to start a business without yer father, though with Miss Rosemary's help of course. It was only when Hannah's mother died and she was sent here from America. How could I have left a tiny little baby in the care of yer grandmother? She disliked the child on sight, because it hadn't bin born in wedlock for a start."

"Well, you disgust me Father and you have made up my mind for me because of it. Mother, I would like to take up a commission in the Army. I will send for the papers tomorrow and I would be obliged if you will furnish the necessary money to pay for it. Oh, and by the way Father, perhaps you would like to know where your by-blow got her information? She had a secret assignation on Wednesday in Chester with the uncouth fellow who lives at the inn."

Michael walked away with a look of scorn on his face, narrowly escaping a blow from Jack who had jumped up in anger, ready to hit out with his clenched fists.

"Leave him, Jack. Don't do something that you'll regret later. Mikey's hurting like we all are at the moment. Mikey," his mother called. "I'll make us all a cup of tea and bring you one up when it's ready. Thank the Lord, the servants are off this evening," she said to Jack. "We don't want all this being stirred up again."

Jack sat with his head in his hands, while Maggie left the conservatory and Hannah studiously stared at a leaf on a palm tree. He felt gutted, as if the wind had been knocked out of him. Wasn't there a saying, how chickens came home to roost? Well, his chickens had certainly come home today. What he could do to put things right, he just didn't know. Nothing would be the same again. He wanted to go down to the Brown Horse and knock seven bells out of this blackguard, but he knew he was as much to blame as the lad.

"Papa," came Hannah's voice, full of sorrow. He looked up to see the tearstained face of his daughter, as she reached up to take hold of his hand.

"Papa. Was my mother pretty? And can you tell me why she died?"

"Oh, Hannah," was all Jack could say, then he stood to engulf her into his arms. He kissed the curls that had escaped from the pins that held up her fragrant-smelling hair. "She was as pretty as you are, with the same pussycat eyes. She died giving birth ter you. Some sort of fever they said. I couldn't look after yer, with my work that is and we didn't have a proper home. So I sent yer to live with yer grandma, but it was Maggie who took yer on. I've a lot to be thankful for to Maggie. She forgave all me transgressions, when I came back ter be with you."

"I know," replied Hannah, as they both sat in chairs beside each other, not letting go of each other's hand. "Maggie has been the only mother I have known. I shall tell her how much I am grateful when she brings in the tea. But why has Mikey been so horrid? What you did when you were younger hasn't really affected him."

"It's because he loves his mother and when he was a baby he was separated quite a lot from her. She worked many hours and your grandma was quite mean, by only allowing Maggie ter see him for a few hours each day."

"Poor Maggie. No, I'll continue to call her mother, she doesn't deserve anything less. Ah, here she is."

Hannah moved away from her father and smiled tremulously at Maggie, though inside she was still in turmoil; sad for the woman who had died giving her life, but grateful to her father's wife, who had treated her as her own.

"Ah, that's better," said Maggie, as she sipped her tea. Her colour had come back and she saw that Jack and Hannah were now on better terms. Though her son was still angry, she knew, because he had ignored her knocking when she had gone upstairs with his tea. Mikey would come round, she thought, especially if she allowed him to take up a career in the Army. She would miss him, but she knew that he hadn't been happy at Sheldon. While Mr. Arlington was still around no one could get a look in. Even *she* still had battles with him, if she wanted to change things or amend.

"Now young lady," Jack said, trying to put on a serious voice. "I think yer've served yer time at finishing school and are ready to take some pressure off yer mother now. I think she's got some plan to create a grand building company, so you will be needed here to make sure the household is running smoothly. Then perhaps yer could take over some of her social duties as well."

"I'll try, Father," replied Hannah, in a small voice. "And I'm assuming I'll not be allowed to see Eddie again. Though I'm sure he didn't mean to hurt our family, he was just repeating something his mother said."

"Ah yes, the pot boy. He isn't really the type of person we would choose for the company of our daughter. We prefer yer didn't see him, Hannah, but who am I to make the rules, when I broke them all when I was young?"

"I think we would all benefit from a holiday, Jack, like you were saying before. Let me visit the bank and sort our affairs out, then we'll consider where would be best fer us all," said Maggie.

Chapter 3

Eddie had been devastated when Hannah left him at the cottage. Gone were his hopes and aspirations that one day he would marry her. She would hate him now for bringing up the past, though it had been purely accidental. He had mooched home, furious with himself for causing his loved one pain. Though the person to blame was his mother, who couldn't keep secrets to herself for long.

Five anxious months passed by, with him not even being able to get a sight of her. He had haunted the station every day, until someone told him at the pub that Hannah had finished at the school in Chester. It appeared she was now at home helping her mother.

He had then taken to hanging around Selwyn Lodge's stables, hoping he would see her saddling up to take a ride on her pony, but he got threatened with a pitchfork by a great giant of a man. Eddie decided to call it a day after that.

His father had got fed up with his moody son, and asked around his customers if they knew of any jobs. So now Eddie was a labourer, working for Jimmy Pearson. Jimmy was a builder and Eddie was going to learn the trade. It was hard, back-breaking work, especially that first winter when the ground was hard with frost and it was his job to dig out the footings for the houses that his employer was to build. They were terraced dwellings at the far end of Town Lane and at first Eddie was hopeful that he would see his loved one. Selwyn Lodge was just a walk down the hill; perhaps one morning she would ride his way.

It was one beautiful morning in late February that he saw Hannah again. He was taking a break from being shown how to set the bricks that were to be laid on top of the foundations. It had taken all the day before for the cement to dry, so there was a bit of catching up to do that Saturday. The sun shone weakly through the clouds that were coming in over the River Dee. For some reason he felt cheerful. Was it because spring was on its way, as he listened to a chirruping blackbird on the wing?

She was driving the family carriage, a highly polished black barouche. Eddie looked first to see if there was a passenger sitting inside. No, he breathed thankfully, Hannah was alone.

He ran at the side of the carriage for a few minutes before she reined the horse to a stop.

"What are you doing, Eddie?" she asked in exasperation. "You'll have my father after you if you keep on plaguing me. You've not been forgiven for causing a holy war, saying what you did."

"Oh, Hannah," said Eddie. "I didn't know that your family hadn't told yer. I just want to see yer again. To tell yer how sorry I am."

"Well, here is not the time or the place. I accept your apology, but I have been told not to speak to you again. I must get on now. I have just taken my mother to Clatter-bridge. She has a presentation to make to the Board there and I must pick her up again at one. Then this afternoon I must get ready. I am attending a ball at the Grosvenor Hotel. It is a farewell dinner for Jeremy Adshead, amongst many. He's leaving to do a tour of duty in India. I'll be staying over at Causey Hall and it will take hours to look my best."

"You will always look the best ter me, Hannah. You're looking yer beautiful best at the moment. Please say yer'll meet me again. Could yer come to Lilac Cottage again next Sunday?"

"No, Eddie. Will you not take no for an answer? Anyway, I couldn't possibly. We will be going away at Easter time and I've a lot of packing to do."

"Please, Hannah."

But this time in answer to Eddie's pleading, she snapped the reins for the horse to go forward and he was left standing alone in the lane.

–

It had been arranged that Jack would drive Michael and Hannah to Causey Hall, then the young people would be ferried to the hotel in Chester by the Adsheads' liveried carriage. An old aunt would travel with them, rather deaf, but capable of overseeing the three excited girls.

Hannah's gown was in a saffron-coloured satin. It was low on the shoulders, with short sleeves covered in three-layered lace. The bodice was pointed, over a short skirt trimmed with buttercup shaped flowers: underneath was a floor-length skirt decorated with flounces and frills. Cecelia, her friend, had on a white satin gown in a similar fashion, but with a sash of emerald green pinned across her breast.

Florence, Cecelia's sister, wore a dress of burnished gold that seemed to show off the streaks of chestnut in her hair. The girls all wore woollen cloaks to keep out the chill wind as the carriage was rather draughty.

Jeremy looked his handsome best in his military dress uniform, epauletted and ornamented, with shiny black dress shoes. There hadn't been enough room in the carriage for everyone, so Mr and Mrs. Adshead, Monty and Michael, had gone ahead in a hired carriage. The dancing would begin at half past seven.

Hannah gasped when she saw the luxurious foyer of the newly built hotel. Large crystal chandeliers hung down from the ceiling, with marble pillars with what looked to be ivy wound around them. There were gilt trimmed floor to ceiling mirrors and shiny marble tiles on the floor.

The girls were directed to the Ladies' Powder Room and Cloaks. The same theme of shininess was in there too, with chaise longues upholstered in a deep red velvet, and tiny hand basins and fluffy white towels for the patrons' use.

After tidying their hair and adjusting their gowns, the chaperone lead the way to the ballroom. Here, there were even more sumptuous surroundings, with a pale peach silk canopy draped in folds which covered the entire ceiling, a mahogany wooden dance floor and long gilt mirrors again. There were recesses, which held elegant sofas and upholstered chairs and the dance floor was edged with a russet carpet, which ran the full length of each side of the room.

There was a long table groaning with food, and waiters in black formal dress, white waistcoats and white ties came to each guest with a glass of champagne or sherry, carried on a large silver tray.

The place was crowded with friends of the Adsheads, military personnel from lieutenant up to a colonel. All belonged to the Chester regiment that Jeremy, Monty and Michael had recently joined.

The three young men were standing as part of a group, deep in conversation about their unit departing on Tuesday for Lucknow. There had been a mutiny in '57 and there was need of a peace keeping presence to guard the British missionaries there. The men were excited, like boys looking forward to Christmas. They had heard that the living was gracious, with punkah wallahs attending every whim. Their accommodation was the finest, with Gentleman's clubs, tennis, and plenty of leisure time.

Jeremy was glancing over to Michael's sister. His brown eyes seemed to follow her everywhere, especially as she danced with her first partner around the room. Jeremy was a tall, spare kind of a chap. He had light brown hair that flopped over his brow, with high cheekbones and an outdoor tan, as he liked riding to hounds and rowing on the River Dee.

"I say, Mikey, your sister is looking rather splendid this evening. I've a mind to ask her to marry me, that's if she's not already spoken for."

Mikey's heart sank for a moment, thinking of how his sister was an illegitimate. Was it fair to warn the fellow, or did his loyalty lie with his family? A scandal like that wouldn't reflect very well on him if he spilt the beans to Jeremy. Having a sister related to the Adsheads could only further his own ambitions, he thought, so he smiled at his friend conspiratorially and said, "I can't see why you shouldn't pursue her. Why don't you ask her if she has any dances left on her card?"

"Good idea. I'll go straight over. You're a lucky chap to have a sister such as her."

Jeremy marched to where Hannah was sitting: she was breathless from her previous partner who hadn't danced in the usual sedate fashion. She hoped the man that was coming over had attended a better dance academy than him.

"Hannah, my dear. I do hope you have something left for me on your dance card. Perhaps the last waltz if your card is full?"

"I have the one after supper free and of course you can have the last one, Jeremy. This is all very exciting, isn't it? You all going off to India with your unit to a place that I can't even dream of."

"It's the heat that will get to us, though they'll be sure to provide us with light clothing. It's cooler, so I've heard in the mountains during the summer months. I'll come back and tell you all about it in a couple of years or so, unless of course you would be willing to write to me. A chap can get very lonely, even if he is surrounded by his men."

"I'd love to write to you. Send your address to Cecelia or Florence and they can pass it on." Jeremy looked pleased and, saluting smartly, he asked could he have the honour of escorting her to supper as well?

They sipped sparkling wine together, after partaking of a gourmet buffet, then ventured into a secluded alcove when the chaperone looked the other way.

Jeremy was flushed with the warmth of the ballroom, the wine he had been imbibing and the embarrassment of a possible rejection if Hannah turned him down.

"Hannah," he said, taking her gloved hands in his and placing a kiss on each one. "I have something to ask you. Could you possibly wait for me to come back from my tour of duty? I would find it very pleasing to make you my bride."

Her eyes widened in surprise at his suggestion. He could have his pick of any of the young ladies that were in the ballroom. She said so and was pleased when he shook his head and spoke of his devotion to her.

"I've always looked upon you as much more than a friend of my sisters'. I admire your looks, your candour and the way you have a sparkling wit and repartee. I don't want a dull as ditchwater, well brought-up, little mouse type of a life partner. I want someone who excites me, vivacious and full of fun like you are. We'd have a good marriage and you could continue to do the work you carry out for the various local charities. Oh yes, I've done my homework; though your background is trade you've had every social advantage, which can only enhance our marriage, I'm sure."

"Can I have time to think about it? I should inform my parents first before I say yes to you."

"There is not a lot of time, Hannah. I would need your decision before I leave. Do say yes, my darling and you'll make me the happiest man alive."

They had the last waltz and he held her as if she was spun sugar, whispering loving endearments into her ear and pleading that she tell him if she had made up her mind.

Hannah was dizzy with his impassioned attention, a little too dizzy if truth was told from the drinks she had consumed. And when Jeremy tapped on the door of the guest room at Causcy Hall later, she had made up her befuddled mind that she was going to marry him. So, it was natural, wasn't it, for a couple who had just agreed to a betrothal between them, to show a little passion? Especially when one of them was going overseas.

"Hannah, darling," Jeremy wheedled, as he lay beside her on the bed. "Give me something to remember you by, in my lonely moments before I go to sleep. Let me love you. Let me take the memory of your sweet kisses and your tender warm body with me. I'll know then that you are mine forevermore."

He slid his pyjama-clad body under the blanket to get even closer.

She was won over by his touching declarations, though only expected him to do a little more in the way of kisses; not begin to probe her in her private place, nor begin to knead her bosoms as if she was going to turn into a loaf of bread. Then her senses began to stir and she began to retaliate, thrusting her body about in a very unladylike fashion, as he caressed her in places that she had never thought about before. Though when she felt his hard member, urgently seeking its way between her parted legs, Hannah felt she had to say something. Her mother had told her that this act that Jeremy was about to carry out could bring an unmarried girl's name into disrepute.

"Stop, Jeremy," Hannah slurred her words. Intoxicated she might be, but this thing she was about to partake in could bring on long-lasting consequences. She sat up quickly, causing Jeremy to slither from on top of her.

"What is it Hannah? Can't you see I'm ready for you? A chap could die of agony if his function isn't fulfilled, you know."

"But you might give me a baby and we're not married. Jeremy, I would be mortified if I found that I was expecting."

"Oh, do lie back, Hannah. Everyone knows you can't have a baby the first time. And the next time we do it you'll be bearing my name!"

–

She stretched luxuriously under the bedclothes next morning, as the early morning light filtered through the gap in the curtains. A small clock on the bedside table told her it was just after seven. A few minutes more and she would be attended by a maid.

It had always surprised Hannah when she had stayed at the Adshead's before, that such a wealthy family had not modernised their living quarters. At Selwyn Lodge there was a very pleasant bathroom. Here, they relied on the maid to bring the washing water in a jug. Hannah ran her hands carefully over her body, as her mind relived the passion shared with Jeremy. She was tender in places, sore in another and she looked forward to a deep-filled bath when she returned home later.

But first she must dress and go downstairs to break-fast, there to see her betrothed one, who would probably announce over breakfast that they were to be married the following year.

The maid, who was called Milly, arrived ten minutes later and helped Hannah into the dark blue day dress that she had left in the room the evening before. Her hair was brushed and coaxed into glossy ringlets, which were pinned on top of Hannah's head and ribbons threaded through.

Milly left and Hannah finished her ablutions, then slowly walked down the rather grand staircase into the morning room.

"Good morning, Mrs. Adshead, Cecelia, Florence. It looks as if we shall be having good weather today."

"It certainly does, Hannah. It is a pity that Jeremy, Montague and your brother have had to return to their barracks. I'd a mind that they were planning to go shooting, get some practice in before they go. Help your-self to breakfast, you know where everything is. Is your father coming to collect you as usual, as we will be leaving for church at half past ten?"

Hannah felt deflated. She was certain that Jeremy would have made some announcement. It was too important not to have done.

She helped herself to kedgeree; the Adshead's cook made a delicious one and Hannah usually had to control herself and not return for more. Today though, she played with the fish bits, pushing it with the rice around her plate. Perhaps Jeremy had told his father before he had set out? If he had, again there was no mention, except that Mr. Adshead had left the carriage for the ladies, as he wanted to walk the two miles to church.

"Did you enjoy yourself last night, Hannah?" inquired her hostess. "You seemed to be getting along very well with Jeremy. Pity Lady Lydiate and her daughter Catherine were indisposed at the last moment. We had high hopes of a match between Jeremy and Catherine, but I suppose they will write to each other while Jeremy is overseas. And he's a little too young for marriage at twenty one."

"I heard him telling Monty this morning that he was going to call on Catherine at Lydiate Hall before he goes away," said Florence.

"I did too," chimed in Cecelia and gave Hannah a surreptitious grin. Hannah went hot with embarrassment. Did Cecelia know what had happened between her and Jeremy? The girls' bedrooms were on the same floor.

"I'm sorry Mrs. Adshead, I'm not feeling very well this morning. Perhaps it was something I ate last night, but I'll gather my things up from the bedroom then wait for my father at the Lodge. It will give me time to take advantage of the fresh air."

"Oh, I do hope it isn't the same complaint that Catherine seems to have gone down with."

So do I, thought Hannah, as she walked up the stairs.

What a fool she had been. Carried away with romantic dreams of being married to the son of a wealthy landowner, when all the time there was sweet, simpering Catherine Lydiate being eyed up as a future brood mare to continue the Adshead line. Jeremy was probably at this very moment boasting of his conquest, how he had tumbled the very willing daughter of a jumped-up Irish man. Oh, she had heard the whispers, the giggles behind the hands of some of her so called friends, but she was surprised that Cecelia hadn't told her of the Adshead's wish to marry their son off into the landed gentry. She felt betrayed and very hurt as she walked down the long gravel drive.

Hannah dashed away self-pitying tears, as she saw her father driving the carriage up the country lane. He would be mortified if he knew the truth, that his daughter had behaved like a trollop. Though she was surprised, if she was honest with herself. Her mother had behaved just the same. But the difference was, or so she believed, Kitty May had been in love. She had nursed Jack when he'd been very ill, had been willing to leave her homeland and her family for him, then had paid the ultimate price. Hannah had only been attracted to Jeremy for the status it would bring. Mrs. Hannah Adshead. What an important-sounding name it had seemed.

As she settled herself in the carriage, her father whistling happily above, she wondered if Jeremy had lied, or had he been serious in wanting them to marry? Was his proposal just a ruse to gain access to her bed? Her head swam with unhappy thoughts, confusion and bitterness.

Now that Jeremy was off to serve in India, she felt she might never know.

The house was quiet when they got back home. Olive and Joan had not started work and Maggie had gone with Alice to church. Jack made them both a coffee to drink in the sun-warmed conservatory. He wanted to know all about her evening and who was there at the ball.

"I'm glad yer mixing with people such as the Adsheads, Hannah. Imagine. A daughter of mine staying in a grand mansion like Causey Hall and being invited to rub shoulders with the gentry. Not that we couldn't afford to live in a place as splendid as that one, but yer mother loves Selwyn Lodge so there's not much chance of us ever moving house. Still, one day, who knows, you might receive a proposal from one of those fellows. Do yer like Jeremy or Montague? Which one does yer heart beat the fastest for?"

"Neither, Papa. I thought I had a liking for Jeremy, but he's a cad. Last night we danced and danced and he said that I meant the world to him, but this morning I heard that he's virtually betrothed to Lady Lydiate's daughter, Catherine. He just played with my affections. I'm glad he's going off to India, because I wouldn't want to see him any more."

Jack looked indignant. "I hope he didn't do more than play with your affections, Hannah, because if he has I'll be over to Chester Barracks and he'll get the beating he deserves."

Hannah sat quietly for a moment, sipping her coffee while she wondered if there was any point in telling her father what had happened. He would be very angry, get his shot gun, demand that Hannah's honour would be paid for in the form of marriage. But did she really want that?

Force Jeremy into something that he may regret for the rest of his life? Oh, she'd have the status, and the social life, but he would despise her, scorn her and probably hate her.

And her father, what would he think of her after he knew? Hannah shuddered to think. "No, Papa. All I have is hurt feelings and tired feet. I think I'll go and have a bath, then lie down for a while."

"And I'll go and look the horses over. Hopefully we'll have another addition to the stables soon."

Jack took himself down to the stable block. The horses whinnied in greeting and he fed them each a handful of hay. They were well looked after by Fergal, a cousin of Paddy Fearon's who had worked as a blacksmith in Ireland but had wanted to emigrate, for reasons he kept to himself. Since arriving, he had found himself a young widow in the village; a woman who only came up to his elbow, but who loved Fergal with a devotion that he wouldn't have found anywhere else.

Jack had two carriage horses, black stallions, both fifteen hands high, named Lincoln and Jefferson. There was also Simba who Hannah rode. A bay horse, dark reddish-brown with a black mane and tail.

Secure in a paddock outside Chester was Jack's pride and joy. A racing horse named Fletcher. Brought over from a stud farm in Wicklow, the animal was being trained by Thomas Butler, with a view to bringing Fletcher up to the standard of Jack's other horse, Dalton. Dalton, his first ever horse, had already won at Epsom and the Derby and Jack had plans of mixing business with pleasure, visiting a few places in Ireland on the lookout for another likely winner and taking Maggie back to Killala as well.

Maggie needed a rest. With Betty gone, she had a greater share of responsibility, driving herself to make decisions that would be a daunting task for a man. Not content to sit back and let others do her bidding, Maggie made sure that her mind was a match for Mr. Arlington. Her latest plan was to buy up all the land that was being sold by Farmer Briggs.

Jack smiled to himself as he ran his hand over Jefferson's fetlocks. Maggie never ceased to amaze him; there was always a plan a, b, and c. He had never quite got over coming back from America and seeing how much everything had changed. He had expected her to be taking in sewing or giving his mother a hand, looking after his two babies and never looking at another man. He had been surprised to learn that there had been another man in the background; Eddie's uncle, Johnny. Though Maggie had assured him that Johnny had been the perfect gentleman, the very idea of another man in his wife's life had made Jack very jealous. Which brought to his mind his daughter. Adshead's son had obviously been dallying with Hannah's affections and Jack could see that the girl was upset when he had picked her up from Causey Hall. Her eyes had looked full of anguish and she had taken to her bed when Jack had left her to come down to the stables. If he ever found out the swine had interfered with his darling daughter, and for some uneasy reason he felt that was the case, Jack vowed to get even, whatever the price.

Maggie and Alice walked down Burton Road together, chatting about the service and Mrs. Fielding's silly hat. It was a bright sunny day, so Maggie decided to walk to the promenade with her mother-in-law, rather than head back home just yet. Joan would start the dinner at twelve and Olive wouldn't serve it until two.

Maggie hadn't visited Seagull Cottage since Alice had provided Christmas tea for the family. She had been very busy with her Sheldon interests and the charities that involved fundraising as well. Strange how money opened doors to society; she was always being asked to social events and open houses by the leading wives of the community.

When Maggie thought back to when she had first arrived from Killala, it made her smile. No way would she have been accepted into these circles twenty years ago, probably not even as a serving maid. The Irish were a race that had been viewed with rancour and suspicion, but hadn't she shown them all? Now, half the population of the area had cause to be grateful for her presence. If there wasn't a company like Sheldon, some of the local families would find it hard to exist.

"So, what do yer think, Maggie, should I tell him 'no'?" asked Alice and Maggie realised that the woman was waiting for an answer. The question, Maggie didn't know.

"Sorry, Alice, me mind was wandering. Should yer tell who 'no'?"

"Mr. Arlington of course. He's asked me to marry him. Now that Jack's dad has passed over these last twelve months, Mr. Arlington thought it a decent enough space of time to ask me ter marry him."

Hmm, Maggie thought. Mr. Arlington never did anything unless there was an advantage for him in it. She had learnt that lesson with her dealings with him over many years. He must be after Alice's money or her property, because he already had her cooking, having been her lodger for twenty-one years. Alice was now in a very vulnerable position; a comfortably off widow since Michael, her husband, was carried off by the cholera, the house owned outright and regular money coming in. There had only been one change in the whole time Alice had been a landlady at Seagull Cottage. Mr. Dickinson, one of her first lodgers, had been replaced by a Mr. Andrews instead.

"It's not that he loves me or anything and I'll never love him like I loved my Michael, but I get lonely fer company, especially on a cold winter's night when I lie in me bed."

"Well, put a hot water bottle in yer bed, Alice, it's less complicated than marrying. And yer years older than him anyway, yer know how people will talk."

"I'm not that much older. Anyway he's talking of retiring, so we can spend our days together. Visit places as friends. Now that Seamus, that rascally son of mine is living with that woman in Liverpool, I don't see anybody of me own. Mikey traipsing off to foreign parts, Jack tied up with his horse racing. And you, well, yer have to make an appointment to see *you*. I want somebody I can really call me own."

"I can't see you two making a go of it," professed Maggie. "He's a pedantic old buffer, but you can be as bad."

"What's pedantic? You and yer big words, Maggie. If yer mean that we're both alike with our tempers, just remember I've lived with him as his landlady for all these years. He's not going ter change towards me, just 'cos we're married. It will be as if I have a big bear beside me, that I can cuddle up to in bed."

"And what about the property? If he wanted, when yer legally married he could insist on saying that Seagull Cottage belonged to him."

"No, that can't happen. Jack's name is on the deeds as well. He made sure of that so Mikey could inherit. No, if Mr. Arlington wants to marry me, it will be for companionship. But just to make sure, I'll mention the inheritance. Then if that was his only reason, he can go ter Hell instead!"

Maggie laughed and squeezed her mother-in-law's hand. "Yer don't change do yer, Alice? God help him if that's all he's after. Now, you get inside, you've the dinner ter make or he'll be thinkin' twice about marrying you."

Maggie leant over the railings and stared across the estuary. They never changed, those far-off Welsh hills, not like life did. Always there, even if sometimes they were covered by cloud. So much had happened since she sailed up the river, all those years ago, but here her view was constant and would be in the future for all the generations that were to come.

She remembered how she would look across there and think of Molly, her sister. Did she go to Australia with the Filbey's? Was she still there today? Then there was her brother Bernie, who had run away to sea when he was fourteen. He would be thirty-four or -five now. Was he married, settled down or beneath the ocean somewhere? In her heart she knew he wouldn't be. Bernie was a survivor like her.

Now there was Mikey to worry about; off on a troop-ship to foreign parts. Her son, whom she'd nurtured from a little boy. Would he ever see this view again?

Chapter 4

"Are we all ready now?" shouted Jack to his wife and daughter, as overhead he could hear sounds of a trunk being dragged along the carpet.

"For pity's sake, Maggie, leave it and gather your other bags together. We're only going for ten days yer know, you'd think we were going for a month or more."

He hurtled up the stairs to find Maggie and Hannah still putting things into their valises. Jack became increasingly irritated. They had been up since cock crow that morning and the packet ship from Wales sailed off at two.

"If we miss that boat, there isn't another until tomorrow. Now hurry, Fergal is waiting outside with the carriage. I don't want to be putting the horses into a lather 'cos of you two. Hannah, pick up those bags fer yer mother and hurry."

Jack put the trunk onto his shoulder, tutting irritably. Why did women need to pack everything just in case? His own clothes were arranged neatly in a small valise!

Maggie and Hannah smiled wryly at each other. Jack just didn't understand that they must take things in case of emergency. They were travelling to a land that wouldn't have a village every two miles or so, as the Wirral did. There were many miles in between Dublin and Killala, with vast stretches of countryside where they might never see another soul.

Both women wore day dresses in a light woollen material. It was the middle of April and the time of the year that could be warm one day and chilly the next. Maggie's dress was long-sleeved, edged with a pretty lace ruffle at the wrist, worn with gloves in case it got cold. Her dress was a deep green satin and round her shoulders was a heavy wool magenta-coloured shawl. She had brushed her hair into a centre parting, tied it into a chignon at the back and on her head was a satin-trimmed saucer bonnet. Hannah had on a mauve merino dress, in a similar style to Maggie's, with a matching shawl and trimmed spoon-shaped bonnet tied under the chin with mauve ribbons. Neither wore hoops or a great amount of underskirts, as they might be required to walk along difficult terrain. Hannah had let her hair fall into heavy glossy ringlets and she carried a cream tasselled parasol by her side. Jack, in contrast had only dressed comfortably, in a dark blue suit of houndstooth check, with a small matching deer stalker hat.

Fergal clicked up the horses and the carriage bowled along merrily, following the route into Wales. Jack had asked Alice if she would like to accompany them on this short holiday, partly as a trip of nostalgia and also as a break which might do them all good. But Alice had declined the offer. She was much too busy planning her wedding and running the boarding house to be fussed with all that sentiment. She had left her homeland twenty-odd years ago and had no wish to return!

Fergal followed the Chester Road which soon brought them to the cross roads at Two Mills. There he bore right and drove down the road to Queensferry, the gateway into Wales. They were making good time. Jack, looking at his fob watch, felt pleased. This holiday they were taking would do them all the world of good. Well, he hoped it would. There had been a foiled attempt by the Fenians recently to cause mayhem at the Chester Barracks and there was talk of uprisings around Dublin. But as Fergal said, the targets were the British, not people like Jack who was returning to Ireland with his family. Fergal advised him not to sail from Holyhead though, but he wouldn't be drawn as to why!

To say Maggie was looking forward to the trip was debatable. She was looking forward to being with Jack and Hannah, but there were so many things that she could have been doing if she had stayed at home to which her mind kept harking back.

Sheldon Property Company had recently bought Briggs' farmland that he had put up for sale. The intention was to build affordable property for the locals, backed up by loans that could be repaid over twenty-five years. Maggie had wanted a mix of houses: terraces, semi-detached and detached villas, and she had employed an architect to design just that. But already there had been snags with the parish council, who were drawing up a list of rules that the development must abide by; foundation depth, sewage pipes, water mains, to name just a few. Then there was the builder to be chosen, tenders for the job were coming in and, to Maggie's exasperation, they would be picked by Mr. Arlington. He had argued that dealing with men in the building trade was not a job for a woman and on this, Jack had heartily agreed. Still, she would be back in time to deal with the architect. Mr. Hughes was a very agreeable young man.

Hannah sat looking out of the carriage window, watching the scenery go by. It would be good to visit new places; take her mind off her problems for a time. Three weeks had passed by since she had expected her monthly courses. Not that it meant anything really, because it had happened once before. It was just that this time there could be an actual reason. Hannah was conversant with the mystery of gestation, because Maggie had sat her down and explained it all a few years ago. To have a baby without a father though, would create a mighty scandal and Hannah knew she couldn't marry Jeremy. His tour of duty would be for at least two years, so what was she going to do?

There were two options she kept thinking of. Throw herself on the mercy of her father, or find a woman who could get rid of the unwanted thing. The latter she hadn't a clue how to go about, it was just something she had heard was a possibility. Still, she had ten days in which to make her mind up and it could be a false alarm anyway.

"Look Maggie, Hannah, over there, you can see the beginning of the Wirral. In a few minutes' time you will be able to see our house in Neston. Come over by me, Maggie. You'll have a better view."

Sure enough, as the carriage continued along the road through the village of Flint, they could just make out the black outline of the colliery across the water. Though their house was obscured by the trees that surrounded their dwelling, they knew that Selwyn Lodge was over there, too. Maggie was delighted and moved to the other window, hoping to see the hills that she could see from her bedroom. But the road was lined with forest and thick vegetation, which for the moment made it impossible for Maggie to see.

"It's another few miles yet to Llandudno," advised Jack, who had taken the ship to Dublin from there once before. He usually travelled from Liverpool but wanted Maggie to experience the view of the Wirral from the other side of the River Dee. Besides, Llandudno was a spa town. If Maggie liked it, perhaps he could take her in the future for a short holiday there. They sat for a while in silence, enjoying the surroundings and looking out to sea.

The carriage eventually came to a steep incline and, though the occupants couldn't see it, Llandudno lay below. It was a purpose-built resort town, fronted with grand Georgian style hotels looking over the Irish Sea. The beach was long and sandy, sheltered by the hill called the Great Orme and at its foot was a deep water harbour, where lay the *Irish Maid* packet ship.

Fergal drew up at the pier entrance and helped his passengers down, then handed the family's trunk to a waiting porter. There was ten minutes left before embarking; no time to sightsee while they were there.

"Never mind," said Jack, as Fergal turned the carriage round and saluted his employers before departing. "We can come here again for a holiday, don't those hotels look grand over there? But we must hurry before they put the gangplank up. Time and tide wait for no man, or so they say."

Jack had booked a cabin. Though Dublin was less than fourteen hours away, he didn't want his women mixing with the *hoi polloi*. And he was glad he did, when Hannah began chucking back her breakfast. Strange that she should do that when she was usually such a healthy girl.

–

Dawn was beginning to light up the sky as the ship sailed into Kingston Harbour. They went on deck to look at the islands that were dotted around Dublin Bay. There was

Dalkey Island, an island dedicated to St. Benedict, where the remains of a Celtic church and a Milasian fort could be seen. Another was Muglins Isle, where a lighthouse sat to warn seafarers of the jagged rocks around the bay. Then on to a train that would take them on the coastal route to the city. Jack had reserved a suite of rooms at the Sherbourne Hotel.

The sun was up by the time the family reached Amiens Station. It was only a short walk to their hotel, so a porter trundled a trolley behind them, bearing the family trunk and valises. They planned to stay for a day or two, see the sights, then hire a carriage with a driver, who would take them overland to Killala Bay.

Later, Maggie sat with Hannah on the plush sofas in the hotel's foyer, waiting for Jack to return with their keys, noting the elegantly dressed ladies and the fine furnishings there. What a difference twenty years had made to her life, she thought; she wouldn't have been allowed through the doors of the place all those years before. Dublin, in Maggie's mind, was a refined and cultured city, with Trinity College, splendid buildings, streets with modern gas lighting and a river to promenade by. They would have a short rest, perhaps a little breakfast and then take in the sights before supper. Hannah in particular should be delighted with the place. She was always mourning the fact that she didn't visit Chester any more.

Maggie looked sideways at Hannah. She was looking very peaky and rather forlorn. It seemed that she'd had a falling out with the Adshead girls, because since the night she had stayed over at their mansion, Hannah hadn't seen the two sisters at all. Jack had said it was something to do with Jeremy. That was all he would say and Maggie hadn't dwelt upon it. She had enough to worry her on the business front, without looking for trouble at home. It was probably a silly quarrel between the young ladies and it would all blow over soon. Still, the girl was very pale and had lost her usual colour. A walk by the river would probably do her good.

"Mother," Hannah broke into her thoughts. "Could I lie down when we get to our rooms? I still feel rather sick this morning, but perhaps an hour on the bed will do me good."

"I was just thinking that meself, Hannah. You're looking very peaky. Perhaps we should be lookin' fer a chemist. Maybe some powders ter settle yer tum."

"I'm sure I'll feel better when I've had a rest. I'm looking forward to seeing around the city, aren't you? Did you never come here when you were younger, Mother? Papa was saying he had visited sometime, but only when he was passing through."

"No, I never had the pleasure, Hannah. I've told yer something of me background and when we get to Killala you'll find out why. Ah, here's yer father and I'm glad he's brought a porter with him. It looks as if it could be a struggle ter get the trunk up them stairs!"

The rooms they had been given were impressive, as befitted the status of an Irish emigrant who had made good. From the crystal chandeliers to the thick luxuriant carpets, and the shining tile floored bathrooms attached to each bedroom. Exhaustion began to take over, as no one had slept in the cabin with Hannah retching all night long.

"I think I'll go out and try and find some transport, Maggie," said Jack, as they sat in the room after luncheon, the meal having been served in their suite.

"It will save me time tomorrow, if I were ter have problems finding a driver willing to go that far. Though I suppose we could take the train. I'll not be long. Hannah, yer still lookin' rather weary, perhaps instead of sight-seeing you'd rather go ter bed?"

"I'll be all right, Papa. I'm looking forward to walking out later. I'm sure the fresh air will do me good."

"Hannah," Maggie said gently, when Jack had gone from the room. "Do yer think this could be something to do with yer monthlies? I've brought some cloths fer the both of us, if yer feel you might be comin' on."

"No, Mother," replied Hannah quickly. "It must be the travelling that is causing my sickness. I had my monthly course a week ago." She hated lying and wondered if Maggie was suspicious, as usually both women were on at the same time.

"Ah well, whatever it is, a good night's rest will put it right again. Shall we gather our things and saunter down to meet yer father? It seems a pity to be sitting around and wasting such a glorious afternoon."

Jack came across the foyer as Maggie and Hannah reached the bottom of the stairs. His face was creased with anxiety as he guided them to a secluded alcove in the room. "I think we're goin' to have ter change our plans about staying a while in the city. The fella I've just spoken to says we'd be fools ter stop here, and to get out right away."

"But I thought all that was done with," said Maggie, her face becoming red with annoyance. She had been looking forward to the delights that Dublin could offer, especially the musical recital to be held in the hotel.

"Jack, according to the Chester Courant, the raid on the castle was foiled by an informer and the Fenians never managed to get the arms they wanted, so how are we in peril here?"

"The man said there are small pockets of rebels that are making trouble. There's been a huge explosion in Tipperary, sabotaging of railway lines and attacks on lots of police barracks. If they come into Dublin we could be caught up in it all. We're safer out of the way."

"Do you think we should go home?" Hannah's quiet voice broke into their discussion and startled, the couple turned to stare at her.

"Why should we? Why should a handful of hot-heads spoil our visit back to our homeland? Jack, did the man say there was any trouble in Mayo? Around where we're goin' ter stay?"

"I never thought ter ask him, I was so worried about you both back here. He's willin' to take us in his carriage as far as Foxford. He said he's got a delivery there. Then maybe we could find another driver, willin' to take us further. A local farmer or a carter mebbe. I'll have to forget me trip ter Wicklow this time. I'm not goin' to put us in the face of danger, as it's not too far away from here. No, we'll spend a few days on nostalgia, then back as quick as we can ter Liverpool. You've never bin there, Maggie, so that can be part of yer holiday."

"I'd rather we went back home, Papa. It seems very dangerous to suggest we continue with our journey and I think it would be very agreeable to have a look around Liverpool."

"As yer mother says, Hannah, we shouldn't let a group of anarchists ruin our holiday. We're not the targets, it's the government, but unfortunately innocent people get in the way. If we abandon our plans, we may never get the chance ter visit Ireland in the future and it is your heritage, me darlin', even if yer don't see it that way."

"Your father is right, Hannah and it will do you good to breathe in the fresh country air while yer about it. You've still got that pale look, you're usually so bright and pink–looking. We'll order some tea and drink it here in the foyer and perhaps have a few cakes, before we venture along the banks of the Liffey."

"Are you sure it will be safe, Mother? I don't feel very safe with what Papa has just been saying and I'm not feeling well. Perhaps I should just lie down in my room."

"Tosh! Look through the window at the hustle and bustle. It isn't stoppin' other people gettin' on with their lives. Do as I say, Jack and order us some refreshments. It will be another few hours before we have supper and I for one think we should be fortified."

Next day the family was woken early as arranged, by the night porter. Instead of breakfast, they were given a food parcel to eat along the way. It appeared that Keva, the man who would be their driver, was anxious to make an early start. He had parcels to deliver on a route that was not particularly profitable and was glad to carry passengers, if only to pay for the feeding of his horse.

Their hearts sank when they saw the ramshackle vehicle they were to travel in. The hood was ripped in places, the door was askew on its hinges and the horse looked as if it was ready for the knackers' yard.

"Smile will yer, you two," hissed Jack, when he saw the horror on his wife and daughter's faces.

"This is all I could manage at such short notice. It was this or walkin', there isn't an overland train!"

The man named Keva stowed their trunk on the already loaded roof rack, then helped them all aboard, passing an old blanket to the ladies to drape over their knees. He was a big man with a roguish grin, a heavy weight who looked as if he could defend himself in times of trouble. Maggie felt herself relax and vowed to enjoy the journey; she had Jack as well to protect them. No ruffians would get past these stalwart men.

"The first stop is Mullingar, Sir, so it is. A farm on the outskirts, but we'll stop in the hamlet for a drink and to rest old Rebel here. Not that he's much of a rebel any more, but I've heard he was in his younger days."

Hannah shivered in apprehension. Even the horse was called Rebel. What kind of place had her parents brought her to? Still, it was taking their attention away from her for a while. It was beginning to dawn on Hannah that what Jeremy had said, about not getting caught the first time with a baby, wasn't remotely true!

The carriage manoeuvred its way down busy Balfre Street with its dray carts, pedestrians and shoppers all getting in the way, through Grafton and onto the quieter roads that would take them out into the country. They sat in silence, staring out of the carriage, as the morning light began to filter through the darkened clouds.

"Papa," Hannah began hesitantly. "Papa, why are these people rising up against the government and making trouble? Mother said they were trying to cause problems in Chester a few months ago. What has it got to do with people like you and me?"

"Shush, Hannah, keep yer voice down. We don't know which side this man supports, we don't want him turning on us. The problem goes back fer years, because a lot of Irish people think they've bin treated badly by the British government. They want to be independent, set up a sort of republic. That means to rule themselves, without the

71

Queen. And it's true, the Irish have suffered for decades. Think of the famines that Ireland has had. The very reason why me and yer mother left our homeland. There's never been much help given from London. In fact at one time if it hadn't have been for voluntary groups, a lot more people would have starved. The Irish have bin left to fend fer themselves on many occasions and that's why they resent being ruled by uncaring politicians and greedy landowners, who only think of themselves."

"But how does blowing up railways and stations help their cause?"

"It's a way of bringing attention to themselves, their aims and justifications. When I was in America, a lot of the emigrants joined the Fenian Movement, raising money to support their brothers who had stayed in Ireland. The money went to purchase weaponry and food, because a lot of the men had no employment or were on the run from the authorities."

"That's enough now, Jack. I think Hannah has bin told all she needs ter know about the situation. She'll be havin' nightmares if yer continue. It's best if we can, to steer clear of all these politics."

"I was only answerin' her question, Maggie. I agree with yer, but we were very lucky to get away like we did. It could have bin us, struggling ter survive when the crop failed again that summer. As it was, we've done alright fer ourselves, but there are many thousands that aren't here, to be able to tell their tale."

Jack's words were bitter. If the truth was known he had supported the Fenian Brotherhood when he was in America. It was hard not to do so, when tales of evictions, poverty and starvation due to the high prices of corn reached the emigrants' ears. They heard of the callous indifference shown by the British government to the plight of the Irish, heard of their refusal to provide cheap food, heard that the problem was transferred to the Irish landlords, who seized on the chance to evict as many poor tenants as they could. Healthy Irish fields were given over to cereal growing and pasturing livestock, gone were the smallholdings that relied on the potato yield. Demand for Irish produce was at its highest ever, but it was hard for a starving peasant to see cart loads of grain and other products being shipped over to England, while all they were offered was the grimness of the workhouse to ease their woes. The country became a hot bed for the revolutionary. It had worked in France, the overthrowing of an uncaring hierarchy, it could happen in Ireland as well. Names like O'Connell, Mitchel, Meagher and O'Brien were spoken of in reverent tones by the peasants. These men were their only hope of making Ireland great again. Then O'Connell died and the other men were transported to Australia. Another generation had to grow before the Fenians became strong again.

"How long before we make our first stop, Jack?" asked Maggie, when they had been travelling for about an hour. "I could do with the privy and this seat is giving me jip. A cushion or two would be welcome as well."

"Be thankful you and Hannah are wearing all them underskirts. How do yer think my bum is feeling with just me trousers on? I'll shout up and ask if we can stop at the next village. I don't fancy stopping here. These trees are so tall and thick, who's ter know who'll be hiding behind them."

For many miles that morning, they had been travelling through lush and green countryside. There was certainly no evidence of a land blighted or spoiled. Cattle grazed on pasture, crops were beginning to show their heads and everywhere looked peaceful. Hard to imagine that very scenery just twenty years ago. Now the carriage was taking them through the forest at the foot of the Kilcock Hills. An eerie place; dark, shadowed and spooky. Not a spot to linger in, if you were able to choose. It was a relief to see the sun again when they eventually drove from the gloom.

"We'll be making a stop at Enfield," shouted Keva, from his place above. "This old nag's started a quiverin'. I'll have ter give him a rest."

"Thank heaven fer that then," said Maggie. "And perhaps we can eat some of this food we've bin given. The way this thing is rattling, our tummies must be all tangled up!"

The carriage drew to a stop in the middle of a small village, a hamlet really as it didn't boast a pub. Keva jumped down from his platform and helped to get his passengers out.

"There's a privy over there, ladies, behind Widow Cusack's shebeen. Me and your man will wet our whistles while yer gone, if it's all the same ter you." With that, he unharnessed Rebel, letting the horse wander to a water trough that was sited outside a cottage further up the road. Hannah went to pat him, as he greedily drank his fill. How sad he looked, she thought, an old horse forced to continue with its labours. If it was up to her, Rebel would be in retirement, spending his last days in a grassy field.

She followed her mother behind the widow's cottage, where Maggie had already finished her ablutions in the small brick building and was on her way back.

"*Shebeen* is the Gaelic for an unlicensed house that sells liquor, if yer were wonderin', Hannah," she remarked, as she passed the young girl by. "A place that attracts men like bees round a honey pot for some reason. Though I've never found out why that is."

Maggie stood outside the carriage, chewing on a piece of cheese and looking over at the view. The fields were vast and full of crops, whoever owned them must be doing very well. It was all so different from the way she remembered her beloved country. In those days, these fields would have been divided into smallholdings or tenant farms of less than thirty acres. Potatoes, rather than these cabbages, would be planted here instead. There were workers dotted around the fields, stooped low at their task of weeding or throwing some things onto a farm cart, though she couldn't see what it was. The overseer astride his horse watched them all vigilantly. It reminded Maggie of the slaves she had read of in Mikey's story book. Her heart went out to each one of them.

"A bit different to when we were children growing up, eh, Maggie?"

Jack had come up behind and rested his chin on her shoulder, in order to share her view.

"See those workers, they're what they call itinerants. Keva was just tellin' me. They're dispossessed folk, too poor to find the money for emigration or to find the rent for a bit of land. Instead of being housed and fed by a caring master, they wander from place to place finding work, in return fer a daily pittance. It's a brutal life by all accounts, out in all weathers, never knowin' what the next day will bring. It's a changin' world, Maggie, from the one we knew. Now anyone can buy up the land if they have enough money, thinkin' just of profit and not their fellowman."

Maggie turned to him, seeing the sadness in his pale blue eyes. She wanted to hug him for his sense of underlying goodness, tell him something to heal the hurt that he was feeling for his fellow countrymen.

"Jack," she said laying her hand comfortingly on his arm, keeping her voice low, as Keva began to wander by.

"Jack, I feel very humbled when I take a look around me. It could have bin us if you'd not taken your chances the way that yer did. Though until today I would certainly not have admitted it, yer did me a favour when ye dragged me off to a foreign land."

He laughed out loud then and slapped his hand on his thigh with delight at what he was hearing. He kissed her quickly on the cheek and she noticed that a tear had come into his eye.

"You made me the happiest man alive when yer took me back again, me darlin'. It was a dream come true fer me, when yer decided to forgive the way yer did."

Chapter 5

They arrived at Longford in the early evening, having lunched in Mullingar, while Keva had gone off to deliver a parcel to his customer at a farm. He had left them to sit on the shore of Lough Ennell, where they had finished off the remains of a cold chicken provided by the Sherbourne Hotel.

The skies were growing dark as the carriage pulled up outside the 'Pot of Gold' tavern, a small creeper-covered building on the edge of a deep silent glen. Keva jumped down to inquire of the landlord if there were any rooms available, then came back to tell them there was one, but he himself would have to doss down in the tap room. He didn't mind, he was used to sleeping on a washing line, but there was no way that he was going to risk life and limb by continuing on in the dark! And Rebel needed to rest as he was all aquiver again. Not that Keva was worried about being set upon by foot pads or vagabonds, as he told his weary passengers, but it was remote and desolate terrain on the way to Ballaghaderreen and they would need daylight to see that they kept to the road.

The landlord of the small but homely hostelry gave them a cheery welcome, setting his wife to preparing a meal of soda bread and mutton for his unexpected guests. The bedroom they were given was tiny, no bigger really than their storeroom at Selwyn Lodge. The rickety bed

77

was just big enough for all three of them to share. Hannah couldn't believe that there was no bathroom provided by the tavern, just some scummy water in a basin and a chamber pot in full view! Jack, sensing her discomfort, suggested he join Keva. His daughter had been brought up very differently from the surroundings she was experiencing now.

"You'd have bin horrified to live in me old place, Hannah," remarked Maggie, as she rummaged around in their trunk to find a nightdress each for them to wear. "With an old palliasse to lie on and that was on a mud-packed floor. The only time we had a bath was in the river and that was usually once a year. It makes me shudder just to think of how we used to live, compared to the luxury we live in now."

"I don't know how you managed it, Mother. I'd die if I had to live in the squalor you must have lived in. Though what could you expect, if what Papa was saying was true, that you had to rely on your landlord to provide housing and such things."

"We didn't know any different. We were brought up in the cottier system, where we rented land and relied on the potatoes to give us our food. Oh, there were many other people better off than we were. The farmer that I worked for, for example, my friend who had her own cottage and the inhabitants of Ballina, the artisans and the shop keepers. But you just made the best of the life you were given and most of the time we were happy. It wasn't until I was fourteen and went to work at the Filbey's, that I realised we were having such a miserable existence down in Killala. Then the blight affected our crop. And yer know the rest of the story, yer father took me off to be his wife."

"Were you happy, Mother, when Papa took you away from Killala? Michael told me once when we were younger that you missed your birthplace greatly and didn't know where your sister had gone."

"'Tis true enough, Hannah. I mourned for me homeland for ages after and it wasn't until Michael was born that I felt settled. He seemed to replace the need I had, to be lookin' after a little one like I used to look after Molly. But I know she's well and cared for, someone told me where she had gone."

"How old would your sister be now? Perhaps she's married and got a family of her own."

"She was three when I left Ireland, so she'd be twenty-three or –four. Not much older than you are really. I do hope she's found someone considerate and kind if she did marry. Come, we'll go and see what the landlord's wife has provided fer our dinner, then we'll leave the men to their drinkin' and you and I will retire."

"So what brings yer to Longford?" inquired Jimmy Naylor, the dark-bearded landlord of the Pot of Gold. Maggie and Hannah had gone up to their bedroom and the three men were talking alone. He passed Jack a jug of the local brew and topped up Keva's glass of whisky that he had already started on.

"We don't have many passin' travellers, just the labourers from the Fanshaw estate and the odd tinker now and again. Keva here, of course has been known ter visit, but we've not seen him in a while."

"We lived in Mayo until twenty years ago," Jack explained, settling himself comfortably on the settle near the fire. "Both our parents were cottiers, but as you'll know fer yourself it was either emigrate or die. We got the chance ter go ter England and that's where we settled. At least me wife did, I'm a bit of a wanderer and spent some time in Chicago, but as they say, 'Love conquers', so I felt meself being drawn back ter me wife again. Then as time passed by we had a hankerin' to visit our homeland again and here we are, but it seems very different from when we were here before."

"How so? I've bin here eighteen years and nothin's changed much. Well, yes we've had a new land owner, but we never see him. This one changed a lot of things through his agent, but we never had the cottier system round here anyway, everyone worked fer the estate."

"It was different in Mayo. In Killala people rented their own bit of land. That's why they were so hard hit when the potato crops failed."

"And why there's bin uprisings ever since," broke in Keva bitterly. "But how can ordinary folk take on the might of those that have got the power? I know I tried it meself along with others, but I was left a broken man." Both Jack and Jimmy looked in surprise at Keva, but the man continued. Seemingly the whisky had loosened his tongue. "I was one of those at the battle of Widow McCormicks. Jimmy here knows all about it, as his son Danny was there as well. Where did they send him, Jimmy? Australia. A boy of barely sixteen. Me, they banged up in Dublin Jail for a year or so. I wasn't one of the main players, though they brought in people who said I was. But I maintained I was passin' by with a delivery and just got caught up with all the fightin', and my employer kept sayin' that that was so. I'm no hero anyway, I left that to the likes of O'Brien and Meagher, but I couldn't stand by and see all those half-starved people when Ireland was exportin' food, instead of feedin' their own."

"It's best ter keep yer head down, Keva. I've told yer that before. Get on with yer life and leave the rebellion to the youngsters. Nothing will change in Ireland, because of the system that we have here."

"It's a system that needs changing though," said Jack, heartily sorry for the landlord who seemed to have accepted that he would never see his son again. At least Mikey was in a peaceful place with his regiment in India, so they knew they would see him again one day.

"Yes and it *will* be changed by these young Fenians that are causin' mayhem at the moment in all corners of Ireland," Keva continued, passing his glass over to Jimmy for another refill. "The government will listen when disruption is caused to their railways and telegraph links and when the Fenian Army arrives from America."

"So that was what the fundraisin' was all about when I lived in America. To help recruit an army to send over here?"

"Well, yes and to raise the money to send arms across. There was quite a surplus of guns ter be had after the American War."

Keva suddenly turned around and looked over to the kitchen doorway. He lowered his voice, asking Jimmy, were there still folk around? "There are spies every-where," he said dramatically. "Government spies. The man yer thought was yer friend could be one. Who's in the kitchen, Jimmy? Yer wife? You, Jack. What side would you be on, now that you've abandoned yer homeland for the enemies'? What are you doin' in Ireland, I'd like ter know?"

"Come on now, Keva," remonstrated Jimmy, as he could see Jack sitting there looking embarrassed. "You've had enough ter drink fer one evening. This man is employing you to drive him and his family to their destination. And I'm sure he'll be payin' yer well."

"No, I'll answer his question, Jimmy. Yes, I am a Fenian sympathiser, Keva. Wouldn't anyone be who had ter leave their homeland 'cos of the famine and no help offered from those who rented yer the land? But I've done with fighting. I was a pugilist fer many years, earned me livin' at it and when I was in America I gave towards the fund. But me rule in life is to never get involved in politics. Nor join in discussions about religion or the Queen. I'm just thankful that I can go about me business back in England, without lookin' over me shoulder fearfully all the time. And Keva, I'm certainly not a government spy, I believe in freedom fer everyone."

"Sure I was just testin' yer, Mister. Sorry, Jimmy's right. Too much of the nectar. I'll say goodnight and bed down over there." And Keva lurched unsteadily to the mattress that Mrs. Naylor had earlier put down.

–

The drizzly rain set all hearts plummeting the next morning, as the carriage continued on towards Ballaghaderreen. The scenery was one of desolation, with mile upon mile of peat bog and open moor. The small hamlets they passed through were deserted. Grass and weeds grew entangled around dilapidated cabin doors. The carriage moved slowly with Keva hunched over the reins, as he suffered from a dizzy head, each pot hole in the road causing him to wince with sudden pain. Rebel ambled with his head down, only making an effort if his master's whip reminded him of what he was there to do. Both human and animal were saturated, neither with adequate covering to keep out the very wetting rain. Not so his passengers, nor the remaining parcels. The Haineses were snug inside beneath a blanket, a tarpaulin covered the trunk and Keva's precious goods.

Conversation inside the carriage was scant. Jack was feeling bilious having overdosed on the local brew. Hannah felt similar, although not for the same reason and Maggie wished she was back in Neston. There were so many things she wanted to do back home. Home. She had spent more years of her life in England than she had in this country, Ireland, the place that she had always thought of as home. It came to her then that it wasn't; it was just the place where she was born. It was situation and circumstance that decreed she was to grow up in Killala. The elder daughter of cottiers, she had known what it was like to be poor. But now, thanks to Miss Rosemary she was wealthy and making this trip back to Ireland seemed somehow all wrong. What was she going to find when they reached their little hamlet? Her mother, friends and sister would all be gone. It was dragging up the past for no good reason, better if they had stayed in Llandudno with its genteel buildings and golden sands.

The carriage suddenly lurched and juddered and the occupants were thrown onto the floor. Rebel neighed indignantly at whatever had caused his delay.

"What's going on?" shouted Jack angrily, as he picked himself up and helped Maggie and Hannah up again. He craned his neck through the window to find himself staring into the barrel of a well-polished rifle.

"Good morning, Sir, Ladies. Sorry to have to inconvenience you on your travels, but I would like you to disembark from your carriage while we carry out a search."

Two soldiers, their helmets and capes running with water from the continuing rain, sat astride their horses beside the carriage. Keva had jumped down in terror and was waiting for his chance to run, but the soldier who hadn't spoken yet had his rifle trained on him.

"We have information that weapons are being transported along this route, so our orders are to stop all vehicles that pass along this way."

"So that gives yer leave ter stop law-abiding citizens and search their possessions. Is that what yer tellin' me?"

"Look Sir, we can do this politely or we can cause offence. You choose. But I insist you get down from the carriage, though we will allow the ladies to sit out of the rain. You, driver, get up aloft and start handing down whatever is under that cover."

Keva rushed to do as he was ordered. First the trunk was passed down to Jack and then the three oddly-shaped parcels; one a bolt of fabric for a farmer's wife, another a replacement head for a pitchfork and the third a shiny large kettle. The soldiers grunted their apologies after searching through their trunk and told Keva to be quick about reloading and to get the carriage on its way.

Throughout this, Maggie sat with Hannah, silently fuming. The indignity of having to show the contents of their luggage, especially her and Hannah's underwear, was an unwelcome intrusion into their lives. She could feel the familiar red mist starting to appear in front of her eyes. She began to get up from her seat, gathering the folds of her skirt to her so that she could easily manage to jump down, but Jack put his hand up to stop her. He knew what Maggie could be like when her temper was aroused.

"We're to go on our way now, Maggie. Isn't that so, Lieutenant? I'll just help the driver to reload his parcels, then we'll be on our way m'dear."

The soldiers saluted and rode off back towards Longford, leaving the two men to heave the trunk and parcels back on top of the carriage again. Rebel had welcomed the break from his journey, contentedly chewing on a clump of grass at the side of the road.

"A good job they didn't climb up to have a proper look," whispered Keva. "Or stop us before we got ter Longford. That package I delivered while yer were havin' yer lunch had a couple of rifles in it and there's one under the blanket destined fer a Brother in Mayo. Sure, there's a box of ammunition too. It's no good havin' a rifle, if you've nothing in it ter fire."

Jack's face went crimson. Here was the man putting them all in danger, just for the sake of his bloody cause. He balled his fists, his temper matching the one before of Maggie's.

"How dare you put us all at risk, yer bloody fool. What would have happened if the soldiers had bin more thorough? You'd have had us all hauled to a magistrate before nightfall. If it wasn't for the sake of me family, I'd knock yer senseless. Now, drive on ter the next town or village and we'll find someone else ter take us the rest of the way."

Jack climbed back into the carriage beside Maggie, trembling from head to foot at the thought of what could have happened to them all. Maggie had calmed down, though looked very grim. She had heard some of what Jack had said but didn't dare mention it, as Hannah's eyes were full of concern. She accepted the hip flask that Jack had shakily drank from then passed on to her. The contents were fiery, but it seemed to help in calming her down.

"Papa," Hannah began unhappily, "I wish we hadn't come to Ireland. It's a frightening place. I wish I was back at home."

Maggie put her arm around her comfortingly. "I'm sure we both agree with yer that we'd be much safer back at home. The problem is, we haven't much in the way of choices. Though I think it would be safer, Jack, if we sail back from Sligo, rather than return overland."

"It's sorry that I am to have brought yer. I was taking this as a chance fer Hannah to see where we came from and do a little business along the way. Still, we can't be very far now from Ballaghaderreen, I've just seen some women gathering peat blocks for their fires."

Craning their necks through the window brought them untold relief. At least this village was inhabited. Alongside the road was a fast-flowing river, and Jack swore he could see salmon leaping up the craggy rocks towards the hill side. The carriage drew up beside a row of poorly-constructed cottages, the more substantial one in the middle being the tavern, where they were to stop to rest the horse and let him drink his fill. It was time for Jack to make a decision. He disappeared with Keva, leaving Maggie and Hannah to stretch their legs by the riverside.

The mist began to lift as the two women stood by the river, and soon a spot of blue could be seen in the cloudy sky. They wandered a little, pointing excitedly if they saw a flash of silver in the frothy water, glad of their warm clothing against the morning chill.

"Hey up," shouted Jack from the tavern entrance. "Do yer want to come in where it's warm or drink this in the carriage?" He was carrying two cups of tea on an old tin tray. There was no sign of Keva.

"We'll sit in the carriage," replied Maggie. "Here, Hannah, you go ahead with these. I want to speak to yer father."

When Hannah was out of earshot, Maggie asked what had been going on when they had been stopped by the soldiers. It was as she had suspected. Keva had been gun running, using his passengers as a cover, and posing as a delivery man.

"So, what can we do, Jack?" asked Maggie, a little fearfully. "We're taking a risk by travelling with him, what if some soldiers stop us again?"

"Keva says t'would be foolish to be rid of him now, though he's mortally sorry that we got caught up with it all. We can make Foxford by nightfall, then he'll leave us ter make our own way. We'll find somewhere to rest fer the night, then we'll ask around to see if anyone is travelling beyond."

"Well, all I can say is that I'll be glad when we manage ter get there and all of us in one piece. Why I let yer talk me into this Jack, I just don't know. I should have been like yer mother and stayed in the country we've got used to. I'm beginning to think there's no sense in looking into the past."

The rest of the day was uneventful. The landscape became one of open moor, peat bogs and distant forest covered hills. Small streams meandered beside the roadside or loughs glistened with the rays of the afternoon sun. Except for the occasional cottage, there was no sign of habitation along their way. Maggie and Hannah dozed; they had slept fitfully the night before, not used to the proximity of sharing the double bed. Jack tried to nap; he felt exhausted. The bench that he had tried to sleep on at the tavern had been narrow and he had been wary of landing on the floor. And Keva, only a foot from him, had been open-mouthed and snoring. If Jack had been given a pillow, he would have smothered Keva, he was sure!

The carriage seemed to be slowing and, with a jolt, stopped as it had done so before. The road had become narrow, the tree branches overhanging creating a dark and sinister tunnel where no sun could be let in through the leaves. As a family the occupants groaned. What was the delay this time? Not more soldiers they hoped. Jack and Maggie exchanged glances. Would they find the guns that were hidden this time?

Keva was shouting something in Gaelic, then stopped as he was hauled from his perch above. A mighty thwack was heard and he cried out with pain. Jack flung himself out of the carriage to offer his help if he could. Maggie and Hannah hugged each other in silent fear, while Maggie fingered her rosary, surprised that she had slipped it unconsciously from around her wrist.

It seemed that Jack too had been rendered speechless, as there was no warning for the women when two dirty tattered brigands leapt in from either side, with cudgels in their hands. Hannah became hysterical, screaming for her father, while Maggie sought to bravely push them off, as the men tried to drag them from the carriage. They were hauled unmercifully to their feet then thrown into a muddy ditch, where they sat for a few minutes, stunned.

From there they could see what had happened. Both Keva and Jack were nursing sore heads, while their attackers were picking through the contents of the trunk, that they had thrown down from the roof rack above.

Keva shouted again in Gaelic, clutching his head as he spoke, but whatever he said it stopped the men from their looting and, surprised, they turned to listen to him. One of the men then pointed to above the carriage, then grabbing a still-reeling Keva, shoved him against the side of the now-trembling horse and urged him to climb back up into his seat again. That done, the men hoisted Jack to his feet, then kicked the back of his knees so he stumbled into the ditch beside his horrified wife and daughter. Two minutes later the carriage was gone, the men shouting and waving to them from their newly-acquired transport, as they went on their way triumphantly!

There was silence in the ditch until Hannah started sobbing. Jack sat in a daze and Maggie was struck dumb. All that had happened in literally minutes; was it a nightmare or a devilish dream? Wordlessly, Maggie climbed up onto the road, ruefully inspecting her now-wet gown, glad she hadn't put her high-heeled slippers on. Then she helped Hannah. The shoulder seam had come away from the girl's gown and the whiteness of her trembling skin showed through it. Maggie looked at the muddy contents of the trunk now strewn all over the rutted ground, as she patted and soothed Hannah, thinking of how she had packed everything so carefully. Where was she going to get them cleaned again, was all her mind could say?

"Mother," Hannah seemed to be the first to come to her senses. "What about looking at Papa? There's a cut on his face above his eye and he seems to have fallen asleep. What are we going to do about him? He can't sit in the ditch for the rest of the day."

The fear in her voice alerted Maggie from wherever her mind had taken her. She had to do something; get Jack some help from somewhere, find them all a safe place to rest their heads. She crouched down to look at her husband. He was moaning quietly and it was true; there was blood trickling down from the cut on his face.

"You must get help, Hannah. I will stay with your father, but first we must try to get him out of there and make him comfortable. Here, take my shawl and lay it over by that bush where the grass is more flattened. Then you run to the nearest village and find someone. Anyone will do, just make it quick in case your father is really ill."

"But, Mother," the girl protested. "We haven't passed through a village or a hamlet as you call them for miles, nor have we seen a soul pass by for hours. I could get lost in the dark. Not find my way back, even if I do get help. Can't you go, Mother, I'll stay here with Papa?"

Maggie was about to say no, that the girl's legs were younger than hers, but the legs that she was talking about seemed about to buckle under. Hannah's face looked grey and it had seemed a great effort on her part to help haul Jack up from where he lay. Maggie stood up with a sigh of resignation and promised to be back as soon as she could. As she walked away, she looked back to see Hannah kneeling beside her father, cradling his head in her arms and crying over him piteously.

Maggie walked for at least twenty minutes before she came across a small slate roofed cottage. She was beginning to tire as the way had become hilly, and her breathing was laboured as she rounded a bend. With a sigh of relief she knocked on the door, hearing a dog barking from somewhere within. Hopefully the occupants would have a cart they could lend her, to bring Jack to their dwelling and let him rest for a while. A face appeared at the cottage window. An old woman's face; she looked guardedly at Maggie then shook her head.

"Please Missis, will yer listen ter me fer a minute. Me husband is injured, he needs help."

But the woman shook her head once more and disappeared.

Dear God, thought Maggie, as she trundled dejectedly on. What am I going to do, if no one's willing to help me? He could take a fever lying there in all his damp clothes.

Another two cottages later and still the same response. No one was willing to open their door.

At least though, Maggie was walking into civilisation. A row of cottages and a shebeen had appeared – and was that a church in the distance? Well, something to do with religion, as the Holy Cross was up on the roof. She decided to make for the church; no man of the cloth would refuse to lend a hand.

"Can I help yer in anyway, Missis?" A small girl pulled back the grill in the heavy oak door and peered at Maggie through it. She looked anxious and a little suspicious. It was not often a fine lady travelled along that way – not that Maggie was looking like a fine lady. Her hair had come down and her face was smeared with mud, but her clothes were of the best quality. No skirt made of common drugget for her.

"Could I speak with someone in authority? It's urgent I find help fer me husband. He's lying in a ditch some miles away."

"Oh, Jesus, Mary and all the Saints," and the girl crossed herself piously. "The Sisters are all getting ready fer Vespers, but I'll go and find someone fer yer."

With that she shut the grill and left Maggie on the doorstep to wait impatiently. As Maggie looked around she saw then the statue of Mary, standing on a marble plinth in the small gravel garden, and realised it was a convent she had come to. Maggie had never had anything to do with nuns, though she had seen them in the town of Ballina, usually walking around in pairs.

Heavy footsteps began to sound coming towards the doorway, then the door swung open to reveal a woman dressed in black from head to foot, except for a white wimple framing her face. She looked to be in her fifties, tall and large boned. This was the person in authority that Maggie had asked for.

"I'm Mother Immaculata, in charge of the convent. Matilda said something about your husband being in a ditch somewhere."

"Yes, Madam," and Maggie curtsied to the woman. "We were set upon by two vagabonds and the driver of our carriage and me husband were beaten about the head. Then the men took our transport and the driver away, leaving us in a ditch beside the roadside. Me husband seems terribly injured, his eyes were closed and he has a cut above his eye."

"And you left him like that to get help? How far away was that? There were cottages all along this way who could have given you a hand."

"No one would help us. Oh, I'm sorry, each moment that passes means he could be in terrible danger. Will someone here help? Does anyone have a cart or something that he could be laid upon?"

"Well, of course I would like to help, dear, but we are about to start Vespers. Just a moment, I'll see what I can do. Perhaps some of the girls from the dormitory can assist you. One or two are due out any day."

Maggie was left on the doorstep again, to puzzle why she should be helped by girls from the dormitory. Perhaps it was a boarding school and the nuns were all teachers;

perhaps some of the girls were due to leave any day. It was chilly standing there anxiously waiting, with desperate thoughts of Jack and Hannah. How much colder must it be for them?

"Hey up, Missis!"

Maggie turned to see a small wagon pulled by a brown and white pony, being driven by a plump girl in her twenties. The girl drew up in front of the convent gate and beckoned Maggie to climb aboard.

"Which way are we goin'? That way or this? The old woman said you'd been set on by the Fenians, the buggers are living up there in the hills. They're forever robbin' decent people. Folk round here are terrified of them, though she encourages them. Always feeding them from the back of the kitchen door. I'll be glad when I can get back to Galway; there's no sign of the troubles over there."

Maggie directed the girl onto the road out of the village and soon the wagon and its occupants were bowling merrily along. Maggie learnt that the wagon was used to convey the vegetables that the Sisters grew to the market at Ballina. She also found out that Bella had been a naughty girl and had just given birth to a child.

"That's why I'm at the convent, me and a few like me are there. Got sent away by me lovin' parents, to return with a flat belly and a bit of religion as well. Baby will go to a childless couple and I'll be welcomed back to the fold. 'Til I get found a husband that is. How far along here did yer leave him? Good job yer found the convent; no one else will help yer in this God-forsaken place."

Maggie agreed with the girl wholeheartedly; she had been beginning to despair of any help at all. Visions of being left to die at the roadside had been uppermost in her mind.

"Mother, oh Mother, thank God you've brought someone to help us." Hannah ran towards the wagon happily as she saw them coming along.

Maggie got down as soon as Bella had stopped the pony and ran to Jack who had his eyes open this time.

"How's he been, Hannah? Do yer think we can get him to the wagon between us? This kindly young woman has come from a convent to collect us, though I don't know what'll happen when we get there."

"Oh, they'll take yer in, like they do with all waifs and strays," imparted Bella. "They'll cluck around yer 'til he's better, then they'll put yer out again. As long as nothing interferes with their Matins and their Vespers, they're there to dole out good to the less fortunate. I'd help yer with himself, but as yer know I've just given birth."

Hannah gave a shocked glance to Maggie, who gave her stepdaughter a look that said "don't ask". Between them they managed to lay Jack down in the wagon, then they hauled the trunk up together. Hannah had put back the contents while Maggie had been away.

"They've taken Papa's money belt and most of his clothing. I hadn't noticed until I was picking everything up that most of his things had gone." Hannah was close to tears again, as Bella turned the vehicle round to head for the village. "I wish we had never come to this hateful place. Now we'll be stuck here forever or at least until Grandma hears about us and sends some money for us to get home."

"Shush Hannah. Everything will be all right again, don't you worry." And Maggie lifted the hem of her skirt to show Hannah. "There's twenty golden sovereigns in here."

"Thank God," whispered Hannah. "And Papa's looking better, though he hasn't said anything yet. He just keeps staring ahead."

"We'll all be fine when we've been looked after for a few days in the convent. Then we'll continue on our journey, as we wanted to before. Don't yer worry about anything any more, Hannah. God works in mysterious ways, but His plans are not fer us to see."

Chapter 6

The wagon drew up in a courtyard at the back of the convent's main building. It was almost dark now and from some of the windows came the flicker of candlelight.

On their arrival a nun came out to greet them, dressed in her habit and an all-enveloping white pinafore.

"I'm Sister Agatha. The Mother said she'd instructed Bella ter bring yer in. Is he dead, the manny? Let me take a look at him."

Maggie and Hannah gasped as they took in the import of her words. They both fell on their knees at the side of Jack. Surely he wasn't dead, though he was staring upwards with a vacant look in his eyes.

"Help me get him down, will yer," said the nun briskly, after she had climbed on board to feel Jack's wrist and satisfied herself that he still had a pulse.

"He's to go to the infirmary seeing he's not dead and I'm ter be his nurse. Bella, these ladies are ter be housed in the west wing. Put the horse back in the stable, then come up and take them to their room. Ready ladies? One, two, three. I've got him, steady, steady, now take his head and shoulders. That's it, now it's this way."

The three women carried Jack with difficulty, up two flights of stairs into a large, cheerless long-windowed room. The nun directed them to one of the six iron bedsteads, where they placed him carefully onto the clean mattress made of ticking, then placed a bolster under his head to support him. They were all breathless from their exertions. Sister Agatha had to sit for a moment on a wooden chair that was placed at the side of the bed.

"I'll look after him, don't you worry," she said, when she had got her breath back. "You'll both feel better after a good night's sleep and you can look in on him in the morning. Now, here's Bella, go with her and she'll see you're comfortably settled. Let's pray that the good Lord looks down on him with His favour and delivers him whole again."

They followed Bella to a small room on the first floor corridor. It was bare, except for two narrow beds. There were no curtains at the window or a rug on the wooden floor.

"You're lucky ter be given a room with only two beds in it," remarked their escort, when she saw their dismayed faces.

"What did yer expect, a comfortable hotel? I have ter share with five others, in a room not much bigger than this one and if yer stay more than a day or two they'll be after you helping out with the chores."

"Mother," said Hannah, after Bella had gone. "What kind of place is this that we've come to? You heard that girl saying before that she'd just given birth."

"Well, we're in a convent, Hannah. A place where nuns live together and pray for the souls of those who live in this world. They seem ter be taking in fallen women. Those girls who have got themselves in the family way, but are not married. Their parents must have sent them away from home, so as not to bring shame and disgrace to their good name. I feel very sorry for Bella. She was telling me that her baby will be given away to a childless couple; she didn't say if it was a boy or a girl. Now, let's not talk about things that don't concern us. We should be grateful that the nuns have been kind enough to take us in. And yer father will be fine once he's rested, then we can continue on our journey. Look, someone has brought our trunk up, we can change our clothes for some that are cleaner, though there'll be muddy marks on a lot of them."

It was hard to sleep that night. Maggie lay awake worrying that Jack might not recover. Hannah was concerned about her father, but finding out that the convent was a place for fallen women had brought her guilty secret to the fore. It had been easy to forget her condition while they had been travelling, but the tale of Bella and her illegitimate baby made her fear that she would be sent to such an institution too. Both her and Maggie's stomachs began to rumble, as no one had been sent up to their room with something for them to eat. They had heard some bells ringing in the distance then all had gone quiet.

–

Next morning came quickly, though it seemed to them that they had only been asleep for a couple of precious hours. A bell woke them first of all, then they heard the pattering of many scurrying feet. Maggie sat up quickly, wondering initially what she and Hannah were doing there. Then it all came back with swift remembrance. The theft of their carriage and driver and her husband lying upstairs in a hospital bed. She thought for a moment of Keva. Was he lying alone somewhere beaten senseless, or was he in on the kidnap, covering his tracks from the authorities? Whatever, it wasn't her problem. He had put them all in danger, carrying those rifles as well as them.

"Mother, I have to go to the lavatory. They don't seem to have provided us with a chamber pot and not only that, I'm beginning to feel sick again."

"Oh no, Hannah," Maggie replied, feeling a little exasperated. "If it wasn't that we are already in a place fer fallen women, I would be suggesting as a joke that you must be one of them."

Her heart nearly came up in her mouth to choke her, when she turned to Hannah to find that she wasn't smiling as well.

"You're not are you? Expecting a child? Hannah fer God's sake, is that what's the matter with you?"

She ran her fingers through her hair in complete bewilderment and looked over at her stepdaughter who had turned her face away.

"I might be." The girl started to whimper. "Oh, Mother, it was just the once. He told me he loved me and wanted to marry me."

Hannah started to cry properly then, remembering her hopes and dreams of marrying into society, then finding Jeremy had only used her. It was Catherine Lydiate he was set on plighting his troth to.

"How many courses have yer missed?" asked Maggie, clinging on to the hope that Hannah was only late, perhaps due to the excitement of their holiday. "Only when I was your age I never kept track of when me bleeding was due."

"Well, only the one, but I have had a lot of sickness since we started our travels. Perhaps I'm not expecting. He did say no one fell for a baby when they did it the first time."

Hannah began to look a bit more cheerful, though she couldn't quite bring herself to meet her stepmother's eyes.

"Oh, Mother, I really do need to find a lavatory. Can we talk about this later, after I've managed to find one?"

"We certainly will, young lady. I thought you understood what happens when yer lay in bed with a young man, when we had that talk about the birds and the bees. What yer father will say when he knows about it? I'm assuming that it was that Eddie from the tavern?"

Hannah was spared from answering Maggie's question as someone came crashing through the bedroom door. Bella stood before them, smiling cheerfully.

"Top of the morning, ladies. I see the Angelus has already woke yer up. They're all over in the chapel. Nothing much changes here. The Angelus three times a day, breakfast at six, dinner at noon and in between they get on with their duties. I'll be glad when I'm gone from here, I wouldn't make a good postulant anyway! Sleep well, did yer? Breakfast in the Refectory in ten minutes, so look sharp."

She began to walk back through the door, then remembered.

"Oh, the lavvies. You'll be needing them. On the right at the bottom of the corridor."

—

Later Maggie sat with Hannah at the long wooden table in the place that Bella had called the Refectory. Her mind was in an anxious whirl as she brooded on the consequences of Hannah's revelation. What was Jack going to say? What would they do with Hannah? How were they going to hide such a scandal in the small village where they lived? Well, if it was true that her stepdaughter was expecting, then she would have to marry the boy from the tavern. Though what a waste of that expensive education Hannah had just completed, to have to marry such an uncouth lout of a man.

She looked around at the other people present. There seemed to be a pecking order amongst the women who sat there on the benches. Mother Immaculata at the head of the table, Sister Agatha to her right, another older nun on the left. There were four other nuns dressed in black habits and two young girls dressed totally in white. Then came the 'sinners' in various stages of pregnancy – or not, as in Bella's case. The two visitors, Maggie and Hannah, were placed at the bottom of the table and of course were to be served last. Maggie cast her eyes over the nuns as they sat there, heads bowed and hands together, as they waited for their Superior to begin her prayer of thanksgiving. Each wore a wooden cross on a length of twine around their necks, along with their necklaces of black rosary beads. The young postulants, or candidates to become 'Brides of Christ', sat serenely, the light of their eager devotion shining from their eyes. Not like the other girls of around their age. One girl whose stomach was quite enormous seemed full of misery; another was giggling to her friend. Mother Immaculata shot her a look of disapproval and silence began to reign in the hall.

The grace was said, then a servant came with a huge platter of potato cakes and disappeared to bring fried eggs and soda bread for everyone. She served the head of the table first with her breakfast, then the platters were passed along for everyone to help themselves.

The soda bread seemed to be sticking in Maggie's gullet. By the time the pot of butter had reached the end of the table it was empty and no one seemed anxious to ask for another one. The bread was very dry, so she dipped it into the egg that was beginning to congeal before her. She felt like crying; those damn Fenians had a lot to answer for.

Maggie looked at Hannah, who hadn't yet touched a morsel; she just kept drinking from a pewter mug, her shoulders hunched, her eyes downcast. Maggie felt a certain sympathy. Who wouldn't, towards a girl who had been taken in by a young man's glib and lying tongue. Like the others sitting there, persuaded no doubt, to give away their innocence with the promise of marriage, or to prove to the man their undying love. They were left with the shame and consequence to be shunned as easy women in their communities. But, Jack would go mad if Hannah was expecting; his little princess who could never do any wrong. There would be hell to pay and Maggie would bear the brunt of it. She was the one that people would point at; the gossips in the village would have a field day. How could Hannah let this happen? They had such high hopes for her; possibly she would marry someone like the Adshead boy. A gentleman, to say the least, who would rise through the ranks in the Army and Hannah could have had it all. Maggie began to feel angry; she would take the blame for Hannah's action. People would say that she had spoilt her, letting Hannah's luxurious upbringing go to her head. Well, Alice, Jack's mother would anyway. Alice would say, what do you expect from a girl that was illegitimate? Fancy clothes and an expensive education won't change the truth of the matter. Hannah had her mother's blood.

Maggie tried hard to pull herself together. Didn't Miss Rosemary used to say, never trouble trouble, until trouble troubles you? Hannah would have to miss another month of her courses before she was going to let it trouble her.

For the moment it was Jack who needed her attention, though if he didn't get better in the next few days, what was she going to do?

She was summoned to the Mother Superior's office an hour or so later. Hannah was left with Bella, as Maggie hoped that some of what the poor girl had been through would be discussed with her stepdaughter if the two of them were left on their own.

"I don't have your names, my dear. Oh, Margaret Haines, Jack Haines and your daughter, Hannah. Thank you." The nun wrote their names carefully into a large brown book on the table in front of her after Maggie had given her reply.

"Sit down for a moment, will you. I have to keep an account of the money our community spends, to show our benefactor. A devout man and a Christian but a businessman just the same. Now, you can see your husband after our discussion, but from what Sister Agatha tells me, there is little change in his condition since you brought him here. He has control over his faculties, but his mind seems to have gone to a different world. Maybe that is well, if he has been set upon by vagabonds, but if there is no improvement in a day or so, I'll send for the local doctor. He will advise you on what to do, because as you can appreciate we cannot give you sanctuary for long. We are not an hotel. Each person here has to make a contribution towards the running of the place and I'm sure I cannot see you or your daughter scrubbing the floors on your hands and knees."

"But we can make a donation in return for your kind hospitality," Maggie hastened in. "We are a family who are not without means, though the creatures who hurt me husband stole his money belt and clothes. I am anxious, though, to continue on our journey. Our servants and the people we employ will be worried if we don't return when we said we would. Although, perhaps I could send a letter of explanation to the man I left in charge."

"Yes, yes, well let us see how your husband responds over the next day or so and then we'll have a further discussion. Do make yourself comfortable. I take it you are of the same faith as us, so you are welcome to visit our chapel and join in with our prayers. You might like the peace and quiet of our small community, though I would keep your daughter away from Bella. She might hear things that are not for her innocent ears."

Hannah was sitting on a bench with Bella in the vegetable garden, her 'innocent ears' agog with what she had heard. At the side of the bench sat a willow cleeve, or a potato basket, that the two girls had filled with spring cabbages. Bella was on light duties and out of sight of the kitchen nuns.

"So didn't you want to keep your little baby? Did you see her, where is she now? What was it like giving birth?"

"No, I didn't want ter keep her, in answer to yer first question, Hannah. Our house is full of babies. I'm one of ten as it is and me father told me to clear off the farm when me mother went behind me back and told him. I thought she could have passed mine off as one of hers, because it would have got lost in such a big family, but no, I got a hiding with that belt of his and I ran ter me aunt, who paid fer me to spend me time here."

"And what of the father of the baby? Did he want to marry you? Were you in love together, or was he spoken for and you are dying of a broken heart?"

"Romantic piffle, Hannah. I'm not saying who the father was. Let's just say there was no romance involved. Just a coupling, like any bitch or cow."

Hannah looked at Bella in horror. Was that what she had done with Jeremy? Behaved like a bitch on heat, his for the taking, happy to drop her drawers? No, she had loved Jeremy, hadn't she?

Especially when he had told her that they were to be married one day.

"Oh, yer don't have ter look at me like that, Hannah," said Bella, her face hardening as she replied to the girl. "I could have got rid of the poor little mite and meself if I'd wanted to. There's plenty of deadly nightshade on the hedgerows where I come from. But I thought no, I'll give it life and make some old childless couple happy and that's what I've done. She'll be going off soon to a farmer that's got no children and that'll be the end to it. I'm going back ter live with me aunty and that'll be me finished with men."

"You don't mean that, Bella. One day you'll find someone who loves you, then you can settle down and raise a family with a steadfast, caring man."

"Do yer think I'd go through all that again so that I can raise a stuffin' family? You'd blow the brains out of a donkey if he was suffering that kind of pain. I thought me stomach was goin' ter burst when I was near the end of it, but havin' ter push it out is something I'll remember forever. Those nuns, my God they were cruel. Prodding and poking into yer private parts, shouting at yer when yer wantin' a rest, forcing yer ter push when you've no strength left ter push with. No, I'm finished with men, as I've said to yer and I hope what I've said will be a lesson ter you."

"Well, you've certainly frightened the life out of me, Bella, but I'm sure you are just exaggerating because of your circumstances. If giving birth was so awful there wouldn't be any people left on the earth."

"Ah well, Hannah. That's where the Catholic Church has got yer now. It is your duty when you marry to have as many children as possible, because every child born comes in to the family of God. You watch when yer marry. The priest will be around yearly to see if there's another babby on the way. Oh crumbs, I can see Sister Izzy watching us. Let's get over with the cabbages or she'll make my life hell."

—

Maggie and Hannah stood at Jack's bedside. The cut above his eye wasn't so prominent now, but his jaw and left cheek had a terrible bruising. It was his eyes that frightened them both though; open and staring, occasionally blinking. But Mother Immaculata was right, Jack's mind seemed to have withdrawn to a different place.

"What are we going to do about him, Sister?" asked Hannah anxiously. "He can't stay here forever; we've got to get him home somehow."

"We must pray for Himself, Ladies," said Sister Agatha who was hovering around her patient. "Sure, we must be grateful that he's not a cabbage. At least he's not wet himself or soiled the linen. I've managed ter get him to the lavvie, with Sister Isabel's help of course."

"I'm in your debt, Sister Agatha, I'm sure me husband is getting the best of nursing care. I wonder though if he could be taken out of his very dirty clothing. Perhaps you know where I could lay me hands on a clean nightshirt. I'm sure he would be more comfortable."

"A clean nightshirt, now where do yer think I'd get one of those from? Do yer think I could perhaps magic it from thin air?"

"You probably don't know this, Sister, but me husband's clothes were stolen by those ruffians who caused me husband to be lying there. If you could think of someone locally, perhaps an inhabitant of the village or maybe a farmer who would be willing to sell me one. Perhaps the village has an haberdashery store?"

Sister Agatha laughed at Maggie's suggestion. "Where do yer think you've come to? This is Foxford not Dublin town. No, I've got an idea of something clean and comfortable. I'll put your manny in a shroud!"

Maggie sat with her head in her hands at the back of the convent's dark, but peaceful chapel. Her spirits had sunk to a depth that she hadn't felt for years. Her husband was lying in a world of his own and might never even come back to them and Hannah had committed a terrible sin that might ruin her life forever.

"God help us," she whispered. "Be merciful. I might not have loved Jack as much as I should, but he's made it up to me, for his sin with Kitty. Don't let him suffer; bring him back to us and forgive Hannah for her trespasses." She looked about her, waiting childlike for a sign that God would promise to help her; but there was nothing. Only the sound of her breathing and a bird chirping merrily on a tree outside. Then the Angelus was rung and the nuns began to file in quietly. Maggie left them to their devotions. She didn't stay, that would be to intrude.

The doctor appeared the next morning, whether he had been summoned, or happened to be passing, he didn't say. He stood by Jack's bedside, pulling on his goatee beard while looking at the patient ponderously.

"In my opinion, the man won't get any better lying here, because he hasn't been damaged physically. It's his mind that has been affected and he needs to get out in the fresh air. People and surroundings that are familiar to him are the best medicine. Those things could make him snap out of it. Are you far from your destination, Mrs. Haines? Mother Immaculata said you live in England normally."

"We had intended visiting Killala, where we both were born, Doctor. Perhaps seeing the place where he comes from might bring his mind back?" As Maggie clung to this hope, she could feel her spirits begin to soar again. "Yes, we could take him back to the headland, he might benefit from all the sea air."

"And do you have relatives in Killala? Somewhere you could stay while your husband is recuperating?"

"No, I'm afraid there is no one left. No one who will remember us anyway."

"There's a good hotel in nearby Ballina," piped up Sister Agatha. "My cousin runs it with her husband. I'm sure they could find yer transport to visit Killala, it's only really a spit away."

"Thank you, Sister," said Mother Immaculata. "I will write a letter immediately and you can deliver the Haineses on Thursday personally into their hands. You would be going to the market anyway, so you'll be killing two birds with one stone, as they say."

It was hard waiting around for Thursday to come, but there was no choice but to wait for Sister Agatha's weekly trip to the market at Ballina. Maggie contented herself with sitting by Jack's bedside, talking to him about their life together in Neston; his horses and the race meetings he had attended and how his mother was looking forward to marrying Mr. Arlington. Now that was a strange old how do yer do. Sometimes Jack's eyes would flicker, giving Maggie hope that he could understand, but then it was back to the vacant look, staring upwards to the ceiling as if he was finding something of interest there.

She borrowed a needle from one of the nuns and took out the twenty gold sovereigns from her skirt hem, putting them in a secret compartment in her reticule, just in case they were set upon again. The weather was fine and sunny, so she walked along the narrow village streets with Hannah to sit together by the riverside. They kept off the subject of Hannah's possible pregnancy. For the moment they must concentrate their thoughts on Jack, the person that was so dear to both of them.

There was a final parting between Bella and Hannah. Bella had been pronounced fit enough to leave. Her aunt would be coming to collect her; Mother Superior had sent her a letter earlier that day. The two girls sat on their favourite bench overlooking the vegetable plot, watching another poor young woman sweating, whilst digging up the turnips for Sister Agatha to sell on her market stall. Instead of looking happy, Bella's face was thoroughly miserable and she looked as if she had been crying, because Hannah could see the tracks of tears down her cheeks.

"Are you not looking forward to leaving, Bella? I thought that was what you wanted. To get far away from here."

"'Course I want ter go, silly. Who'd want ter stay in a convent unless yer were going to take yer vows? No, I was thinking back ter yesterday, when that couple came for me babby. I saw them through the window They looked older than me mother does! He had a face on him like a busted boot and she looked like a timid mouse. I know I shouldn't, but me heart went out to me little daughter.

What kind of life will she have with him? I know, I know, a better life than she'd have with me."

"At least you know that she'll be living in this area and who knows, one day you could come back this way and look for her. The convent will keep records. You might marry a rich handsome man, who will worship the ground that you walk on. Your every wish will be granted and then you could come back for your daughter and whisk her away!"

"Oh, Hannah, you are such a romantic. Real life isn't lived like that. Some of us haven't been feather-bedded like you have. No, I'll marry some smelly old farm labourer, probably a widower whose got a hoard of kids. That's what happens to bold strumpets like I am. Widowers aren't so particular about used goods like single men are. Ten years from now, yer won't even recognise me. I'll be the spit of me mother, with a big fat hanging belly, droopy tits and a rake of children as I'll be giving birth every year. That's if I have to. Aunty's a kind old bat, she'll probably let me live there for nothing. For company yer know. She's never married. Me Mother's put her off marriage. No, I'll settle for leading an easy life, without a man to bow down to."

"I'm really going to miss you, Bella. I'll give you my address and you can write and let me know how you get on."

"Fiddlesticks to writing, Hannah. I never took to it meself. Aunty can write though," Bella said hastily, when she saw that her friend looked rather crestfallen. She put her arms round Hannah and they both gave each other a hug.

–

Thursday came along at last and as usual they were woken by the sound of the bell. They had put their travelling clothes out the night before and hurriedly changed into them. The mud had been brushed off quite easily and Maggie had repaired the shoulder on Hannah's bodice. Then they both dashed off to the lavatory where they brushed their hair and washed their faces in order to make themselves look as best as they could. Breakfast was a hurried affair with Sister Agatha anxious to be off, so she and the visitors were served, unusually, before the Mother Superior. Then they assisted an unsteady Jack down to the waiting wagon, all loaded up with the convent's produce, but at least a pillow had been supplied to give him support.

Jack looked a sorry figure, sprawled amongst the baskets of cabbages, turnips and potatoes, though someone had bothered to clean and repair his clothing, so that he didn't have to travel in the ghostly shroud.

Maggie prayed she would never see him in one again, at least not until he was ninety. The thought of Jack dying made her heart do a somersault. She hadn't realised the strength of her love until this sorry time.

Mother Immaculata came to see them off, smiling sweetly as Maggie handed a sovereign to her. Bella waved from an upstairs window, then the pony set off at Sister Agatha's command.

The wagon bumped along the narrow road that led to Ballina. Jack appeared to be sleeping, at least his eyes were closed. Maggie and Hannah spoke in hushed tones while they decided what they would do when they got there. It was rather early in the morning to expect the landlord of the hotel to let them in, even though Sister Agatha assured them that he would do. Maybe they could help the nun at the market and take it in turns to keep an eye on Jack?

They crossed over the stone bridge at Meelik.

"Not long now," Sister Agatha told them. "We've just gone over the River Moy."

Maggie's heart soared when she heard this information. The River Moy. That was the name of the river that flowed past the hamlet where she was born. "Look, Hannah. It's only a narrow stream here, but further on it gets wider and wider, like the estuary at Neston does. Then the Moy meets the Atlantic Ocean at Killala Bay. Just think that is where your father and I lived. Jack, oh Jack can yer hear me, we've just gone over the River Moy!"

Jack's eyelids flickered for a moment and his body did a little shudder, then he relaxed back into sleep again. Maggie and Hannah held their breath. Perhaps he had understood something of what she'd said.

"Along here are the Ox mountains and further on are the Oweniny hills," Maggie explained to Hannah. "See the peat beds between the forests? That's what we used in our cabins to make ourselves a fire. Every May, when the weather started getting warmer, me father and the other men of the hamlet would take their slanes – that's like a thin spade – and cut hundreds of squares of peat sods nearby. Then they were stored under sacking to keep out the rain. The drier the sods got, the better the fire. It was like a day out fer them all. Oh, look, there's some men over there working on their peat beds already. Usually we lifted ours a bit later in May."

"It's going to be a lovely day," remarked Sister Agatha. "I'm sure you'll remember though, if we started off with a good summer, it usually rained in July. But I can tell from the formation of the clouds that it will be hot by dinner time. That means I'll have this lot sold much quicker. Not many people like to venture out when it rains."

"Is it always your job to come to market, Sister Agatha?" asked Hannah. "You seem such a busy person, working in the infirmary, dashing off to prayers and looking after the women in the Baby House as well."

"As they say, Satan finds things fer idle hands to do, Hannah," the nun replied, chuckling. "But there's not many of us at the convent and plenty of work to go round. No, it's usually me and I'm glad of it, though sometimes another sister will accompany me if she can be spared. Oh, look, we're nearing Ballina already, I can see the ruined castle in the distance. Look over there on the hill."

Chapter 7

Jack felt as if he was floating... Yes, that was what he was doing... floating along on a slow moving tide. The tide was taking him nearer... To what, his mind kept asking? Was he travelling through a mist or had a fog come eerily down? He could hear voices; gentle, caring voices, concerned voices, voices of loved ones, but who he didn't know. Now they had gone, there was nothing; just a silence, but he felt warm and comfortable; drowsy. Happy to be lying there in a world without a sound.

"So, what are yer plans now?" asked Sister Agatha, as she stopped the wagon outside the Heaney Hotel. "Will yer be staying fer one night, two? Bridget, me sister, will have to know."

"Probably two nights, Sister. Then we'll have to make arrangements to get over to Sligo. We'll sail back to England from there. It'll be easier than travelling back to Dublin overland."

"Just wait with the wagon then for a moment while I nip in the back door. They'll be in the kitchen having breakfast. I can ask Bridget's husband, Francis, to come and help us with Jack."

The nun scurried off and a little later came back with a big mountain of a man who introduced himself as Frank.

"*Cead Mile Failte*," he said. "Welcome to our humble hotel. I take it yer'll be wantin' a double and a single. Well, that's all we have anyway, so I hope they'll suit."

"Yes, thank you, it's very kind of yer to take us. You will have noticed by now that me husband isn't very well, but he'll be no problem. We'll take care of him between ourselves."

"Sister Aggie here has told us a little; poor man has got me sympathy. But this is a quiet law abiding town, where they'll be no trouble. Not any more anyway, not since 1798."

Frank began to roar with laughter, then he picked Jack up as if he was a baby and began to carry him through the front door of the small hotel.

Maggie, Hannah and the nun looked at each other quizzically. Then Sister Agatha shrugged her shoulders and said she must be on her way.

"We'll come down to help on your market stall later," said Hannah. "If that's all right with you, Mother, and you'll be bound to know the way?"

"You can, Hannah, but I'd like to stay with yer Father. I'll say goodbye now Sister Agatha, and I'd like ter thank yer for all yer care."

"God bless yer Maggie and yer little family. We'll be saying our prayers for yer husband at the convent. Perhaps yer could let us know of his recovery. Write to us when yer get home."

She began to drive off down the high street and Maggie and Hannah waved until she rounded the bend.

"Do come in. I've made enough for you to share in our breakfast."

Bridget Heaney, the nun's sister, stood on the hotel doorstep. She was similar in looks to Agatha, but had a bit more weight on and her dark brown hair had a few streaks of silver in it. Not that anyone had seen Sister Agatha's hair colour; it was presumed it was dark brown because of her black eyebrows. The woman could have been in her forties or fifties as her face was unwrinkled; just laughter lines around her eyes.

"I heard that dote of my husband mentioning the siege of Ballina. He does that to all our guests, likes to appear knowledgeable about the town's history and covers up the fact that he's a shy old thing at heart. It's through here. Come and sit down and make yourselves comfortable. Frank will be back in a minute and I'll get him to take your trunk up as well."

"We had our breakfast at the convent, Mrs. Heaney, but I'm sure we'd both be grateful fer a cup of tea. But before yer pour it, do yer think yer could take me up to me husband? I'd like ter see him settled then I'll come back down again."

"Oh, what am I thinking of. You'll be wanting to see your rooms. And call me Bridget, everyone else does. Do forgive me. I just get carried away with myself, don't I Frank?" she said, as her husband came into the room.

Frank nodded. He looked rather sad and his eyes were full of compassion. These two had a hard field to plough before their man came back into the living world again.

–

Hannah walked along the street a little later, keeping a lookout for the road that would take her down to the River Moy. Her mother had said that the market was held on some open land in the middle of the two bridges. She would see 'The Font' on the corner, a right, then a left would take her through the town. Hannah looked with interest at the shops she was passing. There was a haberdashery, a chemist and a small dressmaker's with a window display of pretty little christening gowns. Her heart gave a thud as she saw them. She had forgotten all about her possible condition. In nine months' time her baby might be wearing one of those! Oh God, what was she going to do if her courses didn't start again? Jeremy was miles away in some steamy tropical jungle and probably wouldn't be home again until the child was almost five. What a rat he was; an uncaring rat. No, not even a rat; a dirty horrible toad. Bella was right. She had filled her head with romantic, fanciful piffle, wanting to believe that what Jeremy had said that night had been the truth. But he probably wouldn't have done it with Catherine Lydiate, her inner voice came to her in mockery. She would have kept herself chaste for marriage, which is what *you* failed to do.

Hannah found herself down beside the river. She looked to the right of her and could see the salmon weirs. To the left was a big stone bridge and in the distance she could see a ruined castle and another stone bridge nearly facing a cathedral or a large church. There were many people walking along the riverbank and she realised that must be where the market lay.

"Hannah! Over here, Hannah." It was Sister Agatha calling from her stall. It looked to be fairly busy as housewives milled around, handling the cabbages, feeling the firmness of the potatoes then handing over the coins if they were satisfied.

"Put this apron on, will yer? I could do with a breather; thank heavens yer came along. I haven't got any scales for weighing on. Let people pick what they want, they usually bring a bag. A cabbage is a penny, about six large potatoes, two, and the turnips are two for thruppence. I'll be over there getting a drink of tea if yer need me. Thank God yer've come, I'm parched."

Hannah did as she was told and found she was really enjoying herself, especially as the customers she served were a cheerful lot, with lots of banter and repartee.

"Ee, thanks fer that," said the nun gratefully when she came back a bit later to join Hannah. "Pity you can't help me every week. The customers must have taken to yer, judging by all the money in the bag."

"Oh, I enjoyed it. Now I know what I will do for a living. I will find something to sell from a market stall. We have a market in Neston, that's on the Wirral, near Liverpool, that's where we come from."

"Tut, tut. I don't think a girl like you will have to work fer a living. Me old eyes tell me that yer from a refined background."

"I'm sure there's a saying, Sister Agatha, about not judging a book by its cover, or something of that nature. I have a feeling that it won't be too long before I will be taking responsibility for myself."

Hannah left the nun feeling a little puzzled, but that was how she usually felt around young people. They were complicated souls; full of perplexities and hornswoggle. Lots of phases they had to go through before they found their inner self.

Maggie sat with Frank and Bridget eating lunch of buttered soda bread and a chunk of yellow crumbly cheese. Maggie and Hannah were the couple's only guests and Maggie had turned down their request to eat lunch in their dining room.

"So, Maggie, what are yer plans?" asked Frank chewing his bread hungrily and taking big slurps from his mug of local black beer. "Your husband seems to be in no condition to take in the sights, but what about yerself? I'll keep an eye to him if yer want ter look around."

"We came from round here, Frank," said Maggie sadly. "This was meant to be a trip down memory lane. Show Hannah her roots and make sense of the life that we have carved out fer ourselves. You know, close the chapter on our past, that sort of thing. But now that Jack seems to have lost his senses, it's all a waste of time. Though I suppose I can take Hannah down to Killala, she can share *my* memories, if not her father's. The doctor at the convent said it may do Jack good to see the old places, but it's how to get him there. It's a bit far to walk, though when we were younger we walked to Ballina often. In fact, Jack worked at the quarry so he walked it every day."

"I can sort yer transport out, Maggie," Frank replied eagerly. "If yer don't mind handling our stubborn old donkey, yer can take Bertha. There's enough room in the cart fer three people and as long as yer firm with her, she'll get yer there and back again."

"Oh, that's wonderful," Maggie said gratefully. "Hannah's the one that is good with animals, she has a pony of her own back home. If yer sure, I'll be grateful for the lend of it. Though I don't think Bertha would be able to get us as far as Sligo. I think we'll head back to England the day after tomorrow. Is there someone who could take us to Sligo? Of course we're willing to pay."

"I'll ask around. Sometimes people journey over to Sligo to visit their relatives at the weekend. Or I could ask Billy McDermott. He has a carriage that he hires out, but it might cost a pretty penny fer him to drive yer there. It's over thirty miles."

"Where did yer actually live in Killala, Maggie?" broke in Bridget. "I have a cousin who lived near the harbour. Yer know the road that goes down to the quay?"

"We didn't live near the village, in fact we lived nearer to Ballina, than Killala, but fer some reason the hamlet we lived in was called that. You know the headland that juts out over near Moyne Abbey? Well, it was about a ten-minute walk from there. We overlooked the place where the River Moy joined up with the sea at Killala Bay. Me parents never seemed to take me in that direction when I was small; we always came over this way. I worked fer a farmer with the name of Filbey fer a couple of years – that was, until the potatoes failed and you'll know the rest if yer came from round here."

"Neither of our families relied on the land fer a living," said Bridget. "My dad was a shoemaker and Frank's dad had this place, but we saw the poor people who suffered. Many came to sell their possessions on the market to raise money for their fare abroad. We were just about getting married then, weren't we Frank? You'd done two years in the Army, but came back because yer dad wasn't so well."

"Aye, don't remind me, Bridget. Whatever possessed me ter join the British Army, I'll never know. I feel ashamed of meself when I look back ter those years. Anyway, we won't get on to politics, when yer daughter gets back we'll get Jack on his feet and put him in the donkey cart. Bridget'll make yer a bottle of tea to take with yer, won't yer Brid?"

The sun blazed down from the sky as Hannah chivvied up the donkey to get her to walk down towards the Killala road. Maggie felt Jack's forehead. He was sweating, so she helped him out of his jacket and loosened the collar on his shirt. She was going to take him to the tailors the next morning and see if they had something off-the-peg to fit him there. She had remembered there was a tailors on the high street and hoped it was still trading after all these years.

The fields they were passing on the outskirts of the town were full of yellow gorse bushes. It was heath land; wild and rocky with small dense copses that Maggie remembered she used to skirt around. In the distance she could see the small islands that were dotted along the far coastline. Except for poor old Jack, she felt contented. Suddenly she felt glad that she was coming home.

"How far along, Mother? You said we would see a narrow cart track once we had passed St. Patrick's Well."

"It's a bit further on yet, Hannah. I never used to walk along the road ter Ballina. I used to cut along the footpath by the waterfall and passed those woods over there. Filbey's farm where I used ter work is over that way and have yer heard me mention Mrs. Dockerty? Her cottage was further up the path, near the farm."

"Mrs. Dockerty? Isn't she the mother of Eddie's Uncle Johnny?"

"Yes, that's true, but I doubt if she'll still be living there. The poor old dear will be up at the cemetery, and that's another thing I want ter do."

"What, go to the cemetery?"

Maggie nodded. "I grieved fer years 'cos I wasn't there to see me mother's burial. Now, I can go ter see if they're taking care of me parents' graves."

"Were they buried nearby in Killala?"

"No, in Ballina. We used to worship at a church at Inishpoint, but the ground there was never consecrated.

Possibly because the church was so close to the headland, that they thought that one day the whole lot would fall into the sea."

"Is this the lane, Mother? It's very narrow and bendy. Hey up, Bertha, leave that pretty plant alone."

As they travelled along the rutted cart track, Maggie felt full of nostalgia. She kept gripping Jack by his shirt sleeve, pointing out this and that to him.

"Look Jack, over there, see there's Baunrosmore Island. Do yer remember when you and our Bernie walked out to it and you couldn't get back because the tide came in? Look at the sand hills in the middle of the river. Remember when we used to catch those tiny eels? They only used ter come to Killala around harvest time. Oh, there's the Filbey's farm; we'll stop here Hannah and I'll help yer father down. Come on Jack, we'll walk over and have a look at it all."

Jack got down unsteadily and leant on Maggie, as they walked over to the farmyard. He rubbed at his eyes with his left hand as if he was clearing a mist away. He stopped and looked about him, Maggie held her breath. Was his memory returning? Had he remembered how he used to pass this building on his way to work every day? She caught his hand and looked into his face. His eyes began to focus on her and her heart leapt. Was this a beginning, a recognition? Then his gaze dropped and Jack looked down at his feet.

"Hannah, I think something happened then. Your father, I thought for a moment that he knew me. His eyes looked into mine for at least ten seconds. Oh, Hannah. Perhaps this place is going to help him. Get his mind back again!"

"Where else will he remember?" Hannah said excitedly. "What about the hamlet where you lived?"

"All gone now, me dears," said a voice from within the farmyard. The person who the voice belonged to came up to the farmyard gate.

A tall thin man with light brown hair growing down to his shoulders, but not a lot up top, came out to meet them. He nodded pleasantly at Jack and Hannah, then looked puzzled when Jack turned away without acknowledging him.

"You'll not remember me, but I knew your family. Maggie Mayo, isn't it? Me parents had the pig farm up at Crosspatrick. I was just a tiddler when you upped and went. This place lay empty fer years after the Filbeys left, same with the row of cottages, except fer the Dockerty widow's. But she's bin gone this past two year; found her dead in her chair one winter's morn, when I was passing bringing in the herd."

"Oh, poor Mrs. Dockerty. Did yer get in touch with her sons? One of them was a friend of mine."

"Didn't have no address; couldn't have written to him anyway. No, I had ter call on the parish to bury her, though her son wasn't happy when he did turn up in the spring. But, I said to him, 'What else could I have done?' Not seen him since. There's the question of who owns the property now. It was hers, but it's on my land. He sold her stuff to one of me labourers. That's where Sean lives, in the middle house. Anyway, what brings yer to Killala? I'd heard yer hopped it to England when yer lost yer crop to the blight that summer. When we took over here, them cabins had just about caved in."

"Hannah, take yer father for a walk whilst I speak for a moment with the farmer. We'll have to leave the donkey cart here anyway. Bertha will never make it down the path to the hamlet. Would it be all right with you if we leave the donkey tied to your gate?"

The farmer agreed that it would be, then Maggie asked him her burning question. Had anyone else from the hamlet ever come back this way?

"Ah, that's why you've come back then. Looking up yer relations, is it? Well, I can't say that I remember anyone. All the time I've bin here, I've only seen the Dockerty son visit. Though there was a man hanging around about five years ago. Tall and sunburnt, not a black man with curly hair, but a man who's spent his life in the sun."

"Bernie, that will be me brother Bernie! He left fer a life at sea twenty years or more ago. Did yer speak to him? Did he say where he lived?"

"No, I shouted at him to get off me land or I'd set the dogs on him. I thought he was one of them gypsies that sometimes come around."

"If he ever comes back again, will yer tell him that Maggie, his sister, was looking for him and that he can find me in Neston on the Wirral? That's England, by the way. I had better dash off now and catch up with me husband and our daughter. I'll see yer later when we come back fer the donkey. We should only be an hour or so."

Maggie walked quickly along the footpath, feeling excited that her brother was still living and had come back to Killala, even if it had been after a very long time. She knelt at the shrine of the Blessed Mary on her way. It was still there after twenty years, still there for travellers to say their prayers. She prayed that Bernie was healthy and happy wherever he was and that one day they would meet again.

"And me sister, Molly, wherever she is. Look down on her, dear Mother Mary, bring her back to me one day." Then with a prayer for the soul of her friend Mrs. Dockerty and one for Jack to be restored to health again, she continued down to Killala, back to the memories of yesteryear.

Hannah was helping her father down towards the 'Giant's Tub' as Maggie caught up with them. Subconsciously, Jack had walked towards Killala. Years of habit, Maggie supposed, as she looked down before her. Her eyes met nothing. No cabins, no plots of land, even the stone walling had gone. Just a grassy headland and the sea beyond.

"Oh Jack, it's all gone," Maggie moaned and sat down amongst the bluebells and celandines that were growing in profusion around her.

"Hannah, when we left there was a row of little cabins, made from the turf cut by my ancestors. Poor dwellings I grant yer, but what we considered to be our homes. Now there's nothing. Someone's come and cleared the land, there's not even a stone bin left behind."

"Oh, come Mother," said Hannah practically. "You didn't expect the place to have stayed the same. From what you told me everyone moved out anyway. The person who owned the land wouldn't have wanted to be reminded of the bad times, would he?"

"Him?" Maggie snorted, getting up and brushing down her clothing. "He was away in his fancy house in England most of the time. It was us and the tenant farmers that supplied his lavish lifestyle. Anyway, let's go down and have a look for any clues that might tell that we once lived there. We can sit on the cliff and look out to sea. We don't want to waste such a glorious day."

"I'll be glad of a drink from that bottle you've got in your reticule, Mother and I'll take off my jacket. Papa can sit there while we have a look around and I've got a notion to make a daisy chain."

The warm floaty feeling was passing. Jack felt he had been left high and dry by the tide. He was hot, very hot; his head throbbing with pain and his eyes had filled with a mist, then they cleared again. A young girl was kneeling, picking flowers at his side.

"Maggie?" He put out his hand. "Maggie, you are goin' ter come with me, aren't yer?"

The girl rose quickly to her feet and cried out to someone that they were to come over quickly!

"Mother," he heard her cry. "Mother, Papa has spoken again!"

Jack looked around to see a woman running towards him, then as she bent over him, he saw she had tears in her eyes.

"You're not me mother. Where's Alice? Maggie..." he turned and clutched at Hannah's skirt. "Where's me mother gone, Maggie?"

"I'm Maggie," the woman said gently. "This is Hannah, yer daughter. We've come all the way from England to visit our homeland. I'm yer wife, Maggie. Alice is back in Neston where we've lived fer twenty years."

"No, no," cried Jack. "We're off ter England tomorrow, we're leavin' on the mornin' tide!"

"Yes, all right then, Jack, we'll be going off ter England tomorrer. You just sit there with Maggie and enjoy the sunshine. Have a drink of tea from the bottle, it'll cool yer a bit from the heat of the sun."

She nodded to Hannah, when the girl looked in surprise at Maggie's reaction, hoping that she realised she had a role to play.

—

Back in Ballina, Maggie sought out Frank and Bridget. Her heart was heavy as she explained to the couple what had happened earlier on. That Jack had recovered for a few minutes, but he had got Hannah mixed up in his thinking and didn't know that Maggie was his wife.

"He's gone back into his dream world again, I've put him to bed and left Hannah with him. He seems happy to have her near him. He keeps wanting to hold her hand."

"Well, that's something," said Bridget gently. "An improvement surely on what he was like before."

"I know and I must try to build on that by taking him back to England. I'll get the best doctor, one that knows all about these sort of things. Did yer ask around about someone to take us to Sligo, Frank? I know I said we'd go on Saturday, but I feel useless sitting around."

"I spoke to Billy McDermott. He said he was free to drive yer, but it'll cost. Do yer want me to go and ask if he can take yer tomorrow? Now, you just sit and stop frettin'. Bridget, make her a cup of tea."

"I could do with taking Jack to the tailors; he's only got what he stands up in, thanks to those rotten fiends. Is there still one on the street next to the market? I can't take him back home looking like a farm labourer; he's always been most particular about the clothes he wears."

Bridget said that the tailors had been there ever since she lived in Ballina, but Maggie would have to be sharpish as they usually closed at half past five. So, once again they set off down to the high street, Jack walking with Hannah, holding her hand.

Maggie couldn't help but feel resentful as she walked along behind them. If her husband was going to remember anyone it should have been her. She felt guilty at even thinking it. Poor Jack, it wasn't his fault that he'd been set upon, not his fault that his mind was confused. But still there was this little niggle. Why did he cling to Hannah and not her?

Jack stood in front of the cheval mirror that Mr. Tolan, the tailor had in his curtained off changing room. He was wearing a double breasted jacket in a light grey colour with a darker stripe running through the material, matching narrow trousers, a white winged collared shirt and a light blue cravat. What a handsome man, he thought, as he looked at his reflection. I could do with a haircut though, but all in all, not bad for nearly forty years! Forty years! Jack felt a cold shiver running through his body. He was only twenty, wasn't he? About to marry Maggie and go to England with her?

"Maggie!" he shouted. "Maggie..." Mr. Tolan came running into the changing room and Maggie a step behind him.

But it wasn't the Maggie he had pictured in the dark recesses of his mind, the girl with hair the colour of mahogany, creamy skin and oval green eyes. It was a woman nearly as old as his mother. A fashionably dressed woman though, brown hair pinned up into a neat curly bun, green eyes certainly but smudged underneath with the dark shadows of weariness. She stood at the side of him as he gazed into the mirror. Jack and Maggie, Maggie and Jack. The years came crashing back into his memory, but so did the pain of it all and it caught him unawares.

Jack lurched against her, clutching at his head in agony with his two hands. Maggie and the tailor caught him as he fell.

–

He lay shivering under the bedclothes then sweat started pouring from every part of his body, then back to the shivering again. He was aware of someone leaning over, wiping down his forehead, his neck, his torso, with cooling water. Her hair was hanging down in wild tangles, anxiety showing in her dull green eyes.

"Oh God, it's all my fault," he heard her whisper brokenly. "Taking you out in all that sun, whatever was I thinking of?" She held his head as he sipped from a cup of water, then the room began to spin.

Frank had sent for the local doctor when Jack had been carried back to the hotel by the butcher and his assistant, whom Mr. Tolan had hurriedly called for help. The doctor had said it was a mild case of sunburn, made worse because he was still recovering from the blow to his head. Had the patient been wearing a hat, or had he overheated with too many clothes upon him?

Maggie had felt mortified at her lack of care for Jack, in that bright blazing sunlight down on the headland. She had been so absorbed in her memories; the present had mingled with the past. As children, they were as brown as berries from the hot summer sun. No one was ever taken ill with sunburn, none of the kids had ever worn a hat.

Those carefree days in Killala. Maggie wished she had them back.

The doctor had recommended that Jack should rest for at least two days before Maggie contemplated getting him up again. He would return on Monday and if the patient showed signs of improvement, then travel arrangements could be made. Maggie hoped that Billy McDermott would still be free to get them to Sligo. So did Frank; it was embarrassing having to seek out the driver on a daily basis, especially as Billy was now talking about a standing charge.

Still, what did the man do with himself anyway? Sat around The Font in the daytime and evenings were spent in Moran's Bar.

Hannah sat beside her father's bed the next morning. Maggie had taken herself off somewhere, muttering that she'd had a bad night and wanted some time on her own. She had been waspish with Hannah, saying she couldn't be totally blamed for Jack's condition. Hannah could have made sure that his hat was on, just the same as her. Hannah had been stung by the criticism and was sitting there with tears in her eyes. One dripped on to her father's hand. He blinked and opened his eyelids. She found that he was watching her.

"Don't cry, Hannah. I'll be better soon, I'm sure of it. We'll go home and I promise yer, we'll never go on holiday again. It was thoughtless of me, dragging the pair of you across Ireland, but I thought it would do us all a power of good, seeing our roots, you seeing where your parents came from. I should have listened to the warnings in the paper that your mother read."

He closed his eyes again, weakened by the effort of his speaking. It made Hannah cry even harder when she thought of his hurt to come.

Maggie was sitting on a wooden bench that some thoughtful person had placed by the riverside. It was cooler that morning, she thought, as she pulled her jacket closer. The wind certainly had a bit more of a chill. She watched a little family of ducks as they glided past, a brown-feathered mother and her four tiny chicks. From across the bridge she could hear the high-pitched voices of children, then saw a formation of blue clad convent girls, walking in twos, behind their teacher nun.

Maggie felt really weary. Two sleepless nights watching over Jack were beginning to take their toll. She had snapped at Hannah, because she felt the girl had deserved it. If she was so fond of her darling papa, then she should take some of the blame as well! Her thoughts were on the same lines as Hannah's and she sighed when she thought of all the grief that her stepdaughter might cause them in the months to come. Maggie groaned to herself in frustration as she thought of Selwyn Lodge and her adopted home. There were contracts back in Neston that were waiting for her to sign!

Chapter 8

She was home! Oh the joy of it! Maggie ran to her bedroom window and looked across the estuary. There were the Welsh hills draped in a mist as dusk began to fall and her garden, her wonderful garden, a riot of colour against the backdrop of the grassy fields.

"Will yer be wantin' something to eat?" shouted up Olive, still agog and waiting to hear why the family had been away so long.

"Later," Hannah answered for Maggie, leaning over the banister to answer the servant. "It's a bath each that we'll be wanting first; ask Cook to leave us something on a tray. Papa, you are looking very weary. Sit yourself down and rest for a while. Olive have you made up the beds?"

"They've been airing for the last few days, Miss Hannah. I put a warming pan in each day to take the chill off and I've taken the opportunity to clean the house from top to bottom while you've been away. What was it? What held you up? Fergus went to Llandudno twice to meet the ship. You said you'd be away around a week or so and it's been nearly two!"

"Only two? I feel as if it was a lifetime. We had a few problems that's all and my father has been ill."

"Oh, shall I go and fetch the doctor then? I can be back in ten minutes if I run."

"No, Mr. Haines will be fine after a few days' rest. Now, weren't you going to inform Cook about our meal?"

Maggie lay in her warm comforting bath. She had thrown her travelling clothes into a heap on the floor of her bedroom. She would have them cleaned then pass them onto charity. Never again would she put them on; they would remind her too much of their recent nightmare. A nightmare that had seemed to be never ending.

After she had sat by the river in Ballina, she had decided to walk across the bridge to St. Muredach's Cathedral: chiefly to pay her respects at her parents' grave and to try to arrange a stone memorial. She had been sure that her father had been lain to rest under a beech tree near the far wall of the graveyard, but after fruitless searching she had gone to look for Father Daley. He would know where her parents' grave was and it would be good to tell him all that had happened since she had gone away. The housekeeper at the mansion house had told her that the priest had retired to his sister's home in Westport and the new priest was away visiting his parishioners, and would she like to call back again in the evening? Feeling very frustrated by the housekeeper's news, Maggie had gone to the stonemason's on Nally Street where she was told that the proprietor was so busy that a headstone could not be made for at least two weeks. If she would like to call in on Monday, he would spare the time to discuss what she wanted it to say. Monday? Maggie had thought in annoyance. She had been hoping that the doctor would say that Jack was well enough for travelling on Monday, now she would have to make time to see the stonemason too. What was that saying? Man proposes and God disposes? Well, that saying was well and truly meant for her! Her mood worsened. Not uplifted by the few hours of solitude she had given herself, Maggie had gone back to the hotel to find that Billy McDermott wasn't pleased that he had to wait until Monday for his passengers, and if he was to transport them after the doctor had made his call in the morning he'd be charging for a night in a Sligo guesthouse for himself as well!

And so it had gone on, Maggie thought, as she dried herself on a white fluffy towel, then wrapped herself in her pink satin peignoir. The only good thing had been Hannah's report that her father had awoken earlier while Maggie had been away and had seemed as if he had got his wits back. The doctor had confirmed it to be so when he had visited as promised, but warned that Jack must take things easy. If the family were able to find the money, he recommended that Jack be seen by a specialist who knew about the workings of people's heads.

It was a good job that they were a family with money, Maggie thought, as she glanced over at her reticule that she had placed on her dressing table stool. Her purse held only two silver shillings; all that was left from the twenty sovereigns it had held before. There had been the doctor's bill, Jack's new suit to pay for at Tolans, Frank and Bridget's hospitality, the headstone that Maggie eventually managed to order, the enormous bill of Billy McDermott's for transporting them to Sligo, overnight accommodation for them all, then at last three berths in the ship that would carry them to Liverpool. She hadn't even paused to admire the skyline of the great city, when after a strong tailwind, the ship had tied up at the wharf thirty-six hours later. Instead, she had bundled Jack and Hannah onto the next available ferryboat across the Mersey, frightened that some disaster would befall them if they didn't go directly home.

Spurning Hannah's plea that they travelled by train from Woodside to Neston, Maggie hailed a surprised cabby, who was very pleased to earn on that one journey enough to spend the next day at home.

"Oh, I feel so weary, Maggie," said Jack, as he wandered into their bedroom while Maggie was brushing her hair. "What say we have a lie down before supper? Hannah's going to use the bathroom next and it would be good to hold yer in me arms for a while."

"You could do with a bath too, Jack, yer only had bed baths while yer were poorly. I don't want yer messing up Olive's clean sheets. Why don't we just sit and talk about the future? You're not going to be able to carry on as you've done before."

"Pooh, there's nothing wrong with me, Maggie. Just a bang to me head that knocked me fer six for a while. I had worse done to me when I was on the circuits. Remember that fight I had when I worked fer Belsham? Two days I lay dead to the world, but Kitty May helped bring me round. Oh, sorry Maggie…"

Jack realised his mistake and blushed self-consciously.

"That reminds me. What is the matter with Hannah? The sea was as still as a mill pond when we were coming over from Sligo and still she was chucking up. I think she should be seeing a doctor, not me. Doesn't seem right somehow, a young healthy girl like Hannah. Yer know, I wish we hadn't gone back to Ireland, everything was going so well before. Sorry, Maggie, yer weren't keen to go, but yer gave in to me persuadings. I promise that next time we go on holiday, you can choose."

He put his arm around her, but Maggie shrugged him off and began to fiddle with the ties on her peignoir.

"There isn't going to be a next time, Jack. How could anyone want to leave here? This place in itself is like being on holiday, especially compared with the life that we left behind. No, if yer want you can go off, but let me stay here where I feel safe and secure in me own little haven. At least there's no nasty men lurking around wanting to attack me and mine."

Hannah listened to the low murmurs coming from her parents' bedroom as she walked along the landing to her own room. Poor Papa, she thought. It looked as if he had got over the trauma of the blow to his head by the Fenians, but soon he would be receiving a different kind of blow when she told him that she was expecting. She was convinced now that all her sickness hadn't been due to the heaving of the ocean, but the reaction of her body to the child who grew inside. Her breasts were sore and there seemed to be a change in the colour of the circles that surrounded her nipples.

Oh God, what had she done? What could she do to save her Papa from the misery that he had in store? She was a bright girl, wasn't she? Hadn't her tutors told her so when she had attended her private school? Think of the problem as an outsider would – what advice would she have to give? Morally; she would say that the person needed a husband. Find one quickly, before the baby began to show. Financially; he would have to be someone who earned a living, who could give her the things that she had been used to in her life. Attraction; it couldn't be someone who was ugly; she was going to have to spend the rest of her life with him and there was the coupling part of the marriage she would have to put up with as well.

Hannah sighed. It looked as if she was going to have to throw herself on the mercy of Eddie. Now that Jeremy was out of the picture, who else but Eddie would be happy to be the father of her child? But, for now, she would rest, and try to recover from that very long and arduous journey. What was it with these parents who looked into their past and thought their children would welcome their nostalgia? It was the future and where you were going that was important, not where you had come from.

—

"So, yer telling me yer missed me and couldn't wait to see me again?" Eddie said in wonder, unable to believe his ears when at last Hannah had managed to track him down.

She had hung around the tavern, feeling like a tart wanting business, stood looking into shop windows until the owners had begun to feel uncomfortable at her scrutiny, wandered around all the building sites trying to get a glimpse of him and even walked down to Lilac Cottage, thinking he might be there.

"I did miss you, Eddie. I had time to think whilst I was on holiday and I realised that you are a very important person to me and I wanted you to know that. That's why I've come to see you. To let you know how I feel."

"Well, all I can say is that I'm very cheered to see yer standing there looking pretty, especially as it's me you've come to see."

"What have you been doing while I've been away? Last time we met you looked as if you were working. I'm sorry I was in such a hurry but as I said, I was going to Chester to a function, so I didn't really have the time to speak.

Michael went off to India with his unit you know, so I had to go to the leaving do."

"Ah yes, I did hear you were hankering after that Jeremy Adshead. What is it Hannah? Now he's gone, feeling lonely so thought you'd seek out the second best?"

Hannah had the grace to look a little sheepish, but she quickly gathered herself together to assure Eddie that his jibe wasn't true.

"Oh, Eddie, how could you think that? You've never been second best. I had to attach myself to the Adshead family because that was what my parents wanted, especially as Michael and Jeremy were such good friends. But while I was on holiday I said to myself; just because my parents don't like Eddie doesn't mean I can't be friends with him. I mean, good heavens, I saw where my parents came from; a mean little hovel from all accounts."

"So does this mean you and I are going to start walking out together? Because if it does all me dreams will have come true."

"Yes, of course it does and we'll stand firm together if we start receiving any backlash. Now would you like to walk me home? I've been standing like a statue on this corner for half an hour at least and the people who own the vegetable shop were beginning to wonder why I was here."

Eddie couldn't believe his luck as he said goodbye to Hannah at the gate of Selwyn Lodge, especially as she had promised to meet him at Lilac Cottage the following evening. He had thought he would never hold her in his arms again, after that terrible afternoon when he had blurted out what his mother had told him. Now it didn't seem to matter. All those things that he'd been hearing; how Hannah had been seen in the company of the heir to the Adshead fortune, how she would probably be announcing her engagement; none of it had been true. It had been Eddie that Hannah had hankered after and she was willing to overcome all the problems that undoubtedly they would have to face.

What a vision she had been; dressed in a flowery summer frock with a yellow jacket hanging carelessly from her shoulders. He had spotted her on the corner of Bridge Street as he trundled aimlessly up the hill with another solitary evening to look forward to. He hadn't bothered pursuing any of the local girls to try and mend his heart over Hannah. No one could ever measure up against his beloved; they had no class, they didn't have her style. His heart had leapt at the sight of her, but he told himself not to be too eager. She might have been waiting for her mother, or worse, a boyfriend, but as soon as her eyes met his, Eddie knew that Hannah was to be his destiny.

—

"Mother, Papa. There is something that I wish to tell you." Hannah stood in the doorway of the drawing room as the couple relaxed at the end of the day. Maggie raised her eyebrows at her stepdaughter then groaned inwardly. She moved protectively towards Jack who was sitting on the settee beside her. The specialist who had been called in to assess her husband's condition had said that he must take things easy; no shocks or sudden excitement. If this was the announcement she was expecting from Hannah, Jack would need her support as never before.

He had improved greatly over the month that they had been back from their trip to Ireland. His memory had returned in full, though he was a much more sober man in temperament; spending a lot more time at home or in the garden. There had been no talk of buying another race horse to keep Fletcher and Dalton company. In fact, he had only been to visit Fletcher once at the stud farm outside Chester, saying that Fergal would inform him if any decisions were to be made. Maggie had been busy up at Mr. Arlington's office, signing the contracts for the land purchases and catching up with her various committees, so she had pushed Hannah's possible motherhood to the back of her mind. She sat rigid as she waited for Hannah to start speaking. This would either destroy their little family or perhaps make them stronger. Would Hannah admit to her father that she was carrying Eddie Dockerty's child?

"Papa," Hannah began to speak in her little-girl voice, which she usually used when she was trying to wheedle something out of him.

"Papa. You know you said that I wasn't to see Eddie Dockerty again, because his background isn't as good as ours? Well, I've decided that I'm going to marry him. It doesn't really matter about a person's background, Papa. Look at you and Mother. Eddie asked me to be his wife when I saw him yesterday and I've agreed to his proposal. I know I need your permission as I am under twenty-one, but I've said 'Yes' anyway."

There was a silence in the room as two pairs of eyes stared at Jack expectantly. Maggie was waiting for Jack to explode and lock Hannah in her bedroom forever and Hannah trembled a little as she waited for the battle to begin. Both women were surprised at his reaction, especially Maggie, who was sitting so close she could feel how Jack's body had tensed.

"Do as yer like, Hannah," he said brusquely. "If yer want to leave here and exchange it for a run-down hovel at the back end of Neston, then you do it. If yer want to give birth to a child each year and live off the wages of a labourer, then so be it. But let me tell yer this. When it all gets too much for yer, don't come crying to me and don't expect a big lavish wedding either. You'll be married at St. Winefred's as soon as the banns have been read. I take it you're expectin', or you wouldn't be so insistent at throwing yer life away."

He got up then and brushed past Hannah, knocking her into the doorjamb. Not intentionally, though it looked that way. He slammed the front door behind him and he stalked angrily along the gravel path that led to the stables. Hannah threw herself in the seat that Jack had just vacated and allowed the tears to run.

Maggie felt at a loss, as she listened to the girl breaking her heart over her father's pitiless words. But what had Hannah expected? That Jack would be delighted, buy her a smart new house and pay for a costly wedding day? The man must be mortified, as she was, to see his daughter throw away an expensive education and a comfortable lifestyle to marry an ignorant oaf such as Eddie Dockerty.

"Why did you do it, Hannah?" Maggie put her hand tentatively on the girl's shaking body and attempted to smooth down Hannah's tangled hair.

"What possessed yer to give in to a person like Eddie Dockerty? Your father had such high hopes that you would marry someone like Jeremy Adshead and live like a princess at Causey Hall."

"Oh, yes, someone like Jeremy Adshead," muttered Hannah. It was difficult to hear what she was saying as her trembling hands were covering her face.

"And what would have been wrong with Jeremy, Hannah? He's from a very good family; he'll gain rapid promotion in his battalion and should win a few medals I've no doubt."

Hannah sat up then, her eyes puffy from crying and her face red and blotchy. Glaring at Maggie and poised ready for flight, she said the words that cut into her stepmother like a knife.

"It wasn't only Kitty May that behaved like a bitch on heat with the first man who asked her to sleep with him; so did her daughter. But I didn't give away my honour to a solid gold man like Eddie. No – the father of the child I'm bearing was Jeremy! Prince Jeremy, heir apparent to Causey Hall, who promised that we would be married, but he's beggared off to God knows where. Why do you think I've thrown my lot in with Eddie? At least he'll be around for me and he'll never know that it's not his child."

With that she flung herself out of the door and ran up the stairs to her bedroom, leaving Maggie stunned and feeling horribly wounded. That was twice in the last few weeks that Kitty May had been mentioned. Did she have herself to blame for letting Jack live his own life, like she had? If she had followed him to Liverpool, none of this would be happening. There would be no Hannah, no immoral act committed with Jeremy and Jack wouldn't be hurting with this misery and shame.

She would have to go to him. Follow him down to the stables and try to get him to come to terms with his daughter's decision. They couldn't let her live in squalor, couldn't let her live from hand to mouth on the wages of a labourer. Hannah was Jack's daughter and soon he would have a grandchild. Be it Jeremy's offspring or Eddie's, the babe shouldn't suffer. Maggie would make damn sure that his grandchild would have the best in life. She went into the hallway to put her cloak on, but spotted Olive lurking.

Why would she be dusting the dining room mirror at this late hour?

"Haven't yer got a home to go to, Olive?" she asked crossly. "You're usually away on the dot of seven, or has it been more exciting listening to what's been going on here? Well, let me tell yer, if I hear that one word has been repeated outside to the villagers, you'll be finding another place of employment. Now get yer coat on and be on time tomorrow. I've a coffee morning in aid of the cottage hospital, so make sure there's no stains on yer pinny and give yer shoes a bit of a wipe."

Maggie found Jack with his arm round the neck of Jefferson, one of his carriage horses. His eyes were bright with unshed tears as he turned to face her. Then he gathered her into his arms and wept, bringing forth his anguish as she patted him as if he was a babe.

"Maggie, oh Maggie, this is certainly a case of sin being passed down by the forefathers. Why on earth did I leave you all those years ago?"

"Hush, Jack," Maggie soothed. "It's not your fault that the silly girl has got into the family way. It takes two to make a baby, so it's her problem not yours. But I thought yer were a bit harsh, if yer don't mind me saying so. At least she has a boy to marry; it's not as if she's going to bring shame on us all."

"Not like I would have done if I hadn't run off with Kitty. Is that what yer mean, Maggie? *You* had to cover it all up and pretend yer were a widow for all those years."

"No, Jack, it's *not* what I'm saying." Maggie felt stung that he could even think it. "But if that is going to be your attitude, yes, let's say what is on both our minds. Hannah has behaved no better than her mother did and it will probably be me who has to do a cover up again. Well, I'll leave yer to stew then, I've a girl who needs my attention more than you do."

With that she stalked back up the gravel path like a cat angrily swishing her tail.

The atmosphere in the house was unbearable over the next few days. Jack refused to speak to anyone; even Olive ran for the security of the kitchen if the master was found to be blocking her path. Hannah stayed in her bedroom and had her meals taken up on a tray. Maggie just got on with her life. If there were plans to make for a wedding, she would wait to hear from the daughter of the house. She had tried to talk to Hannah; she had knocked tentatively on her bedroom door after she had left Jack at the stables. But there had been no answer. Either the girl had fallen asleep or didn't feel like talking. Maggie left her to it and smilingly played the gracious hostess, when the good ladies of the village called on her next day. Jack moved his things out to the guest room, so neither of them suffered nights of tension. When Maggie examined her feelings, she found that she was glad.

–

"Mrs. Haines! Oh, Mrs. Haines, will yer come up here quickly!" Maggie could hear Olive shouting, as she walked in from the garden where she had been cutting back a climbing rose.

"Whatever is the matter, Olive? If I was in Neston village I would have heard yer. You must learn to have more decorum, not shouting out like an old fishwife."

By this time Maggie had climbed the stairs to see what all the fuss was about and pushed past her goggling servant, who was in the doorway of Hannah's room.

Maggie took in the scene before her, panicked for a moment, then told Olive to get some rags from the store cupboard downstairs.

"It's Hannah's monthlies, nothing to get worked up about. It's happened before, though why I'm standing here explaining this to my servant, I'll never know. Get the rags like I've told yer, then get about yer business. You can tell me later what yer were doing up here. Yer know that servants use the outside W.C."

"Well, I come to give her a message from her fella, Eddie," Olive retorted defiantly. "She's to meet him at Lilac Cottage after work this evening, but I suppose now she won't be able to go."

"No, she certainly won't be going down to Lilac Cottage, not this evening, nor any other and remember you're not paid to be a messenger. You're here to serve this household, now go and do as yer told."

Hannah was hunched up under her blankets, looking deathly pale and scared at what her body was doing to her. Maggie could see that she had been crying and was struggling to be brave with her obvious pain.

"Do yer think yer losing the baby?" Maggie asked in the lowest voice she could muster in case she was overheard. Hannah nodded, then winced as another spasm caught her, which brought on another bout of tears.

"Maybe it's for the best." Maggie mentally kicked herself for saying it; it was a little baby, after all, that was slowly losing its life. She was saved from saying more and digging herself into a bigger hole that might be remembered by her stepdaughter, with the appearance of her breathless servant. Olive placed the pile of clean rags on the bedside table, her eyes enormous in her thin, pointed face.

"You can go now, Olive, thank you. Perhaps you could find a little brandy in one of Cook's cupboards. Bring it up and tell Cook that Hannah will only need a light supper. Perhaps some coddled eggs or if she has any, some calves foot jelly. I'll be out this evening, so I'll make myself something on my return."

Once Olive had left, she sat on the bed and held her stepdaughter to her.

"It is for the best when you look at it sensibly, Hannah, though you won't thank me for saying so at this very sad time. It wouldn't have been fair to Eddie. It wasn't his child and you would always be fearful that he'd notice. The problem with skeletons in peoples' cupboards is that they often pop out at inopportune times. Look, you'll probably suffer a lot of discomfort for the next day or two then it will all be over. Now, put these wedges between your legs and when Olive brings the brandy take a gulp and it will help yer settle. I've got to go out in an hour or so, but if the pain gets worse we'll send fer the doctor. You'd only missed two monthlies, hadn't you? Let's be thankful fer that anyway. Further on than that and I don't know what we would have done with you."

"Thanks, Mother," said Hannah, in a low voice, as she settled back on her pillow. "You've been good to me over the years and taking on someone else's daughter couldn't have been easy. I must have been a constant reminder of Papa's infidelity and you could have left me with Grandmama if you had wanted to. Couldn't you?"

"No, I couldn't, Hannah," Maggie started to laugh at the thought of it. Olive wondered at her gaiety as she walked in bearing the glass of brandy. She'd never work these Haineses out. One minute they were all doom and gloom and now here was her mistress laughing so much she was falling about!

Maggie hurried across the field in the direction of Lilac Cottage a little later. Her mind was so focused on what she was going to say to Eddie that she didn't experience the pleasure of the fact that all of this land around her belonged to the Sheldon Property Company, and the cottage she was visiting and the other two just up the lane were included in the land purchase. She was intent on meeting this Eddie to try and persuade him that marriage to Hannah would not bring them any happiness. They would hate each other in years to come, when the first bloom of love had withered like a dried-out plant. And there would be no support for the young couple if they went ahead with it; Jack with his silence was making that very clear.

Maggie looked in surprise when she arrived at the cottage. What a state it had got into over the years since she and Jack had lived there. Surely Farmer Briggs could have maintained the place better, even if it had been empty. The door was hanging by only one of its hinges and a few slates to cover those gaping holes in the roof wouldn't have gone amiss.

She pushed her way past the overhanging bushes, the scent of lilac invading her senses, causing her for a moment to hanker after her youth. Hadn't life been much more simple then? A roof over their heads and food in their mouths. The pleasure of waking up each morning, breathing in the fresh sea air, walking along the shore without any shoes on. She forgot the more unpleasant parts; waking up in the chill of the winter and walking through the rain to work at the farm.

"Hannah, is that you?"

Maggie heard a young man's voice calling eagerly from within the cottage. She hesitated. That was the voice of the man who was looking forward to seeing the daughter, not her mother. What kind of reception was she going to receive?

"Oh, Mrs. Haines!"

Eddie gaped at her, looking alarmed. He rose quickly from the old settee where he had been sitting. "Where's Hannah? Did she send yer? Is she ill or something? I haven't seen her for days!"

He began to run his fingers through his hair in a distracted fashion and Maggie's heart softened a little as she looked into his handsome face.

"Yes, Hannah isn't very well at the moment, but she doesn't know that I'm here. I waylaid Olive and got your message that you'd be waiting here at Lilac Cottage. Strange that you should choose this place to meet. My husband and I used to live here."

"I know, me mother told me; seemed fitting somehow that we used it for our secret trysts."

"Oh, so you've met here quite often then. All those long walks with the dogs that Hannah took ended up with meeting you."

"Mrs. Haines, I'm sure yer didn't come here to discuss Hannah's walks in the countryside. To be honest, I'm glad that you and I have met. Rather it be you than yer husband. Hannah told me I'd get a good hiding off him should our paths ever cross, which is going to be difficult seeing he's going to be me father-in-law. I'm sure that Hannah has told yer that she has said she will be me bride."

"Yes, she had told us, Eddie and that's why I've come to see yer. Her father went up in a puff of smoke when she told him and now he's not speaking to her. It's a great pity 'cos the bond between them is a strong one. Well, it has been up to now."

"It's because he thinks I'm not good enough for her. I know it, Mrs. Haines, but she'll never find another who loves her as much as I do. I love her down to her little fingertips. Since I played with her and Mikey in the Selwyn Lodge nursery, I knew that she would be mine one day. I'll work all the hours God sends to give her everything she wants in life. The foreman where I work says I'm a strong and willing worker and I'll end up one day running me own gang of men."

Eddie looked hopefully at Maggie, wondering if his words had gone some way to impress her. He couldn't tell as her face had remained inscrutable and then she started pacing the floor, which somehow made him feel nervous. He felt she was up to something; she hadn't just appeared to tell him Hannah was ill.

"I can see that you're an earnest young man and only want the best fer Hannah, but think what will happen if things don't live up to your expectations. She'll hate yer for it, for taking her away from the comfortable existence she's grown up with and without meaning to sound the proud parent, she's been educated to a higher standard than you have, as well."

"I don't think that's a fair thing to say, Mrs. Haines, if yer don't mind me saying so. Hannah may have had all the advantages, but that doesn't mean we'll be mismatched in our married life. She'll make a good mother and will be able to help our children get a better future. I regret the hours I didn't spend in the classroom, but I'll make sure me kids don't miss out."

Maggie could see that she wasn't getting anywhere with this zealous young man who was so adamant that his future lay with Hannah. She decided to try one more tactic, then she was going to throw the towel in. Perhaps a bribe would work; perhaps Eddie could be persuaded financially to move away from the area. She would feel that it was rather a dirty trick, but it would give her the measure of the man.

"Fifty pounds!"

Eddie's eyes nearly popped out of his head when he heard the sum that Maggie mentioned. But his voice was full of scorn as he flatly turned her offer down. "You're trying to bribe me to give up Hannah. What kind of a man do yer think yer dealing with? If yer said a thousand it wouldn't be enough to make me part from her. I love her, Missis, and I'm gutted that you'd think you could pay me to go away. Anyway..." Eddie's voice dropped to a confidential whisper, "she may be expectin' my child. It's possible, and yer wouldn't want its father to have cleared off and left it, now would yer?"

Maggie's anger reached boiling point when she heard his jeering words. So, the little madam had lied when she had said that it was Jeremy she had lain with. Her hand came up to give Eddie a hard slap across his smug-looking face. Then she turned on her heel to walk angrily out of the cottage.

Chapter 9

Maggie tossed and turned in her bed that night. Her head throbbed with the anger that she was still feeling. She hated being lied to, and she couldn't make sense of why Hannah had done so.

On her arrival back at Selwyn Lodge, she had quelled the urge to rush up to Hannah's room and confront her. The girl wouldn't be in any fit state to listen to her stepmother's ranting and deep down Maggie would have felt a curmudgeon to have added to her suffering.

She decided to get up and make herself a warm drink; maybe a cup of tea would calm her down, or perhaps a glass of Cook's brandy would help her sleep. Maggie looked in on Hannah. From what she could see from the light of the oil lamp, the girl was sleeping, so she closed the bedroom door quietly and tiptoed away.

Someone was sitting at the kitchen table as Maggie entered the room. It was Jack. He jumped as she glided in with slippered feet and set the oil lamp down so she could see him.

"What are you doing here in the dark?" she asked gently. "Can't yer sleep? Well, that makes two of us. What's that yer drinking? Pour me a glass of it, will yer? Anything to make me sleep after a really terrible day."

"Can it get any worse, Maggie? You and me have fallen out over something that we could have worked out between us. I'm sorry, Maggie. I've been acting like a thoughtless idiot because I've got a dent in me pride."

"Well, one of the problems has gone away, Jack. Hannah isn't expecting any more. She'll be poorly for a few days, then probably steeped in misery for a week or two, but that should be an end to it. At least she doesn't have to marry Eddie Dockerty any more and perhaps we could think of somewhere to send her to get over it. I have the address of her old nursemaid, who I'm sure would be pleased to see her after all this time."

"No, Maggie." Jack said very firmly. "Hannah will still be marrying the Dockerty boy. I'm going to insist on it, even if she has lost his baby. He's deflowered her, if that's what yer call it and what other man will have her now? I thought at one time she was more than friendly with Jeremy Adshead and marriage to him might have been on the cards."

Maggie nearly blurted out that Hannah had said it was Jeremy's baby she was expecting, but decided to hold her tongue. She was at a loss now as to whether Hannah had told her the truth and telling Jack would only confuse things.

"So what are we going to do then? She's not going to be up to getting involved with wedding preparations just yet and there's something we've forgotten about, your mother and Mr. Arlington."

"Yes, I know. Poor mother has been pushed onto the sidelines with all this kerfuffle; their nuptials are on the 23rd. We can hardly tell her about Hannah getting wed, that would really put the cat amongst the pigeons. Anyway, what say I come back to our bedroom and make up for lost time? That's why we've not been sleeping well, yer know. No one to warm each other's feet and that bed in the guest room is as hard as hell!"

–

It was Hannah and Eddie's wedding day: 8th January 1870. It was also Eddie's 21st birthday, as Madeline had flatly refused her permission for her son to marry into the uppity Haines family. That had greatly puzzled Eddie when he had asked her to sign the paper. He had thought his mother would have been happy for him, knowing how he had always nurtured that dream.

Over the years Madeline had lost her prettiness. After the birth of seven children her girth had widened significantly and her expression was of permanent sulkiness, as she experienced life married to a pub landlord. Their tavern was the hub of the working-man's community and Ted spent long hours running it.

Madeline's pampered upbringing in Formby was now a distant memory and her dreams of a career as a dress designer dwindled with every birth. She had turned into a bitter, resentful woman and she placed the blame of her misfortune squarely at Maggie's door. For her son to marry into that family was to her a flagrant travesty. She had refused point blank to give the marriage her blessing, and threatened her husband with all sorts of misery if he signed and went behind her back. There was nothing for it but to wait for Eddie to legally be the master of his destiny.

Hannah, on the other hand, experienced none of this hostility from her parents. Jack was glad to be getting rid of her. She was no more than a slut in his opinion and deserved all that life with Eddie was going to bring her. Hannah was his princess no longer; just a constant reminder of his time with Kitty May.

Maggie, however, had been more sympathetic. The thought of Hannah having to live in a tumbledown dwelling, which was all the couple could afford, dismayed her. The fact that Jack was denying her the wedding that all brides dream of was enough in itself, but Hannah was still her stepdaughter; a child that she had nurtured since a babe of eighteen months old.

Behind her husband's back, she had arranged with a team of her workmen to add two rooms and a bathroom to Lilac Cottage, fix the roof and repair the place into an habitable home. Ironically, she had chosen Lilac Cottage, not because the couple had used it for their secret trysts, away from the prying eyes of those who would have frowned upon their relationship, but because the place down there brought out the best of Maggie's nostalgia. It had been a haven, somewhere simple and uncomplicated; a shelter where she could hide away from the villagers who had looked down their nose at an immigrant. Now Hannah and Eddie could embrace the same protection, because there would be those who would make it their business to point fingers as before. What was a well brought up girl like Hannah doing with a no-hoper like the Dockerty boy? Was he after the family money? Was there a Dockerty baby on the way?

–

"Hannah, I've never seen you look so beautiful," Maggie remarked as she put the finishing touches to her step-daughter's hair. "I think I made a good job of yer gown if I do say it meself. I've not lost the touch even after all these years."

She had copied Hannah's wedding gown from a picture in a fashionable London magazine. They had made the journey to the fabric house in Chester and chosen a length of heavy white silk, which Maggie had made into a fitted bodice dress with a skirt that draped across the front in neat swathes and covered Hannah's now-womanly figure. A small bustle sat under a waterfall train that fell to the floor, then trailed a couple of feet behind her. A long-sleeved jacket made of white baby seal skin completed the outfit and Maggie was now fixing some white satin roses into Hannah's chignoned hair.

"It's all thanks to you, Mother," Hannah said brightly, though tears of emotion were welling into her eyes. "Left to father, I'd be wearing sack cloth and ashes, not this elegant dress on my wedding day."

"That's because yer father is still hurting. He's unhappy that yer marrying Eddie, he only ever wanted the best fer you."

"You mean marry someone like Jeremy Adshead? This is all Jeremy's fault that I'm in this situation. Did you seriously think I would have married Eddie, if Jeremy hadn't given me a baby?"

"Hannah!" Maggie said in a shocked voice. "What are yer telling me? Are yer still insisting that the baby yer lost was Jeremy Adshead's child?"

"Why, didn't you believe me?"

"Well, no, not after Eddie told me yer could be expecting his."

"When was that?"

Both women stared at each other aghast.

"I went to see Eddie that day you were losing the baby. He had left a message for you to meet him at Lilac Cottage. I went instead and tried to get him to change his mind about seeing you. That was when he told me that you were probably expecting his child already. Unfortunately I lost my temper and belted him one, because I thought that you had told me a lie. And he was mocking me, making out that you were his already and that there was nothing I could do."

"Oh, Mother, I wish that you had told me. It's true what he said though. Because I needed a father for my baby I sought Eddie out. I didn't want to be the subject of people's gossiping. I purposely let him have his way with me, one evening at the cottage. Then of course I lost the baby shortly after, but by that time Father had issued his ultimatum. So, here I am making the best of it. There's really no choice in the matter, is there? Eddie will be waiting at the church and in an hour I'll be a married woman."

Maggie sank down onto the bed in despair. It seemed like history repeating itself. She hadn't wanted to marry Jack, but circumstances had forced her into it. Now here was Hannah feeling forced into marrying Eddie, because she had let him couple with her.

"You don't have to marry him, Hannah. You can take the carriage and drive down to Malpas. Sarah, your old nursemaid, would take you in until we can think of something. Here, I'll go and get her address. Take Lincoln or Jefferson, you could be there by nightfall and I'll square it with your father after yer gone."

"Mother," Hannah patted Maggie's shoulder gently, her voice all wobbly as she tried to stem her tears. "I can't do that to Eddie. It would break his heart. He has loved me since we were tiny tots and though I don't return his love, I am fond of him. I'll go ahead and marry him and who knows, it could be the making of me. It's not as if I'll be living in a hovel; your workmen have made a wonderful job of the cottage and Eddie will have regular wages with all the building that's going on. You don't know how grateful I am to you, Mother. You could have left me with Grandmama all those years ago and I'm sure she would have made my life a misery, but you have always been kind and I've wanted for nothing."

Hannah put her arms around Maggie's neck and hugged her fiercely.

"Well, if that's yer decision, come downstairs and we'll have a nice cup of something. At least yer father said he'd walk yer to church, so now he can see what an elegant bride you will be."

Meantime, Eddie was getting ready in the living room of his parents' four-roomed accommodation above the tavern. He adjusted his silver-coloured cravat in the flyblown mirror above the mantelpiece. He smirked with satisfaction, then turned to his mother who was watching him.

"What do yer think, will I do yer proud when I take me bride up the aisle?"

Madeline sniffed and smoothed down the dark blue skirt of her best outfit.

"I've told you before, nothing good will come of this marriage. Chalk and cheese the pair of you. Why Miss Goody Two Shoes Haines had condescended to wed you is beyond me. It's not as if she's expecting and her father's after yer with a shotgun. Though maybe the pair of you have been up to no good, seeing he's being mean with the wedding breakfast."

"Oh, Old Sour Puss will soon come round, Mother. Once he sees me and Hannah are happy and there's a baby on the way to make him a granddad, he'll get over his jealousy. That's all it is, jealousy, because I'm taking his little princess away. That's what Hannah has told me anyway. I didn't dare go near him or Selwyn Lodge once he knew we were getting married, though her mother Maggie has been a star. Look how she's let us have the cottage, had it done up fer us and given us fifty pound to spend as a wedding present. That's where me suit came from by the way. Hannah took me to Browns in Chester. I felt a real toff with all the other gents."

"Ah, a kept man already is it?" came a voice from the stairs.

It was Uncle Johnny, who had travelled over from Ireland to be with the family on his nephew's wedding day.

"Not so long now before yer a married man, young shaver. I was wondering if yer were going to ask for the borrow of me suit again."

"No, according to Eddie, he'll be getting a wardrobe full," Madeline broke in. "Thinks he'll be landed once her dad gets used to them being wed, but I know that family. Especially that Maggie. She'll be ever so pleasant, Eddie, then you put one foot out of line and then you've had it. I'd go carefully and not get any big ideas, 'cos whatever she does, she'll do it for Hannah, not you."

"Yes, I can second that, Eddie. Years ago I thought I was in with a chance with Maggie. I took her out, did a spot of courting with her, was prepared to give up the sea 'cos I thought I'd be moving into that great big house and be taking over her affairs. Then before yer know it, her husband appeared. Out of the blue, just like that."

"And we all thought she was a widow, didn't we, Johnny?" said Madeline jeeringly. "We felt sorry for her, me and her were the best of friends, but all the time she was double dealing us. So be careful 'cos you never know where you are with her."

"Well, I'm marrying Hannah, not her mother," laughed Eddie good-humouredly. "Now do yer think yer could round up all the kids? I don't want the Dockerty's to turn up late."

–

At least one side of the church was full, thought Hannah, as she walked slowly down to the altar with her father. She saw the grinning faces of Eddie's brothers and sisters, the disapproving face of his mother, Ted, Eddie's father, who winked at her and gave her an encouraging smile. A whole host of villagers ('come to gawp' as her mother would have put it) and at least ten young men from the building site. On the bride's side were Maggie, Grandmama and her new husband, Mr. Arlington, Sean, Jack's brother with his wife, Matilda, and Fergal whose wife would join them later on. There was no sign of Cecelia and Florence, who hadn't even replied to Hannah's invitation; she had fallen back on an old school friend to be her attendant. Emily Watts, by return of post, had said she would be delighted to come. Of course Mikey was away in India, though Hannah knew he wouldn't have approved of her marriage to Eddie, if he had been here. Well, never mind; it was the people who were here that mattered and Hannah smiled gently at Eddie as he turned to look her way.

"So we meet again, Maggie," said Johnny, as he saw his chance to get her on his own after the wedding, as the other invited guests made a beeline for the church hall.

"I see you've gone to inordinate expense on behalf of the young couple. I thought the do after would be at least at the Grosvenor Hotel."

"Get lost, Johnny," muttered Maggie, stung by his criticism. "It's not as if it's the wedding of the year, it's your nephew Hannah's marrying after all."

"What do yer mean by that?" he asked her, his eyes narrowing as he looked at her. "Eddie's good enough for any girl, especially one who has a dubious background like hers."

"Do you not think we should join the others?" Maggie smiled at him sweetly and began to walk away. No doubt Johnny had been listening to Madeline's gossip and Maggie was determined not to take him on. This day was Hannah and Eddie's, and no one was going to spoil it. She nodded at the priest who hovered by the church hall door and asked him if he would care to join them.

"I don't think much effort has gone in to this," Madeline remarked to her husband, as they waited for the bride and groom to arrive. "Two tables of food to cater for our lot, I could have done better if we had done it all at the pub!"

"Well, yer should of volunteered then, shouldn't yer, but all you've done is bitch and snipe. You and Maggie could have got together, but it looks as if all the hard work has fallen on them over there."

Ted pointed over to Olive and Joan, who both looked tired and harassed. They were filling sherry glasses as fast as they could, while Olive's younger sister, Polly, was still buttering slices of bread.

"At least someone's bothered to make a wedding cake, probably shop bought from the bakery though. I can't see Maggie putting a pinny on, can you?"

"Give it a rest will yer, Maddy and get our Jimmy out from under that table. If he pulls on that tablecloth any more, he'll have the cake on top of him. Ah, here they are. Our Eddie and the beautiful Hannah. Ladies and Gentlemen, make way for the bride and groom!"

"Who does he think he is?" commented Alice to her husband, Mr. Arlington. "At our wedding we had a proper Master of Ceremonies, not any old person who just shouts that the couple has come."

"Well, we had a more refined wedding, my dear Mrs. Arlington. None could better our special day at the Victoria Hotel. And if I do say it myself, we didn't stint on our guests as your son appears to have done. I mean ours was a sit down do, not a help yourself to a buffet, with a choice of meats and a bowl full each of trifle. I'm surprised with all the wealth that the Haineses have that their guests should be treated in this way."

"Ah," replied Alice knowingly. "This is because of who Hannah is marrying. Jack was very upset when she told him of her choice. He had got his heart set on her marrying Jeremy Adshead of Causey Hall. I notice none of their family are present either; just that common lot from the village. He runs that vulgar tavern by the fountain, yer know."

"Hannah, my dear, you are looking just splendid. Congratulations, Eddie, on your choice of such a beautiful bride."

"This is my Uncle Johnny, Hannah. You've not met him yet. Thank you for coming, Uncle Johnny. You'll be staying on at me parents, will yer, for the next few days?"

"Certainly will, Eddie. Now, I'll leave you two to mingle, mustn't hog yer to meself."

Johnny walked away, intending to help himself to some refreshment, but was waylaid by Jack who had been standing nearby talking to the priest.

"So, you're the famous Johnny Dockerty. You won't remember me from Killala, but I lived in a cottage near to Maggie. I heard you'd made a play for her while I was away."

"Get right to the point, why don't yer? No introducing yerself formally as any gentleman would do."

"You might have heard I'm no gentleman. By me face you'll see I was a fighting man. And I'd like to warn yer, don't start sniffing round her again. Me fighting days may be over, but I can take someone like you on any day."

"By the smell on yer breath I'd say you've been drinking, Sir, and I suggest you moderate it from now on. But why you think I'd be interested in a married woman, I couldn't say. I was under the misapprehension that your lady wife was a widow until you made your timely appearance. Now, do me a favour and leave me to sample the delicious-looking spread that your servants have put on for us. I am sure that Maggie would welcome your support on your daughter's happy day."

Jack looked as if he was going to say more to Johnny, but just then Ted announced that the newly-married couple were going to cut the wedding cake and everyone should charge their glasses to toast the bride and groom. There was a great confusion of noise as everyone hurried to fill or refill their glasses, even the children ran to help themselves to some delicious looking lemonade.

Outside, Jack looked up into the gloomy clouds that were threatening to discharge their load in the next few minutes. He'd been mad to even consider attending his daughter's wedding. He'd lain in the guest room tossing and turning all night again, because Maggie had decided to put him out. She had wanted to look her best for the wedding and didn't want him keeping her awake.

Yes, he had been drinking, the swine had been right, but he had needed some fortification to walk his daughter down the aisle. He walked slowly down the path and onto Burton Road. They could all get on with it without him. He was going to go back home.

"Have yer seen me husband, Father O' Brien?" asked Maggie, when she noticed later that Jack had disappeared.

"I was talking earlier to him, Maggie, but I haven't seen him lately. I have to confess I was quite surprised to smell alcohol on his breath."

"Oh, he was extremely nervous about walking Hannah down the aisle, Father. He probably had a nip of Cook's kitchen brandy before he came out. He's not a drinking man as yer know, especially since he was ill in Ireland. I told yer about it a few weeks ago."

"Ah yes, may the good Lord watch over him. Tell me Maggie, are the married couple having a few days away?"

"No, they'll be taking up residence in their new cottage as soon as the guests start leaving. I'm sure you've heard I've had Lilac Cottage done up for them? You know, on what used to be on Farmer Briggs' land?"

"Yes, I heard that you had bought up most of his farmland and will soon be having new houses built upon it. I must say we are very fortunate in having you as one of our benefactors."

"Thank you, Father, I'm very pleased that I am."

"Hannah, Eddie, I have a little surprise for you," Maggie said, as the couple began to open their presents, displayed on a table just inside the church hall door. They had just unwrapped a canteen of silver cutlery and to

Hannah's surprise the card said it was from Grandmama and Mr. Arlington. She was amazed to receive such a handsome gift and she smiled over delightedly to where the older couple stood.

"I've made an appointment at that Photographic studio in Eastgate Row, you know, just a few yards up from Becketts. You can get all dressed up again in your finery on Monday and I'll lend yer the carriage and Fergal. You can park outside the door, have your photographs done and then come back to Neston again."

"Quite the Lady Bountiful aren't you?" sneered Madeline, who had already been watching the bridal pair opening their wedding gifts, so she could see what they had got and who had given them.

"Oh, hello, Madeline. I was going to come over and have a few words. Perhaps we can renew our friendship now we are related by marriage. Perhaps you could come up to Selwyn Lodge one day fer afternoon tea?"

"I don't think so, Maggie. You seem to have forgotten what happened all those years ago when your dear Miss Rosemary give me the push. Ruined my plans, if you remember. I was going to be the best there was in the fashion design business. I could have gone to London perhaps one day."

Maggie ignored the woman's slighting words and plunged on, trying to brush off Madeline as she did so.

"Well, if yer outfit is anything to go by you haven't lost your touch. Anyway, let Hannah and Eddie carry on unwrapping their presents. They seem to be doing very well. Oh, what delightful salt and pepper pots."

But Madeline had put away too many glasses of sherry and she wasn't about to let Maggie off lightly. She grabbed hold of Maggie's arm to steady herself, then glared menacingly at her.

"Don't talk down to me, you uppity bitch. I have to make my own clothes, not like you. Got an account at Browns, no doubt. You may be rolling in it, but look at the pitiful spread you've put on for our Eddie. Aye, if she had been marrying anyone else, the do would be at the Grosvenor Hotel."

"Now then, Maddie," said Ted when a hush descended on the room, as people stopped talking to listen to her words.

"This is a happy occasion, we put away our grievances on such a special day."

Ted could have kicked himself for letting her drink all that sherry. His wife didn't usually drink alcohol, even though they lived over a pub. He had come over quickly when he saw that she was having a go at Maggie, dragging one of the children with him, who he had caught picking the decorations off the top of the wedding cake.

"Well, *you* might want to keep your gob shut, but I've waited nearly twenty years to have my say to this hoity toity madam…"

"Then do it outside will yer Mother," Eddie butted in. "You're not going to spoil it for everybody. Mrs. Haines has gone to a lot of trouble laying all this on and we're grateful for it, aren't we Hannah?"

"Ah, that didn't take you very long, did it son? Gone over to the nobs, have you? Well, everyone listen to what I've got to say. The party continues down at the tavern, if you'd like to follow me. Free drinks all round and it won't be bloody sherry!"

With that, Madeline made unsteadily for the door. Algernon, her next to eldest, was on hand to help her through.

So many people stood there openmouthed that Johnny wanted to laugh. That had put the cat amongst the pigeons, hadn't it? He looked around at the different faces as the guests wondered what to do. He for one had had enough of eating dainty tit bits off porcelain plates and drinking from a glass that only held one mouthful. There were plenty of guests on Eddie's side that couldn't agree with him more.

Eddie's work mates were the first to go, all dressed up in their Sunday best with collars that were too tight for them. They uttered apologetic mumbles as they passed the alarmed couple, some asking Eddie if he wanted to follow too.

Within ten ghastly minutes the hall was almost empty; just the priest and the Haines's guests stood in embarrassed silence wondering what to do next. Eddie comforted Hannah, as she had begun to cry. Alice was the first to have her say from where she stood with her husband and Sean and Matilda.

"Well, Maggie. If this is a sign of things to come, I'll be glad to turn down any future invitations. What did you expect from people like the Dockertys? You surely didn't think they would behave with decorum. People like that just don't know how to behave. And you, Hannah, have brought all this on yourself for marrying one of them. When I think of the expense your father has gone to on your upbringing! Where is he by the way? Still, what do you expect when…"

Mr. Arlington suddenly gripped hold of Alice's arm quite forcefully, so much so that she yelped and seemed to be about to shrug herself loose from him.

"Maggie, Hannah, please accept our apologies, but I think it's time for us to go. Sean and Matilda haven't visited since our wedding, so it would be nice for them to spend some time in our home. Thank you, Maggie, on behalf of all of us."

Then Mr. Arlington shook hands with Eddie, kissed Hannah on the cheek, nodded to the priest, then lead his unrepentant wife away. Sean and Matilda followed after also giving their embarrassed apologies.

"Well, Maggie. In all my years as a priest, people never cease to amaze me. Still, the deed is done. Eddie, Hannah, it's up to you to prove that the choice of marrying each other was the right one. Now, I'll be away to get ready for the next ceremony at three o'clock. No hurry to leave here by the way. Their celebrations will continue back at their parents' house."

"So, that leaves the six of us," said Maggie, who had been desperately thinking what she could do to cheer up the rest of them, especially Hannah who looked as if she had been left in the lurch.

"Fergal, would you be willing to drive the carriage to Chester?"

Fergal nodded that he was willing, provided his little wife Ivy could go along with him.

"Of course she can, Fergal. If you don't mind riding up top with him, Ivy. Olive, Joan, you can go home and clear up here in the morning. Emily, I'm sure you'll be happy to come along with us. Hannah, Eddie, we're off for supper at the Grosvenor Hotel!"

Chapter 10

"So where do we go from here, Sis?" asked Ernie, as they sat upon two rickety chairs in Thistledown Cottage.

"Oh, I can't think about the future yet, Ernie. Give us a break. We've just buried Mam and I would like to sit and do nothing. Anyway, Annie will be over soon when she's got the kids settled. We'll see what she's got to say."

The pair of them sat quietly, each with their own thoughts about their dead mother, Ruthie. They had known that her end was near when the doctor, upon examining her, expressed disbelief that he hadn't been called in earlier. Something to do with fluid that was slowly invading her body, starting with her legs. The doctor had shaken his head and, taking Katie aside, had told her that Ruthie's death was only a matter of time. Katie had done her best to make her mother comfortable, calling on her sister Annie to help with her nursing. Even Ernie had learnt how to change Ruthie's bandages, as the sores on her legs kept pussing and her open wounds wouldn't heal. It had been a desperate time for all of them, especially Ruthie who wasn't a good patient and screamed abuse each time one of them came near her, then cried pitifully when the pain became too much to bear. Katie had broken rule after rule at the hospital where she was staff nurse, harassing the doctors there for advice on how to help her mam, taking time off to be with her, filching bandages and ointment, bringing her woes into work with her. Matron was beginning to wonder if Staff Nurse Tibbs, her shining example to the rest of the team, had been spirited away by some devil and she had been left with a changeling instead!

Ernie's thoughts were on how he was going to miss his mother. Compared to a lot of mothers, Ruthie hadn't been a good one, if he thought of how his childhood friends had been treated by theirs. There didn't seem to be enough food on the table for all of them – that's when they had a table to eat off. It was the same with their clothing; they didn't have a complete set of anything. Clothes were handed down or bought second-hand from the market, birthdays and Christmas sometimes didn't happen in their family. He remembered the clouts, the fearful shouting, the horrible noises coming from his parents' palliasse, but Ernie also remembered the times when Ruthie had stood up for him and how gentle she had been with Lenny, his poor brother who hadn't been right in the head. Ernie had watched her when she had found Lenny dead in his bed one morning, some years ago. He had thought she would be relieved to have her burden taken away from her after all those years, but Ruthie had mourned; mourned terribly, walking around the cottage for weeks on end, without anything to say. She had stood up to his father when Solly, deprived sometimes of his alcohol, would make life hell for his children. But she never found out why Ernie often went missing; some things her son would never tell.

"Yer know why Lilac Cottage has been done up?" came Annie's voice from the front door way. "I've just passed it on me way here and they've added on to it." She walked in to join her siblings who had awakened from their revelry.

"Let's have yer chair, Ernie. I'm fair knackered with all the walking about I've done today. And this one's kicking me something rotten. Thank God I've only a week to go."

Annie sat down with a thump onto the chair that her brother had vacated and asked Katie if she'd make her a cup of tea.

Over the years since she had married Sam Piper, Annie hadn't changed much. She still had the brown straggly hair, the thin pointed face and an air of helplessness that made people want to protect her. After each child that she had given birth to, her figure always reverted back to being thin and bony. Although she was nearly due with her next one, under her smock it hardly showed.

"So why has Lilac Cottage been done up?" asked Katie as she waited for the kettle to boil on a struggling fire.

"It was so Hannah Haines didn't have to live in a hovel when she married Eddie Dockerty."

"I'd heard that her mother had bought all this land from the farmer, so she got these cottages too," said Ernie worriedly. "Well, that's it then Katie, we'll be looking fer a new place to live."

"Why so?" asked Annie. "You've still got a job with Briggs, haven't yer? This is a tied cottage, so you've still got a place to live."

"I was just about to talk to Katie about it before, but she said it was too soon after the funeral. It has to be faced up to Katie, now or tomorrow and with Annie here, she can be in on it as well."

"What is there to talk about, Ernie? As Annie's just said, it's the job and the cottage. Mam going doesn't alter a thing."

"I was waiting until after Mam's funeral to tell yer. Briggs says I have to pay rent now to the Sheldon Property Company. We can still live here if we pay rent."

"Rent!" said Katie derisively. "Rent for this place? Pigs wouldn't want to live here, never mind paying rent."

"Perhaps she'll do it up fer you like she has Lilac Cottage," broke in Annie eagerly. "And there's Ashlea going begging too, 'cos no one's lived at Ashlea fer years. Me and Sam could do with a place of our own, now the kids are bigger. I think I'll go to the office tomorrow and ask what's happening. She's all right, is Maggie. We go back a long way."

"But, Annie, even if she did this place up for us, we couldn't afford the rent she'll be asking for it. Let's face it, we only managed to find the money for the funeral because we all chipped a bit in."

"My wage will be going up a bit according to old Briggs. Compensation he said for losing the cottage."

"Well, there you are then, Ernie, even the farmer thinks you'll be looking for somewhere else to live," retorted Katie, thinking with a sinking heart that she would probably have to live in the Nurses Home.

"You must be getting quite a bit, Katie, now that you've been made up to a staff nurse," commented Annie. "At least you don't have to take in work like I have to do."

"Oh, come off it, Sis. If I had your skill I would have opened up a shop years ago, not settled for a ruck of kids like you have. At least you're sitting on your arse all day, not running around the wards like I have to do."

"Hark to her, Ernie. Her life's work devoting herself to the sick and needy. Let's face it, it's the thought of giving birth that makes yer dedicated. That and the fact that no man has ever looked at you."

"That's enough!" roared Ernie, taking the girls by surprise and making them jump. "Isn't it bad enough that we've just buried our mother without you both sniping and snarling? Pack it in or I'll be giving you the length of my tongue."

Both his sisters had the grace to look ashamed of themselves and Annie, being the elder, apologised. "Sorry, Katie. I shouldn't have said that. What say I go up to the village tomorrow and find out how the land lies?"

–

"Customer, Mr. Arlington," the young girl on the reception desk shouted up the stairs, when Annie presented herself next morning at the Sheldon Property Company. She came back to sit on her chair, rudely declining to offer Annie a seat on one of the couches. Annie decided to sit down anyway, even though she knew she would have difficulty getting up again. She looked around as she waited, thinking how much the place had changed since she was an alteration hand on these same premises. It had been a crying shame when Miss Rosemary, her employer, had decided to close down her dressmaking business. Annie had been happy here and had reason to be grateful, for it was here that she had honed her skills. She smoothed the skirt down on her very drab, rubbed-up winter coat, feeling very conscious suddenly that she was expecting another child. Why hadn't she put on her Sunday best? The colour blue suited her and there was more material in it, so it would have hidden her condition to the world. Then she tutted with annoyance, it was only Mr. Arlington she had come to see. Anyone would think she was seeing God Himself!

"Ah, Annie Tibbs," said Mr. Arlington, as he spotted the young woman from the top of the stairs. "What can we do for you this fine day? Come to buy one of our new properties up on Claypool Road?"

"Annie Tibbs as was, Mr. Arlington. I've been married to Sam Piper fer a few years now. Is it possible that we can speak in your office?" she asked, trying to summon up a bit of dignity. The thought of discussing her business in front of the office girl annoyed her greatly. This was a private matter and that was how it would stay.

"Of course, come up." Seeing her efforts, he kindly came down the stairs and extended a hand.

Annie was overwhelmed by the opulence she found herself in when she finally made it to the manager's room. When she had worked there, the floor had no covering upon it. Now there was a plush green carpet, plain peach wallpaper and drawings by a local artist dotted around the walls. She glanced nervously at the elderly man, who had motioned her to sit on a comfortable chair.

"Annie," Mr. Arlington said gently. "How are you? How is your family? It must be what, nearly twenty years since I last saw you?"

"No, not quite. It was when Miss Rosemary closed the business down that you last saw me, but you've passed me in the street a few times since."

"Well, never mind that. I take it you're not here to buy one of the new houses from the Sheldon Property Company. Is it to rent your mother's cottage, now that Farmer Briggs has sold it on?"

"I've come on behalf of me brother and sister. We buried me mother yesterday and now they're beginning to think of their future. As yer know, Ernie had it as part of his wages, but we wondered what was going to happen to it now."

"The simple fact of the matter is that Mr. Tibbs will have to pay rent now if he wants to stay there. He is actually down for a visit, when our agent can find the time to get over to see him."

"And what about Ashlea Cottage? Will that be up for rent or will it be pulled down?"

Mr. Arlington seemed startled. "Why should Ashlea Cottage be pulled down?"

"Well, it's in a worse condition than Thistledown. No one's lived in it for fifteen year and the starlings have taken over it fer nesting."

"Ah, sorry my dear, I didn't know that. I rely on my staff to inform me of the condition of these places. What would your interest be in it?"

"My husband and I would like to rent it. Where we are living is too cramped for all of us and I seem to remember from when I was a child, there were three bedrooms. We could manage the rent, me husband has a milk round, he probably delivers to you and I take in alterations to make ends meet."

"But you think it will need substantial investment?"

"If yer mean it wants doing up, I think the answer would be yes."

"Then leave it with me. Get your husband to call in here next week and I'll have an answer ready."

Annie was shown out of his office, very politely she thought to herself. Though what had she achieved by making her visit? Nothing that she hadn't known already. She couldn't take her family to live in squalor and Ernie and Katie were going to have to find the rent.

"All I can say is that you must be going senile in your old age, Mr. Arlington," said Alice, when he told her that evening about Annie turning up at his office that day.

"Well, I felt sorry for her. I remember when she used to work for Miss Rosemary. She was like a nervous rabbit in those days. Used to bolt back up to the workroom when I went over to the shop to have a word."

"I'm surprised Maggie's even considering keeping those places standing. They've always been hovels. Briggs never spent a penny on them as far as I know. If I were her, I'd have them pulled down."

"I'm having a meeting with Maggie tomorrow. I don't suppose she's even thought about the other two cottages, what with spending all that money getting Lilac Cottage modernised. But it won't look good for the company if the Tibbses are put out on the street."

"If it were me, I would have let Hannah stew in it. I'd have made her take her chances with the Dockertys. Our Jack won't have anything to do with her now, though Maggie's never off their doorstep I hear."

"Well, if that is so, she must have noticed those cottages' condition. I'll have a word and see if we can make Ashlea habitable."

"Pooh, they won't thank you for it. I'd let Annie stay where she is. If she's anything like her mother she'll turn it into a hovel again!"

It was a wet and windy day as Maggie walked down to Mr. Arlington's office. There was a mist clinging to the hills in the distance and everywhere looked dark and dismal, matching Maggie's mood. She had heard from Hannah that the woman who lived in the cottage up the lane had died. Poor Ruthie. She could have only been in her early fifties; not very old to have died. She hadn't seen Ruthie for many a year, not since Maggie had worked with Annie. There had been no reason for their paths to cross, as Maggie got on with her life. Still, the thought of Ruthie dying saddened her. She had been there in the beginning when Maggie first came to live in Neston. A bit of a rapscallion really, but she had done her best with the cards that life had dealt her. Maggie wondered what would happen to Ernie and Katie. She had heard that Katie was a staff nurse at the cottage hospital and Ernie worked for Farmer Briggs. A sudden thought quickened her footsteps.

Thistledown Cottage belonged to her now, didn't it? But all that land was earmarked for her building project. The cottage would be demolished as far as she knew.

Maggie looked at the plans for the creation of low-priced houses that she was struggling to get planning permission for from the local Town Hall when she arrived at the office. The officials had argued that larger dwellings for the middle classes would be more in keeping with the area. With the train stopping at Neston, it would encourage those with higher incomes to travel to Liverpool or Chester each day. These were the kind of people that would be welcome and would benefit local businesses, jobs, churches and schools. The air here was healthier, especially with the sea breezes coming up from the shore.

She felt at a loss as she gazed at the drawings that the architect had given her. Were the committee members right? Should she have given more thought to what was being built; was she being sentimental as she thought of people like Annie who was still living with her mother-in-law?

She turned to Mr. Arlington, who was aware of her inner struggle. He had been there to advise her for twenty years, even though you would have thought he owned her businesses himself. She had cause to appreciate what he had done for her; she wouldn't have been so successful without him at the helm.

"Well, what do you want, Maggie? Profit, or a statue of a kind benefactress erected in the village? Whatever you decide on, I've been thinking that those cottages will have to be demolished. Not only will the council act, but they're in the way of progress; buyers will want a view of the sea."

"But we didn't have to tear down Lilac Cottage, did we? We've had it done up very nicely, we could do the same with those."

"Let's face it, Maggie. You kept Lilac Cottage for its sentimental value. As I understand it from Alice, you were happy there, but you've earned your reputation as a hardheaded businesswoman in the community. Keeping those cottages will make you a laughing stock amongst those who choose to buy around there. I must admit, when Annie Tibbs came to see me yesterday I felt a certain sympathy. I too thought that perhaps we could make those cottages habitable again. But if I were in your shoes I would have them demolished and build two pretty villas instead."

"You agree with the Town Hall then, Mr. Arlington, don't you? Build large four-bedroomed dwellings and give them an acre or more of land."

"Yes, I do, Maggie and if you want to do your bit for the more poorly paid, there's some spare land along Town Lane. A row of terraces would go nicely there."

"And what about Katie and Ernie? Neither will have a home if they're told to go."

"Oh, pay them some compensation then. Fifty pounds would give them a deposit on a very nice place."

Sam walked glumly into Piper's Cottage a week or so later. He ducked his head through habit as he entered the small cramped living room. His wife had just given birth to their latest addition and she was sitting nursing baby Alexandra by the fire.

"Well, what did they say? What are they going to do with Ashlea Cottage, Sam? Are they going to do it up and let us go and live there?"

"The answer's no, Annie. The man there said it was something to do with the Artisans and Labourers Act, where the Town Hall can pull down insanitary dwellings. So we'll be buggered anyway, because this place is falling round our ears too."

"So, what are we going to do then? Look around yer, Sam. Two cradles now in the living room, four kids top to tail in the bedroom, me and you sleeping on the kitchen floor. You know if yer mother would give up her room and sleep down here, we could move in with the babbies. She doesn't need all the space for herself."

"Annie, that's cruel. It's her cottage and she was good enough to let us share it with her. It isn't her fault that you've been giving birth every year."

"It's not my fault either! Perhaps yer should be keeping your baby maker to yourself, Sam Piper."

Annie was stung that he should even think it was her fault. Didn't he get as much pleasure making babies as she?

She had never turned her back on Sam as they lay snugly together on their mattress; he was so good-looking that she thought she was the luckiest woman around.

"Keep yer voice down Annie, our Joe's twitching, he must be ready for his dinner. Where have the others gone? It's awfully quiet. I'll be glad when they're all school age."

"I should be saying that, but you know they're good kids really. Just loud like all kids are; they'll settle down when they go to school. Your mam has taken them down to the promenade, to run some energy off them, then this avvy they're all going up to Dr. Farrington. He's giving them all injections in case there's a smallpox outbreak again."

"That man at the Sheldon office said that they might be building some places on Town Lane that might suit us. He said that the rent would be low 'cos the woman who will own them all wants to make sure that people like us can afford it. What do yer think, shall I get our name down?"

"Don't see why not. Though you'll have to find somewhere for the cart and a place to stable Dobbin. I know the woman you're talking about. She's Maggie Haines. We used to work together at Miss Rosemary's. Shall I go and see her, put in a word for our Ernie and Katie as well?"

"Best not, let them sort their own affairs out and if we do get a place, we'll be taking me mother as well!"

–

Maggie sat in her bedroom, looking out of the window at the sun dappled estuary and to her beloved Welsh hills. Jack had moved his things into the guest room again, on the evening of Hannah and Eddie's wedding. She felt annoyance at his childishness; he had done it to let her know that he was blaming her. What had he expected? Was she to let his daughter experience the deprivations of being married to a builder's labourer? Where was his compassion for the daughter he had loved so much? She had known that she had made the right decision. Hannah loved playing the little housewife and from what she had told her recently, there might be a baby on the way.

Maggie visited Lilac Cottage often; as often as she could when her diary wasn't full. The place had been changed beyond recognition; her workmen had certainly done a good job. The roof had been re-slated, a modern kitchen range put in, an inside bathroom and water closet and two extra bedrooms built on the back of the place. The original bedroom was now a small sitting room and Hannah had done her best to make the place bright and comfortable. She shopped every day in the village and joined the other housewives looking for a bargain on market days. So now Hannah was living in the real world, but she appeared to be making the best of it with what money Eddie managed to give her.

But what was she going to do about Jack? Maggie's thoughts returned to her very morose husband. He had more words to say to a cat than he said to her nowadays. Evenings were the most uncomfortable times when they sat together in the dining room. Meals were eaten in silence, then Jack would disappear to sit in his room. He had eaten his breakfast and gone out by the time Maggie came down for hers. She wondered where he got to. Had he returned to the horse racing? The carriage and pair was certainly missing every day. She had been reduced to using Sam Owen's transport instead, driving to her appointments in his old black cab. Not very dignified when she was attending one of her Board of Guardians meetings at the hospital. Most members had a servant to convey them, another reason now for them to look down on her. She knew she was only invited to sit on these boards because of the wealth she had behind her, but if it meant that they would be getting the poor man's point of view, then so be it. Maggie had a wealth of experience of what it was like to be poor!

She turned from the window with a sigh and looked at the plans on her desk again. She wished she had someone to listen to her doubts over the houses that she wanted building. Mr. Arlington could only see what was good for the company, though when she thought about it, wasn't that what he was paid for?

Jack had never been really interested in the Sheldon Property Company. Because he had not been part of its development he had let her get on with the job. So long as his own needs were catered for and he had a biddable partner in bed.

But she wasn't even that to him, now he was sleeping in the guest room. Oh well, was she bothered?

As far as she was concerned, he could go to Hell.

—

It was as if Jack had picked up her thoughts, as an hour or so later Maggie heard Olive talking to someone in the hallway and when she looked over the banister it was him.

Jack looked guilty as she came down the stairs towards him, like a small boy whose mother had caught him with his hand in the biscuit jar.

"Oh, Maggie, I didn't expect you to be here. I thought you would be at one of your meetings."

He said the words so coldly and didn't meet her eyes as he said them. Then he asked would she like to sit in the conservatory with him and would Olive make some tea?

Goodness, thought Maggie. How very formal, like he was the chairman at a meeting. She followed him through the dining room, wondering what he had to say.

"This isn't easy for me, Maggie," Jack said, when they had both sat down on comfortable chairs. "But I want you and I to have a separation. It's not working out again, is it? Surely you must have noticed it too?"

"If yer mean you're a moody sod and if yer don't get your own way you'll sulk forever, yes I'd say our marriage isn't working. But you were the one who came back from America, you were the one who said you wanted the dream of us being together again to come true."

"Yes, and at that time I meant it. The thought of us being a family again was one of me dreams. But Mikey has gone to foreign parts, Hannah is… Well, as far as I'm concerned she doesn't exist any more and you, Maggie, are so tied up with your do-gooding and being the big developer, that the wife I knew before doesn't exist any more either. There's nothing here for me now."

"So, what you're saying, Jack, is that we're finished? Fine. Clear off like yer did before. See if I care. What is it? Found another woman to get yer leg over? 'Cos if that's so, don't expect me to bring up her bloody kid!"

"There is no other woman, Maggie. Unless you include Ivy, Fergal's wife, who will be coming with us. Ah, yes," he continued, when he saw Maggie's face taken aback by the mention of Ivy. "I've been planning this from the night of that damned wedding. Fergal and Ivy are coming with me as well."

"Oh. And do yer want to take Joan and Olive, too?!"

"I don't think they'll want to come where we're going." Jack smiled wryly for a second at her. Maggie still had the power to get all fired up, that was why he had been first attracted to her.

"I'm going into partnership with Paddy Fearon. His parents have left him a place out in Wicklow, so we're going to start our own stud farm. I've the money to tide us over 'til we get a reputation and I'm taking Dalton and Fletcher too. Of course I'll leave Lincoln and Jefferson to pull your carriage; it must have been very inconvenient for you recently."

Jack reached out to touch Maggie gently on her hands, which she had balled into clenched fists on her knee.

"You've never really loved me have yer, Maggie? You've gone through all the motions and you've certainly fooled me at times, but deep down it's money and power you've been after. You've never wanted to play the little housewife, even fer me."

"How can yer say that, Jack?" retorted Maggie hotly. "I've never give yer cause to doubt me. I let yer go your own way when yer wanted to be a fighter. I had yer back when yer wanted to come home. I gave you a second chance to be me husband and me lover but let's face it, deep down I've never been enough for yer. It's the wanderlust yer have."

"Well, whatever yer think, I've made me plans and we'll be away by Saturday. You never know, you may miss me so much you'll want to come over and stay."

"I don't think so. Once you go from here, you and I will be finished for good. Pity, 'cos in a few months you are going to be a granddad, so we won't be able to play happy families."

"Maggie, don't give me all that sentimental rubbish, especially as you're being sarky about it. Yer know I've washed me hands of me daughter. She'll end up breeding like a rabbit and we'd be overrun with her brood. That wasn't what I wanted for me daughter, but if she's fool enough, so be it."

Maggie got up then and started pacing the length of the conservatory. There was a silence between them then, only interrupted when Olive brought in a tray of tea.

"Cook says to ask if yer both in fer dinner?" she said looking at Jack with enormous eyes, because she and Joan had heard every word that had been said. Funny how employers thought that their servants were deaf or that walls were so thick that arguments couldn't be heard through them. Joan had told Olive that perhaps the Haineses thought their servants were invisible.

"I'll be out," Maggie snapped. "Ask Cook to leave me a little supper on a tray."

"Thank Joan and tell her that I will be in for dinner," Jack replied.

"I suppose your mother knows yer going," Maggie continued, standing angrily beside him now with Olive out of the way. She felt like hitting him across the head. All that she'd gone through in Ireland with him; worrying herself half to death in case Jack was taken from her. The money she had spent bringing in the best specialist to see him. The care and devotion she had given him after the Fenians had attacked him that day.

He nodded that he had told his mother, then sat stiffly as he waited for the next tirade to begin.

"And am I to say that I'm a widow again, so that she can keep her head high in the community?"

"Sarcasm doesn't suit you, Maggie. Yes, she does know I'm leaving and she does know why, but the story will be that I have to oversee me business interests in Ireland, but it's up to you to say how long I've gone for. How long I'll be away."

"Then you'd better get on with it. I leave yer to yer packing. I'm off down to Lilac Cottage. I take it you'll be taking the dogs as well?"

"Yes, and I'll be putting Simba through the auction at Chester tomorrow. Hannah doesn't ride him now and seeing as I bought him for her in the first place, he is now mine to sell."

Chapter 11

"Oh, Mother, I wondered if you would come over today. I'm just putting the chicken in the oven for mine and Eddie's dinner. I've followed a recipe from that book you gave me on household management. It has been a godsend. Gives you tips on adding more flavour to dishes and there are some scrumptious desserts that I intend to make. Mother, what's the matter? Have you been crying? Come and sit on the sofa and tell me what's happened. Eddie will be a while yet, so I don't have to think about dinner now until he gets in."

Hannah pulled off her pans from the top of the kitchen range and set them aside, then came over quickly to sit by Maggie.

"Has father been upsetting you? You said the other day that he had moved into the guest room and hardly ever speaks to you. Oh dear, it's all because of me, isn't it?"

Maggie's tears began to fall then. She had been burning with anger when she had slammed out of Selwyn Lodge, but her walk across the fields had given her time to calm down a little and she had begun to feel sorry for herself.

She scrubbed at her face with the handkerchief that Hannah took out of her pinafore pocket, then took some deep breaths before she told the girl her tale.

"He's decided to leave and go to Ireland. He says that our marriage isn't working and there's nothing left fer him here. I should have seen it coming, but I've been so busy with all the committee work, deciding what to do with these building plans and all the messing about with the Town Hall. I suppose when you think that your marriage is on solid ground, you start taking everything fer granted. When he came back after all those years away, I assumed we were settled for the rest of our lives."

"But all that changed when you took my side and started helping me and Eddie, had this place done up for us and bought us all this furniture. I suppose he feels he should have had your loyalty and he's angry because I didn't make a good marriage with someone like Jeremy."

"Yes, that's true, Hannah, I have to admit it, but it's the deceit that I can't handle. He's been planning this move with Fergal and his wife since your wedding. That's what I don't like."

"You mean Fergal and Ivy are going with him? What's he going to do in Ireland and why Fergal and his wife?"

"He's starting a stud farm in Wicklow. Paddy Fearon, that's the man who helped him buy his horses in Ireland, has been left some property, so Fergal will go to look after the horses and they'll need a woman to run the house. He is very kindly leaving me the carriage and Lincoln and Jefferson, but now I'll have to find a man to look after them as well. Do you know, Hannah? I don't need this at the moment. I can get used to your father not being there, let's face it I did without him fer years, but I've all these decisions to make as well. Me head feels it's going to burst!"

Maggie was not far from tears again, so Hannah took her stepmother's hand and squeezed it gently. "Mother, I can help you with some of it. What do I do all day but keep this place nice for Eddie? He'll understand if I come up to help you, he won't mind a bit of dust or the occasional crumpled shirt."

"No, Hannah. I can't expect yer to take on my problems. You've only been wed these last four months and it would be unfair to both you and Eddie, especially when you might be expecting a baby."

"Oh, Mother, please don't turn me down," she said eagerly. "I want to help. *You* don't even have to get a man in to see to the horses. I had plenty of experience with Simba. I was always cleaning out his quarters and Lincoln and Jefferson know me very well."

"That's something I haven't told yer, Hannah," Maggie said sadly. "He's selling Simba. Says you don't ride him any more and Simba is his to sell. And he's taking Fang and Rufus too."

She waited for Hannah's reaction. If it had been her she would have stormed over to Selwyn Lodge and brought the animals back here, but her stepdaughter had never been a firebrand; she just got on with life in her own quiet way.

"He certainly knows how to hurt, doesn't he?" Hannah's eyes filled with tears and Maggie pushed the handkerchief over to her. "But in a way I can't blame him. I caused Father pain by marrying Eddie, so it's his way of punishing me."

"Yer know, Hannah. It never ceases to amaze me how hurtful the ones who are supposed to love yer can be. I used to be jealous of the bond you and yer father had, felt hurt at his lack of attention, though I knew that it was a different kind of love. The same with Mikey; we were so close when he was little, I couldn't wait to see him when I got back from Miss Rosemary's, but look what's happened with Mikey. One letter in nearly a year. He could be dead for all I know and it hurts me that he just doesn't bother writing. Never mind," she said with a forced brightness. "We've got each other now and hopefully soon we'll have a little babby that we all can love. Talking of which… Oh, Hannah, I've just had a marvellous idea! Put the kettle on will yer, and make us a cup of tea? I want to gather me thoughts fer a moment. I think I've got a wonderful plan."

A little while later, Hannah nearly choked on her tea that she had started sipping when Maggie made clear her thoughts.

"You're saying you want me and Eddie to move into Selwyn Lodge?" she gasped incredulously. "Are you sure? You don't even know Eddie very well and you must have spent a fortune on this place here."

"Well, I'm not forcing yer to come. You can talk it over first with Eddie. It's the thought of me rattling around in that big house with only Olive and Joan fer company. But you'll be needing help with the baby and your old nursery could be used again."

"Yes, and I'd be nearer the stables to see to the horses and I'd be on hand to drive you around like I used to. But Mother, I've just got used to the cooking, shopping and cleaning and I have to admit I'm happy creating a pleasant home."

"Then we'll sack Joan and Olive," said Maggie dryly. "You can work fer your keep by being me housekeeper as well."

Maggie lay awake that night listening for any sounds of movement coming from her husband's room. Should she get up and plead with him to stay? Did she want him to? It would spoil all the plans she had for the future. Was there still any love between them? Had there been any in the first place? Did she really know what love was? So many questions, and her mind couldn't give her any answers. Perhaps she was just a selfish person and only loved herself. But that wasn't true, she thought to herself, remembering back to when they had been on their trip to Ireland. When Jack had been lying ill in the convent's infirmary, she had prayed that he would get better, realising then that she loved him and needed him in her life. She had prayed that they would be together until they reached their nineties; but was that love or a need in herself that she shouldn't be alone again? Maybe it was all her fault. She had got tied up with her ventures, her meetings and anything else that gave her satisfaction, as soon as she'd got home. She had left him to his own devices and this was her reward. But did she want to give all this up – everything she had worked hard for, to share a kitchen with Ivy over there in Wicklow? Be at Jack's beck and call and give up the independence she had grown to love? The answer was no. It came to her loudly and strongly. If she had to give her independence up, she didn't want to be Jack's wife.

–

Eddie walked along the lane that lead to Lilac Cottage, past the near ruin of Ashlea and the hovel that they called Thistledown. He was tired and looking forward to seeing Hannah. He had been working on the roof of a property on the promenade and the wind had kept buffeting as he had tried to knock the nails in the slates. Eddie whistled tunelessly to himself as he neared his home. What a shock his wife had given him yesterday after he had walked in and Maggie was on her way out. She had smiled at his greeting and turned down his offer that she should eat with them, saying mysteriously that they should have some time to themselves. He had laughed and replied that was all he lived on earth for. Aye, it was true, he thought to himself. These last few months had been a dream come true. Hannah was everything a man could ask for in a wife.

Her time at the college had been well spent. How she managed to be so clever with her housekeeping money and turn out well cooked meals of quality was beyond him. She kept the cottage like a little palace and was never too tired to delight him in bed. His life was like being in a bubble; a bubble they shared when they shut the cottage door on the world; but it was about to be popped. Hannah had a hankering to live back at Selwyn Lodge again.

"So come on then, what's Maggie being all mysterious about?" he had asked, after taking Hannah in his arms and burying himself deep into her lusciousness. "You're looking happy anyway, or is it because I've come home?"

"Go and wash your hands and I'll serve up dinner, then I'll tell you. I think you'll be pleased with the plan."

"But we can't live at Selwyn Lodge," Eddie had cried, with his fork midway to his mouth holding a piece of succulent chicken. "Yer father would make me life a misery and Hannah, we're so happy here."

"Father is moving out. He's moving to Ireland and taking Fergal with him, so Mother will have problems driving the carriage herself."

"You mean you want me to be a coachman? Hannah, I couldn't do it, I'm no good with horses, I've no experience fer a start."

"No, silly. I would see to the horses and drive Mother. You would continue working for Jimmy Pearson, but we would move up into a better world."

"There's nothing wrong with living in this one, Hannah. I don't want our children growing up like you did, like one of those plants that you have in your conservatory."

"Rubbish, there's nothing wrong with the way I was brought up. At least I had a decent education, the fruits of it you can see."

"So you're saying that I was dragged up," he had said, feeling dangerously close to them having their first row.

"I'm not saying that, Eddie, but let's face it, bringing up children over a pub is not how I would choose to bring up mine."

"I'll have yer know me mother was from a very good family in Formby. She was educated just like you, it wasn't her fault that dad wouldn't move from the pub."

"Eddie, Eddie, let's not get caught up in trivial argument. I would like to go back if you will come with me, but not if it means you'll be unhappy in the place."

They had agreed then that they would both give the matter much thought, but not until the next morning as Eddie felt the need to carry Hannah quickly to their bed.

She was there waiting to greet him as he walked up their path. Her face flushed with baking and a little bit of flour on her pretty nose. Oh, she was so beautiful, he sighed to himself, his spirits uplifting at the very sight of Hannah. He would follow her to the ends of the earth if that was what she wanted him to do.

"Have you come to a decision, Eddie?" she asked him eagerly, in the measured tones she had been taught at college that always gave him a thrill.

"I'll tell yer in a minute, come here and give me a hug."

He clung to her far longer than he usually did, when he came home from work. It was if he wanted her back in the bubble, where they couldn't be disturbed.

"I've got some things that worry me, but without them I would say yes. Though, you've worked so hard on this place, Hannah, do yer really want to leave all this?"

"Well, I have my reservations as well, Eddie, but I can see the advantages for both of us, especially in the winter months. Remember only a month ago we were blocked in with snow."

"Hmm, I remember. I didn't have to go to work and we were snug as a bug in a rug."

"Yes, but when we have a growing family we'll need to feed them, take them to school and back again; we can't just spend our time in bed."

"Sounds just perfect to me, Hannah, but you want me to be serious, don't yer? Well, yes I'll give it a go. But what are we going to do about you know what? We'll have the servants and Maggie listening and I know how you cry out in bed."

"The servants don't live in, Eddie, and I'll just have to learn to be quiet. It is a small price to pay, curtailing our lovemaking. Anyway, I think I'm expecting as you know, so it's not as if we'll be doing it every day."

"What happens if Michael comes home? He's not going to be in the Army forever and he might not be happy that we're living there."

"Oh, Mikey will be in India for years yet. According to Mother there's skirmishes all over the place. She reads the broadsheets avidly to see if she can get any news."

"Well, I think you've nearly won me over. There's just me family now. How is Maggie going to like Maddy and Ted dropping in? Not to mention Uncle Johnny, who I believe was a suitor of hers."

"You've hardly seen your mother since our wedding. Only that one time when you went to the village after work. You said she heaped a load of profanities upon your head. I can't see her having the nerve to drop in at Selwyn Lodge."

"Oh, Hannah, I do love you. You do me heart good just to listen. I take it with your 'profanities', yer mean me mother was heapin' curses on me head."

–

Sam tied his horse up to the railing outside Piper's Cottage. He was in the middle of his milk round but he had called in to see Annie, as one of their youngsters was ill. As soon as she heard his footsteps on the path she was standing in the doorway, cradling little Joe.

"How is he, did yer get the doctor, Annie?" The tot was flushed and his eyes were puffy and red.

"I did as yer said Sam, but he thinks Joe's only teething. He's probably right, says it's the back ones that are coming through."

"Thank God fer that then. You'd think we'd know all about teething with having the other three."

"I've give him a hard biscuit to chew on, and I went up to the chemist too and got him a bottle of something to calm him. You'll never guess who I saw up there. Maggie Haines, of all people. I've not seen her to talk to fer years!"

"Is the kettle on, Annie? I'll come in and have a drink. It's so hot today that I'm worried the milk will go off."

"The kettle's just boiled, so take Joe and I'll go and make yer a brew. Anyway me and Maggie got talking and you'll never guess what she said."

"She said she'll do up Thistledown and Ashlea for us all and we can get to know her daughter and go to Lilac Cottage for afternoon tea."

Annie looked at Sam puzzled. How did he know what she and Maggie had been talking about?

"No, she never said that, but Lilac Cottage was mentioned. Her daughter and husband are moving into Selwyn Lodge and Lilac Cottage will be up fer rent!"

"And so...?"

"Don't yer see? We could move into Lilac Cottage. I passed it by on the day of Mam's funeral and they've done it up beautifully. They've added on, so we'd have more space and there's enough land at the side for a stable as well. You know, I could grow me own vegetables and I know there's an orchard, because me and Ernie used to scrump there when we were kids. Oh, Sam, all me dreams would come true if we could move into Lilac Cottage. Will yer go to see Mr. Arlington as soon as you've finished? Sam, will yer do that? Maggie said the tenancy would have to be through you."

–

Katie lay asleep on her new bed that she had bought soon after Ruthie's funeral. It had been bought with a Bounty voucher, a cheque enabling a person to purchase an item, then regular payments being made whilst having the use of it. She and Ernie had gone by train to Chester to the designated furniture shop that dealt with these vouchers from the Sheldon Company. Ernie had ordered a new bed too, as he had taken over Lenny's room when the poor lad had died. Now their mam had gone, they were free to do whatever they liked and they had nothing against her old enemy, Maggie Haines. In fact, if truth was told, many people in the village relied on Maggie's Bounty vouchers. They made a difference giving presents at Christmas time, buying a gift for a happy couple on their wedding day, renewing clapped-out furniture, furnishings and bedding and kitting the children out with brand new clothes whenever necessary.

The old palliasses they used to sleep on had been thrown in the garden, ready for burning. The rickety chairs would be next to go, when they had paid for their vouchers by at least a third. Katie had already seen an upholstered moquette settee and a colourful rug. All they had to wait for was a visit from the agent so they could start paying rent for the property.

Katie had been on a night shift at the hospital. It was easy to sleep down at Thistledown Cottage because there was no one to disturb her there. Ernie was up at the farmhouse helping old Briggs, who still had one or two acres of meadow that he'd not sold on.

She slumbered on in a dreamless sleep, not hearing a persistent knocking upon the front door. If it had touched her consciousness at all, her thoughts would be that it was only Sam, her brother-in-law calling with the milk.

A few hours later and refreshed from her sleep, she spotted a single sheet of paper that had been pushed under the door. Though it was addressed to Mr. Tibbs, not Miss, Katie read it anyway.

"Mr. Tibbs," she read out. "Would you kindly present yourself as soon as possible at the offices of the Sheldon Property Company. I have tried to contact you on a number of occasions, but you have not been in. Please ask for Mr. Arlington." The writer had signed it, Richard Clegg.

Katie's heart plummeted as she sat down and studied the words. So this was it then, the news that they'd been waiting for at last? What if they couldn't meet the rent that they'd be asking? Nurses Home, here I come?

–

"Eddie, there's something I want to discuss with you. Could yer come into the drawing room for a moment? Olive, you can bring in the tea."

Maggie sat on the chaise longue and motioned to Eddie to sit near her on a chair. They sipped their tea from delicate porcelain cups and Eddie felt he was in heaven.

"Eddie, I know you and Hannah have only been with me fer a few days, but there are certain rules we must follow if our life together is to be harmonious. The servants are used to following a routine here, so I would thank you not to hang around engaging them in conversation. They must be encouraged to call you Sir or Mr. Dockerty, especially Olive, who I have heard calling you by your Christian name. Joan must be allowed to get on with her cooking and it isn't your job to bring in coal for the range. Do yer understand what I'm getting at? These people are my servants and that's what they get paid for."

Eddie's face was a picture. His mouth started twitching and Maggie felt sure he was trying to suppress a giggle. Suddenly all Hannah could hear as she came down the stairs was her husband and stepmother beside themselves with mirth.

"What's so funny, you two?" she asked as she came across the pair of them, seeing Maggie with tears of laughter running down her cheeks.

"Ask this noggle head you've brought to live with us, he'll have me in the funny farm the way he's carrying on!"

Maggie sat with Mr. Arlington in the chambers of the Town Hall Planning Officer. Newly created to this position, Mr. Hobbs was quite a pompous young man.

"We have studied the architect's drawings that you resubmitted for our approval, Mrs. Haines," he said importantly. "I must say with only twenty-four houses being proposed for the site, we can now see the wood from the trees!"

He sat back in his chair and smiled widely at his little joke. He realised that neither of the people opposite him at his desk shared his small frivolity and arranged his face back into a serious one again. "As we have said before, so I won't bore you with reiteration, these plans are best for the foreseeable future. The previous ones would have put a great strain on the village's existing resources, for example the sewage system and the water supply. As we are trying to work within our budgets, we don't want the cost of the aforementioned to have to rise again. So if we are agreed, you can now put out for tender to build twenty-four houses on what we shall be naming Claypool Road."

"And what about the proposed row of terraces that we have applied to build along Town Lane?" Mr. Arlington inquired, knowing that Maggie was too annoyed to speak.

"Won't be a problem, Mr. Arlington. There is already that type of dwelling on that road, so your plans should pass through the committee without much discussion. You can take it from me that those buildings can go ahead."

"I told you, Maggie, that your plans for low cost dwellings wouldn't meet with their approval," said Mr.

Arlington, as they walked down the high street from the Town Hall. "You may as well get on with it, or some other developer will come along and they'll be given the go ahead. Just do as Hobbs tells you and forget your dreams of houses for the masses. Think of the money you're going to make from it anyway. Now, is this job going to be too much for our company? Do you want me to approach any other firms to put a tender in?"

–

"Do sit down, Mr. Tibbs, Miss Tibbs. I see you have received our communication regarding Thistledown Cottage. It's good of you both to come in."

Mr. Arlington sat down heavily behind his desk. He was feeling his age today. If it wasn't for all the excitement that was going on with the Sheldon companies, he would go into retirement. Alice was constantly nagging him to give his notice in to Maggie, but who would she get to replace him? Mr. Peel was happy in his Bounty voucher kingdom and Richard Clegg had a lot to learn still. You couldn't throw away the experiences of twenty-odd years.

He smiled encouragingly at the two young people before him, who were looking distinctly nervous. Even Katie felt a bit shaky, and she dealt with her dragon of a Matron every day.

"Can yer tell us how much the rent is going to be, Sir?" asked Ernie timidly. "Only neither of us have well-paid jobs and you'll know that we lived rent-free before."

"It still will be rent-free, young man, but only for the near future. The council in its wisdom has decided that all properties deemed insanitary are to be demolished and your cottage is one of them, I'm afraid, along with the other cottage further up the lane."

"But, Sir," gasped Ernie, looking at his sister in alarm. "We've nowhere else to go and that place is all we've known since we were children. Tibbses have lived at Thistledown Cottage for nearly forty years!"

"Yes, yes we are aware of that, but remember things have changed now. It isn't a tied cottage any more. It belongs to the Sheldon Property Company."

"Then how will we be paying no rent on it for the near future?" asked Katie, puzzlement showing in her pleasant face.

"Because you will be getting first refusal on a property to be built on Town Lane. You can stay at Thistledown Cottage until then."

"But we've got no money to go buying a new place to live in, never mind find the rent if that was to be asked for instead. I told yer before that neither of us have well paid jobs…"

Ernie went pink in the face and hot round the collar. The frustration of trying to make this man before him understand their situation was causing him to break out in a sweat.

Mr. Arlington opened a drawer in his desk and brought out a paper. He explained, as he knew that they had probably never seen one before, that it was a money order.

"Given to you by Mrs. Haines, in memory of your mother. Fifty pounds, a good deposit, and you can borrow the rest at a very low interest from the Sheldon Property Company!"

"Well, I never," said Annie in amazement, as she looked at her two siblings, when they arrived breathless on her doorstep later.

"She's given yer fifty pounds as a deposit on a new house to be built up on Town Lane? How much are they costing? When will yer move in? You look like startled rabbits the pair of yer. Come in anyway and tell me all about it. Then I'll tell you my news, it's just as good as yours!"

Chapter 12

Maggie walked with Hannah along the road to church one Sunday morning. They hadn't been there since Hannah's wedding, as neither had felt the urge to. Maggie, because she felt so angry still at Jack's departure that she couldn't take the Host; Hannah, because she had never been a keen churchgoer anyway. Today, though, the sun was shining and with spirits feeling distinctly uplifted, they had agreed to go together, leaving Eddie to lie in bed.

It had been a big mistake, thought Maggie after. Not only did they see Alice in the congregation, but Madeline, Eddie's mother, was there too. They should have just turned heel and returned later for the second Mass, but surely there would be no confrontation in the House of God?

Alice was the first to stir up trouble. She had made a beeline for Maggie, as everyone spilled out into the churchyard.

"I see you couldn't hold onto him fer very long, Maggie. How many years has it bin?"

"Just ignore her, Mother," Hannah hissed. "You know what she's like, she's only looking for a fight!"

They began to continue together along the path that lead to Burton Road, both staring ahead of them, ignoring people as they walked.

"But you've held onto mine though, Maggie Haines," shouted Madeline, who had heard what Alice had been saying and had run after them.

"Doesn't allow our Eddie to come a-calling now. Thinks our place isn't good enough now he's living at Selwyn Lodge."

That was too much for Maggie. She turned with the light of battle sparking in her eyes.

"Madeline. I've offered yer the hand of friendship. I said yer would be welcome in me home at any time, but no, yer full of bitterness wanting to cling on to the past and try to even old scores. Nobody is keeping your son away from the tavern, but perhaps he prefers it where it's peaceful, instead of living in a menagerie with all those kids and you!"

More insults might have been hurled and physical damage done, if it had not been for the priest, who upon hearing the ruction, hurriedly intervened.

"Ladies, I could hear you from inside the vestry!"

Father O'Brien came hurrying down the path towards them, his cassock flapping around his heels.

"I'm ashamed of you all, that I am."

He gestured towards the small group of gaping onlookers, who had gathered to speculate on the outcome of the affray.

"Go to yer homes now, I'm sure you've all got Sunday dinners to get on with."

Turning to the three guilty-looking ladies and Hannah, who was holding onto her stepmother protectively, he glared at them and said, "Mrs. Dockerty, Mrs. Haines and you, Mrs. Arlington, whatever your differences are, you have just bin in the House of God and He won't be pleased at all at you shouting like a group of fishwives. Neither am

I happy about it and I will visit each one of yer in turn to see what is at the bottom of these shenanigans."

"Well, she started it," began Hannah, feeling that she should protect Maggie from her Grandmama, who she knew had a vicious tongue.

"Never mind who started it, Hannah. We are all God's children and we should treat one another with respect. Now go in peace and don't forget I'll be visiting you all in the next few days."

–

Eddie thought it was funny when Hannah and Maggie told him that they had felt like naughty school girls.

"I don't know. All this fighting is over me, isn't it? It's this way I've got with women, yer see."

Even Maggie joined in when Hannah started hitting him with a cushion, until he cried for mercy, saying two onto one wasn't fair!

–

It was Maggie's fortieth birthday. She didn't feel like getting out of bed to face it, though they had planned to hold a celebration at the Victoria Hotel. Not really a celebration, she thought. It was only the three of them. Just dinner in a different place without one of the people she loved the most. It was Mikey's birthday today as well. How would he be celebrating his twenty-third year in that distant foreign land? Would someone be making a fuss of him, with presents, congratulations and a special dinner, too? His letters, now he had decided to write them, told of voracious heat, diseases, water shortage, millions of mosquitoes and flies. Surly servants, basic quarters, minor skirmishes now and again. It was nothing at all as he had expected and he hoped he'd be back home this time next year. She felt sad for a moment, thinking that in some way she had failed him. Had he joined the British Army because she hadn't given him enough responsibility? Had she driven him to it by taking her step-daughter's side?

She got out of bed reluctantly and stared at herself critically in the cheval mirror. She didn't look too bad, she thought, considering her age. Her hair only had a little grey in it; a few more lines on her face than there were last year; she wasn't fat but slender and curvy and she knew she was still attractive, because of the attention she received from certain men. Richard Clegg seemed to be very taken with her, as was Dr. Farrington, and her new solicitor in Chester couldn't do enough for her!

Her thoughts wandered to Richard Clegg, the young man who was being groomed by Mr. Arlington to take over from him when he retired. It was the admiration in Richard's eyes when Maggie was introduced to him that she remembered. How could she not feel flattered, when Jack didn't even want her as his wife? Still, she chided herself, she shouldn't even be thinking about young men such as Richard at her age. She was going to be a grandma just after Christmas; all her love and affection would be given to him or her.

-

Katie sat in the grounds of the cottage hospital, taking a breather after a busy morning on her ward. She had come on duty at 7 a.m. and would be there until 9 p.m. that evening. It was a long day, but she was used to it now that she had been nursing for a couple of years. She was taking her lunch break, preferring on sunnier days to eat her food on the bench in the hospital garden. That was when Matron wasn't about anyway. But Matron had gone to Chester, something to do with the Medical Board, and Sister Makin was in charge. Though the Sister was a stickler in keeping certain disciplines, she turned a blind eye to a lot of things.

The rays of the sun came through the trees in the shady garden, as Katie pondered over the letter that had come to Thistledown Cottage by post. It had informed Mr. Tibbs of the interest payable on the loan to be taken out on Barleymow Terrace, Town Lane. Katie had felt a great flash of anger when she had read that Ernie was to be the owner of the property, especially when it was her wages that would be bolstering up the repayments. She earned the veritable sum of thirty pounds per year, when Ernie was only earning twenty-four. Being a woman was so unfair, she ruminated. Why was it that women were treated so badly? Not every woman had a husband and a family. What became of single women who wanted a place of their own?

She thought of all the women who worked in the hospital; Matron, Sister, Rebecca Flynn, the probationer, Celia Rankin, the almoner. All women without property; all reliant on their professions to give them a home. Though there were the exceptions she knew. There was Maggie Haines, who seemed to have her fingers in every pie in Neston and that woman Matron was always banging on about, Elizabeth Blackwell, the first female to become a doctor. And there was their own dear Queen. All strong women who hadn't relied on a man to achieve their status.

Katie moodily chewed on a piece of cheese and thought about her situation. Should she confront the

Sheldon Property Company and demand that her name was put on the deeds? Or should she let her brother become the sole owner and just pay him rent for one of his rooms? What if he found himself a wife in the future? It was possible. Ernie was a good-looking man when he bothered to make an effort, but strangely enough there had never been a hint of a woman in his life. But that didn't mean there wouldn't be, when he got the keys of the new house in a month or so. Katie brushed the crumbs from the skirt of her uniform, feeling trepidation at the uncertainty of the years to come.

It was nearly Christmas and the berries on the holly bushes hung in large red clusters, glowing brightly against the white of the snow that had been falling for the last few days.

Eddie sat companionably with his mother-in-law in front of a roaring log fire in the drawing room of Selwyn Lodge. They had just eaten a satisfying dinner of roast pork and all the trimmings and Eddie, who was sitting with a large glass of port in his hand, was feeling that his world was complete. Well, not quite complete, he thought, as he listened for sounds from the marital bedroom. Hannah had been up there for a few hours resting. The baby had been due two days ago and the nurse, who Maggie had employed for the birthing, had insisted that Hannah took the weight off her feet. Eddie sat and counted his blessings. He lived in a comfortable, well-run house, he was now in charge of his own gang of workmen and before long he would be father to a little baby that he and Hannah had made together. Be it boy or girl he wasn't really bothered, but a boy would be the ticket if Eddie managed one day to realise his secret dream. The Sheldon Property Company was becoming a big name in the building industry and he was hoping that soon he would be given a bigger role in it. He was grateful for what he had, no doubt about it; at his age it was a great honour to have such responsibility. But if Maggie was to be presented with a grandson, wouldn't she want her grandson's father to have more say in the running of the company? Foreman maybe, but the title Works Manager had a better ring to it. This new man, Richard, who had taken over from Mr. Arlington, was all right when it came to running the business for Maggie, but he hadn't any manual experience like Eddie had and wasn't very popular with the ordinary working man. Still, for now Eddie was content with the way things had worked out for him. If he hadn't have married Hannah, he wouldn't even have been made a ganger at the young age of twenty-one.

—

Richard Clegg sat at his desk chewing on the end of his pencil as he waited for his employer to appear. She had said she would come in on New Year's Day to go over a few details with him; check that each of the businesses were running well and to talk about new ideas for the future. He couldn't see why she bothered making her regular appearances. The woman was loaded and didn't need to oversee the work he did for her. The Bounty vouchers were popular with the locals still, the Loan Department was raking the money in and already there was a list of people waiting for their homes to be built. Besides, Mr. Arlington, although now an old man, still popped in to keep an eye on him, which annoyed Richard greatly. Why couldn't they both leave him to get on with the job?

Richard brushed back the hair that flopped over his eyes and busied himself with the loans ledger. They had taken sixty-three pounds in the last week of 1870, not a bad little sum. He was glad that a branch of the Chester Bank had opened locally a few months ago. Maggie had entrusted him to ride to the city with the takings up until then, but he had always felt nervous. Especially walking through certain streets in Chester where the unemployed seemed to hang around. He was lucky really that Mr. Arlington chose him to be his successor. Mr. Peel could have taken over, but he liked the outdoor life, visiting shops to collect the vouchers, and really the man was getting too old. He was also training up a young man to follow in his footsteps. A chap called Penswick. Strangely enough he had been in a lower year than Richard. They had both attended the Caldy Grammar School.

Richard heard footsteps hurrying up the staircase, unannounced, as the dratted girl who called herself the receptionist hadn't appeared this morning. That was one of the things he needed to talk to Maggie about. Should they advertise for another girl?

"Good morning, Richard. Happy New Year. Did you have a pleasant evening with your family? Or did yer celebrate with a secret lady love?"

Maggie breezed into the office with a happy smile on her face. Her grandson, Edward John Dockerty, had made his appearance into the world on the penultimate day of the old year and Maggie was tickled pink with him. He had been born with a shock of silky brown hair and navy blue eyes and had been a good weight of seven pounds, nine ounces. Hannah had been exhausted after a labour of thirty-four hours, but she had come through it unscathed and was even talking about having another! Eddie was delighted, like a cat with two tails.

"Yes, thank you, Mrs. Haines, a very pleasant evening was spent with my family, though unfortunately I don't have a secret lady love. And may I wish you a Happy New Year too? Let us hope it is as successful as the last one. You are looking very chipper today, Madam, if you don't mind me saying so. Is this something to do with the expected happy event?"

"Yes, I have recently become a grandmama! Edward John Dockerty will be his name when he is christened. Mother and babe both doing well. I'm glad to see you've lit a fire in here, Richard. It's freezing outside. I'm a bit worried the weather is going to delay the finishing date on some of the houses up on Daisy Bank; the ones on Town Lane are already behind."

"Firstly, may I say congratulations on the safe delivery of your grandson. But I can't see any of our clients wanting to move in in this weather, Mrs. Haines. I wouldn't want to contend with all the business of moving when I could be sitting around a warming fire."

"That's not the point, Richard. I pride meself on sticking firmly to the date we have given our clients and not everyone has a warming fire to sit around. Take the Bradleys for instance. They've come up from London; he's been sent to set up a branch of their manufacturing business. How do you think his wife will feel having to live out of a suitcase in the hotel?"

"Well, their house is nearly completed, Mrs. Haines. We're only waiting for the finisher to tile the door step and stick some up around the archway in the porch."

Richard began to feel annoyed with Maggie. Did she used to pester old Mr. Arlington with her petty fogging in this way? They'd just had Christmas and New Year to celebrate. Was he to go around to the tiler's house and drag him out of bed?

"Is that all that is stopping the Bradleys from moving in, then? Have they signed all the necessary documents and got the loan they wanted? I take it we have agreed to a loan."

"Of course, Mrs. Haines, that was done months ago, when Mr. Bradley first approached us. Mr. Arlington agreed it, after taking up references with the company Bradley works for. Begging your pardon, Mrs. Haines, but I have been trained very well by my predecessor, it is just the weather that has put everything behind and I hear that a lot of our workmen have been off ill."

"Pooh, I'd say it was more like having a few too many in the taverns celebrating Christmas that has caused the problems, not just the weather. I grant that the weather can cause havoc when footings are being dug out, or when the men are having to work at fixing the drains, but inside work should have continued despite the weather. Some of the roofs are on for heaven's sake."

Richard sat dumbly then waiting for Maggie to finish. What did she want? Someone who sat in the office and ran her day-to-day business, or someone who visited the building sites for her? He said as much when she had finished pacing. Maggie never liked to sit at a meeting; she was like a dog worrying a bone.

"I think the responsibility should rest with the gangers, Mrs. Haines. That's their job, isn't it? To keep an eye on their men?"

"You'd think so, wouldn't you? That's what they're paid for. But I only know one ganger that's worth his salt; the other two are as bad as their men. Right, I know what I'm going to do, Richard. I'm going to create the position of

Site Manager. It will be his job to visit each development and check over each house nearing completion. He'll have what we will call a chase list and it will be his responsibility to let you know when the buyer can expect to move in. Now, I think we'll call Milly and get her to make us a cup of tea. Have you heard from the Town Hall yet regarding those demolitions? I'm sure the Tibbses will be pleased when they get a date to move out."

Maggie tutted with annoyance when she heard that young Milly had not turned up for work. She hurried down to the small kitchen that she had provided for her staff and waited for the saucepan of water to boil on the newly-installed gas hob. It was a good job that it was New Year's Day. Not many folk would have surfaced from the previous day's celebrations to be thinking of a loan or even a repayment. If the girl didn't turn up tomorrow, Maggie would make sure she was out on her ear.

The outer door banged shut and Maggie put her head around the kitchen door, frowning slightly. She had been wrong; someone had bothered to stir their stumps. A woman in her twenties stood looking about her hesitantly. A fairly tall, plumpish girl, who wore her brown hair in a fetching chignon. She looked familiar, thought Maggie, taking in the shabby navy cloak, the long grey dress that showed beneath it and the comfortable-looking lace-up shoes.

"Do I know you?" Maggie inquired, walking up to the girl, who seemed nervous now she had been spoken to. The girl nodded.

"I'm Katie Tibbs, Ruthie's daughter. I was passing by and decided to call in. I was surprised that the office was open on New Year's Day."

"Ah, Katie Tibbs, pleased to meet yer. Happy New Year to you. I heard about your mother, poor soul, but you'll know that, as I have arranged a deposit on one of our houses for you and your brother. It was the least I could do, seeing Thistledown was bought by me. Call it compensation, with the Council wanting to demolish it but being too mean to pay. Have you been up to Town Lane to see where you'll be living?"

Maggie stood waiting for an answer and was surprised to see that Katie didn't look grateful or pleased with her good fortune, but distinctly put out by it all.

"Have I done something wrong? Aren't yer pleased? I didn't have to go to this trouble, as you'd do well to know."

"I was wanting to say, Mrs. Haines, that Ernie and I are extremely grateful. It is more than enough that you're doing this for us; totally unexpected. You didn't have to, seeing as Mother could be a spiteful old besom at times. But I just feel annoyed that the house is in Ernie's name and not mine, because I'm the one who will be contributing the most to pay the loan back and should he marry, I could find myself without a home."

"Oh, I didn't know about that. Sorry Katie, I just assumed that Mr. Arlington had completed all the necessary documents, making both of you the owners. It was foolish of me really to think that he would do that, seeing as he was always such a pedantic man."

Maggie sat down on one of the comfy couches and beckoned Katie to sit with her.

"I know how yer must be feeling. I've been in your situation meself once, having another person holding on to the purse strings. Mine was similar to yerself as I didn't have a husband around to support me. Everything's geared for a man to take charge, isn't it? Where is the house purchase up to, Katie? Have the deeds been signed yet? Do yer know?"

"I'm sorry to be putting you to all this trouble, Mrs. Haines, truly I am, but I thought you'd be best placed to know how I feel. I was going to write you a letter, drop it into your home like, but I plucked up the courage to come in when I saw the lamp on here. As to where the house purchase is up to, all Ernie's had is a letter saying how much the repayments are on the loan. I believe the house costs £95, so after your very generous contribution, we owe £45. We can easily afford to pay back the money over a period of twenty years, but as I said, I was annoyed that my name wouldn't appear on the agreement. Can you do anything to change it, Mrs. Haines? I have good employment. I'm a staff nurse at the local hospital."

Katie looked with new-found hope at Maggie. Her mother had always been scathing if Ruthie's old neighbour was ever mentioned, but this woman was being kind and gentle; not the ogre that local gossip made her out to be.

"What does Ernie think? Didn't he understand that the gift was for the both of you? Was he not surprised that the letter was only in his name? Have yer discussed it between yer, about if your futures were to change?"

"The problem is that Ernie is not a great reader, can't read at all if the truth was told, and relies on me to sort out problems such as this one. He probably doesn't even realise the implications of my name not being on the documents, but I've told him I can move into the Nurses Home if my name's not on them, where I can live for nothing. Then where would that leave him property-wise, Mrs. Haines?"

"It would leave me withdrawing my gift to you both, if I thought there would be problems with the repayments. I honestly didn't give any of this serious thought, Katie.

214

Just wanted to see Annie and the rest of you settled, as it were."

"Oh, Annie's over the moon with Lilac Cottage. Was singing your praises all the time when we visited on Christmas Day. Like me, she's grateful for her good fortune, there's so much more room there than in the place they had before."

What a pleasant girl, thought Maggie, as she told Richard later to expect new instructions regarding Mr. Tibbs's home ownership. Certainly a bit of a likeness to Ruthie in her appearance, but none of her mother's uncouthness about her at all. In fact, if Ruthie was still alive she would be very proud of her daughters, especially Katie. Though how the girl had become a staff nurse, Maggie would never know!

Maggie made her announcement after dinner. Hannah had been allowed to join them, though she was only three days into her lying in. The nurse was left to watch over little Johnny, as they had begun to call the baby; Edward John was such a mouthful to keep on calling him.

"I've decided to give yer a promotion, Eddie, seeing as it looks as if you're here to stay and you're not doing a runner as Hannah's father did. Let's raise our glasses to me new Works Manager. Do yer think yer up to it, Eddie? It will mean a nice warm office down at Sheldon and the use of the carriage to get around in."

Her son-in-law could only gape for a few moments, then he began to thank Maggie with delight once her words to him had sunk in. "What made yer think of me, though?" asked Eddie, after he and Hannah had exchanged surprised glances. It had been something they had discussed together, a bit of promotion to foreman perhaps, but to be made Works Manager? That was a leap in status in anyone's book! "Though, don't think that I'm not up to the job, but I thought this Richard bloke was in charge of everything, just as Mr. Arlington was before."

"I'll let you in on something, Eddie," Maggie said confidentially. "For years I took orders from Miss Rosemary and Mr. Arlington. I listened while they made all the decisions and believed they were right, because let's face it, I was just an ignorant girl. But it was my money that started the Sheldon Loan Company and it was my money that helped to start the property side. Now Mr. Arlington has gone and I'm left with Richard, his successor. A pleasant young man I grant you, but still a bit wet behind the ears. He knows nothing about the building trade, though he's very good at ledger work and dealing with the public. But you, Eddie, have been at the sharp end. Been out there in all weathers, learnt your trade and get on well with your men. I can just see Richard in his top hat and tailored suit wading through a muddy site inspecting a house for completion. No, you're the man fer the job, Eddie and perhaps now I'll get more of a say in things."

"He'll make a fine Works Manager," said Hannah, with a devoted look at her husband. "He won't let you down, Mother. Edward John will have a father to be proud of."

A little while later, as Hannah prepared to take herself off to feed the baby, leaving Eddie and Maggie to talk a few things through, there came a sudden knocking at the front door.

"Who can that be at this time of night?" tutted Maggie. "You go, Eddie. It must be revellers who are knocking at the wrong house. Probably for the Wickhams; they usually have friends around at this time of the year."

She settled back and drained off the contents of her glass, preparing to have one more sherry before she too headed for bed.

"Johnny!" Maggie gasped as she saw her visitor. "What a surprise! What are you doing here?"

"Thought I'd come to offer my congratulations to the new parents, seeing we only just heard through Olive's dad tonight in the pub."

"I was going to come down, Uncle Johnny, wasn't I, Hannah? But we've been rather busy up here what with the little fellow settling in."

"Sit down, Johnny, and have a sherry with us," said Maggie, after she had got over the shock of seeing Johnny again. "I didn't know yer were over in Neston. Did you know, Eddie? You could have had a meal with us if I'd known."

"Didn't know us Dockertys were welcome. After all the ill-feeling at the wedding we thought we were barred from Selwyn Lodge, so I was elected to throw me hat in the ring."

"No doubt Eddie's mother didn't tell you how she tried to show us up at church one Sunday morning," broke in Hannah. "We've not been since for embarrassment and I have to go in the near future as I must be churched!"

"Oh, you know Madeline, tough on the outside, but really deep down she only wants to be loved. Anyway, congratulations you two. Am I allowed to see my new little relation? Or have you got a dragon upstairs standing guard?"

"Olive's dad has told yer about Nurse Moffatt then," laughed Eddie. "I'm the child's father and I've only been allowed a peek or two."

Later, after the proud parents had retired to bed and little Johnny had been settled, Maggie stood on the doorstep saying goodnight to their unexpected visitor. He was looking uncomfortable, as if he had something more to say.

"So, perhaps we will see yer at the christening, Johnny. Now that you've made the effort to break the ice, perhaps some of the other members of the Dockerty family will want to do so too."

"Yes, you could be right, Maggie. Maybe the little chap will bring the family together again. Maggie... Can I say how bad I feel... um... For making those unkind remarks at the wedding? It was unforgivable of me. Especially as..." Johnny suddenly went red in the face and turned away.

"Go on, Johnny... Especially as what?"

Maggie felt secretly pleased at his discomfiture.

"No, it's nothing, I'll say goodnight then."

He began to walk away while Maggie stood and watched him. He was still an attractive man, though his hair was almost white, still smartly dressed and a catch for any single woman. Single woman, she told herself. You're still married to Jack!

Sighing to herself, Maggie turned to go back indoors, letting her mind dwell fleetingly on that night so long ago in Killala. It had been dark like this, as Johnny and she had made their way back to the hamlet. She had dared to think that one day she might be married to someone just like him. Someone who had made her heart skip a beat and her pulse race rather quickly; someone kind and considerate who would live his life for her.

"Maggie."

She jumped in surprise as she felt a gentle hand on her shoulder.

"Maggie. Let me come back into your life. Can you forgive what has gone on in the past?"

Chapter 13

"I've decided I'm going to treat meself to a small holiday in the not too distant future," Maggie announced to Hannah a few weeks later. They were walking companionably along the promenade together, Hannah proudly pushing the new perambulator before her, a present from Maggie, containing her sleeping son. The air was invigorating as a strong breeze blew in from the estuary and baby Johnny wrapped up well against the elements, was benefiting from the refreshing ozone smell.

"That's not like you to be thinking of holidays, Mother. You do surprise me, especially as Sheldon may crash about our heads without you at the helm. What's brought this on? Whatever are you thinking of?"

It was said tongue in cheek, as Hannah had great faith in her husband's ability to run his side of the business and from what he had told her, he, Richard and Mr. Peel's protégé were getting on famously.

"Since Eddie became Works Manager, things seem to be going more to plan and with the Christening over I'm feeling a little at a loose end and in need of a change. It was remarkable how everyone got on so well with each other last Sunday, wasn't it? Though I was glad that the Arlingtons declined the invitation; I would have been more on edge than I was if Alice had decided to come. I think Eddie's Uncle Johnny must have had a word and put the Dockertys on their best behaviour. I was holding me breath for Madeline to start having a go again, but fer once she was quite pleasant and positively glowing when yer let her hold the babe."

"And the children were little angels, weren't they?" Hannah agreed. "It was a good idea of Eddie's to ask his sister to be godmother and of course his uncle was as pleased as punch to be made godfather as well. So, where are you planning to take your short holiday, Mother? Llandudno seemed a pleasant place that time we were passing through."

"Oh, don't remind me. Your father said we'd go on holiday there one day, but I rather fancy booking into that big hotel in Liverpool. Do you remember when we were coming home from Ireland, some of our fellow passengers were going to stay at the Adelphi? No, you wouldn't remember, you were too busy being sick. Oh sorry, I shouldn't have mentioned that again."

"Mother, that's all in the past." Hannah squeezed Maggie's hand. "And I don't know if I've ever thanked you enough for the support you gave me when I needed it. You could have disowned me like my father eventually did, but look at us both happily pushing little Johnny out for his constitution. I'm content with the way my life has turned out and grateful for all you've done."

"Go on with yer, Hannah, yer making me feel all weepy. I should be grateful to you for giving me my beautiful grandson. Anyway, enough! Let me tell yer about this plan of mine."

Maggie fiddled with the ties on the fur tippet she wore around her neck as she thought about what she would say. She felt nervous and a little guilty; this idea she had was so unlike her that Hannah would know straight away she was being lied to. When had Maggie Haines ever taken time off for her own good?

"I'm thinking of staying a week in luxurious splendour and I've heard the shops in Liverpool are equal, if not better, to our favourite department store. I can just imagine meself being cossetted and pampered and spending a lot of money on a new wardrobe of clothes. I hear that Bond Street is the place to be, according to Mrs. Peters, who's on the Hospital Board. She was telling me of a little shop that's just opened there. Bespoke tailoring would yer believe?"

Maggie waited, blushing, for Hannah's pronouncement, ready to hear of the girl's disbelief.

"Well, I have to admit that it will be pleasant to have some time alone with Eddie. Now that the nurse has gone, we can play happy families on our own."

"Yes, I've been thinking along those lines meself, Hannah. It can't be much fun fer yer both having me hanging around. No, let me finish..."

Maggie put her hand on her stepdaughter's arm as the girl began to protest.

"Though I adore the little one, I've been thinking I might look around fer a country cottage. Something that we could all use for holidays or when we want to get away from it all. I was thinking perhaps in Wales or on the banks of the Mersey. I don't know yet, it's only a thought fer the future, but it would give yer time on yer own."

Hannah looked thoughtful and hesitated over her next words, but things had to be said if they were being honest with each other. "Tell me to mind my own business if you want to Mother, but do you ever think of going over to Ireland to be with Father? I know he let you down, he let us all down, but I wonder if you still have any feelings for him? I know… That's what you're doing, isn't it?!" Hannah stopped walking and turned quickly to face her stepmother, her eyes wide open in surprise. "Going to meet Papa in Liverpool! You'd never leave the business behind if it wasn't so important…"

"No, Hannah, that's not it at all. Your father and I are finished and I am amazed that you could even be thinking of it, but I suppose now that you're a married woman I can speak frankly to yer. You're a bit of a romantic, perhaps seeing us living happily in our old age together, but no, that will never happen. You know the story of our early years together, how I took him back when he came home from America, but I'll not do that again. I've too much pride to let that happen and, who knows, he might even have a new love in Wicklow. So he wouldn't want me turning up and messing his life up for him."

"But you must have loved him once, Mother," Hannah insisted. "Before all the misery he caused you. Would it be too difficult to try again?"

"Let it rest, Hannah. Just thinking of your father aggravates me. Besides it's too nice a day to be dwelling on him."

—

Maggie stood for a moment at the bottom of the marble steps that led up to Liverpool's grandest hotel. She had turned down the cab driver's offer of carrying up her two heavy valises to Reception, tipping him well as he shook his head disbelievingly. Her heart was hammering as she realised the enormity of what she was doing. But this had been planned for weeks now and she was going to see it through. Why shouldn't she and Johnny be together at last?

He had told her it was what he had wanted since he'd first met her, though she'd taken it all with a pinch of the proverbial salt. How could he have loved that raggedy, wild-looking, tattered girl?

That night when he had come back to speak to her had been a revelation for the both of them. So many years had passed since their time in Killala. Was it really the truth that Maggie was hearing from him?

"Why do you think I never married?" Johnny had asked her. "Because you were there in me mind, whatever I did. When I left you at the 'Giant's Tub' I worried for your future. I told me mother the next morning that I'd visit where you lived."

"But yer didn't, did yer?" Maggie had replied, quite unable to believe that the pair of them were sitting with a glass of sherry each at midnight in front of the drawing room fire. "Nor did yer want to take me back to Ireland with yer, when I met yer that day by the pier."

"Oh, Maggie, how could I have done that? You had just married Jack. What if there had been a baby on the way?"

"I'm still married to Jack," Maggie had said flatly. "So it doesn't change the situation, though it does me heart good to hear that you care for me."

"And what about you? I know you have some feeling for me. Every time we meet we're drawn to each other. Remember that time when we danced on the bowling green?"

"Aye and remember all those hurtful things that were said at Hannah's wedding? Not words I should hear from a man who professes to care."

"I know, Maggie and I'm sorry. I was jealous that I wasn't in your life and you'd changed so much from the girl I loved. You were confident, poised, none of the things I remembered about you. And with Jack as your husband, I didn't have a chance."

They had talked until the milk churns rattled, as the farm cart passed by on its way to the village, eager to hear of life's journey that each of them had made.

"And here I am," Maggie said to herself. "About to start the next stage."

–

"Let me help you with your bags, Madam."

Maggie turned to see the concierge of the building, a tall man dressed in a blue and silver uniform, gazing at her with some concern.

"Surely the cabbie didn't leave you to carry these up on your own?" He tutted disapprovingly and began to climb up the steps to the hotel with her valises.

Maggie watched him go, suddenly unwilling to follow. Once up those steps she'd have committed herself to a man she was unsure of, even if he did have a handsome face. That was what it was, she thought. She was attracted by his looks and stature, left over dreams from her girlhood, when she imagined the man she'd marry one day. It was still there in her memory, still feeling cheated that she had been whisked away by Jack and his mother. Had there been a glimmer of hope that last night in Ireland that Johnny would come to rescue her?

What harm would it do? A few nights of passion. To feel the heat from another man's body, when for too long she had slept alone. She was hurting no one, except perhaps herself in the future, if Johnny was playing a duplicitous game.

"Madam, are you waiting for somebody?" A voice from above broke into Maggie's daunting fears.

She walked slowly upwards, her head tilted bravely, unsure if she could cope with the challenge that lay ahead.

–

"So," said Eddie after Hannah had come down from settling their baby. "Did Maggie get away alright? What time train was she catching?"

Hannah snuggled down beside him on the big sofa that had just been delivered. They had complained that the chaise longue was uncomfortable, so Maggie had ordered this one and banished the chair to the little-used sitting room.

"Oh, don't remind me. She was in a real snappy mood before she left. Said she was going on the eleven o'clock, but was still here at half past. Interfering with my plans for this evening's meal, telling Joan that she might be here for it anyway. I kept saying, 'Leave it, you'll be at the Adelphi eating from an á la carte menu', but she kept muttering, 'That's if I go'."

"I thought she was looking forward to getting away for a while. Spending some of her millions on new gowns and fripperies, or whatever you women do."

"I just don't know what got into her," Hannah yawned and stretched her body beside him.

"She deserves a break from all these decisions she's been making, especially now she's got you overseeing the developments and from what you say, Richard seems to have got everything else in hand. But I heard her talking to herself in her bedroom while she was doing her packing, saying why on earth had she agreed to leave her beautiful view?"

"She'll enjoy herself once she gets there. A week spent in the lap of luxury and all those shops to wander through. She'll come back feeling pleased that she made the effort... Meantime, what about you and I making another baby together?"

Eddie drew Hannah into the circle of his arms and began to nuzzle her.

"Let's forget Maggie for the moment and concentrate on you and me."

–

Maggie anxiously paced the floor of the sitting room in the suite she had reserved for her and Captain Dockerty. It had all seemed so easy when she had written her letter to the hotel all those weeks ago:

> *The Captain and Mrs Dockerty would be staying*
> *in Liverpool for a short holiday and would they be*
> *so kind as to reserve them a suite?*

Or something like that, she couldn't remember her wording. This day had crept up on her so quickly and now she was waiting for her 'husband' to appear. Johnny had said his ship would tie up at the docks around five-ish and now here it was; six o'clock and there was no sign of him. How long did it take to walk from the docks to the Adelphi Hotel?

She still had on her travelling coat, round saucer hat and wrist-length gloves. They all matched in colour, a blueish grey in an attractive brushed velvet. The maid had hung her clothing in a vast wardrobe in the large bedroom adjacent to the sitting room, but on two occasions Maggie had thought of repacking them and taking flight. What was she doing there, she kept asking herself? She knew nothing about Johnny, other than he was the son of her old friend, Kathleen Dockerty. Yes, he was Eddie's uncle, her grandchild's godfather, but that didn't mean she knew a lot about the man.

What had he been doing since they had parted all those years ago? Oh, she knew when he had finished running cattle across from Ireland that he had captained anybody's vessel who would have him, that now he sailed a steamboat to Dublin every other day, but what about the man? What had he been up to? Had there been a girl in every port, as was said about sailors, or had it been true what he had said to her? She had always got in his way. Did she really believe there had been no other woman he had called his beloved, no girl he had slept with or lived with? An attractive man such as Johnny, charming and dashing, still good to look at almost fifty.

Maggie groaned at the thought of him; he was everything she had dreamed of as a young girl. But she was a married woman, wasn't she? About to start something with another man, when Jack was only a short sail across the Irish Sea. And Johnny would expect that thing that she had disliked when she had shared a bed with her husband; the mauling, the sweating, the messing about with her private bits and the worry of finding herself expecting. She was forty now for heaven's sake; she was too old to get in the family way.

She stopped her pacing and started for the bedroom. If she was quick it would only take her minutes to get her clothes back into the valises. They would be surprised to see her back in Selwyn Lodge, but she still had time before Hannah and Eddie retired to bed. Her breath came in little gasps as she flung open the tall doors of the wardrobe, pulling down her evening gown, her warm wrap, her two elegant walking dresses, throwing them haphazardly into her bag. Next the drawer with her underclothes in. Don't forget your nightie and your shoes, her mind said. Finished! All she needed now was a porter and a cabbie. She'd leave a message to say she'd been called away!

Too late. A knock came at the door of the sitting room. Maggie trembled from head to foot for a moment. What was she going to tell him? He'd be angry, she'd seen him in action at Hannah's wedding. What could he be capable of? He seemed a strong man, would he strike her for messing him around?

"Sorry to disturb you, Madam." It was the manager; a small man in a stiff black suit, with a toadying air, whose eyes seemed to dwell somewhere around Maggie's shoes.

"I was wondering if you would like to take dinner here instead of in our restaurant. I noticed that your husband hasn't put in an appearance yet and…" he coughed. "I'm sure you wouldn't like to have attention drawn to the fact you are dining alone."

Maggie stood for a moment and stared at him, relieved that it hadn't been Johnny. But what was wrong with dining alone? Was he suggesting something? Something impolite, for heaven's sake?

She was saved from answering him, as Johnny came walking briskly up the hall.

Her heart began to pit a pat as she saw his elegant stride. He looked a little windblown and had changed from what she imagined would be a smart sailor suit to evening dress. Black tails, white frilled shirt and a top hat that he carried in the crook of his arm. In his hand was a large masculine-looking overnight bag. The thought crossing her wildly thrashing mind that it would have a change of clothing and his nightwear in.

"Ah, you must be the manager of the establishment," Johnny said a little breathlessly. "I'm Captain Dockerty. Got caught up in stormy waters out in Liverpool Bay. Here now. Did you want something? My wife and I will be down at eight thirty for our evening meal. Sorry darling…"

He shut the door firmly in the surprised face of the manager, then after looking Maggie up and down quizzically, he hugged her to him, then kissed her warmly on her gaping mouth. When he had finished, he looked over her shoulder with appreciation at the surroundings they were in.

"Well, you've certainly done us proud, Maggie. I couldn't believe it when the man in the lobby said we had been put in the Crosby suite on the first floor. Is that a bathroom over there. That bed that I can see looks far more comfortable than my bunk on the *Irish Maiden*. So, what are you doing with your outdoor clothes on? Why hasn't the maid put your clothes away? Have you only just got here like I have? I thought you were leaving Neston early so you could have a look around the shops without me hanging around?"

Maggie pulled away from him and sat down in a small gilt-edged chair. She covered her face with her hands and began to sob quietly.

Johnny stood in amazement, wondering what she was doing. He knew he was later than he said he would be, but he had expected her at least to have changed into an evening gown, or even have a maid on hand pinning up her hair. What had got into her all of a sudden? He shoved his bag aside with his foot and knelt down on his knees in front of Maggie, trying to take her hands in his.

"What's the matter with you? Was it that man that was hanging round the door? Has he upset you? Come on Maggie, out with it." Johnny started to get angry. If someone had hurt her in some way then he'd go straight down and deal with it.

Maggie rubbed at her wet cheeks distractedly and tried to take command of herself. This was silly. She was acting like a child.

"No," she said hastily, keeping her eyes averted from his in case she softened her resolve.

"It all got too much for me, sitting around this afternoon waiting for you. I should have gone shopping like I said I would, but I didn't and it gave me time to think. We shouldn't be doing this, Johnny. I'm a married woman and I don't even know yer properly. The thought of all this was exciting. You and me together, pretending to be Captain and Mrs Dockerty. It all seemed a world away when we were planning this in Neston, but now it's happening, I don't think I can go through with it. I think I should go back home."

She brought her eyes up to meet his, expecting an angry face, waiting for a tirade from him saying that she had played him for a fool. But there was none of that. He was smiling kindly at her, nodding with understanding. He raised her to him and kissed her on both cheeks slowly.

"Maggie, do yer think I'm a monster? Did yer think that I'd drag yer over to that big bed through there and have me way with yer? This week is for us to get to know each other. I lost yer once to that eejit from Killala but I'm not about to lose yer again. I know yer married and yes, we're both Catholics, so we're bound to do the guilt thing.

But you only get one chance at true happiness in this life, so let's take it while we can. I've arranged five days leave and in that time we'll do the sights, tramp round the shops and take our loving very slowly. We'll even put a bolster down the middle of the bed, if yer think that I'm just after your body. Now come on, Mrs. Dockerty, I'm starving. Shall I ring for a maid to help you with your dressing? I believe that's what they do in fancy hotels!"

Maggie reflected on Johnny's words as the maid fastened her into the wasp waist corset, then placed the bustle beneath the underskirt of the peach-coloured, shot silk evening gown.

She had bought the dress on impulse last time she had visited Chester, thinking she could wear it at one of the many charity balls she was always being invited to. But with no one to escort her, it was difficult to summon up the courage to go alone and the dress had sat forlornly in her wardrobe for quite some time. But here she was, about to go to dinner with a very handsome escort, throwing caution to the wind, embarking on this second chance of happiness, hoping it wouldn't come to a bitter end. Because what had happened when she had taken Jack back into her heart again? Betrayal and treachery, from a man who had insisted they take their marriage vows in the first place, when she had been prepared to sit out the famine in her family home. Was she expected to live out her days as a spinster would, although Jack could have a lover at his stud farm? If there was a God, did he want her to live her life growing older and bitter, only concerned with business and how much money she could earn? No, she and Johnny deserved this time together. He had said he had loved her for twenty-four years!

She felt calmer as she looked in the cheval mirror, patting the curls on top of her head where the maid had entwined peach satin ribbon. Johnny had disappeared somewhere, but was not disappointed when he returned clutching a small delicate posy.

"These were the last the woman had in her basket," he said gruffly, "though I don't think violets go with the colour of your gown."

He thanked the maid and tipped her a few pennies. Maggie had whizzed around before she came to help her, putting all the clothes back into the wardrobe again.

"Maggie, you look beautiful. I can't believe I've got you back in me life again."

He took her in his arms and kissed her cheek.

"I aim to make this week the happiest you have ever had."

—

They were greeted by the Major Domo as they hesitated in the restaurant doorway. The place seemed to be in an uproar, with white-gloved, uniformed waiters rushing about with tureens, silver platters and bottles of wine or champagne.

"It's the Aintree Races this week, Sir. I must apologise if your table isn't ready yet, but I'll set one of my staff to it as soon as one of them is free. Meantime, would you and your good lady wife like to sit in the drawing room? I could bring you an aperitif, on the house of course."

Maggie felt herself relaxing as they entered the comfortably-appointed room, with its pretty fabric-covered sofas, occasional tables and heavy rugs on the shining wooden floors. Couples sat nursing their after-dinner coffees or drinking from fluted glasses. A man sat at a grand piano quietly playing a popular tune.

"I would like a small glass of sherry, thank you," Maggie said to the young man who had been summoned, while Johnny ordered a tot of rum.

"I was a little worried just then, Johnny. Jack could be here on business from Ireland. Did you know he had a stud farm in Wicklow?"

"Yes, Eddie's dad told me when I was contemplating calling to visit you. I'd heard he'd cleared off again. Must have caused a lot of heartbreak, Maggie. Not only just for you."

"I'm over it now," she shrugged. "It was Hannah who suffered more than me. She had always been Jack's princess and this business with Eddie brought out the worst in her father and I have to admit we were going through a bad time."

"Not happy, I suppose, that you'd managed to exist without him while he was off in America all those years," Johnny said dryly.

"Well, what was I supposed to do without him, Johnny? I'm sure the Dockertys filled yer in with all the details; told yer about Miss Rosemary and me rise to fame."

"Yes, of course they did," he replied gently. "You were the enemy as far as Maddy was concerned; she was bound to tell me all she knew. But I thought we were putting this behind us; starting afresh as it were."

"To face the future we have to talk about the past," Maggie said quietly. "You must know all there is about me and I need to know all about you. No hidden secrets from each other, nothing that could rear its head and cause any problems. I had enough of that with me husband. You know that Hannah is only Jack's?"

Johnny was saved from making further comment as their drinks arrived on a silver salver. They both took a sip from their respective glasses gratefully.

"It all sounds rather lively in the restaurant," Johnny said to the waiter. "We can hear the noise from here."

"We've got two parties in this evening. One belongs to Lord Belsham and the other is part of the Earl of Sefton's group. One of their horses won on the steeplechase at Aintree and they all turned up unannounced on our doorstep. The manager couldn't turn them away, of course, because of who they are. But they'll be going soon. Off to one of their regal residences to continue their celebrations, I'm sure."

Maggie tugged at Johnny's sleeve as the waiter walked away from them.

"Johnny," she said urgently, a blush appearing in her cheeks in her agitation. "Johnny, we can't eat in there if Lord Belsham is there with his party Can we go somewhere else fer dinner? I'd rather not be where he is... I might see someone I know."

"Why, does he know yer, this Lord Belsham? I hadn't heard that yer mixed in such exalted circles, Maggie," he replied teasingly.

"No, I don't know him, but Jack did. Jack went over to America as his agent. It would be just my luck fer Jack to be in contact again with him, especially as he's in to racing now. He mentioned Aintree as one of the meetings where he raced his horses."

"Oh, all right, Maggie. Let's not spoil our evening with you peering over yer shoulder and jumping at the slightest sound. I'll ask for a menu and see if we can have our meal served in our quarters. Mebbe even better, hey? It's not every day that I get me dinner served in the Crosby suite. I'll take advantage while I can."

—

After they had finished their meal of pheasant paté, cod creole and lemon crumb pudding, Johnny poured the last of the wine into the two silver-stemmed goblets before them.

"Ah, that was a wonderful meal, Maggie, wasn't it? And this Burgundy is a good drop of stuff too. I don't usually drink wine, but I might take it up if this is anything to go by. How about you? Are you a wine drinker? Have you got a cellar full of interesting wine?"

"We haven't got a cellar," Maggie replied, lethargically. "No, I've never been much of a drinker. A drop of sherry before a meal, maybe another after, but Miss Rosemary didn't drink wine at all, so I've never bothered to try it. Yes, the meal was very pleasant. I must ask Joan if she knows how to make that lemony thing. A drop of sauce of some sort would have been nice with it though; I've a bit of an aversion to cream."

"I'll ring for someone to clear these dishes away, Maggie, and I'll ask fer another bottle of this, unless you've had enough and want to retire now."

"No, it's still early, but even if it wasn't, I think you and I should use the time fer talking, but perhaps I'm being selfish. Perhaps you'd prefer to go to sleep instead."

As they waited for someone to come to their suite, Maggie began to feel rather self-conscious. This was ridiculous really. Here they were, all dressed up in formal clothes; she in a tight restrictive gown and high-heeled boots, Johnny sat there like a mannequin in a tailor's window. The room was warm and a pleasant glow emanated from the gas lamps. The food she had eaten was having a soporific effect on her and the wine had made her limbs feel heavy. There was a silence hanging companionably between them. Neither wanted to break it, talking maybe of unpalatable things.

The young man who had served them their meal arrived. "Everything all right for you, Sir, Madam? I'll clear these away shall I and then I'll uncork the wine? You'll probably be pleased to know the gentry have departed! It's always like this when the gee-gees are running. They seem to follow one another around all of the racecourses."

"Jack used to do that," remarked Maggie, once the rather familiar Liverpudlian waiter had gone on his way. "I never knew whether he was at Epsom, Derby, Cheltenham or Chester. He would tell me he was away fer a few days of racing, then I'd not see him until he turned up again!"

"Well, let's not talk about Jack, Maggie. I'd like to know what it is like being at the head of a vast business empire, because when I first met you, you hadn't got a pot to piss in."

He laughed when he saw Maggie's face redden in annoyance.

"That may be so, but it's taken me years to perfect this cultivation," she snapped. Then she smiled ruefully at him, as she realised he was teasing.

"Oh, come on, Maggie. We may be sitting here pretending that we were born to this kind of lifestyle, but you and I know our backgrounds all too well. So let's not put on airs and graces while we're alone. We'll not be disturbed until the morning now, so let's say I change into something more comfortable and you can do the same."

She nodded tentatively then Johnny bounded off to the bedroom, coming back a little later wearing a pair of brown moleskin trousers and a plain cream collarless shirt with nothing on his feet.

"Phew, that's better, Maggie. I don't think they need a fire burning in each room like they have here. We'll let them die down a bit, shall we? Now it's your turn. What will you change into?"

Maggie had been pondering on this all the while Jack had been away changing. Would it seem too forward of her if she was to wear her nightdress and her matching robe? Or should she put on one of her day dresses? The muslin one was fairly simply cut, but it did have a garish pattern on. The georgette one had far too many ruffles and flounces and it was a bright yellow. She would look just like a daffodil in this pastel shaded room. She decided on her nightwear. If Johnny thought it was a signal for any tomfoolery, it was his hard luck.

"Pour me another drink, would yer, Johnny, while I go and choose from me vast array of clothing."

She giggled at her joke as she made her way unsteadily.

–

So that was what it was like to be made love to with a passion. Maggie lay quietly in Johnny's arms, listening to his even breathing. Had he lied when he'd said he wouldn't have his way with her? Had he plied her with that wine, so that she'd be panting for his love? And she had been, hadn't she? She had gloried in the admiration

238

from his eyes, when he'd seen her in the silky robe, its plunging neckline showing him a great amount of her rounded breasts. She'd burnt as his fingers touched hers briefly, as he handed her the goblet. They had moved over to the sofa on the pretext of being more comfortable, but as they'd sat sipping their drinks, both knew there would be no need for a bolster in the bed. Johnny had made the first move, taking her glass away and placing it back with his on the tray. He had moved closer, putting his arm around her waist and drawing her tenderly to him. Then had come those little kisses, placed lovingly on her neck, then forehead. Each one caused a tingling sensation, desire flaring in her down below. Her nipples had hardened quickly under her nightdress as Johnny had firmly put his mouth on hers, then probed it open with his tongue. She had felt his hands move gently underneath her, to pick her up and carry her through to the bed. Gone was the tenseness of their situation, gone was the pretence of getting to know each other first.

There was not a squeak of protest; Maggie had just lain pliant in Johnny's strong, muscled arms. Their bodies then took over, like a raging thirst in the desert that must be quenched before the person can then stagger on. They had given into a sensuous abandonment. Maggie had been tearing at her nightie before Johnny had taken his trousers off.

It had surprised them both, this intensity; this almost craven desire. It wasn't until they were sated did they wonder where the hunger for each other had come from. But both knew then it had been an irrevocable plunge into the waters of unknown.

"I cannot believe it, Muirnan," Johnny whispered sleepily, as Maggie lay later in his arms. "To think that you're here beside me after all those lonely years. It's a wishful dream come true."

Chapter 14

The sound of a hotel waking caused Maggie to stir next morning; rattling sounds, murmured voices, someone clanking about in the room adjacent to hers. From the street below came the noise of the city, horses clip-clopped and footsteps scurried. Another day was beginning for them.

She raised her head from the pillow then sank back with a moan as the pain of a terrible hangover clutched her forehead as if caught in a vice. She moved her leg a little to see if Johnny was still there beside her as the memories of the night before came immediately rushing in. She contemplated her next move as she found the space beside her empty. He must have been gone for quite some time as the sheet that he had lain on was no longer warm. There was a chill in the air and she shivered. She felt for her robe or nightdress, remembering as she did so that the fire in the bedroom would have gone out by now.

"The top of the morning to yer, Maggie." Johnny appeared, carrying a small white cup, his voice sounding happy as he stood by her bed.

"Oh don't shout, Johnny," Maggie gasped, covering her nakedness quickly. "Me head feels as if someone's hit me with a hammer and me mouth has turned to acid drops. I just want to lie here and never get up again. What have yer got there in that cup? Not more wine I hope.

241

Don't even think I'll touch an alcoholic drink again. I might even go and sign the pledge!"

"This will put yer right, Maggie. Water with a dash of pepper. An old cure for a hangover given to me by a Polish shipmate. They drink a lot of vodka, yer know, in their country, so I'm sure he knew what he was talking about. The maid has been in and lit a good fire in the sitting room. She's sending up someone with our breakfast and, while you're drinking this, I'm going to draw you a nice hot bath."

He placed the cup on the small bedside table then bent to kiss her cheek. He raised her chin so that she would look at him.

"You don't regret what we did last night, do yer?"

For a moment she saw a flash of fear, as she met his steady stare. She smiled weakly, then caught his hand to her. "I regret nothing about our time together, except this pounding in me head."

Johnny smiled and she sensed his relief at her answer. Had her answer been any different it would have wounded him to the core. He left her with instructions to gulp down all the drink at once as it didn't taste very pleasant. Then he set about his task of running a bath tub full of water, taking delight in doing so as he poured some of her perfume in.

"Well, Johnny, that tip from yer Polish friend certainly worked," remarked Maggie, as she walked in from the bedroom, newly bathed, attractively dressed in yellow, her shining hair firmly caught back in a chignon. There had been a moment when she had wanted to throw the mixture back up again and had dashed quickly to the bathroom, but her wobbly stomach had soon settled down as she slowly completed her toilette.

"Good, I'm glad, Maggie. Perhaps you would like some breakfast now. I've had mine while it was hot, I hope yer don't mind."

She looked under the silver lid of the dish which held a few congealed sausages, a bacon rasher and a hard, pale-looking egg.

"Uh, I don't think I could eat any of that stuff, Johnny. I'll make do with some apple from the fruit bowl. I'm still rather full from yesterday's meal."

"I thought perhaps we could take a walk along Ranelagh Street. Have a look in Lewis's, then maybe stop fer lunch in a restaurant? I'm in desperate need of a few bits of clothing so as not to show you up in your finery."

"You've only just eaten breakfast, you greedy hog, but what's wrong with what yer wearing? You're looking very handsome to me, though perhaps yer could do with a different jacket. That one doesn't match your trousers, does it? A fawn maybe or a lighter brown, but certainly not navy. It just doesn't go at all."

Johnny laughed and caught her hand in his. He pressed it to his lips slowly with a look of something akin to adoration. Her heart lurched as she saw it. Jack had never looked at her in this way.

"I suppose I'll have to get used to you helping me choose me clothing. Oh, Maggie, will that ever happen? Could we make a life together? Is it possible that we could be together for the rest of our days?"

Maggie chose her words carefully before she answered him.

"I would like us to be together, Johnny, I'm sure of it. I've been very lonely since Jack abandoned me again. I know I've got me family, Hannah, Eddie and me little grandson and the businesses of course, but yer showed me last night the strength of your love. You said yerself that it was a dream come true fer us to be together, but I remember the scandal when Jack appeared, after I'd convinced everyone that I was a widow. I don't know if I can weather another round of gossiping and yer have to admit that you were one of the one's to point a finger too."

Johnny grabbed her fiercely into his arms, his voice trembling with emotion.

"Don't yer think I was cut to the quick when I learnt of your masquerading? When I found you again, heard that Jack had died on the fighting circuit, I was over the moon with happiness. At last, I thought. I could give you an old-fashioned courtship, then me world crashed around me when I found that Jack was still alive."

"It wasn't my fault, Johnny. It was Alice, his mother. Couldn't bear the thought of the family being laughed at when Jack ran off with Kitty May."

"Kitty May? No, yer don't have to live the pain again by telling me, Maggie. Come over here with me."

He took her to the window of the sitting room and asked her to look across the rooftops to the River Mersey. It lay glittering there in the distance, beyond church spires, housing, offices, newly-built structures vying with the old. Rows of docks and warehouses lined the banks of the wide estuary, cluttered with the masts of schooners, brigantines, barques and the funnels of heavy steam ships. It was the busiest port in all the world from what Maggie could see.

"Over there's the river on which I've spent most of my working life, sailing up and down. It's bin in me blood, the Mersey river, since I sailed out of Liverpool on a slave ship in 1843 under cover of taking emigrants to the Americas, as it was after William Wilberforce introduced his Bill to abolish slavery. It was the only ship to take me on as I was an Irish Mick. I saw the depths that man will sink to in the degradation of other human beings. Not only the treatment of emigrants, but the slaves we then brought back with us to sell. I won't sicken yer with the sights I saw, Maggie, just to say that I couldn't wait to get off the ship and go back to me homeland. That's why I took command of a vessel that only delivered cattle. I couldn't bear the sight of people crowded like animals in steerage, to line the pockets of their fellow man. As yer know that venture ended when the Dee started really silting up, so I coasted along the Mediterranean for few years, visiting ports with cargo and bringing fruit, the oil of olives and wine back with me. Then yer know the rest, don't yer? I have a part share in the *Irish Maiden*, which is making us quite a good living, bringing passengers from Dublin across the Irish Sea. I've been lucky. Apart from being exposed to a few violent storms and nearly losing me life off Blackwater bank, the sea and this river have been good to me. But I'm willing to give it all up to be with the woman I love."

Maggie felt choked with tears after Johnny had finished telling his story. Would he really do that just for her? His certainly seemed a powerful love. Was she as willing to give up everything that she'd worked so long and hard for and turn her back on it all for him? The property company, the voucher trade and the loan business. Would running off together really fill the emptiness that she had recently begun to feel?

"I know it will be difficult," Johnny rushed on, seeing Maggie hesitate as she thought of all she'd be leaving behind.

"I know it won't be easy living in sin as they call it, or handing over the reins to Eddie or whoever you'd have in mind. But we could build a new life, just the two of us, where no one knows us. We'll go back to Ireland and start afresh somewhere. I have some savings and there's me mother's house I could raise money on. I'd like to get a ship's chandlers maybe, that perhaps we could run ourselves…"

He heard his voice pleading and became angry. With her, or with himself, he wasn't sure.

Maggie left the lee of his arm and walked calmly towards the bedroom.

"I'll just get me coat, shall I and we'll go on that walk you were proposing before?"

She sat on the bed for a moment, composing herself, worrying about his reaction over her hesitancy. What was she supposed to do? Commit herself now on the strength of him declaring his everlasting love for her? Hadn't Jack come out with a similar declaration, when he'd come back from America?

Johnny came quietly into the bedroom and sat beside her. He tilted her face towards him so that he could look into her eyes.

"Are yer playing games with me, Maggie? Is this how you behave in business? Like a game of chess maybe, where you think about every detail before you make your move? Why did you agree to spend this week with me, if yer didn't think I'd declare me love for you?"

"No, Johnny, you've got it wrong," she replied hotly and shook his hand away. "You don't know anything about me. You've talked about yerself and told me what you'll be giving up if we run away together. That I can hand me business over just like that and walk off into the sunset. I agreed to spend the week with yer, because… because I am attracted to yer and I must admit that, all those years ago, you were my childish dream. I was prepared to see if I could love yer. Last night yer brought it home to me that we could be good together, but I tried so hard with me marriage, believed everything Jack told me when I took him back."

"It sounds as if I should be listening to you then," Johnny said gently. "I'll ring fer a pot of coffee, then you can put me straight."

She told him of their trip back to Killala, of the Fenians attack, her husband losing his mind because of it and her desperate entreaty to God.

"We actually passed your mother's cottage on the day that Jack started to remember. We met a farmer, who told me he had seen yer and the man who lived next door had bought her furniture from you."

"Maggie. Do yer think we could leave me mother out of this?" The pain of his loss was still unbearable. "Could we save the discussion of me mother to another day?"

"Of course, Johnny, I'm sorry. I loved yer mother too, yer know."

She kissed his cheek, then held his hand while she told him why it was hard for her to commit to him.

"I believed everything Jack had to say to me and in the end they were all lies."

"Then you'll just have to trust me, Maggie," he said abruptly.

He rose to his feet then pulled her up gently to him.

"I've still some days to convince you so."

—

It was Friday morning and Olive was cleaning the floor tiles inside the porch of Selwyn Lodge. Nearly time for a cuppa with Joan in the kitchen. It was warm for the time of the year and she looked with satisfaction upon her work, thinking that within a few minutes the tiles would be dry.

"Hey up, Olive." She smiled up the drive at the cheeky new postman. He was a cocky bugger, she thought to herself, but she wouldn't mind getting to know him better.

"Hey yerself, Alec. Got some letters fer us then?"

"That's the reason I'm here, Olive. I've not come all this way to take tea with her Ladyship."

"You can have a cup of tea if you were wanting one. There's only me and Joan around. One of them's walking the baby out and the other's cleared off to God knows where."

"I'll go round the back then, shall I? Wouldn't do to get yer nice clean floor mucky."

Alec whistled happily, clutching the letters he had for Maggie, with his near empty bag dragging on the grass.

He startled Joan as he tapped on the window, but Olive had careered quickly through the house to anticipate him.

"It's our new postman, Joan," she cried. "Be nice to him will yer, get him a cup of tea."

"So, Olive," Alec said, after he had gulped the tea down that Joan had made him and had finished tucking in to a warm slice of bread. "How long yer bin workin' here then?"

"A couple of years, haven't I, Joan? But she's bin here fer a lifetime."

"Hardly that," replied Joan, as she poured herself a cup of tea and sat her heavy bulk at the table. "I was here when

Miss Rosemary was alive, then Mrs. Haines kept me on after."

"I've just started fer the Post Office, as yer know. It's a great job, I love it. I know I'm out in all weathers, but look at today fer instance. I love springtime. All the trees come out in bud, flower heads start peeping through, sea breezes coming off the river and everything starts to look brand new!"

"Yer sound a bit of a poet," Olive said alive with interest. "I hated poetry at school though, more than I hated reading and sums."

"That's why you've got the job of a skivvy," Joan remarked, dryly. "You could have been working in an office if you'd put your mind to yer lessons, yer know."

"Like you did?"

Olive glared at the cook, annoyed with the woman. She felt she'd been shown up in front of this very pleasant young man. He had a good job, with chances of promotion probably. Make an ideal husband for someone. Alec looked so handsome in his uniform; she wondered if his brown hair was curly under that black peak cap. She tried to change the subject and smiled provocatively at him. "So what do yer do in yer free time?"

"Oh, I read, help me father in his vegetable garden, go with me mother to Birkenhead market on a Saturday and help her with the shopping. Take long walks along the beach as far as Heswall or Caldy. You want to come with me one Sunday?"

Olive's eyes lit up as she heard his words. She hated walking, but she'd make herself do it for him.

"Do yer not have to work at the weekends? Or go to church or visit yer grandparents with yer Mam?"

He shook his head and boasted proudly. "No, they look after their employees at the Post Office. We finish at midday on a Saturday and I don't start again until five o'clock on Monday morning."

"Not like you eh, Olive? Work your fingers to the bone in this house, one day off at her Ladyship's whim. Anyway, talking of working I need a hand with the peeling. Of yer go now, young man. Oh, did yer bring us any letters, by the way?"

Hannah came through the conservatory, leaving baby Johnny sleeping soundly in his pram.

"Hello, Miss Hannah. Did yer have a nice walk then?"

Olive took a break from peeling potatoes in the kitchen. She was excited as a flea on a cat after Alec had asked her out.

"The postman's been. I put the letters on the table in the hallway. There's one come all the way from India. Fancy that. Do yer think they have postmen in India too?"

"Have you been rifling through the post again, Olive? You know it's not polite to look at someone else's letters. Anyway, it will be for my mother, not for me."

Hannah ran upstairs to use the W.C. Although it was a lovely spring morning, there had been a chill in the air, which always seemed to affect her bladder somehow. She looked thoughtful as she sat on the toilet seat. Maggie hadn't heard from Michael since last August; why was he getting in touch with her now?

She said as much to Eddie when he came in at lunchtime. He was rosy-cheeked from walking around the development with the finisher. A cold wind had been blowing from the estuary, making him glad to get home to a warming fire.

"Perhaps he's missing us all, Hannah," Eddie said wryly. "Perhaps it's a late Christmas greeting, as he couldn't get it in the post on time."

"I shouldn't think so. I don't think they celebrate Christmas in India. Well, the regiment might do so, but there won't be any shops where he could get a card."

"Funny that, isn't it? No one sent cards to each other before Prince Albert brought the practice over from Germany. Still, I suppose it keeps people employed, doesn't it, cutting card in factories and thinking up fancy words."

"Have you ever thought what would happen if Michael came back to live in Neston, Eddie? I'm not sure he'd be happy to have us living here."

"Why so? It's Maggie's house, isn't it? He'll know that we're living here, anyway. Maggie will have told him, I hope."

"She hasn't, unfortunately. I think that's why he joined the regiment, because he found out I was his half sister. She didn't even let him know we were married or had little Johnny. She said she didn't want to upset him, with him being out there."

"I don't think Michael left because of you, Hannah," Eddie said trying to reassure her. "If yer remember back, his pals Jeremy Adshead and Monty Renfrew were itching to join up and you said yerself, he hated working fer Sheldon. He probably seized his chance to go off and have a great adventure. They're all doing it now, yer know. Look at that Livingstone chap exploring up the Zambezi in Africa, then that fellow, Stanley, meeting up with him in the jungle and all these people upping sticks and taking off to places they've only heard about. No, I wouldn't worry about it Hannah. Neston will be too tame fer him."

"All good things have to come to an end I suppose, Maggie," said Johnny, as they sat having dinner in their suite that Friday evening. "Though I hope they'll continue fer us, long beyond this moment in time."

"Let's raise our glass to the future," Maggie replied, smiling happily. She had taken to drinking champagne these last few nights, as it didn't seem to give her a bad head like the wine did. This glass was her second one this evening, as they waited for the waiter to bring in their food. They had decided to forgo eating in the restaurant after Maggie had a scare on that first evening. Who knew who would be dining there, unless she went through the guest list herself? Besides, she and Johnny felt more comfortable there after a long day sightseeing or shopping. Her mind went to the bags they'd put in the bedroom. What they'd spent this week would have covered the annual budget of a Poor House, but at least Johnny had offered to pay his share.

"So, what were the best bits of our holiday, Maggie? Besides being made love to by a skilled and practised artisan."

Johnny ducked as she threw a napkin at him.

"No, seriously, was there a favourite place? Did yer like the Botanic Gardens fer instance?"

"Well," Maggie considered for a minute. "I enjoyed our stay in this place obviously. It was good to be able to shut the door on the world and be alone together. But I think I loved walking with you around Sefton Park, with its little bridges over prettily laid out ponds and the pagodas where we could shelter from the stares of other people and so much grassland, trees and bushes. You could close yer eyes and swear you were nowhere near a city. The Botanic Gardens were pleasant also, especially as we have plants from far off shores in our conservatory."

"And what about the Brown's Library and Museum, Maggie? I knew you'd like that," broke in Johnny. "I've been going there since it opened over ten years ago. What did yer think of those Roman coins they'd found, when they'd been digging up a cemetery? I thought that the Romans only stayed round Chester, but obviously people used the coins here in Liverpool!"

"I thought it all fascinating," replied Maggie, a little on the bored side. There was a part of Johnny that caused her irritation, especially when he had wanted to drag her around the galleries. She'd really preferred to spend her days shopping, as the stores around Bond and Lord Street were filled with a vast array of products that she'd never seen before. It was a wonderland for those that had the money and she'd spent hers as if the purse she was carrying had holes in it. To give him his due, Johnny never had seemed tired of carrying her loaded bags for her, though he begged from time to time to stop for coffee, or repair to his bank to draw more money from his account.

She'd bought him a solid gold fob watch and had it engraved with their Christian names. He bought her an amber-stoned pendant, with a set of earrings to match.

She bought him a jacket, a smart, single breasted one; he bought her a swishy silver gown, trimmed at the neckline with little tiny pearls. She bought a cashmere shawl for Hannah and a black silk topper for her son-in-law. She found the baby department in Lewis's and bought up half the shop. Johnny bought some low-heel boots, a new jersey that he spied in the outerwear department and little bits of toiletries that he could use upon the ship.

"So where do we go from here, Maggie? The time has come fer an answer, don't yer think?"

"Yes and I've given it a lot of thought while we've bin together. I think you've been as honest as you could be with me, but I don't think I'm ready to throw the towel in yet. I want to finish off me projects first, talk to me solicitor, perhaps transfer some of me money to a Liverpool bank. We haven't even talked about where we're going to live. It's got to be with a view of the river. The Mersey or the Dee."

Johnny leant forward and caught her hand in his.

"So you've got as far as that with yer thinkin', Maggie. Oh, Muirnan, you'll make me such a happy man!"

After dinner, he made love to her. It was done with a compelling need by Johnny, as if he doubted it would happen again. The thought came to him after as they lay together that perhaps she had conceived his child. Then perhaps not; he wasn't sure about women's matters. He'd never known a female long enough to find out about these scary things.

–

"So we met on the Woodside steamer. I'd just tied up at Liverpool and was making me way over here. You were loaded with bags and I helped yer carry them, then we shared a compartment in the train. I then hailed yer a cabbie, but I accompanied yer to Selwyn Lodge so I could help yer at the other end. That's our story then, and I'll stay fer a cup of tea and play with me godson if he's not sleeping. Then when will we be together again?"

Johnny looked over to Maggie who had her back to the engine and was staring out of the window. She'd been very quiet on their journey as if she was regretting their time spent together. Or was it his imagination? Perhaps the girl was just tired.

"I can't answer yer, Johnny. I've already said to Hannah I may get a country cottage somewhere fer us all to use as a holiday home, but if I go in telling her that it's going to be sooner than later, she'll get suspicious. Before I left, she was asking was I meeting up with Jack."

"I'm sure Eddie and her would be delighted if me and you got together. They must know that yer lonely sometimes and I know Eddie would love me to be a married man."

"But we wouldn't be married, Johnny, you keep forgetting that. Divorce is difficult for a Catholic woman anyway. We'd have to wait for Jack to die, and I'm certainly not wishing that."

Johnny shrugged. "Whatever. Perhaps in a month or so we can go back to the Adelphi, or maybe we can stay at the North Western Railway Hotel. We passed it, do yer remember? It's just opened up on Lime Street. It'll be cheaper than the Adelphi; I can't expect yer to keep on paying our hotel bill."

—

Maggie felt a lump in her throat as the porter put their bags on a trolley and trundled it up the incline to look for a horse and cab. She looked at the shops on the high street, her eyes coming to rest on the place that used to be Miss Rosemary's. Then across the way to the building that housed the Sheldon Company. How could she leave this village of Neston that had been home for longer than Killala had, with its familiar smells of horse dung, hops from the taverns and the tang of salt that came from the estuary? She thought of Selwyn Lodge where the buds had been appearing in her lovely garden. The daffodils could have bloomed for all she knew, since she'd had this week away. If only, she thought, then shrugged the idea from her. There was no way these people of Neston would accept her living in sin.

–

Hannah was wearing a cream pintucked blouse and a dark bombazine skirt as she carried little Johnny in her arms around the garden. It was a beautiful day; too warm really for springtime. Eddie watched her from the comfort of his cane armchair that he had dragged out onto the lawn from the conservatory. The sun lit up glints of gold in her shoulder-length light brown hair as she crooned a lullaby to their baby. Eddie sighed as he thought over this week that they'd had alone together. It wasn't that he disliked his mother-in-law's presence; really it was because they were only lodgers in this fancy house. But hadn't it been bliss, just the two of them? Especially once the servants had gone in the evening and they had the place to themselves. His mind briefly touched on the letter that was waiting for Maggie on the hall table. Would it be bad news for them if Michael was to come home? Perhaps they should be thinking about their future, he and Hannah, in case it was the return of the prodigal son.

"Eddie, take little Johnny off me, will you? I've just heard a carriage draw up at the top of the driveway. I'll run to meet her and you open the front door for me."

Hannah dashed off along the side of the house, as Eddie carried the baby in.

"Mother, you're back and look who you've got you!" she cried in surprise as she saw Eddie's Uncle Johnny loaded down with bags behind Maggie.

"Did you meet on your way up here then? Oh, I can see by all these bags you've enjoyed yourself shopping, Mother. Eddie's somewhere about, I'll call him. Eddie, there you are. Look who's here with Mother, your Uncle Johnny! Here, give me the baby and help your uncle with the luggage and everything. Come on then, I've got the kettle on, we'll sit at the kitchen table and you can tell me all about it. And there you were last Monday, Mother, making out you didn't want to go."

Chapter 15

Katie walked along the site road that lead through the new development. It seemed strange to be treading on quarry stones and rubble, instead of tramping through country lanes and grassy fields. She was on her way to see her sister, Annie, whose home at Lilac Cottage would soon be surrounded by luxurious villas. Not yet, though; there was still a lot of clearance work to be done. Over to her left stood Farmer Briggs' old farmhouse, still occupied by the elderly man who kept his livestock in the yard as he had before, which was a blessing, really, for Ernie. He still had a job there fortunately, though there were no fields for ploughing and no seeds to sow. Just a few milking cows on two marshy fields that the developer hadn't wanted and the pigs and hens, that helped to pay the wages. Though why hadn't the farmer sold up completely? He must have plenty of money now he had sold his land.

In the distance, Katie could see a group of men cutting down the copse that had surrounded her old cottage. She willed herself to look away; there was no use in being emotional now. Annie had told her weeks ago that the place had been demolished. At least she and her brother had been well-rewarded for their removal, even if it had been forced. The house on Town Lane was a little palace, with its big front room, dining room-cum-kitchen, two large bedrooms, a tiny box room and a W.C. in the yard.

Katie sighed as she dodged a pothole and clambered across the trunk of a tree that had been left where it had been uprooted. This would be her in a few weeks' time, she thought, pulled up by her roots again, leaving Ernie to cope alone.

She quickened her pace as a few spots of rain dropped upon her uncovered head. Typical. Her one day off and she was going to get caught in a shower.

Luckily her sister had just returned from the village, though Mrs. Piper, Annie's mother-in-law, had been pottering in the garden anyway. Lilac Cottage was warm and muggy-smelling as Katie dashed in through the open doorway. A row of drying baby wear sat on a clotheshorse by the fire.

Alexandra, the youngest child, toddled around in the lean-to, watching her grandma bring in a basket of vegetables. Joe, her elder brother, sat on the overstuffed sofa playing with a struggling kitten. The older children had been put into school by Annie, who was relaxing in an easy chair trying to get her breath back.

"Katie," Annie cried, when she saw her slightly damp visitor. "If I'd known yer were coming over, I'd have brought me shopping to your place and you could have helped me carry it down. Didn't yer think to put on something better than that jacket? Yer only had to look at the storm clouds to know it was going to start pissing down. Ma... Move that washing, will yer, and let our Katie see the fire, then a cup of tea would be nice if the kettle's boiling. Alex, get out of me shopping bag."

Katie smiled to herself. Poor old Mrs. Piper. Annie's willing slave, because she had been allowed to move to Lilac Cottage with the family. The woman was getting on in years, but she was devoted to Annie and Sam's children.

"Here, I'll make the tea, Mrs. Piper, after I've said hello to these two. Have you both got a kiss for your Aunty Katie? And what's this I've got in my pocket?" Katie drew out some slightly soggy gingerbread men.

The children sat down on the peg rug chewing contentedly while the kitten made its escape out of the back door. Peace reigned for a few moments as Katie made the women a cup of tea.

"So, what brings yer here then Katie?" Annie inquired, as the two of them settled on the sofa. Mrs. Piper sipped at her drink, as she began to prepare a cabbage and some potatoes for their meal at the kitchen table.

"Ernie's all right, isn't he? Hey," she continued, before Katie managed to open her mouth. "Have yer seen those houses they've built near where Ashlea Cottage was? There's two of them finished now. I walked round that way from the village yesterday morning and I had a look through one of the windows. What I'd give to live in summat like them. I spoke to a fella who was working on the garden wall; they've got four bedrooms, a study, two big rooms downstairs and, listen to this, a separate kitchen with a pantry off it. And they've got a bathroom upstairs with a separate room for the W.C! He said that the people were moving in this week and there's a push on to get the road up there finished, so that the delivery men can bring along the furniture. I said what were they going to do fer stabling? Because if they've got that kind of money, they'll have a horse and carriage as well. Do yer know what he said? People like that will pay fer a horse and cab to come down from the village to collect them! I'm thinking now that Sam should give up his milk round and buy an old carriage instead!"

"T'would be too much fer Polly, pulling the weight of a carriage," Mrs. Piper remarked, who had been listening to the conversation avidly. "She's getting too long in the tooth to be carrying people around."

"Don't be daft, she's used to carrying full churns, isn't she? Anyway, if we got really busy, we'd get a younger horse instead."

"I wonder how the new folk like the idea of the colliery being only a spit away?" asked Katie. "I wouldn't like to pay all that money and worry about underground tunnels beneath me feet."

"Oh, they never came that far inland," answered Mrs. Piper. "That's why it never made the owners rich yer know, because they never dug deep enough seams."

"Yea, and half the workers died in the cholera outbreak of '66. Beset with problems that mine has bin, but anyway I'm sure they'll have trees planted as a screen. Now, Katie, yer haven't told me yet what brings yer."

Annie's attention turned to her sister, the subject of the new houses beginning to pall.

"Well, I'm here to let you know that I'm going to have a big problem soon looking after Ernie. Matron called me into her office yesterday and told me I'm to be transferred to Clatterbridge Hospital. I don't have a choice in the matter now that we're under the Hospital Board. If I want promotion I have to do as they say. It's all to do with numbers, according to Matron, and as they are short of staff nurses over there, she put my name forward. She says it's for my own good, because I've a better chance of being taken on as a Sister once I've passed my next exams. I told her that we'd only just moved into Barleymow Terrace a few months ago and that I was keeping house for my brother. She asked me what was more important? My brother or my career?"

"And you said your career, didn't yer?" Annie said scathingly. "Then legged it down here to my place to see if I'll help yer out."

"I'm going to have to live at the hospital, Annie. Matron said it was a residential post and even if it wasn't, it would be too far to walk everyday."

"There's the omnibus from Heswall. Calls into the village every afternoon to take people up to visit…"

"But I'll be on shift work, Annie. Be sensible. I can't see them letting me start my work every day at three."

"Ernie could come here fer his meals, Annie. Surely we can help them a little, they are family after all?"

"Ma," Annie cried, feeling aggravated. "Not only do I have five children, a husband and all me alteration work, there'd be the house to see to, cleaning and his washing as well. Perhaps you'd like to volunteer fer the job then, or better still you move in with him!"

There was a silence for a moment. Mrs. Piper took the peelings out to the garden to put on top of the compost heap. Katie could see from the woman's shoulders that she'd be weeping out in the rain. Honestly, Annie could be unbearably rude at times.

"I know!" shouted Annie, her eyes gleaming with a possibility that had just occurred to her. The children turned their heads at her outburst then tried to scramble upon her knee.

"Get down, Joe, go and sit on Aunty Katie's knee, Alex. I'm thinking of something that would benefit all of us!"

Katie looked at her sister doubtfully and Mrs. Piper groaned to herself quietly as she listened from the lean-to.

"Go on." Whatever Annie came up with it would only benefit her.

"We'll do a house swap!"

"A house swap," Mrs. Piper wailed. "We've only just settled here this last twelve month and here yer are wanting us to move again. How's that going to help your Ernie?"

"Well, it's only a short walk fer him from here to the farm, isn't it? If we were to move to Town Lane it will be nearer fer the school, the shops fer me and nearer to me customers. They've got a yard fer Sam to stow his milk churns in, so that would save paying the rent on the lock-up, and Polly could be turned out on that bit of wasteland by Bull Hill."

"I thought yer were talking before about Sam starting up a cabby service?" her mother-in-law sniffed.

"One thing at a time, Ma!"

"You've forgotten something here, Annie," Katie said gently. "The house is in our names, mine and Ernie's and we've still got a loan to pay."

"A mere detail. Ernie will be living rent-free here at Lilac Cottage and he can pay me something fer his meals if he comes to us each day. I'll go up to Sheldon weekly and hand over whatever you're paying to them. And we'll have all that space to live in."

She rubbed her hands together gleefully.

"Wait 'til our Sam comes in!"

–

Maggie sat at her bureau in the drawing room, trying to compose a letter to Johnny. She had not seen him since that day he'd returned with her to Selwyn Lodge.

"*I can understand you're hurt,*" she wrote, "*but Hannah was only teasing me. I did so enjoy our time together. Forget her words please, Johnny. I was nervous, I'm sorry. Can't we meet again?"*

She addressed the letter care of The Mersey Docks and Harbour Board, Liverpool, stamped it with the correct postage, then put it in the top drawer of her writing desk. She would give it to Alec, Olive's new beau, next morning. By Friday, Johnny will have read it and perhaps he'll come to visit at the weekend, she thought. If not, it'll prove that he doesn't really care enough for me, so we'll both carry on with the rest of our lives.

Sitting there in the peaceful oasis of the room, somehow it all didn't matter. She was where she wanted to be after all. Why would she want her boat rocking by men, whom she seemed to manage without very well? Men were so needy; they wanted your soul and your body. Look at Michael: from her son's latest letter, he had wanted something from her as well.

Maggie had spent the time since she read it thinking. Her son wanted her to buy him out, it wasn't what he had been lead to believe. It was a living Hell.

How did she go about that then? Buy him out? Did she go to the Chester Barracks with a fist full of money and hand it over to someone in authority? Her head was buzzing alarmingly. She'd have an early night. Shouting to Hannah that she was making her way to bed and she'd see her in the morning, she slowly climbed the stairs. Perhaps everything would feel differently when she awoke.

"Did you notice that my mother wasn't looking very well at supper?" Hannah asked Eddie, as they settled down in bed.

"Well, I noticed that she left her bread and butter pudding and she was having a lot to drink."

"She's been very quiet since she came back home from Liverpool. I thought she'd want to tell me all about it and she seemed about to I'm sure, then your Uncle Johnny left without a word. That was odd, don't you think, Eddie? The way he dumped all the bags then disappeared?"

"Oh, Hannah," Eddie said sleepily "You do look fer mysteries when there are none. It'll be all these penny dreadfuls you keep reading. Yer know they go way back, Maggie and Uncle Johnny. They probably had a disagreement over something. Something from twenty-odd years ago, just to even up an old score!"

—

Maggie awoke the following morning with a sore throat, a thumping head and her body ached from top to toe. First she pushed her blankets off, as the sweat was pouring off her in buckets, then pulled them up quickly around her as she began to shiver with the cold.

"It's probably influenza," Hannah pronounced, when she heard Maggie croaking her name from the back bedroom.

"Shall I send Olive for the doctor? These things can get nasty; turn into pneumonia if you're not careful. You haven't got a rash on your chest have you, or spots on your tongue? No? Then it's just a case of resting, don't get out of bed."

"Thanks, Nurse Hannah," Maggie said weakly. "You've missed yer way, yer know. Do we get a professional in or will I be nursed by you?"

Hannah laughed at Maggie's attempt at light-heartedness.

"Let's get Dr. Barnes in first, shall we, and see how serious this is? I'll probably be told to keep away because of passing it on to little Johnny."

The doctor was summoned and he agreed with Hannah's verdict, though he was surprised that Maggie had caught influenza at that time of the year.

"We had a lot of this last winter, in fact I remember Olive, your maid, went down with it, didn't she?"

Hannah nodded. As soon as she had seen the girl shivering she had sent her back home to her bed.

"Well spotted anyway, Hannah. Did they teach you this kind of thing at college? I'm very surprised to be called out to a case of this in April though. Has any other member of the household come down with it recently?"

"No, Doctor, but Mother has just come back from a holiday," Hannah answered. Thank heavens she'd paid attention at college when they'd had a doctor come to lecture them.

"Well, that's the reason then, she's picked the virus up from her hotel! I'll leave her this mixture. If it gets any worse, send Olive down again for me. It's only a mild dose from the look of her."

"Can we get a nurse in, Doctor? I daren't get too close to Mother, because of my little boy. In fact," Hannah lowered her voice. "I think I may be expecting again. Shall I visit you when Mother gets better and you can confirm if I am right?"

"Oh, I think your mother will get better in the next three or four days. No need to bring a nurse up here. Get Olive to bring her plenty of boiled water to drink, she'll not feel like eating, but she'll be strong enough to crawl into the bathroom. Olive can change her linen, but otherwise leave her alone. This mixture contains a little opium and rest will do the trick."

The plump middle-aged doctor smiled kindly, as Hannah passed him his tall silk top hat. "Another one already, eh? Are you planning to fill the nursery?"

—

Johnny lay in his bed in the room he rented on Grafton Street. He'd been feeling groggy since he came off his ship at Kingstown Harbour that afternoon and instead of walking from the docks to the city as he usually did, he flagged a passing cabby. Settled with a bottle of whisky that he had hurriedly bought before he mounted the steps to his chilly room, his foggy mind conjured up thoughts of Maggie. What the Hell had she been playing at? There was a name for women who behaved as she had done. He had really believed it, hadn't he, that he and Maggie were going to be a couple? Sod the scandal, forget the Church, two fingers to Jack and their marriage. Maggie was going to leave her business, her family, her committee meetings and her fancy life to start afresh with him!

He threw another glass of whisky down his burning throat. Damn the woman. Just when he had opened his heart, wore it on his sleeve, made declarations of his undying love, her daughter had told the truth about her. Maggie hadn't wanted to go to Liverpool in the first place. So why had she been there in the Adelphi? Why bother to go to all that trouble and expense?

Johnny poured himself another drink. His body was shaking with cold, but sweat was pouring off him. When this was finished, he promised himself, he'd get another. *Try* to block out her lovely face.

"Hello Maggie, Hannah said I'd find yer in here. How yer feelin' today?" Eddie came into the conservatory, where his mother-in-law sat in one of the cane chairs with her feet resting on a footstool.

"Well enough to sit in here, thank you," Maggie replied a little hoarsely. "Your wife's a dragon though, give her a bit of power and her bossy streak comes out."

"Oh, she's only concerned about yer. Doesn't want yer rushing about like yer did before. Anyway, yer looking better, the warmth in here has give yer a bit of a flush. I've been over to see the Bradleys at Ashlea House this morning. See how they're settling in. There's one or two things they're not very happy with. The front door doesn't fit properly, looks like the bottom was shaved too much 'cos the winds bin whistling under it. And she's not too happy with her kitchen, not enough space to put their table in."

"Well, she's been enough times to measure up. I'd say it's her fault if her table's too big. Yer mean a kitchen table, don't yer, one fer working on?"

Eddie nodded, pleased to see he'd lit a spark in Maggie. She'd been so listless according to Hannah, wasn't eating, couldn't be bothered reading the broadsheet or any of her books that she normally loved to read; staying in her bedroom staring out of the window, or sat in the conservatory just looking into space.

"I'll take one of the carpenters off and get him to fit a thresher on the bottom, that should cure it. But I'm afraid she'll have to sort her other problem out herself."

"Was Mr. Bradley there? Yer know he's setting up a branch of Thursco Textiles in Chester, don't yer?"

"Yes, his missis told me. He's one of the Directors. No, he wasn't there. She told me he took a bracing walk up to Neston Station this morning to catch the eight o'clock train. That's why they'd chosen the area, she told me, fer its convenience, location and view!"

"Oh, good. And did yer go next door to the Taylor's?"

"I did knock, but no one answered. What does he do, Maggie? Does he work in Chester the same?"

"No, he works at the bank in the village. He's the manager. In fact when I'm feeling better I'll pay him a visit. Let him know who I am."

"That's my girl," smiled Eddie. "Now can yer manage a little soup? Joan's got a pan of broth on the go."

–

"Here you are, Mother, a small bowl of broth. Now eat it up. I know you put most of your oatmeal this morning down the sink."

"I threw it back, Hannah, that's why it went down the sink. I've got all this phlegm at the back of me throat and down on me chest and that stuff yer give me brought it all up."

"Uh, disgusting. I hope Joan didn't see yer doing it."

"I didn't do it in the kitchen sink, I spat it into the bathroom bowl!"

"Anyway, Mother. Can I talk to you about something?"

Hannah drew up another chair and lowered herself into it. "You know I told you yesterday that I think I may be expecting again? Well, I am. I went to see Dr. Barnes this morning and he says I'm two months gone."

"And is Eddie pleased?" Maggie tried to look pleased herself, but found it an effort to put a smile on her face today.

"Oh, he just gave me a great big kiss and said, 'Well done little mother', but he went out looking cheerful. He's gone back to the site to look at some footings; one of the men sent a message for him to come."

"So, what do yer want to talk about?"

"Well, with me expecting I thought you'd like some of my rags. Only there wasn't any of yours in that basket we share, so I thought you'd perhaps burnt all yours and needed some more."

"I've been thinking, while I've been lying in me bed, that I'm over having monthlies," Maggie said. "I'm sure I was due two weeks ago and I've seen nothing. I put it down to that damned flu or whatever it was that attacked me, but thinking about it, maybe I'm starting the change."

"How would you find out, Mother?" asked Hannah, quite awed at the fact that here she was, wanting lots of babies, and that Maggie was at the end of things.

"I don't know, I don't want Dr. Barnes poking around in me private bits. I'll have to find someone older than I am and ask them."

"Joan," they both said in unison.

"If nothing happens in a day or two, I'll ask Joan about it then."

–

"Staff Nurse Tibbs, can you come here a minute?" Sister Gill called to Katie, as she began to put her cloak on, preparing to walk over to her room at the Nurses Home. Katie groaned to herself. What now? She'd been on her feet since seven that morning and was looking forward to her evening meal.

"I've just had a message from the colliery. It seems that a miner fell out of the cage as it was being lowered into the excavation. He's still alive, as they managed to throw him a rope and haul him back up again, but the doctor is sending him here in case he's suffering any ill effects from the cold or dirty water."

"But the new shift will be here in a minute, Sister. Can't one of them see to him?"

"Yes, one of them could, but as you know one of their team is ill and we have limited bed space. I was going to ask you to put him in a side ward and make him comfortable before you leave. He'll be here in twenty minutes or so. Surely you can do that for your fellow man?"

"Yes, Sister. I'm sorry, Sister. I'll get a probationer to make up the bed. Could I perhaps make myself a drink though, to give me a bit of energy to carry on?"

Katie walked slowly to the kitchen. Sister was always asking for that little bit extra. She had been on Men's Ward now for four months and it always seemed that they were short of staff. An extra hour here and another there. Her old hospital seemed like a paradise when Katie compared it to this place.

"Sister wants you to make up the bed in the side ward," she said to Winnie, her underling, who was sitting sipping tea. She took the cup off the girl and shooed her on her way.

"I'll finish this tea off for you, Win. I'm parched and I've got to stay behind again."

One morning in the middle of May, as the rain lashed down against the conservatory windows, the two ladies of Selwyn Lodge were absorbed in some fashion magazines that Hannah had ordered from a London store. They were both a little bored as the weather had kept them cooped up in the house for days. Hannah longed to walk down to the promenade with little Johnny; Maggie would have liked to visit Chester to see her solicitor. She still hadn't done anything about Michael's release from his regiment and it had been preying on her mind. Eddie had taken the carriage, so it meant walking down to the train station. Nowadays, that kind of effort was just too much to bear. Where had all her energy gone? She kept wondering. Even playing with her grandson was too much at times.

"That would suit you, Mother," Hannah remarked, pointing to a day dress modelled by a pretty dark-haired girl. "If you made that up in a silk, perhaps a pastel shade for when the summer comes. Blue maybe, you always look good in blue, or try a deep pink this time and I could make up one for myself with a similar cut, though maybe a little fuller across the hips. I know, we could both have a draped effect across the front."

"Are you saying I'm fat, Madam?" Maggie asked. She said it lightly, but had to admit to herself that the middle-aged spread that Joan had mentioned seemed to be now applying to herself.

"Well, you have put a bit of weight on, haven't you? Even though you're not finishing up what's put on your plate."

"I'll easily get thinner by Ladies Day. Once this rain stops and we can get out again, I'll take long walks with you and the baby. Though, Joan warned me about something she called middle age spread, when I talked to her about women's changes. I think she was probably looking fer a reason to excuse how fat she is."

"Meow. Keep your voice down, Mother, she'll hear you. You know that in this house our walls have got finely-tuned ears. So, shall I send for the patterns? I'll order this one for both of us and we should be able to make a start by next weekend."

"I suppose so. With me being chosen to carry a banner at the parade this time, I'd better have something new to wear. Though I'm going to feel embarrassed with everyone looking at me."

"Mother, you deserve the honour!" Hannah declared stoutly. "Half the charities around here benefit from your largesse; none of them would exist if it wasn't for your hard work."

"I know, but I've never really got over the feeling that people look at me with scorn. Look, there's the great and good Maggie Haines. She was an Irish immigrant, yer know."

"Oh, tosh to that! You've spent more of your life here than back in Ireland. Not everyone has a memory like you have, except Grandmama or Maddy that is. Anyway, come on, let's measure each other before the little rascal wakes up and starts crying. Stand tall, stand still. No, put your arms down by your side. That's it..."

Suddenly, Hannah stopped what she was doing, leaving her hand dithering somewhere around her stepmother's waistband. She pulled Maggie gently towards her, so that they were facing each other. Her voice were full of disbelief as she looked intently into innocent eyes.

"You did meet my father in Liverpool, didn't you?"

Maggie's heart lurched for a moment at the memory of her guilty secret, then wondered why on earth had

Hannah decided to bring up the trip now, after all these weeks had passed. And why accuse her of meeting up with Jack? What had happened to make Hannah think that she had had an assignation? Maybe someone had seen her in Liverpool. She answered her stepdaughter indignantly, "What are yer talking about, Hannah? Meeting up with yer father, indeed! He made it very clear that it was a different life he wanted. I've not seen him since he cleared off over to Wicklow and how long ago was that? Listen to yer, you wouldn't think that I'm a grown woman who's entitled to some private time on her own, the way yer clucking over me!"

"Then you must be expecting a baby through immaculate conception, if it wasn't Father."

She turned her back on Maggie and slowly walked away. "Hannah, come back. Just finish measuring me or you and I are going to fall out."

But Maggie's cross words fell on deaf ears, as Hannah ran up the stairs to the nursery.

"Are yer all right, Mrs.?"

Joan, the cook, looked at Maggie with concern in her eyes. She stood uncertainly in the dining room doorway, wondering if she was over stepping the divide between herself and her employer, but surely there had been anguish in the voice she had just heard. Probably a spat that she should keep her nose out of, but the missus had been through the mill recently, what with Mr. Haines clearing off like he had and then her coming down with a nasty dose of flu. Joan watched as Maggie clutched at the mahogany table, then sat down in a chair with a thump.

"What is it? Is it them hot flushes? I'll get yer a cool drink from the larder; that should do the trick."

Without Maggie's agreement, Joan waddled through the kitchen, shooing Olive away as she passed the inquisitive girl.

"Mrs. Haines'll be wanting lunch laid out in a minute, Olive. Go and ask her if yer can move all them things from the table and keep yer mouth shut; she's not very well."

Maggie was sitting staring out of the window as her maid crept in. She nodded her head numbly when Olive asked if she could clear the table and put the magazines on the bridge table by the door. She thanked Joan politely as a glass of lemonade was placed before her, then waited with trepidation as Hannah was called down for her lunch from the nursery.

She hated falling out with her stepdaughter. She could count on the fingers of one hand the amount of times there had been sharp words between them. And that in a house full of women, if you counted Olive and Joan. Surely Hannah couldn't be right, could she? Accusing her of expecting a baby, of all things. She was forty-one, nearly forty-two, and in all those years after having Michael there had been no more babies. It was as Joan said. It was the changes that women of her age went through that were causing the extra weight, her lack of monthlies, the loss of appetite and energy. Once the sun started shining she'd feel a whole lot better. Plenty of walks in the fresh air would give her a new lease of life again.

She smiled tentatively at Hannah as the girl came in carrying little Johnny. "Look, we're having your favourite, Hannah. Braised beef and onions, with delicious garden peas."

Chapter 16

Katie tucked a stray hair beneath her nurse's bonnet and straightened her apron in the sluice room. Another few minutes, then it was away to the Matron's office. She and Sister Gill had been summoned to a meeting at ten o'clock. Perhaps there had been word of her proposed promotion or a date to be agreed for another exam. She knew she could do it. All those hours spent in her little room revising from the "Notes on Nursing" that Sister Gill had given her, while the other girls were slipping out to meet various beaus or attending the dances at the local village hall. Or perhaps it was just an appraisal of what Katie thought was her very hard work. Whatever it was, her mood was very buoyant. It was a lovely day at the beginning of June.

"Ah, Sister Gill and Staff Nurse Tibbs." Matron Fairhurst smiled over her half-moon spectacles at her nurses kindly and beckoned the pair of them in. She was a tall, thin woman in her fifties, dressed totally in black from head to toe, except for a white, laced, detachable collar around the neckline of her gown and a white, frilly cap pinned firmly in place on her naturally curly, shoulder-length greying hair. She stood behind her desk and showed them a telegram that she had received that morning.

"It's from the Hospital Board in Chester. We are to be advised that a troop ship will be arriving in Liverpool, within the next forty-eight hours from Bengal. The men aboard have various conditions, but we have been assigned the ones that have succumbed to dysentery. The Hospital Board are trying to arrange it that the men can be treated in the area that they come from, so we probably won't be receiving that many cases. However, to be on the safe side, I'll be opening the Hinderton Ward, so I would like you, Sister Gill, to arrange for a team of cleaning women to go in and bring the place up to our very high standards. And you, Staff Nurse Tibbs, are to brief the probationers and auxiliaries on what will be expected from them. Plenty of bedpans need to be available at all times, plenty of bowls for the sickness and, depending on how far gone their illness is, plenty of jugs of water at their bedsides. It is possible that some may have delirium, as although they will have had nurses travelling with them, conditions on a troop ship are not like ours at all. Now, are there any questions from either of you? Sister Gill? Staff Nurse Tibbs?"

"Well, I was wondering how on earth we were going to manage, Matron?" said Sister Gill worriedly. She was voicing Katie's worries exactly, who didn't think it was her place to air her fears.

"Of course you will manage; I've every confidence in your team. How many are there in the Thornton Ward now? Three, four? One old man with a broken hip, another with a chest complaint, that miner with the damaged leg and the fellow who came in with the scalded face. Hardly wearing you out, are they? Well, we'll see how many men are assigned to our care before we make a fuss about it, then I'll borrow some staff from another ward if I have to. Come back to me, Sister, if there's a problem."

She dismissed the women with an encouraging smile. They didn't know they were born, she thought. Let them try and cope with what she had had to in the Crimea. At least there were bedpans here and decent mattresses for the patients to lie on. The soldiers *she* had tended to in Sevastopol had nothing, other than a few thin blankets and a kind word from the nurses that had volunteered to go out there.

Matron let her mind wander back to that incredibly cold winter back in 1854, when the snow lay so deep around their encampment that nothing could move in or out for days on end. They prayed constantly for a ship to arrive at the nearby port, at least to rescue those that had not succumbed to disease or hunger and to bring equipment, food and medical supplies. At last their prayers had been answered, when the steam ship, *Cambria*, had managed to cut a swathe through the ice of the Black Sea and sent a party of brave young men to seek them out. She had travelled back to Liverpool with the sick and the wounded, along with the body of General Adams, then helped to restore good health to some of the men.

The woman shuddered as she remembered it all.

–

"That's what I like about Matron," Sister Gill said, as she and Katie walked along the stony path back to Thornton Ward. "She knows what she's talking about, though she should do after being a nurse for thirty odd years. Did you know she trained under Florence Nightingale? Well, she was at Crimea anyway; whether she ever met the woman,

I'm not sure. Matron keeps herself to herself, as you will have noticed, but she knows her job all right. Knows exactly how many patients are on each ward and what's wrong with all of them; knows that we're overstaffed at the moment with summer being here. Not so many accidents and illnesses once the sun starts shining and I've noticed how little there is to be done, once the ward work is finished each morning. I think I'll take over the Hinderton Ward myself and leave you to run our ward with the help of Win and Mrs. Mottram, the auxiliary. I'll take Janey, the new probationer and I'll make do with Mrs. Kane. Though I'll not be far away, so you will have my support if necessary and it goes without saying if we cannot cope with the new influx, you'll have to help me out in there."

"Yes, Sister, thank you, Sister," replied Katie happily.

To be left in charge of a ward was such a great honour, her heart soared at the thought of it. So what if she only had four patients to care for? She'd be an Acting Sister, wouldn't she? The committee of the Hospital Board would be impressed as well.

–

Johnny stood on the bridge of the steamer, *Irish Maiden*, watching as his partner, Dermot Ryan, steered the vessel deftly into port. So this was it then, he thought to himself sadly. The end of an era, the closing of a chapter, exchanging it all for a life on shore. Minutes from now it would all be over, except for saying goodbye to the present crew. He had resisted the calls of a farewell bevy; something that normally he would have been glad to do. But he needed a clear head for the following morning, when he was to take over as owner of the ship's chandlers;

here on the very harbour, that he had sailed out from for some years now. This business with Maggie had given him the shove that he had needed; a kick up the backside to make changes in his life.

He had lain for days in his room all those weeks ago, drifting in and out of delirium, not really wanting to live if he couldn't have Maggie by his side. He'd be dead now if it wasn't for Dermot, who had come to 'dig the bugger out' after Johnny had missed two sailings across to Liverpool. He'd been a good mate, calling on a doctor, who had the sick man transferred to the City Hospital. There had been plenty of time since then to dwell on his near-death experience and realise that he was lucky to have another crack at his life.

"Penny for them, Johnny," Dermot broke into his thoughts, before the ship lunged uncontrollably against the solid wall of the berth, sending the pair of them flying.

"Bloody old tub, you'd think she'd know how far we were off that wall by now, wouldn't yer? Let down the gangplank, somebody," he roared, as the wheel righted itself once more and the ship settled down with a sigh.

"What was I saying? Oh, yes. If it doesn't work out, yer know you can always come back and work fer me – this time scrubbing decks though. You'll have spent all me buy out money on that bloody business, by then I suppose."

He held out his hand and murmured softly. "Don't let her get to yer, Johnny. There's plenty other mermaids in the sea."

Johnny felt choked at this unexpected show of sympathy from his shipmate. His advice had always been to love them, then leave them. "Saves getting yer heart all broke" was what Dermot usually said.

He just nodded, too full with emotion, shook hands then climbed down the steps to the gangway. He took one last look at the steamer as he set off for his digs in the city, listening with amusement as some of the crew hung over the stern to wave and shout at his back. Some good humoured joshing, some perhaps tinged with resentment. Dermot could be a harsh man who would lash out at the drop of a hat.

"Oh, damn yer, Maggie," Johnny swore, as he pulled up the collar of his jacket against the wind that suddenly blustered. The only woman he had ever loved, beside his mother, had made him feel a lovelorn eejit.

–

"Mother, we've got to talk about this," said Hannah pleadingly. She was hovering outside Maggie's room, where her stepmother lay on top of the bed, pale and exhausted.

"Let me come in. You need somebody to talk to, or better still we'll sit in the garden. The sun's still warm, even though it's late in the day."

"Go away, Hannah. I'm not up to anything – talking or sitting in the garden. Just leave me alone, will yer. I wish I'd never gone to the Parade today."

She groaned, as Hannah came in full of determination, flinging back the bedroom curtains and letting the sun come flooding in.

"Right, we've been pussyfooting around for long enough and it's time someone took control of the situation. Look at the state of you, Mother. That was your moment of glory carrying the banner, all dolled up in your elegant dress. You've worked hard enough for that attribution and it shouldn't have been taken so lightly. I was horrified when you passed it on to Mrs. Featherstone. What has she ever done to deserve the honour, except snipe at anything good you've done for the place?"

Maggie sniffed back her tears at the humiliation she had felt, when the banner had been so heavy that she had realised she'd not carry it more than a yard or so. Her, big strong Maggie Haines who could do anything she set her mind to, had felt as weak as a kitten. Of course she had used her recent illness to excuse herself, but that hadn't stopped the accusing glares.

"Too big for her boots, too beneath her to carry the banner." She knew what would be said about her. That's why she was lying with the curtains drawn, blocking out a damning world.

"This isn't like you, Mother," said Hannah tenderly, sitting on the side of the bed, stroking Maggie's hair.

"You've not been the same since that week you had in Liverpool and I'm sure that something happened there. Something that you are not willing to tell. I'm sorry I was rude to you, call it a trick of the light, but to me you looked as if you could have been expecting. I know, I know, it was thoughtless. I know that you and Father are through."

Maggie sat up and made herself comfortable with a pillow at her back. It was time she faced up to her future and her stepdaughter owed her, didn't she? Jack had walked away from their marriage because she had taken Hannah's side against him. Now it was Hannah's turn to listen to her sorry tale.

"Do yer remember, Hannah, when you turned to me for help that time over Jeremy?"

"Yes," the admission was given hesitantly.

"Well, I think it will now be your turn to help me."

Hannah sat in a state of stunned silence, while Maggie shamefacedly told the girl about Johnny Dockerty. From the meeting all those years ago, to their secret tryst at the Adelphi Hotel. To give Hannah her due, the only time she winced was when Maggie spoke of Johnny's defection.

"So, you don't know what would have happened if I hadn't mentioned your unwillingness to go that morning?"

"It wasn't that I was unwilling, Hannah; it was because I was just nervous. I've built a cosy nest here at Selwyn Lodge and all this is because I worked hard fer all those years. I've got used to not having a man around telling me what to do. But, I'm a Catholic, and there's no getting away from the fact that I'm married, and now I'm guilty of committing adultery. Johnny, poor lamb, was just happy that we had finally admitted our love for one another and was weaving a magical future for the two of us to share."

"So, is it possible that you could be expecting? I think you are; you have that look about you."

"Well, you'd know about it, Hannah, seeing that's the state you're in."

"This is serious, Mother, so don't joke about it. How on earth could we pass off your baby? Father's been gone for nearly two years."

There was a sudden silence between them as they both realised the importance of her words. Hadn't Maggie been shown that morning just how prevalent the antipathy towards her still was? After all those years, there was still a lot of envy towards the woman she had become. Her good name would be reduced to the level of the gutter. She'd be thrown off her committees; shunned if she attended church. The ladies of the parish would have a field day if Maggie was in a certain condition. She would have to think of going away.

"Of course, I may be worrying unnecessarily, yer know. It could be that I am as Joan has told me, suffering from middle-aged spread."

Maggie looked at Hannah hopefully, who snorted, "I don't think so. You should get in touch with Uncle Johnny. It's his baby and he should be responsible. He's the Captain of the *Irish Maiden*, isn't he? Eddie says he ties up in Liverpool every other day."

"Well, I did write him a letter, just before I went down with influenza, but he hasn't bothered to reply to me, so why should he do so now?"

"And where did you send it to? Perhaps he never received it... Oh, the offices of the Mersey Docks and Harbour Board. Well, he certainly should have received it by now. You'll just have to go to the House for Fallen Women, Mother."

This joke was quickly retracted when Hannah saw Maggie's face.

"I'm sorry, this is no time for me to be joking, but I can hardly take in what you've just told me. It's like I'm in some sort of play, where I'm acting out a role, I can't believe that you and Uncle Johnny... Wait 'til Eddie hears."

"Oh, you can't tell Eddie!" Maggie clutched at Hannah's arm, her voice rising in alarm. "I couldn't face him ever again; he'd be horrified. No, we'll have to think of something else to tell him, another reason if I was to go."

"Look, you're worn out, Mother. Lie back now and I'll fetch you a cup of tea. It's time I woke the baby up from his afternoon nap anyway; he's not going to sleep tonight if I don't wake him now. Oh Glory! Did you hear that? There's someone in the hallway. I'll have to go downstairs."

"Whoever it is, tell them I'm not up to visitors. Leave me to try and make some sense of the mess I may be in. And Hannah, put some brandy in me tea."

"Mrs. Featherstone and Mrs. Gee, for Madam, Hannah," shouted Olive. "I've put them in the drawing room and Cook wants to know if she'll be wanting me to serve them tea."

"Not so loud, Olive," whispered Hannah, leaning over the banister. "I'm going to get little Johnny up and yes, take them in a tray of tea."

She hurried to the nursery, where the dear little chap had awoken. Her body began to tremble as she hugged him to her breast. Her mind felt seized with doubt as she pondered Maggie's dilemma. Wasn't she the one who had put thoughts of a pregnancy into her stepmother's head?

What if there was no baby? There had been no sickness had there, or nausea on Maggie's part, Just an admission that she and Uncle Johnny had spent a week together; perhaps they'd had separate beds? What if it was true that she was suffering menopausal symptoms? All this panic would be for nothing and she'd be the one to blame.

Maggie was also trembling under the covers in her bedroom. So the women from the committee had come a-calling had they? Was it possible that they could smell a scandal? They always seemed to be good at that. The dress that she'd been wearing this morning had indeed been fuller, but at Maggie's age, lots of women were stout. Oh, why had she listened to Johnny's silver tongue, gone along with staying at the Adelphi Hotel, then shared his bed? It had been foolish and stupid to be looking for affection, when she had it from her family here at home. She had acted like a simpleton and was about to pay. What was that saying of Father O'Brien's? Disobedience brings punishment, obedience brings rewards. Then she would be getting a bucketful of punishment, for adultery was a sin!

"Nosey old biddies," Maggie said, when Hannah returned to her bedroom. "I suppose they were having a look at me stuff and putting a value on it."

"Oh come, Mother. I think that they had called because of genuine interest in how you are faring. They were concerned about your disappearance from all the festivities. You know you've always tried to be there on Neston's Ladies Day."

"Hmm, well I've been thinking whilst you've been entertaining them, that yer could be wrong, Hannah, and you've been talking me into something that might just go away."

"And what if I'm right? If I'm aghast at the situation and I'm one of your family, how do you think the locals will act? There'll be whispering, pointed looks, and fifty years ago they'd have you burnt at the stake! Here, drink your tea, then perhaps you'll feel up to coming downstairs for an hour or so. You know how Olive likes to gossip. Don't give her any reason to, except for her knowing that you're not very well."

—

Katie sat at the Sister's desk thinking of how well she had done. It had been ten days since the admission of the soldiers from Bengal. Matron had been quick to tell her staff nurse that she had coped extremely well.

"You have the makings of a first class Sister and I will submit a letter to the Hospital Board, saying just that. And I hear that you give attention to your studies also. Well done, Staff Nurse Tibbs; I have a great faith in you."

Katie had blushed self-consciously. She had thoroughly enjoyed herself, being mistress of all she surveyed, but did Matron's visit signal an end to it all? Was it back to making beds and carrying bed pans for the patients yet again?

"How are the men in Hinderton Ward, Matron? We've not been allowed any contact with the staff there, as you know."

"Better than we'd hoped, though of course I've only spoken to Sister from the doorway. It is an Isolation Ward after all. She tells me that after the initial assessment made by the ship's doctor, most have reacted favourably to his recommended treatment. Of the seven admissions, only one is causing her concern."

"So when do you think Sister will return to take over this ward again, Matron? I'm only asking, because I put in for some holidays at the end of June."

"I think that will be in order, Staff Nurse Tibbs, though I warn you that Sister Gill will be looking for time off too. She and her staff have not been able to leave the building, taking it in turns to sleep in one of the side rooms. But I'll mention it to Sister tomorrow when I visit, if I think on. She thinks that now the tide has turned, I can include the ward on my rounds."

Katie looked around her, checking that every patient looked clean and tidy and in carefully made up beds. The cleaner had been in earlier and everywhere looked polished. Win was tending to old Mr. Biggins and, behind her in the sluice room, Mrs. Mottram was washing out the bedpans. It couldn't have been easier, Katie thought. The miner had gone home to his family to be replaced by a labourer who had dropped heavy bricks on his toes. The man whose face was scalded had gone as well; there had not been a lot that could be done for him. The chesty man was waiting to be seen by a doctor who was travelling over from Liverpool. His problem was being dealt with by inhaling the steam from kettles. And Mr. Biggins was really no trouble, except he had a bad habit of wetting the bed.

"Psst, Auntie Katie, over here – I've a message from me mam."

Katie turned to look down the corridor. Inside the open doorway was her eldest nephew, Luke.

She hurried to him as fast as her legs would carry her. If Matron caught him on the premises there would be Hell to pay! "What are you doing here, Lukey? You know children are not allowed. Shouldn't you be in school today?"

"Naw, it's nearly time for the holidays. They're teaching us nothing, so I'm pretendin' I've got a toothache. Mam sent me to ask when you're coming down to see us, 'cos you've only bin once since we moved in."

"She knows I'm busy. I'm in charge of this ward now and will be for the foreseeable future. Anyway, why is she sending you? Her legs are stronger than yours are and she could have come up on the visiting bus."

"Oh, Auntie, I'm nine now yer know and it's easy coming across the fields. I keep to the footpaths, so the farmer can't shout fer spoiling his crops, and if I'm thirsty I stop at the little streams. I'm terribly hungry now, yer know." He looked at Katie hopefully.

"Well, I can only spare you a copper, 'cos I've eaten my lunch already. If you walk back down through the village, there's a small bakery where you should get something to eat for a penny. Tell your mother that I'll be over at the end of June; that's when I'll be getting some time off. By the way, how's your Uncle Ernie settling in?"

"I think that's why she wants yer to go and see her. They had a terrible barney when he walked with his dirty boots over the living room floor that she'd just bin cleanin'. She shouted at him and he took himself off and hasn't called at our house since. She's supposed to give him his dinner and wash his clothes, well Granny does that really, but she's worrying if he's eating properly, though she'll not go down to Lilac Cottage to see if he's all right."

"Have you not been down to see him, Lukey? You used to get on well with him, didn't you? Didn't Uncle Ernie take you out in his punt?"

The boy hung his head and took a while to answer. There was a strange look on his face and he avoided Katie's eyes.

"I don't like him any more; he says things to me that I don't understand. He started crying once, just sat there like a baby. Mam'll go mad when she sees his place. Me and Freddie Jones looked through the back window last Saturday and it looks like a rubbish tip. Right, I'll tell her that you'll be over soon. Thanks fer the money. Bye."

Katie stood for a moment in the doorway, watching her nephew run along the walkway that separated each building. His words had made her feel uneasy. There was something strange about her brother, but she had got used to him after all these years. It was just his craving for solitude that made him different from other people; he had only ever wanted a simple life. Not like her, who wanted to make something of the chances she'd been given. Go places, see places before she stepped off this mortal coil. With a bit of luck she could rise to the position of Matron, be given her own hospital in a different part of the world. But she'd look in on Ernie next time she visited Neston. Perhaps something was grieving him; perhaps her brother was missing his Mam.

–

"Good Morning, Staff Nurse Tibbs. Oh, you look surprised to see me. Didn't Matron tell you that I'm out of Isolation and I was coming back today?"

Katie had just wandered in at the start of another morning. She was looking forward to a nice cup of tea before she began her shift. "Oh, hello, Sister Gill. No, she didn't tell me, but I'm happy to see you anyway."

The two women went into the little kitchen where the kettle was boiling merrily.

"I've done the changeover for you, Staff Nurse. Nothing to report other than Mr. Biggins has wet the bed."

"Nothing changes on the Thornton Ward, Sister, but tell me about your time on the Hinderton Ward. Was it gruesome having to look after those poor unfortunate men? How are they now? They must be better if you're allowed out again."

"I felt desperately sorry for them, Staff Nurse, as you can imagine. When the wagon brought them in, I just felt full of despair. And the stench from their vomit and other orifices was overpowering. We had to wear masks, all covering aprons and everything had to be thrown away. We got through more sheets and blankets than the store room could cope with and I had to shout a message through the window to be left some more. Mrs. Kane was constantly mopping with Lysol; Janey was forever changing the beds; I was boiling kettles, trying to get some liquids into them, the bedpans were constantly in use and I lost count of the bed baths. I'm fair worn out I can tell you. But this is what I've really come to tell you, I'm going to stay at my sister's for a few days, she lives in Birkenhead. You'll be in charge of the men that are left and your existing patients. We've checked their stools and we think there's no infection; they're eating well and some will be discharged in a day or two. There's only one who must be put in a side ward. They say that he's an officer and must be treated in a special way."

"A special way, Sister?" Katie frowned. She disliked being told that patients were to be given better treatment than others. As far as she was concerned, everyone should be treated the same. "If he is to have special treatment, why hasn't he been sent to somewhere like the Officer Wards at Chester?"

"Because we didn't know he was an officer when he first came to us. All the men were in a terrible state, none of them were in uniform and the underwear they had on was burnt at the receiving hospital in Liverpool. It was one of the charitable institutions that provided them with clean under clothes and blankets. He was the one we were treating for delirium, so we couldn't make any sense of what he was saying for days on end. However, we now know that he has family living in Neston, so I'm to take a note to his mother when I go for the Birkenhead train. Put him in a side ward will you, so that he and his mother can have a little privacy."

"And the others? Are you visiting *their* families with little notes, Sister?"

"If I didn't know you better, Staff Nurse, I would think you were being sarcastic. No, Matron has already written to their relatives telling them of their son's admission, but warning there was to be no visitors for a couple of weeks or so."

"But now the men are being transferred to this ward, I can expect hordes of their relatives at around three?"

"Just two people at their bedside as usual, Staff Nurse. Visiting hours between three and four and no exceptions. The doctor will make his assessments tomorrow morning, so expect him with Matron then. I can't see there being any problems, most of the men just need bed rest, so when I get back they'll probably have gone."

Let's hope so, thought Katie, 'cos I can't see when it's my turn for a holiday that I'll be getting much of a rest!

Chapter 17

"Good Morning. May I speak to the lady of the house? A Mrs. Haines, I believe."

Sister Gill stood at the front door of Selwyn Lodge speaking to Olive, who had been in the hallway, brushing down the stairs.

"I'll get Miss Hannah," she replied and, rather rudely, she thought, shut the door in her face.

"I'm so sorry," a young dark haired woman said, as she came to open the door again a few minutes later. "Can I help you? The maid said you are here to see Mrs. Haines. Did you have an appointment to see her? I'm Mrs. Dockerty, her daughter. Can I be of any help?"

"I'm Sister Gill, from Clatterbridge Hospital. I don't have an appointment to see your mother, but it is urgent that I speak with her if I can."

"Perhaps you would like to come in for a moment then. If it's a donation, Mother usually makes those at the committee meetings I believe, but anyway do come in."

Hannah took her into the drawing room, wondering why on earth a nurse would come all the way from the hospital to visit Maggie. Not just an ordinary nurse either; a Sister, if the woman was to be believed. Though she wasn't wearing uniform, the pleasant-faced woman had the manner of someone used to giving orders. Hannah gestured to the sofa, asking politely if her visitor would like a cup of tea.

"That is very kind of you, dear, but I must catch the twelve o'clock train after I have spoken with you."

Hannah noticed now that the nurse was carrying a small carpet bag, which she had placed carefully near the settee.

"To get to the point, I have a patient who says his name is Michael Haines."

Sister Gill paused as the young woman in front of her gasped, then watched in concern as Hannah virtually collapsed into a fireside chair.

"Are you all right, my dear? Shall I call your maid? Good Heavens, I thought someone would be glad to hear that he is safe and well."

Sister Gill leant over Hannah, grasping her wrist to check her pulse rate, noting as she did so that the young woman had a roundness to her stomach. It was probably due to her condition that she had begun to faint.

"I'm fine, no, no, don't worry. My maid will be busy seeing to my little boy while I'm in here with you. I'll be all right in a moment. It was just the shock, you see. As far as we are concerned, Michael is serving in India. In fact my mother received a letter only a few weeks ago. It seemed then he was very well."

The nurse sighed to herself then sat back onto the sofa. She wouldn't be catching the twelve o'clock train to her sister's house after all. Wasn't it her duty to help her fellow man?

"Michael has been in a state of delirium until a few days ago, while riddled with dysentery and sickness. He was one of those who came over in a ship from Bengal and sent to our hospital. He told me that he had taken a

294

detachment of men on a reconnaissance trip, because of reports of a rebel group further north, who were intent on causing trouble. As you probably know, since the Raj was given his power, the region has been mostly peaceful, but there's a small minority who dislike this collusion with the British and Michael unfortunately fell foul of them. I believe there was a skirmish, but your brother managed to escape, then found himself in jungle conditions along with others who had got away. They trailed around for days, hungry, thirsty and desperate to find their unit, but they never did. It was a group of natives who were out hunting that found them eventually, but as you will understand, by then the soldiers were in a desperate state. They were reunited with their platoon and given medical care, but a sickness was already rife throughout the company and their condition didn't help matters as well."

"So, this patient of yours said that his name is Michael Haines, of this address. Can you be sure of that? Has he any papers to prove it?"

"Why, no," Sister Gill replied, taken aback. "But why would he make up such a story anyway?"

"I don't know," said Hannah, dully. "It just seems strange that he's making this claim when it was only a few weeks ago that Mother received a letter from him."

"Well, when you think about it, the letter would have had a long way to travel. It isn't like our post that can be on your doorstep the very next day. Perhaps he wrote it the day before he embarked on his mission and it was carried there and then by a messenger to the nearest port."

"I don't know what to do," Hannah said, after a few seconds silence, while Sister Gill looked appreciatively at the furnishings in the elegant room.

"My mother has gone away and I don't know when she'll be back again. I can't possibly nurse a sick person myself; you can see the condition I'm in."

Sister Gill looked at her askance. "We're not asking you to nurse your brother, Mrs. Dockerty. I've been asked by Matron to call and inform your mother of his whereabouts. Is it too much to ask if *you* would be prepared to visit him, seeing as your mother has gone away?"

"No, I'm sorry, Sister, I'm not prepared to come up to your hospital on what is probably a wild goose chase. As you can see I'm expecting a baby and I will not put it at risk, nor my six-month-old son, by putting myself near an infectious man who says he is my relative. If he is who he says he is, he can wait until he is clear of any infections. He might have something else lurking, typhoid or cholera for all I know. I'm sorry, but as I say, I'm not prepared to put my family at risk."

Sister Gill rose from her chair abruptly and picked up her bag; she was trying not to show it, but she was raging inwardly. The poor man, who had nearly died for his Queen and country, was being given the brush-off by his sister. And she had a train to catch, didn't she? There was no way she was walking back to the hospital to give him the bad news today.

"Well, thank you, Mrs. Dockerty, for sparing me your time, but I must be away to the station. I'll pass on your good wishes to your brother, shall I, when I return to the hospital in a few days' time?"

With that, Sister Gill saw herself out of Selwyn Lodge, leaving Hannah in a state of bewilderment, wondering what she was going to do. Michael turning up in their lives couldn't have come at much worse a time.

Katie tiptoed into the side ward to check on the young officer that had been admitted to her ward that morning. His eyes were closed, but she knew he wasn't sleeping. Win had told her that only moments ago the man had been close to tears.

"I took him a drink and he asked me when he could expect a visitor. I told him that visiting time was over and he sort of groaned and turned away."

"Sister Gill only went to see his mother this morning, so he couldn't expect her to come dashing down so quickly. I know her; Maggie Haines, she's a very busy woman. Owns the Sheldon Company. You know, loans and vouchers and property, that kind of thing. She lives in a big house on Burton Road, called Selwyn Lodge, with her daughter Hannah and Hannah's husband, Eddie Dockerty."

"Oh, he's from a very good family then. I'm surprised he's here slumming it with the rest of us. You'd think he'd be sent to one of those Officer Wards at the County Hospital."

"Nobody knew who he was until one of the soldiers told Sister. There doesn't seem to be any airs and graces about him, though, and he's not kept ringing the bell."

Katie stood at the side of Michael's bed, trying to put a face to his name, though she couldn't recollect ever seeing him really. He and his sister were brought up in a different world to her. Though his handsome face still had a pallor of sickness and his short brown hair was damp with grease, Katie knew that his condition must have improved dramatically in the time he had lain in Isolation. She had seen from the sketches in her 'Notes on Nursing' what a body looked like suffering from dehydration. Not a pleasant sight; but this body could look splendid once he had been fattened up. She blushed at the thoughts she was having; they were not a dedicated nurse's thoughts at all. She tucked in the sheet where it had escaped from the bedstead to cover the confusion in her mind.

The man's eyelids fluttered, then opened fully. He smiled weakly at Katie and in that moment she was lost. Staff Nurse Tibbs, career nurse with spinsterhood looming, looked into her patient's eyes and promptly fell in love.

–

Hannah sat for a long time in the drawing room after she had seen Sister Gill off the premises. She was in a state of shock, with no one there to turn to. It would be hours before Eddie came home and Maggie had left the morning before. Her thoughts were racing and her heart thudded painfully as she considered what it meant if Michael came back home. The woman must have thought her a cold-hearted bitch, seemingly not interested in her brother's welfare, but Hannah knew her brother well. It would be him and her against each other as he asserted his right to take over the company, asserting his right to live at Selwyn Lodge as well. He'd be arrogant, pompous and overbearing, riding roughshod over Eddie; belittling the hard work that her husband had done. Then there was the unthinkable to dwell on. Michael might have known about her and Jeremy. What if he told Eddie, that she, Hannah, had slept with his upper class friend? Their marriage would be over; her children without a father. Hannah shuddered at the thought of it all as she tried to take it in.

"Miss Hannah, will yer be wantin' your lunch soon? Only I can't set the table and carry little Johnny too."

"Sorry, Olive, I'm coming now. Don't set the table in the dining room, there being only me. I'll eat my lunch in the conservatory today."

Olive's face took on a 'hard done by' expression. She was expected to carry out her household duties, but be a nursemaid too. She'd been saying to Alec, her boyfriend, only yesterday that she was considering looking for another position. What with the Missus clearing off like she had, Miss Hannah walking around in a daze and Mr. Dockerty coming in at all hours expecting to be waited on, it was all getting to be too much for her. She wouldn't mind if she was privy to the reasons for all this upheaval, but she wasn't. And what was that nurse doing here from Clatterbridge this morning, she would like to know?

"It'll be something to do with Mrs. Haines's charity work," Joan had said. "With her going off to recuperate with relatives in Ireland, she probably hasn't had time to let anyone at the hospital know."

But Olive didn't think it was that. The nurse had looked angry as she had walked away from Selwyn Lodge and Miss Hannah had looked downcast, as if she had been given some serious news.

When Eddie got home later, Olive was convinced that she was onto something. Miss Hannah had bundled him into the drawing room, as soon as Mr. Dockerty had put his key in the lock. She hovered as near as possible, listening first to the muted voice of Hannah, then Eddie's, raised and angry. Whatever it was, it was causing a quarrel. Olive didn't wait to hear any more.

Eddie stood staring at Hannah in disbelief as she quietly told him of Michael's reappearance. "Didn't yer say that your mother had a letter from him just a few weeks ago?"

"Yes, but she told me she didn't answer it because he was asking her to buy him out of the Army. I think she couldn't face the fact that he would want to come back again."

"So she's cleared off to God knows where and left us to deal with the situation?"

"Well, it may look like that, Eddie, but how could she know that he'd take ill and wind up in the local hospital?"

"Oh, men like Michael always find a way out of anything that doesn't suit them. I've heard of men injuring themselves so they could be discharged on medical grounds. Did the Sister say what kind of condition that your brother is in?"

"It sounded as if he had picked an infection up. That's why I said I wouldn't visit, because I'm in the family way, but besides that, Eddie, I don't want to go and see him. You know what this means, don't you? He'll take over everything; the businesses, this house. As Maggie's son, he has the right to. Even if he's never done a thing."

Hannah began to cry as she contemplated leaving this beautiful house that she had spent her life in. Her dream had been to fill it with her and Eddie's sons.

Eddie paced, his head, like Hannah's, filled with desperation. He couldn't let it happen, their paradise would be snatched away.

"So, he's expecting his mother to visit? Is that what the woman from the hospital said? And you told her that Maggie had gone away and you don't know when she'll be back again?"

Hannah nodded dumbly.

"Then we've got time to do something about it!"

"How?!"

"Well, before Maggie went away she visited the solicitors in Chester. *You* remember you went with her, because she wasn't feeling very well. Then next day she went to see Mr. Taylor at the local bank. I met her there at eleven o'clock and I had to give a sample signature. I'm the only one who can sign for any payments or authorize the sending of any cheques! So, Michael can huff and puff as much as he wants to, but until Maggie gets back, there is nothing he can do."

"Except make life unpleasant for us," Hannah said, thinking of her secret liaison with Jeremy. If things got nasty, she was sure her brother would blackmail her with that.

"Oh Hannah, don't worry. You can write to Maggie and tell her of Michael's homecoming. Get her to sign something to say that we should be living here. By the time he gets out of hospital it'll all be sown up nicely and your brother then will see that I'll be calling the tune."

"Eddie, this plan of yours will only give us a little time, you know. We should have something up our sleeve for the future."

"No, I've just told you, Hannah, you mustn't worry; we'll never be thrown out of our home."

"There's something I haven't told you, but I'm tired now. There's little Johnny to see to and I'm sure you're hungry, Eddie. I'll tell you later when we've had our supper and baby's been put to bed."

–

Maggie lay on her bed in the room that she had booked at the Adelphi. She'd been given a suite on the second floor. Her mind kept whirling in a dance of anxiety, as she contemplated the journey ahead. Not only the passage to Sligo but the months of being holed up in Ballina until the time she might give birth. What could she have done but go along with Hannah's blunt suggestion? Write to Bridget at the Heaney Hotel and ask if she could rent a room? So, here she was, waiting for the packet steamer that didn't sail until the morning. The letter she had written to Bridget would precede her by a day. What if she got there and found that Bridget had let all her rooms to the summer visitors? What if Bridget didn't believe her tale that Jack had passed away? What if she told Bridget that she was expecting Jack's baby and there wasn't one? How foolish and what a waste of time it was all going to be. Why, oh why, had she listened to Johnny's silver tongue? Look at where it had got her. Men were all the same, when she came to think about it. Jack had fed her a broth of lies then had walked out on her when it had suited him.

Maggie closed her eyes, hoping that sleep would come so that her mind could get some rest from all its troubled thoughts.

–

"So you're telling me that your Mother is expectin' and the father of the baby isn't my father-in-law, but it's me Uncle Johnny! Hannah! You're kiddin' me, aren't yer? Both of them are as old as Methuselah. So, this is what you were waitin' to tell me? Does he know? Does Uncle Johnny know that Maggie's expectin'? No, Hannah, you must have got it wrong somehow. Did yer Mother tell yer this story? She's made it up, hasn't she?"

Eddie felt totally bewildered with Hannah's explanation of Maggie's sudden flight. He kept running his fingers through his hair and pacing up and down.

"Get me a drink, Hannah. A drop of that brandy will do. How long have yer known that that was the real reason? She told me her trip was to do with a friend."

"Well, she could hardly tell you that she was in a certain condition, could she? Not her son-in-law. She might not be anyway; all this could be to do with her age."

"You've lost me, Hannah. What has all this got to do with Uncle Johnny then, or her age?"

"Mother and Uncle Johnny spent a week together in the Adelphi. He hadn't just met her that morning as he'd said; they'd both come over from Liverpool."

Hannah turned away from Eddie, feeling a bubbling of hysteria. This was a serious explanation she was giving him, but the weeks of agonising with Maggie had been just as painful for her.

"You're saying that they were lovers, Maggie and Uncle Johnny, but because of their ages a baby may or may not be a possibility? I don't understand, Hannah. Surely a woman knows if she's having a baby? If they've been lovers it's probably true."

"Not necessarily, Eddie. When a woman reaches Maggie's age, their monthlies stop and that could be Mother's problem."

"Oh, please Hannah, spare me the detail, some things I don't want to know about!"

"I'm just giving you an explanation. I persuaded her to go to Bridget's in Ireland. You know the people I told you about, who we stayed with in Ballina? No one else knows her there; she'll see a doctor and if she is expecting she'll say that it belongs to Jack."

"And if she isn't, she'll stay a few weeks until she's feeling better, then she'll come home again?"

"Yes, that's right, and meantime we've got the problem of Michael."

"And Uncle Johnny. Strange if they were lovers that he's not been seen again."

"Well, they've had a bit of a misunderstanding. She did write a note to apologise, but it seems she forgot to send it. If you remember that was before she caught the flu."

"Oh, Uncle Johnny'll pop up again, you wait and see, then we can tell him of his baby son or daughter."

"No, we mustn't, Eddie," cried Hannah in alarm. "You're not supposed to know, she swore me to secrecy! She's going to write and let me know what the doctor says, then I've to tell you how long you'll be in charge of the company. Remember, it's very important that no one else knows what is happening. It'll cause a scandal if any of this gets out."

"So, what do we do with Michael then? Do yer want me to go and see him and explain his mother's where-abouts?"

"Oh, would you, Eddie?" Hannah kissed him grate-fully.

"Tell him that you're in charge and there's to be no changes while his mother's not here. Tell him that you'll arrange somewhere for him to stay in the village, when he comes out of hospital. Tell him there's no room for him at Selwyn Lodge."

–

Katie jumped up from her seat in alarm as she heard raised voices from the side ward. At long last Sub-Lieutenant

Haines had received a visitor; not his mother who he had hoped would come, but a young man who she recognised as Eddie Dockerty from the Brown Horse Inn. She had heard through Annie that he had married Maggie Haines's daughter so had welcomed him with relief when he had said who he was visiting. A week had passed since Sister Gill had called at Selwyn Lodge and, as she had confided in Katie on her return to the ward, Mrs. Haines had gone away and his sister, Mrs. Dockerty, hadn't seemed too pleased to hear of her brother's return.

"I couldn't tell him that, could I?" Sister Gill had said sadly. "News like that could give him a relapse and I was hoping that he could be discharged into his family's care."

Katie walked briskly along the corridor. She wasn't having a patient upset, especially to Michael, who was important to her.

"Is there a problem?" she asked in her sternest voice, as she took in the scene from the doorway. Michael was raised on one elbow, glaring at his visitor, anger written all over his face.

"Not from my point of view, nurse," retorted Eddie calmly. "But perhaps yon man here could do with some smelling salts after what I've just told him."

"Do you realise that Sub-Lieutenant Haines has suffered severe trauma due to his time spent serving on behalf of his Queen and country in India? If you have come here to be unpleasant, I think you should be asked to leave!"

"It's all right, Staff Nurse," Michael said, through what sounded like clenched teeth. "I can fight my own battles; don't worry about me."

"That is what I'm paid to do whilst your in my care, Sub-Lieutenant." Katie turned to go, glowering at Eddie.

"Ten more minutes, Mr. Dockerty if you please, and then you'll have to go."

Michael fell back onto his pillow, seething at having to be polite to his one and only visitor. He couldn't believe what he'd just heard. What a betrayal. By his own mother! He had only been away, for what, eighteen months? And in that time, his father had gone to live in Wicklow, Hannah had married this pot boy from the Brown Horse and the Sheldon Loan and Property Company had been signed over to a bloody stranger, while the owner, his mother, had gone away! Where was that going to leave him in the scheme of things? If he was medically discharged from the Army he'd have no income. He couldn't move back to Selwyn Lodge because of these usurpers and unless someone informed his mother of her son's return, there'd be no place for him at Sheldon either.

Michael felt angry and dismayed at his mother's treachery, though he supposed grudgingly, that if she had known that he was here in the hospital she wouldn't have gone away. His mind worked quickly as he thought of the position his sister and her husband could put him in. He could be left to moulder here 'til the hospital threw him out, go back to the barracks to honour his obligations, be sent overseas to a firing line and fall prey to the diseases that lurked there. None of it appealed and he knew he had to play for time.

He forced a friendly grin on his face and held out his hand to Eddie. "I must congratulate you on your marriage to my stepsister. Are there any children? Am I an uncle by any chance?"

"Oh yes," Eddie nodded eagerly, grateful that his brother-in-law seemed to have accepted the situation so quickly. It would have come as a shock to him, poor chap, even more so when you consider the state he must have been in.

"We have a six-month-old son called Johnny, he's been named after my uncle, and Hannah is expecting another baby at the end of September, or maybe beginning of October, we're not sure. It was quite a surprise really, her getting caught so quickly, but we're looking forward to a big family anyway."

Michael shuddered inwardly at the thought of Selwyn Lodge being full of mewling babies. He'd be rid of the lot of them when what was rightfully his was given back to him. "And the business? Is it doing well? What is your role in the company?"

"It's doing extremely well. We've a big development underway on what was Farmer Briggs's old farmland. Luxurious dwellings for the middle class and a few bungalows fer the not so wealthy. We've built a terrace row on Town Lane and have a thriving business with loans and mortgages. As fer me, I'm the Site Manager, overseeing the snagging lists and ensuring all goes smoothly. Your mother has not been very well, so I've been gradually taking more and more off her. Not her committee meetings though," Eddie said with a smile. "I haven't been roped in fer them just yet."

"Sounds an up and coming company. She's done very well for herself, has my mother. Is there any room in this great establishment for another family member? Me?"

"Oh, I didn't realise that you were thinking of coming out of the Army..." Eddie felt at a bit of a loss. What would Hannah say?

"I did write to my mother to tell her that I wanted to give up my commission. She obviously didn't receive my letter because I am sure she would have pulled all the strings to get me out. The conditions were quite appalling over there. I realised my mistake as soon as we were taken to our quarters. Some of the officers just got on with it, but I couldn't take to the place somehow."

"Well, I'll let yer know what's decided. Hannah can't make any decisions without her mother knowing that you're back. She'll write to her…"

Michael nodded, suddenly weary. He could see Staff Nurse Tibbs hovering anxiously at the door; this was a good time to send this uncouth person on his way. "Whatever… Oh, by the way, Eddie. Something for you to think on while you're both planning what to do with me. Hannah isn't my mother's child, you know. Your wife is illegitimate. One day Sheldon in all its glory will come to me."

Chapter 18

Maggie hurried up the stairs of the Heaney Hotel, trying to get to her bedroom before Bridget or Frank waylaid her. The shock of having her pregnancy confirmed had knocked the stuffing right out of her. All she wanted to do was hide herself away until she could come to terms with what she'd just heard. It was true then; Hannah had been right all along.

The doctor had looked at her quizzically when Maggie explained in his consulting rooms that she thought she might be expecting. He was the same doctor who had attended Jack and he had been most sympathetic when he heard that Maggie's husband had recently passed away.

"It could be that his death has brought on bodily changes in you, Mrs. Haines. It is highly likely that your bleeding would cease forthwith due to the grieving you will have done. However, if there is the slightest possibility that you may be bearing his child, I shall investigate. If you wouldn't mind undressing behind the screen, I will examine you at once."

It had all seemed a sort of nightmare as Maggie had submitted to the doctor's examination. She had held her breath, hoping that he would say that there was nothing he could find to confirm her fears. It had felt like she was walking through a shadowy mist when she had come from behind the screen again. Her hands were shaking as she skewered her hat back on with its diamond-encrusted pin, then fiddled with the ties on her tippet, hoping that the doctor couldn't hear her heart that was beating like a drum.

"I think I'm right in saying that your baby should arrive at the end of November, or possibly December. You said you couldn't be sure what the date of your last bleeding was?"

"That's true," Maggie admitted shakily. "I caught the flu after my husband died and everything became a bit of a blur."

"Poor lady. Have you got someone to take care of you? I think you told me you were on your way to England, when I attended your late husband that time at the Heaney Hotel."

"Yes, I have good friends in Frank and Bridget," Maggie assured him. "I hope to be staying with them until after the birth."

She had felt so ashamed as the doctor had murmured his sympathies and told her to call into his rooms in a few months' time, to arrange a local midwife to attend her.

"Not that I want to alarm you, but you did say that your last confinement was over twenty-three years ago. Isn't it strange how the God above works in His mysterious ways?"

He certainly did, thought Maggie, as she lay on top of the bed worrying her miserable heart out. This disobedience to all she had been brought up to believe could bring her the ultimate punishment in the end. How dare she commit adultery? It was the seventh of the Ten Commandments. She knew them all, didn't she? The Bible was the first book that she had ever read.

Katie left Michael to himself after she had heard his parting shot to his visitor. Goodness, she felt all of a tremble. Fancy that nice young officer having such a bitter tongue.

It was none of her business, she knew, but what he had said would be such a scandal if it ever got around. How he must be hurting though, to be denied his home because his mother wasn't there. What a homecoming. All the other men had received flocks of visitors during their time on Thornton Ward, so much so that she'd restricted them to two persons by each bed.

–

"So that's what he thinks, Eddie," said Hannah, when her husband had reported back to her. "He thinks that if anything happens to Mother then he'll get the blooming lot. Well, not if I have anything to do with it. I'm just as much Maggie's daughter as he is her son. She took me in when I was little and brought me up as one of her family. He'll have to prize me out with a toothpick before any of it falls into his hands."

"Hannah, there's not a thing you can do if Maggie has willed the lot to him. Not a court in the land will come down in your favour. You must see that, sweetheart. Anyway, I said you'd write to her and let her know of his return. Then it's up to Maggie to say who can live here and who runs the businesses."

"Well, she won't know anything if I don't write to her, will she? Did he say when he was coming out and what his plans will be?"

"He didn't say, but I should imagine he would be discharged into the care of the Army. He's still an officer and it will be up to them if they think he's still fit enough to carry on or be let go on medical grounds. Hannah, don't yer think we should be looking around somewhere, to maybe set up on our own? I have the knowledge to start a small business now in the building trade and I'm young enough to begin again."

"But I don't want to leave here, Eddie," Hannah cried. "This is my home as well as yours and the babies'. It would take us years to have the same standards as we're enjoying now."

"We're probably getting ahead of ourselves anyway, Hannah," he said reassuringly. "Maggie'll be back by Christmas and we can sort things out together then."

—

The next morning, as Katie was inspecting her patients in readiness for Matron's visit, Sister Gill came in with an official-looking paper.

"Staff Nurse Tibbs," she called. "Could you come over for a moment?"

She allowed Katie to read the letter that had come from the Chester Barracks. It said that a medical officer was to visit the very next day.

"We did have one that poked his head round the door way in Isolation, but he didn't stay more than two minutes. Probably this chap will have Sub-Lieutenant Haines moved now he's not infectious. Shall I break the news to him or do you want to do it? Poor chap, I feel so sorry that that sister of his didn't visit him, and her husband's visit didn't do him much good, from what you told me."

"I'll let him know when I go in to check that his room's all shipshape," replied Katie. "He'll probably be gone by the time I get back from my holiday. I'm going to catch up with our Annie and see what she's been up to. Or what the children have been up to! My little house was as clean as a new pin when I left it, but it'll be just like her old place by now. All scuffed and worn-looking, I'll be bound."

–

Michael perked up when Katie walked into the side ward. He had been looking despondently out of the window at the honeysuckle that was climbing up the side of the next building. He seemed to remember honeysuckle at Selwyn Lodge, entwining itself with a climbing rose around a bower in the garden. Not that he was interested in gardening, but it was a pleasant sight that he remembered from two years ago. So many things about his old home had become precious now that he was denied living there. The glorious view of the Welsh hills from his bedroom window; the conservatory where Miss Rosemary's father had brought tropical plants from his sojourns abroad; Joan, the cook, who could be relied upon to fill a growing boy's belly. He wondered if there had been a change of maid; he didn't remember the last one's name.

He wished he'd never left the place now. It was hard to remember why he had. Probably because Jeremy had filled his head with the daring do's of becoming a cavalry officer and Montague urging him to see the world and get a life. They had mocked his position as the 'go for' in his mother's company and ridiculed his provincial ways.

Michael smiled at Katie as she asked him to get back into bed before Matron did her rounds. This staff nurse was a pleasant young woman indeed. Not attractive like some of the young ladies he had met on the social circuit, but passable. He liked the way her eyes twinkled as she spoke to him, her capable manner and her aura of peace and gentleness. She was tall like his mother, though that was where the likeness ended. This young lady was a little plump, where Maggie had always been slender, but there was something about her; perhaps the colour of her hair? He didn't know, but what he did know was perhaps Staff Nurse Tibbs could come in very useful one day.

Katie felt the colour rush to her face as Michael smiled as if he was pleased to see her. She and Win had given him a bed bath the day before and though she had performed this duty for many male patients since her training days, something had been different this time. She couldn't say what, but her dreams last night had been filled by a man who had whispered endearments. To her, Katie Tibbs, who was making nursing her career.

"I have some news for you, Sub-Lieutenant. A medical officer from your regiment is coming to see you tomorrow. That will be something to look forward to, won't it?"

"Not really, Staff Nurse," Michael answered glumly. "With your tender care I'm nearly back to full recovery, so I'll be sent back to that God-forsaken country to finish my commission off."

"Oh, I didn't think of that. Never mind, perhaps they'll think of something else for you to do. Are there no wars being fought nearer home, or perhaps you could do some peace keeping over in Ireland?"

Michael grinned at Katie's attempt at light heartedness. "I'd rather shoot myself in the foot."

They both knew that he was also attempting brevity, but the thought of Michael wounded brought a lump into

Katie's throat. She took his hand, making sure her body shielded the action from any passer-by.

"Please don't do that. If I can be of any help, do ask me. I knew your mother and I have cause to be very grateful to her. I'll be pleased to help you in anyway I can."

–

Katie sat in the kitchen later eating her lunch, chewing on a sandwich thoughtfully. She hoped she hadn't made a fool of herself by holding the Sub-Lieutenant's hand, but her heart had just gone out to him. He had looked so vulnerable when she had given him the news of the medical officer visiting. A bit like her brother, Ernie, used to look before their dad was about to clout him around his ear.

Sister Gill had advised her long ago not to get too close to the patients. A nurse was there to relieve their discomfort. Not to take on their problems; be only a listening ear. But could she do that when this man had no one else to turn to? Or abandon him in his hour of need when she knew that she was in love? Her last thought made up her mind for her. She would give him an address where she could be contacted. He could write. They would get to know each other by being pen friends for a while. Then maybe, one day in the future, she could tell Michael of her love.

–

Dear Hannah,

 It is with regret or joy, I'm not sure which, that I write to let you know that you were right in your suspicions. The doctor here has confirmed that I am to give birth around the end of November. I made him aware that the last time I had a child was twenty-three years ago, so he is arranging for a midwife to be present in case there are complications.

This has brought to mind the fact that I didn't reply to Michael's letter, but I'm sure whatever was troubling him will have been resolved by now, so I have decided to let him continue with his commission.

I have been toying with the idea of buying that little cottage that belonged to Mrs. Dockerty. What a surprise Johnny would get if he turned up one day to find me and his baby living there! My bank has sent funds, as I requested, to the Ballina bank where I have opened an account, so purchasing it wouldn't be a problem.

Bridget and Frank send their best wishes. I have told them the story that you and I concocted, although I feel rather ashamed to be playing the grieving widow yet again.

Hope Eddie is coping with all the demands that Sheldon can bring to a body. I have to admit it is pleasant not to even think about the pressures of business at all.

My thoughts are constantly with you and little Johnny. Strange to think that we will be producing another Dockerty in the Autumn.

My love to you all.

Mother.

Eddie was frowning as Hannah finished reading him Maggie's letter. It had made him feel uneasy, as if this was the lull before the storm. As much as he loved Hannah, he was beginning to see a mean and petty side to her.

"Yer know, Hannah, I think you're storing up trouble by not letting Maggie know about Michael. It's wrong that you've done nothing to help him and I did tell him that you would probably write."

"Is that all you can say, Eddie, after I've taken the trouble to read you her letter?" Hannah's eyes glinted in anger at him. "Didn't you hear me say she's going to have a baby? See, I was right all along."

"Yes, I heard, I was listening, but I can't help feeling sorry fer your brother. We've left him in the hospital and we should have offered him a home."

"Eddie, how can you say that after what he said about me being illegitimate. Yes, I know you knew already, but what if you hadn't? It was a nasty thing to say and it could have caused a lot of trouble between you and me. Do you think he would have any mercy if the boot was on the other foot? No, he wouldn't. He'd have us out on the street as soon as look at us. Michael was always jealous of me, you know, because I was Papa's little princess."

"Come here, Hannah," Eddie said and put his arm around Hannah in an effort to calm her.

"You're my princess now and all I want is fer you to be happy. I just want you to face it; that one day Michael will inherit Selwyn Lodge and all that goes with it. You might not like it, but it will happen, so I think we should have a contingency plan."

"Like what?" Hannah snorted and pulled away from him impatiently. "Don't think you're going to get me to live in a hovel somewhere. If it's not as good as here, I won't be moving with you. I've told you before, Michael will have to prise me out of here with a toothpick."

"Yer have to face it, Hannah, we're just caretakers here until your brother comes out of the army, or if Maggie decides differently and lets us stay. But yer have to let her know that he was in the local hospital, because she'll find out one day and you'll have to take the consequences. Yer may have been brought up as brother and sister, but bloods thicker than water, or so they say."

"I'll think about writing," Hannah answered him sulkily. "But when I get round to it and I've heard more about your plan."

"That's more like it," Eddie said briskly. "Now how about a kiss to show that you still love me? You're looking tired, Hannah, yer need an early night."

–

It was the day of Maggie's forty-first birthday. She had decided not to mention it to Bridget and Frank as she knew that they would want to make a fuss. Instead, she had treated herself to coffee and cake in the tea rooms she had found by the River Moy, then wandered over to the churchyard later to lay some flowers on her parents' grave.

She had sat on a bench that someone had thoughtfully placed under the shady branches of a horse chestnut tree. It was cool away from the scorching rays of the August sun and peaceful to sit in contemplation, thinking of her son who shared her birthday too. That's what Maggie needed now; peace and welcome quiet. Away from people and intrusion in her life.

That was the day she decided to inquire about local property. She had been with her friends now for nearly four weeks. They were kind to her, supportive, and only charged her the bare minimum for her board and rent. But Maggie knew that they relied on the letting of their guest rooms for their income. It was time she looked for a property and stood on her own two feet.

Bridget was surprised when Maggie broached the subject. "I thought you'd be wanting to go back to Neston, dear. Back to your family and businesses. I thought this time here was to help your grieving and make some decisions in your life."

"That's just it, Bridget. I don't want to go back where I'm known and be looked upon with pity. I want a new life for myself and the baby. Somewhere I can start again and make myself a home. Hannah and Eddie will fill Selwyn Lodge with their own babies, the company I know is in safe hands, so what's the point of returning when I'm not really needed at all?"

"Well, if you're sure," her hostess said doubtfully. "If I can help you, let me know. I'll help in any way I can."

"I have a mind to go and look at a cottage on the way down to Killala. It belonged to a friend called Mrs. Dockerty, but I believe she's passed away. How would I get the keys to the property? I know the land belongs to the farmer, but if the cottage is not sold already, how would I know if it's up for sale?"

"Hmm, I'll have to ask Frank about that, he could ask around for you. But why down in Killala, Maggie? It can get very lonely in the winter, as you'll already know."

"Call it nostalgia, Bridget, or a need to be where I belong."

Dear Staff Nurse Tibbs,
*   I am writing to let you know that the medical officer passed me as fit for duty and I am now*

awaiting orders at the Chester Barracks. I don't think they'll be sending me back to India, as the Regiment's tour of duty will be over in six months' time, so they will find me something to do while I am waiting for their return.

I wrote to my Grandmama, who lives on the promenade at Parkgate, to let her know of my situation. When I receive her reply, I will be requesting leave, in an effort to sort my personal life out. I hope it will be possible to meet and I will contact you in the near future.

Yours in appreciation.

Sub-Lieutenant Michael Haines.

"So, who is it from, Katie?" asked Annie, all agog at the official-looking letter that had been delivered by the postman a few minutes before.

"None of your business, Annie. It's to do with work. I asked for any correspondence to be sent over here."

"Is it from a man friend? That's why he's writing here, so that your Matron won't find out."

"I've told yer, it's to do with work, don't be nosy. Now, are we going down to the cottage? I want to see if Ernie's all right."

"Oh, he'll be at work, Katie. Let's leave it fer today and go down tomorrow. It's too hot to be walking and we'll have to drag these two along with us. Sam's mother's gone up to the cemetery to visit her husband, yer know. She'll look after them tomorrow for me."

"You've been putting me off since I arrived, Annie. Have yer got something to hide? He's still at Lilac Cottage, isn't he?"

"That's the thing, I don't know, Katie. Since I told him off fer messing up the floor here, we've not seen him. He's not been fer his dinners and Lukey said he's been down, but couldn't see him anywhere."

"I might have known this would happen," Katie cried. "I should never have let yer do the swap. He was happy here, you know. And now I come to think of it, you and your kids have made a right mess of this place. There's dirty marks everywhere and that rug's in a terrible state."

"Well, what did yer expect?" Annie fired back. "There's five kids, a cat, a granny and me and Sam living here. Yer didn't think I'd pay fer a daily to come and clean fer us?"

"The deal was that you looked after Ernie for me while I was away at the hospital. Cook fer him, wash his clothes and do the cleaning at his place. Now, if yer can't manage your part of the bargain, just say so, Annie. It's Ernie's name on the deeds as well as mine, yer know, and he can always come to live back here again."

—

Hannah groaned as she saw who was on her doorstep. It was Grandmama Haines, looking every inch of her seventy-two years, with Mr. Arlington close behind her. Hannah braced herself for the visit, by putting a smile on her face.

"Why, Grandmama, to what do I owe the pleasure? How long has it been now since last I saw you then?"

"Don't get clever with me, young lady. I know I'm not welcome in this house; your stepmother has always made that clear enough."

"Alice, get to the point, dear, of why you've taken the trouble to call on Hannah," Mr. Arlington said, looking embarrassed. "Perhaps we could come inside for a moment, if that's not too much trouble for you?"

"Maybe you would like to sit in the garden with me instead. It's pleasant in the sunshine and little Johnny is fast asleep in his perambulator. Perhaps you would like to take a peek at him."

Alice muttered something under her breath but meekly followed Hannah. Her husband gave her a warning look, but she took no notice of him.

"The reason I'm here is because I've had a very distressing letter from my grandson," Alice began, once she had settled into a chair without even looking at the sleeping baby.

"We've just been up to church, haven't we, Mr. Arlington? And I said to you, didn't I, it's not right what's been happening? So I decided to see what's been going on. We've only just got back from staying in Llandudno with Mr. Arlington's cousin and there it was; a letter from Michael. It had been posted to me a couple of days ago."

"And?" said Hannah frostily, knowing what was coming. She could almost hear the accusations that were about to start ringing in her ears.

"Is it true that you refused to visit him in hospital? And where has his mother gone? He says that she's away visiting some relatives. Doesn't Michael know there are none now?"

"Well, if you'll let me get a word in, Grandmama. I sent Eddie to visit Michael, because as you can see I'm expecting another baby. I didn't want to go myself in case my brother was infectious."

"I can see you're expecting, Hannah, but that's no reason to turn your back on yer brother. He has more right to be in Selwyn Lodge than you have, yer know. I've a good mind to write to your father, let him know what you're up to. He's still married to Maggie and he can still have his say."

Hannah lost her temper then, with her grandmama mentioning her father like that. If it hadn't have been for his defection, the family wouldn't have got in this mess. "Oh, do what you like, I can't stop you. And let me say it for you, shall I, since you try to remind me at every turn? I must remember I'm illegitimate, not entitled to a sausage, because of Kitty May!"

Eddie found her later, crying bitter tears as she cuddled little Johnny on her knee. He'd seen Alice and her husband go as he'd driven down to the stable. Alice had been shouting something and Mr. Arlington was looking annoyed.

"I see you've had a visit from Atilla. What's she said now to upset yer then? You only see her when she's up to mischief. I suppose this has to do with Michael and you not going to see him."

"Yes," Hannah sniffed, pulling her baby closer as he tried to slide off her knee. "Look he wants to come to you now. Go on then, go to Dada."

She passed the baby over to Eddie then began to walk a few feet away to deadhead a couple of roses.

"I don't know why I put up with her, for all she is my grandmama. All she did was pick and poke and never even acknowledged our little baby. You know, I'm beginning to think you're right about leaving here and starting afresh somewhere else together. Somewhere no one knows me and can remind me who I am."

"Oh, Hannah. Come here, will yer." Eddie's voice broke as he saw the hurt in his adored wife's eyes. She went into his arms and he hugged her and their child together.

"Now sit yourself down, Hannah and let me tell yer something. Never feel that way about yourself again. It wasn't your fault that your Dad made Kitty May pregnant. It happens. There's selfish men out there who only consider themselves and not the consequences. You, Hannah, are the best wife and mother that anyone could ask for and it doesn't matter which side of the blanket yer were born on and it certainly doesn't matter to me."

Hannah went pink at her husband's praise and she picked on some threads in her dress to cover her embarrassment.

"If it wasn't for my mother, Eddie, I would leave here. I mean it, but it seems so cruel when she's relying on us so."

"Ah, but yer don't know where I've bin today, do yer? I was going to wait until you'd written to Maggie, to tell her of Michael's untimely appearance. But if Joan has left us some dinner, we'll eat it now and then I'll show yer what I've found fer us!"

Chapter 19

Katie felt really cross with her sister as she walked down Bull Hill's leafy lane to get to Burton Road. Poor Ernie. He'd never been able to stand up to Annie. She'd been selfish and mean to treat him that way. Katie opened the top button of her long-sleeved blouse, realising she was sweating profusely. No wonder Annie hadn't wanted to stir out of the coolness of the terrace; it was the hottest day they'd had that summer. It was a good thing she'd remembered to put her boater on her head.

"Aunt Katie! Up here, Aunt Katie." A disembodied voice came shouting from the trees above.

"What are you doing up there, our Lukey? Do yer want to end up in my hospital with a broken leg?"

"No fear," called back Katie's nephew, as he swung from the lower branch like a monkey.

"Where yer going? Can I come with yer? Or do yer know if Mam has got any grub?"

"Well, she hadn't been cooking when I left home, but I think she's waiting fer your granny. Why don't you come with me to Uncle Ernie's? Then we'll come back together and have some tea."

"Oh, I don't know about that, Auntie. It's Sunday anyway and he'll be out in his punt. I'll go and see if Freddie Jones is playing. His mother makes him go to Sunday school, but he should be back by now."

"Oh, go on, Lukey. It'll be company for me and besides I don't see yer very often now that I'm working away."

"No, I'm not comin' with yer. I'll see yer later," her nephew said firmly and ran very quickly to the top of Bull Hill.

I wonder what's got into him? Katie thought, as she carried on walking. He'd been like this when he'd brought a message to the hospital. It was strange how he'd taken a dislike to her brother that way. Still, being on her own gave her chance to think about the letter she'd had from Michael. And wasn't that his house she was passing? She was sure that house on the corner was called Selwyn Lodge. It looked deserted, but what a pleasant-looking place to live.

Katie came to the site entrance of the new development. There were a lot more dwellings now than the last time she had been this way. A row of four substantial houses lined the perimeter and she could see the footings ready for another three. Each house was set on a half acre, with a sweeping stone-chipped drive and extensive gardens enclosed by walls and impressive gates. Unfortunately for Katie, these gardens were blocking her journey down to Lilac Cottage. The developer must have forgotten to leave a right of way.

She gazed for a moment at the half-timbered, gabled residences, wondering how she was going to get through, unless she went back along the road to Briggs's farmhouse which she could see in the distance through a gap in the trees. But her skirt was clinging damply and her shoes felt very tight. She turned in disappointment; she'd best be starting back.

But first she would think on Michael's letter, while there was no nosy sister or a house full of kids. She savoured the pleasure of receiving it as she sat for a moment on a fallen log. She could feel her senses stirring with his memory inside her head. He must have felt the same towards her if he had taken the trouble to write.

She sighed; there was no point in weaving happy fantasies. She knew her place in the scheme of things, she would be wasting her love on a man like him.

–

"So, did yer see him? How's he coping?" Annie asked as Katie let herself into the house, which smelled appetisingly of roasted chicken. "I don't know how yer did it, walking all that way in this heat."

"I didn't get that far, Annie. They've blocked the way with those new houses. You were right, it's far too hot today to be out walking, so I'll have another go tomorrow. But this time I'll walk down past Briggs's farm."

"Did yer see any sight of the kids while you were down there, Katie? Luke and Matthew went out together this morning, said they were going fer a paddle, but I suppose their bellies will bring them home."

"I saw Luke, not Matthew. He was hiding in the trees at the bottom of Bull Hill, but he said he was off to Freddie Jones'. He didn't want to come with me. Why is that, Annie? Why doesn't Lukey like his uncle any more?"

Her sister laughed and lowered her voice so that Mrs. Piper couldn't hear her in the kitchen. "He's suffering with what I think is embarrassment. He was spying through Ernie's bedroom window and got a bit of a shock. Ernie was doing what Sam said was called 'wanking'. Our Lukey's never been back to the cottage since then!"

Eddie drove the carriage quickly along the Chester High Road, intent on getting his wife to their destination before she could change her mind. As much as Eddie loved her, he knew that it would be hard to convince her that they should leave Selwyn Lodge. Hannah could be stubborn once she had set her mind to something. But the visit from Alice might just have swung her towards thinking his way; a new start in a new place and leave all that silly feuding behind.

Hannah felt hot and sweaty sitting with her little boy in the confines of the sultry carriage. Johnny's clothes were sticking to his small damp body and his hair lay in slicks about his head. He nodded on her lap from the lull of the carriage's motion, sucking at the bottle she'd remembered to bring.

Where was Eddie taking her? Hannah wondered, as they passed through the village of Heswall and trotted alongside the acres of farmland that undulated down to the sea. She hoped it wasn't where people could see her, because she hadn't changed out of her morning clothes.

The air became fresher and cooler as a breeze came off the estuary and Hannah looked over with interest, past the stooks of yellow corn in the fields and across, to the church spire at Thurstaston as it appeared above the trees.

"How much further, Eddie?" Hannah cried, as the horses began to labour up an incline and her view changed to heathland and scrub. The journey seemed never-ending; this was more than just a little jaunt.

"Not far now sweetheart, and I promise it'll be worth the wait. Watch out fer the windmill and an old red barn, past a duck pond and then we'll be there."

Hannah looked out of the window as Eddie had said, but all she could see was a forest of trees. The track they were taking was potholed and rough and jolted the carriage all over the place.

"Sorry, Hannah, I'm taking a shortcut. There's a better road just over the hill, but it's the long way around, through a village. We'll be there in a minute, I promise you. Watch out fer the windmill like I said."

Sure enough the jolting stopped, as Eddie turned the carriage onto a narrow highway. He brought the horses to a stop and jumped down from his seat with a smile on his face.

"Well, what do yer think of it, eh? Hand me Johnny and step outside. You'll see more if yer down from the carriage."

"I don't know what I'm supposed to be looking at, Eddie. All I can see is an ancient windmill, a disused quarry and old decrepit cottage."

"Ah, but feast yer beautiful eyes over there, me darlin'. Across those fields. Do yer see it now, the Irish Sea? You have to admit it's a breathtaking view."

Hannah nodded, too rapt to comment on the rolling meadows and sparkling sea that lay before her. Eddie took her hand in his; he was clearly delighted with it.

"So, now what do yer think of it? Would this be a good place to start afresh, away from the folk that cause yer pain?"

"Well, it might be if yer showed me a different house. You didn't want us to live in that tumbledown cottage, did you?"

"'Course not, come with me. Nothing is too good fer my Hannah," Eddie winked at her secretively. "You take

Johnny and walk behind and I'll lead the horses the rest of the way."

Redstone House stood in an acre of gardens and woodland. It was a splendid residence made from local sandstone, squarely built with narrow leaded windows, a grey slated roof and an archway leading to a large oak door.

"Oh, Eddie," Hannah gasped, as they stood looking through the tall iron gates at the stable block and outbuildings at the top of the gravel drive.

"You're never thinking of buying that; there's no way that we could afford it. And I hope you're not thinking of going in there neither. I look terrible in my old cotton dress and my hair all of a straggle."

"I just wanted yer to see it, that's all, Hannah. If yer like what yer see we'll come back another day. Well, what do yer think then, just on a first sighting?"

"I think it looks wonderful, but like I said before, there's no way we could afford it, Eddie. This would only be a pipe dream for both of us, so I don't know why you brought me here."

"Leave that worry to me, will yer, Hannah? I've got a plan which I'll explain later. Now, when I was here before, I saw a tea shack outside one of the cottages near the heathland. We'll break our journey, shall we, and have a cup of tea?"

–

Maggie too, was standing outside a dwelling that day, weighing up the advantages of living there. The cottage that had belonged to her old friend, Mrs. Dockerty, was in need of some tender repairing. Slates had come off on part of the roof and the front door wanted renewing.

"I don't know why you want to bury yerself down here, Maggie," Bridget said, who had volunteered to ride with her in the donkey and trap. "You're welcome to stay at our place fer as long as yer like. I just can't see the sense in this at all."

"I know I'm welcome, Bridget, but you and Frank are running a business. I don't think it's fair to be taking up a bedroom, especially with all the visitors around at this time of the year."

"But even so, you'll not be able to move in straight away. You'll need a man to do it up and that could take more than a few days, couldn't it?"

"I know what you're saying, Bridget and if I was going to live here, I'd need a bit more room. Maybe something built on the side and the back. I'd need a proper kitchen and another bedroom."

"There you are then," Bridget sounded relieved. "Wait until you've had the baby, then you can come back and have another look. I'm sure no one will have bought it off the owner by then."

"You're probably right, though I wonder if I should purchase it anyway fer the future. Let's go in, shall we, and see what needs doing? That window needs replacing there and that rotting sill."

The memories came flooding back as she stood with Bridget in the small bare living room. The kindnesses of Mrs. Dockerty to a thin, poverty-stricken girl; the hours she'd spent here learning, when she should have been up at the farm and the crush she'd had on Johnny, her elderly friend's son.

She could see it all in her mind's eye as the years flew back with a flashing clarity. She had stood on this same spot twenty-odd years ago, wondering what she should do. Just like she was doing now, wondering and worrying, not sure of her future and the nature of things to come.

It was chilly in the empty room and as Maggie shivered, her baby moved within her, reminding her that any decision had to be based on her or him.

"Come, Bridget, we'll go back now, shall we? It's cold in here, isn't it? Let's get back into the sunshine and warm ourselves up a bit."

—

Eddie and Hannah sat with their baby on a bench outside the tea shack, soaking up the afternoon sun which had grown cooler as the day wore on. The woman there had been friendly, filling up little Johnny's bottle with water from the well and allowing Hannah to change his cloths in the shed that held the lavatory.

"You're not from round here, are yer?" the middle-aged woman observed, as she served them tea in earthenware cups on a tray. "We get a lot of visitors at this time of the year. It's because of the view from the Common and we're not so far from the shore."

"It's very peaceful here," remarked Hannah, feeling relaxed now inside the pretty cottage garden. "We've been looking at a house at the far end of that lane over there. A beautiful place with a lovely view of the Irish Sea."

"That'll be the Kennet's house you've been looking at. They want to move further up to the village now he's retired. The children have flown the nest and I suppose they think the place is too big fer them."

"What about schools around here? And churches? And are there good shops in the village?" Eddie decided to ask the questions that Hannah would want to know.

"There's a small school, down near the church of St. Bartholomew. My youngest, Harry, goes to that, it's just a short walk down the hill. There's a chapel in the grounds of a farmhouse on Mill Hill Road, or yer could travel down to Greasby where I think there's a Catholic church. As fer the village, there's one shop that sells oil, candles, tea, sugar. Anything that yer can't get from the farms. Do yer want another cuppa, there's plenty left in the pot? Or maybe a homemade scone with cream and jam? It'll take yer on 'til your supper time."

-

Two weeks later, Michael was granted weekend leave. He had written to his grandmama, inviting himself to stay at Seagull Cottage. Now that he was feeling better he decided he needed a spy within the vicinity. Someone who could keep their ear to the ground and let him know of anything that could get him back into Selwyn Lodge; his mother returning maybe, or his bitch of a sister running off with the milkman. He wouldn't put it past her; look what happened with Jeremy. Shame that piece of information had lain dormant in his mind. Her ignoramus husband didn't know what he'd taken on!

It had been decided by those above Michael that he was to take on a role in recruitment. An office job, probably as boring as it had been with Sheldon, but it would keep him away from danger if the regiment was sent to the front line.

Besides a spy, Michael felt he needed a sentry. Someone who could report the to-ings and fro-ings, someone who could tell him what was going on. That honour would pass to Staff Nurse Tibbs; he was certain that Katie had a crush on him. He had written a carefully worded letter, hinting that his feelings were far more than just friendship and the pleasure would be his if she agreed to meet with him.

—

Dear Mother

I am sorry that I've not replied to your letter, but Eddie and I have been very busy. We don't want to cause you alarm, but we have decided to move away from the area and set up home elsewhere. We have found a place that has its own quarry and quite a lot of land, so Eddie would like to start a builder's yard, which will mean us moving away.

You might not understand why we are doing this, especially as you have always been so kind to us, but Michael has returned from the Army and I know you wouldn't want us to stand in his way of working for Sheldon again.

To this end, we have decided to wait until I have had my baby, with Eddie overseeing the developments meantime.

I know that you too are in waiting as I am, but Eddie thinks all we will need is a letter from you for the solicitor and the bank to hand over the legalities to your son.

Hope everything goes well with the birth of your baby. Will send new address when we've settled in.

Your affectionate daughter,

Hannah.

Eddie stood at Hannah's side while she sat at the writing bureau reading the letter to him. "You know Hannah," he said worriedly. "This could bring Maggie rushing over, and in her condition I don't think yer being very fair."

Hannah looked at him, askance. She had spent a long time composing the letter, and here he was finding fault with it. "What else do you want me do then? Say nothing, let Michael come in and walk all over us? We are the ones who have to hold the winning cards, or we'll be the losers at the end of the day. While he doesn't have his mother's address, we are sat in the driving seat and this way we can do the negotiating. Anyway, Maggie will be as big as I am by now. Can you see me rushing about or wanting to travel across the sea?"

"No, that's true, me little apple dumpling. *Yer* know, I love yer even more than ever when yer carrying my babies. There's something about yer... I don't know... I want to eat every bit of yer."

Hannah laughed and caught his hand to her face, nuzzling it gently. "That's all I need to hear! You only love me properly when I'm carrying your babies. Does that mean I'll be in a constant state of expectancy, Eddie?"

Eddie laughed with her, thankful that his joking had made their spirits light. Hannah was right on this occasion; Michael must be dealt with, but in a devious way. Their future depended heavily on the decisions that they were making now. There had already been one set back when he had gone cap in hand to Richard Clegg. You'd have thought it was the man's own money when Eddie had asked for a loan of £530. Not Sheldon's money or Maggie's, and he'd even asked for collateral!

"Do yer know who's paying your wages at the moment?" Eddie had said, fixing his strongest glare on the young office manager, though his feet were quaking in his boots. "It's me. I'm Mrs. Haines's second in command whilst she's away on her holiday. I'm the one who makes all the decisions around here."

"I'm sorry, Mr. Dockerty, but for such a large amount we always ask for collateral. It was what I was told when Mr. Arlington trained me. And I was under the impression that I was in charge of the Loans Department and you were responsible for the building company."

"That is as may be, but I'm the one who holds the purse strings, so just remember that."

They had held each other's gaze across the table in the Sheldon office until Richard was the one who gave way. He was dealing with the boss's son-in-law after all, so he had to make an exception, didn't he?

"Perhaps you could get a letter of authorisation from Mrs. Haines?" Richard had made one last attempt at covering his back.

"I'll be in to sign for the money on Tuesday," Eddie snapped and purposely strode away.

He hadn't told any of this to Hannah. How could he tell his little pumpkin that if the business he planned fell by the wayside, they'd be homeless and mortgaged for twenty-five years? Especially now she had set her heart on Redstone House. It would be like taking an ice cream away from little Johnny and that was something he could never do.

"Did you find someone to dig out a drain for the lavatory, Eddie?" Hannah asked, as she sealed the envelope in readiness to send to Ireland the very next day.

"I wasn't happy that we didn't have an inside water closet at Redstone House, as you know, but it's such a perfect spot for your business that I didn't mind making the odd sacrifice like no boiler. But as they have a room with a hip bath in, the lavatory can go in there, can't it? And this maid we'll be having looks strong enough to be carrying the water up the stairs."

"Yes, that's sorted, Hannah. The drain will be laid and will run to the brook near the crossroads. Someone will come and install a lavatory as soon as we take possession, along with the cupboards in the kitchen that you wanted making and that wall yer wanted knocking down so that we could have a conservatory. And I hear that the Kennet's cook would like to stay with us too. She's been with them fer eighteen years, yer know."

"I do know; Mrs. Kennet told me when we were looking the place over. The cook lives nearby in one of those farm cottages and Sadie, the maid, lives down Arrowe Brook Lane. And the beauty of it all is that I won't have to trudge up to the village, like I have to here at Neston. The farmer's wife delivers all the things we need. Oh, Eddie, I'm getting all excited now! I never ever thought we'd get a place of our own."

–

Katie had felt in a whirl of excitement all morning. At last! Michael had written the week before to see if she could manage to meet him on Sunday. He'd been given weekend leave and she was to be outside the Custom House on the promenade at three o'clock because he was taking her to meet his grandmama. His grandmama! She couldn't believe it. Their first date and he was already going to show her off to a member of his family. Well, she thought it was a date. Young men didn't usually ask to meet a girl unless they had those sorts of intentions. And luckily it was her day off too, so she hadn't needed to change her shift.

She ran her hands down her best navy skirt, hoping that it didn't look too fussy. It was an ankle-length layered skirt, made of a thin taffeta, and with it she wore a cream, high-necked, pin-tucked blouse. Being the middle of September, there was a possibility that the afternoon could be cool by the river, so she had teamed her outfit up with a navy woollen jacket, hoping that it didn't look too obvious that the navy was a different shade. Her button boots were black, so she carried a matching-coloured reticule and her hair was pinned up neatly under a cream, saucer-shaped hat.

The church clock struck the quarter hour as Katie hurried up the high street, passed the fountain at the Cross and down Parkgate Road to the Custom House. She had stayed the night at Annie's, having the use of the sofa again, as all the beds were full and there was no room to swing a cat. The problem of what to do with Ernie still hadn't been resolved to Katie's satisfaction. He hadn't been seen by the family, though Sam was down at the farmhouse collecting milk every day. She wondered if Ernie had gone back to his old ways, preferring to be a fowler or fishing in the sea? Her brother was a loner; only really happy when he was out in his punt with a gun.

She suddenly felt nervous when she saw Michael waiting where he had suggested. She had expected to see him in uniform, but he wore the clothes of a gentleman; a dark frock coat over narrow grey trousers and a shiny black top hat. He was carrying a cane and, as he saw Katie come around the corner, he tipped it towards her in greeting. A simple gesture, but that action made her bashful and ready for immediate flight. After all, Michael was an officer and she was just a lowly girl. He lifted his hat in deference to her as she walked towards him with a quaking heart.

Oh, why had she agreed to see him? They had nothing in common at all.

"Staff Nurse Tibbs, or may I call you Katie?" He smiled engagingly at her and proffered an outstretched hand. "I must thank you for your kindness in agreeing to meet me today. And may I take the liberty of saying how fetching you look in your outfit? Very different, if I may say so, from the drab uniform you nurses have to wear."

Katie went pink at the compliment, then thought she was ready for fainting when Michael put out his arm.

"Shall we walk together to my grandmama's? She is expecting us to take tea with her. She would like to thank you personally for the care that you gave to me."

"But it was Sister Gill who looked after you in Isolation," Katie replied feeling a little guilty. "Surely your grandma should be inviting her for tea."

"Ah, but you were the one who helped me to full recovery and you are the one to be rewarded. I am sure my grandmama will have already written to Sister Gill to thank her for her part."

A silence fell between them then as they walked the few yards to Seagull Cottage. Katie's spirits plummeted when she realised why she was there. It wasn't a date she was having with Michael. It was afternoon tea with a grateful patient's grandma. Made a change from the flowers or biscuits or whatever her discharged patients usually gave. Oh well, she sighed, she'd make the best of it anyway. It was better than searching for her missing brother instead.

Alice was waiting in her doorway. Her face was a wreath of smiles as the couple came into view. The years had not been kind to Alice; her skin was wrinkled and she had put on a lot of weight. But her smile seemed really genuine as she shook Katie's hand. She led the way to the dining room, where a man stood formally near where a table was laid for tea.

"Welcome, Staff Nurse Tibbs," he said, and gestured her to a seat beside him. "A bit of a chill in the air today, isn't there? Looks like Autumn is on it's way."

Katie nodded wondering who the person was. Michael had never mentioned a granddad before, so who on earth could this person be? She felt her knees shaking nervously as she sat down near the fireplace. She was feeling so self-conscious in front of everyone. What if she dropped a cake or scone or slopped her tea all over the place? An afternoon with strangers: it was the first time in her life!

"I'm sorry," apologised Alice. "I haven't introduced you to Mr. Arlington. He's my husband, by the way. Take her jacket, will yer dear, she'll be roasting hot in here. Michael, do you want to come and help me with the tea things? No, no Miss Tibbs, Michael can help me. You sit with Mr. Arlington by the fire and have a chat together. There's not very much to carry, we won't be very long."

As soon as Alice got into the kitchen, she shut the door and gripped her grandson by the arm. "She's perfect, Michael, just perfect. Good child-bearing hips, of pleasant appearance, trained in nursing, she can look after me when I'm old. An asset to the family, Michael, just what you're looking for. If you can get her to marry yer before that mother of yours comes back to Neston, there's no doubt about it; everything will be yours."

"But, Grandmama, do you think that this plan of yours will work? I don't want to get saddled with just anybody if there's a chance the plan won't work."

"We've been over all this, Michael, but I'll tell yer again. You've still got three years left of your commission, so you need someone there in Selwyn Lodge to keep the place warm. Once you have a wife, you can go to a solicitor and tell them that you're being denied access to the family home. You can say that Hannah isn't even related to the owner, Maggie Haines, but you're her legal son. If worst comes to worst they'll get a policeman to eject them, then you can take up the strings again and claim what's rightfully yours."

"And how will I run the businesses from Chester?"

"Mr. Arlington will go back to help yer. He's getting under my feet here and he needs something to do."

Chapter 20

The front door of the hotel slammed shut from the force of the ferocious wind after Frank took the letters from the postman.

"One fer you, Maggie," he cried, as he walked down the hallway to the dining room. "The rest are bills, Bridget. One from the butcher and one from Fred Ellery. He'll be needing to come back again to fix the roofing. One of the slates has come off again."

He sat himself down beside Maggie, who had just finished her breakfast of oatmeal and honey. "Are yer not going to open your letter then?"

"Oh, it's only from Hannah. I can tell by her writing. It'll be something and nothing. I'll read it later when I've helped Bridget finish in here. Then I need to go over to see Mr. Ellery, see how he's coming along with the roof at the cottage. He won't be down at Killala, will he, seeing as it's blowing a gale?"

"Not if he's sensible he won't be, Maggie. I wouldn't like to be on the headland in this weather, it could blow a fellow right into the sea. In fact I'm surprised yer even asked him to go ahead with everything. With winter coming, he'll find it hard enough to find a day that won't be blowing or lashing it down with rain. I'd have left it until next April, after Easter or early spring."

"Yer know I want to be in the cottage as soon as the baby comes, Frank. It isn't fair to you and Bridget. You've a living to make from your lodgers and they'll not be happy with a crying baby keeping them awake at night. Besides, I lived down in Killala fer sixteen years and the weather didn't harm me then. And that was in a tiny turf cabin, not a strongly-built cottage like that one is."

"It was a bit of luck Frank finding out who was selling fer Mr. Dockerty, wasn't it?" Bridget said as she brought them in a fresh pot of tea.

"Yeah, and I only got that from Fred when he was bringing around the slates. I didn't know that the solicitor on Tebling Street sold property for other people. Still now we know, don't we? Did yer ever meet Mr. Dockerty, Maggie, when yer worked at the farm?"

Maggie coloured slightly and played with the teacup in front of her. "Only briefly," she said, keeping her head down so she couldn't meet Frank's eyes. "I knew his mother better, Mrs. Dockerty. She was very good to me."

"Well, I'm sure he'll be pleased to hear that someone has bought his cottage. Does anyone know where he's gone to? Did the solicitor say?"

"No, he just took the money order and got me to sign a few forms. I suppose it wasn't necessary to tell me where the owner lived. Bridget, leave those dishes; I'm still capable of clearing a table and washing up, yer know."

Maggie heaved her bulk from the table, glad of the excuse to get away from Frank and his scrutiny. If the couple ever knew of her deceitfulness and falsehoods, they'd be chasing her down to Killala, blowing gales or not!

The two women worked companionably beside each other in the kitchen, Maggie washing the dishes in the stone sink by the window and Bridget drying them with a cloth.

"Are yer sure you want to go out in this, Maggie? From the way those trees over there are bending, you could be flying through the air!"

Maggie laughed at the picture her words had conjured. "I don't think so, Bridget, it would take two strong men to lift me at the moment. Besides, I need to know if Mr. Ellery has managed to find some matching stone fer the two new rooms he's building me."

"I'm sure he will have or he'd let yer know. Leave him to it, Maggie, that's what you're paying him to do."

"I suppose yer right. I'll stay in then. I'll read the letter from Hannah then I'll settle down to some sewing. I do miss my treadle, yer know, Bridget, sewing by hand is awful slow."

"Why don't yer go into the sitting room, Maggie? I've lit a fire in there and you can use the table if yer need to. Then in an hour or so I'll bring yer in a cup of tea."

–

Maggie read Hannah's words in disbelief. Michael had come back from the Army? How had that occurred? What was he doing back in Neston? Why hadn't Hannah written the reason for his return? Well, this must have put the cat amongst the pigeons. His stepsister married to the pot man from the village and living with their son in Selwyn Lodge!

Oh, why hadn't she written a reply to Michael's letter? His return would cause a magnitude of problems and from the sound of Hannah's letter, it seemed it already had.

Maggie chewed on her lip, thinking back to the day when Michael had heard of his father's infidelity. He had taken it very badly. It was one of the reasons he had insisted on taking a commission up. That and the fact that he had found out Hannah was illegitimate. One of Michael's bad points was his failure to forgive.

She sat for a moment reminiscing with her hands resting on her distended stomach. This baby seemed much larger than when she was carrying her son. It kicked a lot and hurt her ribs, pressed on her bladder so that she'd wee herself. Had Michael been this much trouble? Had he turned somersaults in the womb and given his mother a fright? Sadly, she couldn't remember. It had been twenty-three years ago.

Bridget came in later to see Maggie staring ahead at a painting on the wall. "I've always liked that painting, Maggie. Frank's mother did it, yer know? Couldn't read or write, but a dab hand at the artistry."

"Sorry, Bridget, me mind was wandering. Yes, it's a very pretty painting, isn't it? Looks like she's sat on the bridge over the River Brosna while she did it, 'cos there's the castle up on the hill."

"I've brought yer some coffee, Maggie. Just to cheer yer up as we're stuck in the house today. Did yer have good news in your letter from Hannah? Is she well? You said she was expecting near the same time as you."

"Bridget, did I ever tell yer I had a son who was in the Army? No?" Her friend shook her head. "Well, I have this son who is twenty-three. I bought him an officer commission two years ago. He thought it would be exciting going off with his friends to see a bit of the world. I think he got caught up with the thrill of it all, then found he'd made a big mistake. He wrote to me about seven or eight months ago, asking me to buy him out. Unfortunately, I was so tied up with other things that I forgot to reply to him.

Now Hannah has written to tell me that he's come back home from India. I was just thinking that it will put the cat amongst the pigeons, 'cos Hannah and him don't get on."

"So what is Hannah saying? Does she want yer to go back to England? She must know that you'll not be in any fit state to do so."

"That's the problem, really, she's not telling me very much, other than she and Eddie have found another place to live and will I do the necessary legalities from here, so Michael can take over the running of the firm? But I don't want Michael to take over running Sheldon Property. I have a perfectly good man in Eddie. He made sure the houses were completed when he said they would be; he made sure the snagging lists were kept to the minimum; he oversaw the ganger's work and drew their weekly wages. I couldn't fault him as my manager, but Michael's got a lot to learn. He must have been causing a lot of trouble already 'cos Hannah says Eddie has found a place with its own quarry and quite a bit of land, so he's going to set up a building yard. Though she does say he'll carry on working fer Sheldon until after she's had the baby. So where is Michael living? That's what I'd like to know."

Bridget poured their coffee from the silver pot, something else inherited from Frank's dead mother. She passed Maggie a dainty china cup, then sat down beside her, trying her best to think of a way to reassure her worried friend.

Maggie suddenly slapped a hand to her forehead, making Bridget jump. "That's it! Alice! She'll be in this somewhere. He'll be living with her at Seagull Cottage, waiting for me to send them something official. Well, I won't, Bridget. I'll make them sweat. If Eddie's willing to

346

stay on at Sheldon, while I'm here waiting to have the baby, then so it shall be."

–

Katie sat at her desk on Thornton Ward, thinking back to the previous Sunday with mixed feelings. It was strange how she'd been treated by the grandma and Mr. Arlington. It was as if they were trying very hard to please her and she couldn't for the life of her see the reason why. All she had done for them was nurse their sick grandson; something that she did every day for the patients in her care. Take for instance Peter Robertson, a young man brought in yesterday with gangrene in his foot. Would Mr. and Mrs. Robertson be inviting her around for Sunday tea in the future? She thought not, though maybe Peter wasn't a good enough argument. The poor lad would probably die next week if the surgeon didn't cut off his leg.

Then there was Michael's behaviour towards her. He had treated her like a china doll, or at least someone who belonged to the gentry. Asking was she comfortable, would she like another scone? Helping her on with her jacket and walking her back to Annie's house. She had thought that the afternoon had gone well, considering that they were virtual strangers. She'd relaxed a little when she was asked about her job and she had told them all of her hopes of becoming a nursing sister one day. The only thing that had brought a frown to Michael's grandma's face was when she had asked about Katie's family. Something she'd said maybe, but there was a coolness in the room from then.

Never mind, Katie sighed, it had all been a new experience. To see how other people lived and to see inside their homes. And did it matter if his grandma had taken a dislike to her? Michael had said he'd write again and that's what mattered, didn't it?

—

After Michael had taken Katie back home, he walked slowly back to Seagull Cottage.

Something was puzzling him about his grandmama. One minute she was praising Katie to the rooftops, then she seemed to push the girl away. His grandmama could be quite peculiar sometimes. Look how she'd married Mr. Arlington, a mismatch if there ever was. Him, a gentleman used to giving orders, dominated by his little wife who was several years older than him.

He remembered back to his childhood, when in his early years Grandmama seemed to figure in everything. She took him on walks, played silly games, sat on the shore while he paddled in the waves. Then suddenly there was no more Grandmama. Only Mother and a dainty doll of a sister and they had moved to a great big house with a garden to play in and a nursemaid. There was someone else too, who looked as old as his grandmama, but he had to call her Aunt Betty. She didn't play or walk with him and he had to be good if she looked after him. It had been like that until his father returned, then back came Grandmama, appearing once more in his life.

"Is that you, Michael?" Alice called, as her grandson walked into the hallway.

"I'm in the kitchen cutting yer some sandwiches for your journey tomorrow. Come through and I'll make yer a cup of tea."

"Grandmama, you don't have to make me sandwiches," said Michael, as he walked through to speak with her. "I've only got half an hour on the train to Chester, then I'm nearly at the barracks. I can get breakfast in the Officer's Mess when I get there."

"Yer need your strength, Michael, after all that sickness. Yer need building up again. These will keep the wolf from the door. And while I think about it, yer don't seem to have good judgement seeing as you are an officer. That young woman yer brought here today, a gold digger if ever there was one. Coming here, pretending that butter wouldn't melt in her mouth. I know what she's up to."

"But Grandmama, you were the one who invited her here," said Michael, looking at his elderly relative in astonishment. "I thought you wanted to look her over so that she could be part of the plan."

"Well, yer didn't tell me she was Ruthie Tibbs' daughter, did yer? Her father was the one who tried to diddle your father out of the takings, after a fight at the quarry in '48."

"That was years ago, Grandmama. How could Katie be held to account for something her father did?"

"They were rubbish, them Tibbses. The father a drunk and the mother a big fat loud mouth. Did yer know they lived in that tumbledown cottage, near where your mother used to live?"

"I can't see how it's got anything to do with Katie, Grandmama. She's worked hard to become a staff nurse. If what you're saying is true, I admire her for pulling herself up from her humble beginnings, and when you think about it, Grandmama, so should you."

"Well, whatever," Alice huffed, having the grace to look a little ashamed of herself. "When will you be coming back again, Michael? It doesn't do to let the fire go out, yer know. You have to keep fanning the flames and letting them know you intend to get what's due to yer."

"I know that, but the problem is I have no recourse. Not when they've got permission from my mother to live in the place and to oversee Sheldon. I need to find her address from somewhere or maybe visit her solicitor."

"I can help yer with that one, Michael. I can send Mr. Arlington up to see that fellow that he trained up. Richard Clegg, I think he was called. He can tell yer who the solicitor is, then you can go to see him and make your claim."

"Oh, Grandmama, what would I do without you?" Michael stooped to kiss Alice on the cheek, who pushed him away with a satisfied smile on her face.

–

Hannah lay on her bed at Selwyn Lodge, her face perspiring as her contractions began coming every minute or so. The hired midwife wiped her client's forehead with one of the birthing rags and smiled at her in encouragement.

"Come now, Mrs. Dockerty, you've done all this before. Keep breathing in and breathing out. That's right, don't start pushing yet."

Hannah gritted her teeth and tried to do the midwife's bidding. Though each searing pain was in itself the very devil in its agony, Hannah knew they would bring her nearer to the end of it all. She tried to fix her mind on somewhere or something that gave her pleasure. Redstone House, it had to be, and little Johnny. She conjured up pictures of her child riding on a pony; pity her father had gone and sold Simba; trotting around the paddock at the back of the house. Another pain, another picture; Eddie standing at the front of his quarry, a contented smile upon his face. Redstone House blurred with Selwyn Lodge. Which one had the apple orchard, which the conservatory?

"Mrs. Dockerty, it's time fer pushing. I can see the head, now push again." The midwife was crouching at the bottom of the bed.

"Now pant, stop pushing, pant again, stop pushing. Now big push, I can see its shoulders. Now rest, now pant, another push. There, you've nearly done it. One more big push..."

Hannah felt as if she was being split in two as the baby made its way into the world. It slithered with a mighty plop into the midwife's hands.

"It's a boy, another boy, Mrs. Dockerty, let me just see to the cord fer him. There, you can have the little lad when I've wiped him down. Oh, wait a minute he isn't crying. Let me give him a slap on the bum... Sorry about that. Here, take him from me, he's fine now he's crying. Put him to yer breast, there, that's right, let him suck while I get the other lot out." The midwife busied herself, wrapping up the afterbirth in a Chester newspaper and throwing away the contents on the blazing bedroom fire. "Well, I think I've nearly finished. I'll go down to the kitchen and get a cup of tea, if yer don't mind. Shall I bring yer some and then we'll dress him, then I'll tidy up all the mess? Unless yer want me to do it fer yer now, but I thought you'd rather be alone fer a time."

"I do, thank you, Midwife Thompson. We need to get to know each other, don't we, Georgie? Don't let my husband come up until we have had a little tidy. I want to look my best for him, not a total wreck."

Hannah lay back gazing with affection at the tiny features on her little son's wrinkled face. His skin was red and his cheeks looked blotchy, his eyes had pouches underneath, but the rest of him looked strong and healthy as she pulled back his blanket to satisfy herself. Well, that hadn't been as bad as she thought it would be. A few cramps this morning after breakfast, a stronger back ache by lunch time when she had sent for the midwife, a few hours of pushing and panting and lots and lots of pain, but look what she'd got at the end of it all. Another little Dockerty to put in the nursery!

–

Across the sea in Ballina, her stepmother began her birth pangs a few weeks later. This time in the back bedroom of the Heaney Hotel, with a doctor and a midwife in attendance.

The hotel was shut in the winter months, allowing Frank and Bridget to take a rest from it. They sat in the kitchen listening to the moan of the wind in the garden treetops as they waited for the midwife to come downstairs.

"Surely she'd be down by now wanting a kettle of water," whispered Bridget, scared to speak at all, in case she missed any of the noises that came from overhead.

"I don't know much about it, Bridget, as yer know. I don't know why yer want me here at all."

"Moral support or if there's a problem, Frank. Though the doctor's up there with her anyway. Poor Maggie, she's been at it now since Thursday morning. I think that's why the midwife's got him here."

"Well, how long does it take fer a woman to have a baby? Hours, days, weeks? Never having been in that position, I'm not sure what is going on."

"Yer want to hear of the tales that Agatha comes out with. Yer know, tales of the girls giving birth in the convent. She was only telling me about this young woman who…"

"No, Bridget! No more." Frank put his hands over his ears, so he couldn't hear his wife. "I think I'll go down to the river and drop in fer a drink at Matty's. His wife's got six, yer know and I've never heard him complain."

"Get me some fish from Hancock's then on yer way back. Maggie always likes a bit of fish on Fridays, so I'll steam her some fer after the birth."

Bridget was left alone, waiting anxiously. Should she go up to the bedroom and offer to make them all a cup of tea? They must be really needing one by now. Poor Maggie. It was after she had got out of bed yesterday morning that she had complained to Bridget that her back was sore and aching. Bridget had ordered her back to bed and sent Frank down to Mrs. Murphy's to say that Maggie's time had come.

Upstairs in Maggie's bedroom, the doctor shook his head in despair at the woman who lay white-faced and weak with her efforts to bring her baby into the world.

"I should have been called earlier, Mrs. Murphy. It's lying across her instead of down. No wonder there's been nothing happening for the past few hours."

The plump, round-faced midwife jerked her head at his accusation from where she was standing at the end of the bed. "I was under the impression that Mrs. Haines has not had a child fer twenty-three years, Doctor," she countered coldly. "This means the birth is bound to be a slow one, just like it is her first."

"Yes, that is a probability, but did yer check its position and listen to its heart?"

"I did all that and I've been trying to coax the child into the birth channel, but every time I do that it goes across again. That's why I sent fer you, Doctor. The patient has had hours of fruitless pain and agony and now she needs more help than I can give."

"Yes, well, you were right to do so," Dr Kerrigan said, mollified. He drew himself up to his full height of five feet nine inches and grimaced at the task he had ahead.

"There's an opium mixture in my bag, give her some of that so she's out of it a little. Then whoever is in charge of boiling water, I want a bowl for washing my instruments and I think we could do with a hot cup of tea."

The midwife nodded and, after coaxing Maggie to take a good slug of the doctor's brownish-coloured liquid, sped down the stairs where Bridget lay in waiting.

"Is Mrs. Haines all right, Mrs. Murphy? Can I be of any help?"

"Yes, yer can be of help, Mrs. Heaney. Your friend needs your prayers; she's barely coping. The little one's lying across her, so all her efforts have come to nothing. We need a bowl of hot water and the doctor's asking fer a cup of tea. I'll have one too if possible. Me hands are shaking – look at them."

"Oh, poor Maggie. I'm glad I've never had any babies, Mrs. Murphy. I hear so many awful tales from our Agatha, yer know, me sister who's at the convent where they take in fallen women? I used to think I was missing something by not having any, but we've been so busy with the hotel and that, it wouldn't have been fair to have brought one up in our kind of world."

"Children cope in most places, Mrs. Heaney, but as yer know, not everyone is blessed with a gift of one. I've been lucky really, all mine have reached adulthood and gone off to make new lives fer themselves, but I've never had the problems like Mrs. Haines is having. Mine couldn't wait to get here, they came out like one of Hancock's slippery eels!"

"Do yer think the doctor will be able to help her?" Bridget asked anxiously, while she poured the water from the boiling kettle into a large mixing bowl.

"Oh, he's bound to," the midwife said confidently, as she stood in the doorway of the kitchen, waiting for the bowl to be handed over. "Can yer bring up the tea and leave it outside the bedroom door? I saw a small table on the landing that yer could put it on. I'd better go now; his tools of the trade have to be soaked in this water, then we'll wait until that medicine he's given her starts to do the trick."

Maggie lay on her bed, staring in desperation at the ceiling. Her stomach felt as if she'd been crushed under the wheels of a heavily loaded farm cart. There'd been no respite from it since Bridget had insisted that she went back to her bed. The midwife had been so tender at first, massaging the base of her back, murmuring encouragement every time another pain had gripped, listening intently through her little ear trumpet at the large and rippling mound. But a little while ago – or was it hours ago? – the midwife had seemed to sense a problem. The baby's head had not come down; it was lying across Maggie's stomach instead.

"I might have to send fer the doctor, Mrs. Haines," she had said, trying to keep the panic from her voice. "I'll try me best to bring it round before I do so, but I think he'd best be here anyway. Now breathe fer me like this, while I do it." And she showed Maggie how to breathe in deeply, wait and then breathe out slowly again.

The excruciating pain was too much then, and Maggie screeched as the woman tried in vain to turn the baby. She felt a jolt and then a settling, then the light around her seemed to fade away. The midwife tried again, this time without Maggie's help or caring. She'd gone for a moment to a different place, where there was no sense of time or pain.

She awoke to misty shadows, with a man standing above her, staring down at her face. A familiar face, but one that was looking very grim.

"Mrs. Haines, it's Doctor Kerrigan. A little problem with the baby. Can you hear me, dear? I'll need your co-operation if we're to get the child safely out of there."

She stared back at him dazedly, then nodded, willing him to do anything that would take this pain from Hell away. Then the midwife brought a horrible-tasting mixture and it seemed as if her body had started floating then; floating above the bed, while she looked on down at the scene below.

She saw her legs were raised and parted just like a chicken, a chicken that was ready for the stuffing to be placed inside. Then the doctor putting his head on her stomach while plunging his hand and arm within. An odd sensation, a strange sensation; as if the man was rearranging the contents of her insides. Then a pulling, a tugging, a mighty plop, then the man's head appearing above her again.

"Start pushing, Mrs. Haines! Mrs. Murphy, hold her hand and I'll tell her when to push again! I can see the head, ah, push now, stop, push now, rest. Oh, God, she'll not be feeling her contractions, I'll have to get the forceps and do the rest myself!"

The midwife ran to Bridget's mixing bowl and lifted out a pair of metal blades. She wiped them carefully with a birthing cloth and handed them to the sweating doctor. She watched in fascination as he attached one blade to each side of the baby's little head and started pulling. There wasn't any movement, so he shouted to Maggie to try to push again. From somewhere inside his patient's brain the command began to filter and she heard this terrible mooing sound, like a cow that had its byre nearby.

"Got it! Ah, she's a little beauty," the doctor gasped, then he cut the cord that attached the child to Maggie, turned the infant upside down and slapped it sharply on the shoulder. The child took in a lung full of air and began to cry plaintively.

"It's yellow, doctor," Mrs. Murphy said wonderingly, as she took the whimpering baby off him and wrapped it up in a large square of rag. "Have yer seen this? It's like one of those chinky babies." She lowered her voice and said to the doctor. "Do yer think the father was one of those Chinese men?"

"Not that I'm aware of I met the now-deceased Mr. Haines last year and he looked as white as you or me do. Anyway, see to Mrs. Haines, will you? Give me the child back and I'll call for Mrs. Heaney. She can be cleaning and dressing it downstairs while you make your patient comfortable. I fear that our tea will probably have gone cold now, so perhaps she can be persuaded to make another one."

Maggie groaned as Mrs. Murphy pressed on her sore stomach in an effort to bring out the afterbirth. The feeling was beginning to return in her body and everything that the opium mixture had managed to block out returned with a vengeance. She felt so weary. She wanted to sleep for a million years, or at least until these horrible pains had gone away from her. Something kept dragging in the back of her mind and she wondered why it was that she'd been suffering such a torment. Perhaps an even worse bout of flu than the one she'd caught in Liverpool that time. Though why did her private parts below feel so sore and tender?

"Doctor's taken her down to Mrs. Heaney. He'll be slipping a drop of brandy into his cup of tea by now."

"Taken who? Oh!" It all came flooding back to her. "Taken my baby. What did I have? Oh God, the suffering."

"You had a little girl. A tiny little thing, but doctor says she's a beauty. Yer wouldn't believe that such a little thing could cause such mayhem. We nearly lost yer, Mrs. Haines, in fact at one time I thought we had! But never mind, here yer still are. Now, lift yerself up for me and I'll clear away those dirty rags."

Down in the kitchen the doctor was helping himself to a tot of brandy while Frank did the honours of making the tea. Bridget clucked away like a mother hen, as she washed the tiny newborn on a clean towel laid on the table.

"Poor little thing, what did the doctor do to yer then? Will these little bruises go, Dr Kerrigan? I could put some arnica on. Oh, in a day or two, they'll begin to fade then. Have yer seen her tiny lashes, Frank? They're like little curly feathers, and look at her sweet little nails; they look like tiny shells you'd find on the shore. Oh, the little dote. Come to me, sweetheart, while I wrap yer up in the pretty shawl your mama made yer. Oh, Frank, isn't she adorable? Just come and have a look."

"There is a bit of a problem, Mrs. Heaney," the doctor broke in, as Bridget happily cuddled the child to her chest.

"You'll have noticed that her skin is a bit on the yellow side, which isn't natural at all. I don't know what causes it and it could clear up in a few days."

"They've had that at the convent," Bridget said. "Yer know I have a sister there, Doctor? She's always telling me what goes on with those fallen women that are in her care. Perhaps she could tell us what to do next time we see her."

"A better idea would be to take the baby over," said her husband. "Better to be safe than sorry, don't yer think?"

"I would agree with you, Mr. Heaney, if it wasn't for the fact that Mrs. Haines should be suckling her baby now. Ideally, the child should have gone straight to the breast, but I had given my patient a good deal of mixture to help her through it all and I don't want it to affect her baby in any way. I could bind her breasts though and give her time to recover, then when you bring the baby back we could unbind her breasts again."

"But meantime, what will the baby live off? It's not as if we could lay our hands on a bottle and a teat, is it, Frank?"

"Surely the convent could solve that problem too?"

The doctor looked at his fob watch. It was time he was off; his job was done. His tummy was rumbling and he knew his housekeeper would be keeping his dinner warm for him. "I'll look in on Mrs. Haines next time I'm passing, but meanwhile I'll leave you all in the midwife's capable hands."

"He shot off a bit quick, didn't he?" said Mrs. Murphy, when she came down to burn the rags on the kitchen fire.

"Did he say anything about all this yellowy skin? Oh, look, she's sleeping; she must be as tired as her mammy."

"I was telling him that they've had babies like this at the convent and Frank suggested we took her there so the nuns could take a look."

"I don't know," said the midwife, uncertainly. "She hasn't had a feed yet, but her mother's so exhausted that she's fallen asleep. Do yer think yer could get her back in a couple of hours?"

"The doctor was saying that he'd given Maggie a little mixture, so he was going to bind her breasts up for a little while anyway."

"Oh yes, the opium. I suppose he thinks it would be dangerous if that was passed on through the breast milk. Well, I'll do as he says and *I'll* bind her up, as long as you're back in a couple of hours."

"Does anybody know what Maggie was going to call this baby?" asked Frank, as he took the child from his wife, while she filled a basket with cloths and baby clothes then donned her heavy shawl.

"Yes, she told me yesterday," the midwife said. "It's Rosemary. Rosemary fer a little girl, Bernard fer a boy."

Chapter 21

Eddie came striding into the drawing room at Selwyn Lodge where Hannah was sitting breastfeeding Georgie. Her husband's eyes were angry as he threw himself down beside her on the settee.

"What's got you into a tizzy, Eddie?" Hannah asked, as she pushed little Johnny towards his father. "See, grab Johnny before he falls over, will you? He's taken his first steps today and he keeps falling down and hurting himself."

Eddie lifted the child up on to his knee, feeling himself growing calmer as he stroked his little boy's downy head. "Mr. Arlington's been into the office. Richard said he called in this morning and was wanting to know where Maggie is. Said he wanted her address and the address of her solicitor. Yer know what all this is about, don't you?"

"Well, it's obvious that Alice sent him. Probably on behalf of Michael. It doesn't matter, does it, Eddie? I thought we had decided to make life difficult for him."

"It's not that, it's all this sneaking around that gets to me. Why can't Michael just turn up on the doorstep here instead of getting his grandma and Mr. Arlington involved?"

"Because basically, Michael's a coward. Always has been really. When we were little he was always running

361

to Maggie or telling our nursemaid instead of squaring up to me."

Eddie smiled. "So yer weren't Miss Goody Two Shoes then? That's what you've always told me?"

"No, I wasn't. But he can have the lot in a couple of months when we've moved ourselves into Redstone House."

"It's a pity that Maggie hasn't written back yet," Eddie remarked. "I'd be a whole lot happier if she'd sent over some legal papers for us. We don't even know if she wants Michael to take over the business and the absence of her authorisation is making me think that she doesn't."

"Well, whatever she thinks it's too late now, isn't it? You've put down the money for our new house now. Come on, cheer up, soon you'll be the Master of all you survey!"

That's the trouble, Eddie thought worriedly. Will I be the Master of very much?

"Were you just passing by, Eddie, or are you finished for the day? It looks rather murky outside. I suppose we can't expect anything different at this time of the year."

"I'd popped in to see Richard over something, Hannah, that's when he told me. I'm on me way to Daisy Bank to check out two of the villas. We've two families wanting to move in before Christmas, but with darkness coming so early now there's a bit of a scramble to be ready in time."

"I've every faith in your capabilities, my darling," said Hannah. "On your way out tell Olive to bring me in a cup of tea, will you? Oh and by the way, she's leaving when we do. She's gone and found herself another place."

—

Katie walked down the High street to wait at the Cross to catch the hospital visitor's bus. She had stayed again at Annie's house, hoping and praying that a letter would come from Michael. It had been weeks now since their afternoon tea at Seagull Cottage; something that she looked back upon with an excited little thrill. She was visiting Barleymow Terrace a lot more now than she used to do, making Annie wonder if she was being checked upon. Their brother had appeared from heavens knows where and a repentant Annie now cooked and cleaned for him.

Or rather, Mrs. Piper did, so Katie thought. She had a lot of sympathy for Annie's mother-in-law.

–

It was three days before Rosemary was returned to Maggie. Three days that Maggie hardly noticed, as she lay in her bedroom drifting in and out of a sleep-filled haze. The midwife had tiptoed in apologetically, changing her patient's bindings, smoothing warm castor oil on her patient's tender breasts, helping her onto the chamber pot and wiping down her hands and face.

It was a bit of a shock for Maggie when she suddenly found herself staring down at the trusting face of a tiny infant, its brown eyes staring up at her and its round pink mouth twitching hungrily.

This must be Rosemary, Maggie sighed; her and Johnny's love child.

Bridget was standing at the end of the bed, watching the reunion gleefully.

"See, Maggie. The nuns have worked their miracles. Pinker than pink now they've got rid of that awful yellow. I knew they would, and now our little Rosemary's reunited with her mammy."

She found herself brushing away a tear with her emotion, asked if anyone wanted a cup of tea and quickly ran from the bedroom.

"She's overcome, poor little gosling," said Mrs. Murphy, to no one in particular. "Now, we'll get this binding off yer, shall we, and baby can have a good suck? That should bring your milk a flowing. It'll hurt fer a minute, but the more yer do it the easier it'll get. Now," and she took Maggie's breast in one hand and shoved the hungry baby onto the nipple. "That should do it."

–

It was snowing in Ballina that Christmas time. People scurried off to church for various Masses, bought food to last them for days and chose little presents for their loved ones on the stalls at the market; children made snowmen and played with their friends.

In the back bedroom of the Heaney hotel, Maggie sat in a low chair nursing her baby. Why didn't she love this little child she'd recently given birth to, she wondered? The tiny girl was beautiful and, now she had got into a routine of feeding and sleeping, was no trouble at all. She stared at Rosemary's perfect little features. A button nose, a rosebud mouth, black shiny hair that was already beginning to curl, dainty little hands with fingers that curled confidently around Maggie's and clear pink skin on her lovely face.

Bridget had dressed the child for Maggie. She'd done it willingly every morning, as Maggie couldn't bear to lift or bend. Is that the problem, Maggie thought. I blame the poor child for all my pain?

"I've brought yer a bit of cake and a cup of tea, Maggie. Can I hold the baby while yer drink your tea?" Bridget came in, bustling with energy and eagerly swooped to pick up the baby. "Oh, will yer look at her in her pretty frock. You're so clever with your crochet hook, Maggie. Now, yer will try to come downstairs tomorrow fer your Christmas dinner, won't yer? Frank and I are going to Midnight Mass this evening, which will give me plenty of time in the morning to cook our dinner. I've got a fresh chicken from Hancock's and I went this afternoon to the market fer the vegetables, and Frank and I have bought a little something fer our Rosemary."

"You shouldn't go spending your money," Maggie said wearily. "Especially fer a baby who doesn't know it's Christmas Day."

"Well, we've got something fer you too."

"Oh, Bridget, I've nothing fer either of you being laid up here with the baby. But next week's me third week and I can start getting back on my feet again."

"But yer can come down tomorrow, Maggie, can't you? Just fer a couple of hours? We really want to celebrate Rosemary's first Christmas in the family."

—

"Matron wants to see you, Staff Nurse," said Sister Gill, as Katie was halfway through the first shift of the New Year. "Something exciting perhaps to start the year off well. Run along now; I can see to young Mr. Robertson for you. Pass me over that walking crutch before you go."

Katie sped along on winged feet to Matron's office. It must be a letter from Michael. He had probably been too busy to see her over Christmas time and to make amends had sent one via the hospital. Oh, it would be worth all the heartache she'd been having, just to see his writing and read his words once again.

"Come in, Staff Nurse Tibbs – or shall I call you Sister now? I've had word from the Hospital Board this morning. The examination you undertook a few weeks ago was deemed successful and that, coupled with the tenacity you have shown as Sister Gill's assistant, has made them decide to reward you with the title of Nursing Sister. Therefore, Sister Tibbs, you will be in charge of the Women's Ward from January 6th!"

–

Dear Mother

I am writing to let you know of the birth of George Alexander Dockerty, born on 23rd November. He is a charming little chap, doesn't give me any trouble and has a look of me already. Little Johnny has begun to walk now and seems to be happy with his new brother. I am assuming you will have had your baby by now and hope everything went well with the birth.

We are moving to our new house in February. Eddie wouldn't let me go to Chester to choose our furniture – he said that I have enough to cope with, so I hope his taste in furniture is similar to mine, or there could be a few arguments!

This is our new address, so that you can write to let us know of any decisions you have made regarding the running of the company.

Redstone House, Mill Hill Lane, Irby, Wirral.

Eddie is still overseeing the development, although I think it is nearly finished now, and will

be, Eddie says, by the time we move out of here.
Although I have to tell you that Mr. Arlington
seems to have a great interest in Sheldon all of a
sudden. He has been 'supervising' Richard Clegg
in the Loans Department and I believe that isn't
going down very well.

Please let me know if you have any instructions.
Your affectionate daughter,
Hannah.

Maggie received the letter on the day that she had arranged to accompany Fred Ellery in his pony and trap to look at the progress being made on the two new rooms of her cottage. The roof had been made good, and a new front window put in. She hoped he would be telling her when she could be settling in.

Although Bridget and Frank were the dearest friends that a woman could ever have, Maggie was feeling frustrated. Bridget, in her innocence, was trying to take over the care of Rosemary. It was time they moved to Killala and started their lives on their own.

"Another letter for yer, Maggie," said Frank, who always seemed to be by the door when the postman duly arrived. "Looks like it's from yer daughter again. Open it now and then you'll see."

"I'd rather open it later," Maggie replied. "I need to work me way up to opening this one, 'cos it'll be about Michael. Yer know, me son?"

"Well, I'll see to Rosemary while yer open it, Maggie. Best to do it now. Fred Ellery will be here soon, then yer won't have any time."

Maggie opened the letter, feeling her body tense in anticipation. Something was bound to be wrong. It was as she thought; now Mr. Arlington was hanging around, Alice would be in there too.

"Bad news, Maggie?" asked Frank, who had poured himself another cup of tea.

"It depends on how yer look at it, Frank. I used to have a manager, his name is Mr. Arlington. I was terrified of him at times when I was building up the business. He was full of contempt for me, though he tried to hide it and we didn't get on very well. I suppose it was because I'm a woman, and women in Mr. Arlington's eyes should stay at home and bake the bread. I also had a running battle with me mother-in-law, Alice, and strangely enough they married and it was them then against me. I told yer that Michael, me son, has come back from the Army and now it seems that they've all got together, made life uncomfortable fer me daughter and her very capable husband. So they've decided to move away and start a builder's yard, which leaves me in a mess."

"It seems to me that you'll be back to where you started then, if this Arlington fellow is trying to take over your company."

"No, Frank, that isn't the problem. It's my son that will cause the problems, if he's allowed to make decisions and oversee the men. He's inclined to be rather arrogant, where Eddie was friendly, yer see."

"I suppose your daughter is hoping you'll go over and settle it," broke in Bridget. "Can't yer write a letter, sort things out from here?"

"I could do, but there will be papers to sign and I need to see Mr. Arlington. It's time the man was put in his place – back into retirement with his nasty wife."

"Oh, Maggie, don't go back to England. Don't take Rosemary to people who won't love her like we do. Leave her with us – yer won't be gone too long."

Bridget looked so downcast that Maggie went to put her arms round her. "Don't take on, Bridget, we'll be back in the blink of an eye, you'll see. Besides, she's got used to taking her mother's milk and she's too young yet fer a bottle."

"What are yer going to tell Fred Ellery?" asked Frank, trying for his wife's sake to delay the baby's departure. "He'll be cross; he's been working overtime to get your place ready so soon."

"He'll get paid, he can have me word on that. In fact, if you'll keep an eye on Rosemary for me, Bridget, I'll go to my bank before he arrives."

As Maggie went up to her bedroom to put on her hat and coat, Bridget broke down and wept.

–

It was the second week of February before Michael decided to confront his sister. His transfer to recruitment had proved to be as boring as he thought it would be, and time lay idling in his hands. His thoughts had turned to his mother's fortune and how his life could be so different if some could be made to come his way.

Hannah greeted his visit with trepidation, wishing that Eddie had not left so early and Olive had not been out with the kids. "Michael, can't you see that we are in the middle of moving? Why have you only just decided to come and see me, when you've had all the time since you left Clatterbridge?"

"I was waiting to see what you were up to, Hannah, and now I see it for myself; you're leaving the sinking ship!"

"Oh, don't be so silly. We're leaving because Eddie has found a builder's yard, which means he can set up in his own business. How can you say the ship's sinking, haven't you seen that development over the road?"

"Yes I have, Hannah, and I've also seen there are no plans on the table for the future. Doesn't that tell you something, that Mother doesn't care about Sheldon any more?"

"No it doesn't, Michael. Mother went away for the sake of her health. She'd been ill for months and didn't seem to be getting any better. Anyway, why would you be caring? You left it all for the Regiment."

"Well, I won't always be in the Army and I'm making sure that there's something left for me. Which brings me to the second problem, how are you going to repay my Loan company?"

"How do you mean, your Loan company? I wasn't aware that we owe Sheldon any money. What for? The new furniture? 'Cos Eddie was seeing to that side of things?"

"He seems to have forgotten to tell you, dear Hannah. Mr. Arlington has noticed an entry in Richard Clegg's accounting book. A whopping £530! Do you think that maybe it was overdoing things?"

"I'm sure Eddie got permission from Mother to borrow it, Michael, and the repayments will not be a problem. I still have my allowance, you know."

"Not for long, Hannah, if I get my way."

Hannah straightened up from filling a large trunk with personal effects that had been left by the door in readiness for Eddie to load into the carriage. "Why are you being like this with me, Michael? I don't understand it. You were the one who left Mother to get on with it. You walked away at a time when she most needed you. It's hardly surprising that she was grateful to us when Eddie and I stepped in."

"Grateful enough to let you live here rent-free and give you an allowance. Grateful enough to give a no-hoper like your pot man a top position in her company. Does he know that your little brat, your first born, belongs to Jeremy Adshead? He wouldn't have been in such a hurry to marry you, if he'd have been in the know."

Hannah felt faint. The air seemed to whistle around her, then she snapped and hit her brother squarely across the face. "How dare you," she snarled. "Whatever Jeremy told you, none of it is true. Little Johnny belongs to Eddie and if anyone says anything different, I'll have them sued for defamation. Now, we can do the transfer of legalities the hard way or the easy way, Michael, but I suggest you keep your evil inferences to yourself."

Michael stood in the doorway, his hand across his cheek, looking in hurt amazement at his virago of a sister. "You always were a bully, Hannah, when we were growing up, and I seem to remember that you were the one who always won."

–

The last three days had not been good for travelling and Maggie was thankful to hail a horse-drawn cab at Woodside Ferry and ask him to take her to the village of Irby.

"Where yer wanting to go in Irby?" asked the genial cabby, seeing a well-dressed lady carrying a baby and looking forward to the jaunt into the countryside that would reward him with a rather large fare.

"I'm not sure where it is. My daughter's address is Redstone House, Mill Hill Road in Irby," Maggie replied. "Is it far?"

"Yes, Missis, it's over an hour away and I wouldn't go to Irby village, neither. The easiest way is the road to Greasby and turn left at Arrowe Brook Lane."

"How fortunate I am to meet such a knowledgeable cab driver," she flattered. "Could yer load my trunk on your vehicle then and perhaps we could be on our way?"

"Certainly, Madam. There's a blanket in there to cover you and the baby. Pass me yer bag, then I'll help yer get in."

Maggie sat back inside the worn interior with its shabby leather seats and cracked wooden floor as the cabby set off up the hill and out onto the highway. She cuddled the sleeping baby to her, reflecting on her journey that had seemed to last for days. Was it only Monday morning when she had said goodbye to Frank and Bridget? To tears and condemnation, because she was taking Rosemary away. Not so much from Frank, thought Maggie, but Bridget had been like a woman possessed! You'd think that she had given birth herself and the child was her own, not Maggie's.

It had been lashing down on the way to Sligo and Billy McDermott's carriage leaked; the ship was tossed on waves as high as coal heaps, and the baby had been fretful and set her nerves a-jangling. So it was good to get back on terra firma, though there was still some way to go.

Her eyelids kept drooping as they trotted along, past a small town, the whitewashed cottages of little hamlets, then acres of fields and dark green forests. She made a concerted effort not to sleep so that the baby wouldn't roll off her very weary knees.

"Not far now," the cabby shouted. "Be there in the next ten minutes, as long as we're not held up with cows and things."

Maggie smiled to herself at the driver's words. What else could hold them up in the countryside, other than a herd of cows? A flock of sheep maybe or a colony of rooks? It showed he was a townie; not used to this slower pace. She looked around in interest at the place that Hannah had chosen to live. It might be miles from anywhere, but the view to the sea was magnificent.

–

Hannah looked up from the perambulator where she had just settled Georgie for his midday sleep. The air was fresh on that bright spring morning, with shoots and buds from flowers and trees brightening up the garden of Redstone House. She walked down the driveway to the tall iron gates. Whoever was visiting in the shabby hired carriage would need a hand with opening them. The driver came rushing to the visitor's aid who was alighting, it seemed, with difficulty. The woman carried a shawl-wrapped bundle and an enormous carpet bag.

"Mother," shouted Hannah, the joy of seeing her loved one again making her shriek delightedly.

"Wait, I'll get these damned gates open, then I'll help you in with your things."

The cabbie went to get the trunk, silently amazed that these two women were related. He had seen that the young one had a baby in the pram and the woman, who looked older than his wife, was carrying a baby as well! Still, it took all sorts, or whatever the saying was, he thought, as he carried the luggage to the front door step.

"Let me look, let me look," shouted Hannah, dancing around her stepmother, trying to take a peek at the baby wrapped up in a woollen shawl.

"In a minute, Hannah," Maggie replied impatiently. "I'll pay the driver and then yer can have a look."

The cabbie smiled, then away walked. He was thirty shillings richer and she hadn't even glared at him.

Maggie followed her stepdaughter into the hallway as Hannah rushed ahead carrying the now-whimpering baby.

"We'll go into the kitchen, Mother. It's warmer there and we can make ourselves comfortable. It sounds as if she wants feeding, so you can use the sitting room if you'd rather. Leave your baggage for Eddie, he'll be in for his dinner in an hour or so. Oh, Mother, this is Jenny, our cook. This is my Mother, Jenny. She's travelled all the way from Ireland, so I'm sure she could do with a cup of tea. Here, have Rosemary back, I know who she's been named after, don't I? I'll go and get our Johnny. I wonder if he'll remember you! He's in the orchard with Sadie; they've been looking at the pretty flowers on the trees."

Maggie sat on a chair pulled up to the table and rocked little Rosemary, hoping that the child would go to sleep, rather than having to disappear to a different room to feed her. The elderly cook brought her a cup of tea then off she went to her cooking again. The place was cluttered with pots for washing and the smell of cabbage filled the air. Maggie felt drowsy and tremendously hungry. Her breakfast had been a slice of bread and dripping, from a tea shed on the quay.

Suddenly there was a commotion at the scullery door as a little boy came tottering through, holding the hand of his nursemaid, a pretty young woman with carroty coloured hair and pink in the cheeks from running. Hannah followed, smiling broadly, as her son looked up at Maggie and the baby with curious eyes. He suddenly launched himself against her, making excited gobbledegook noises and jumping up and down. Maggie felt tears begin to well as she looked upon his eager little face.

"Oh, Hannah," she whispered. "I've missed yer so, especially little Johnny. Hasn't he grown?"

"Come, Mother," Hannah said, also feeling overcome. "We'll go into the other room and leave Sadie and Jenny alone."

"So, how was it, Mother?" asked Hannah sympathetically, as she noticed the dark smudges of tiredness and the hopeless look in Maggie's eyes.

"Difficult, Hannah. A woman of my age shouldn't get into situations like I did. She's a beautiful child, but I don't have the energy I used to. Serves me right fer falling for Johnny's silvery tongue."

"Poor Mother, I really do feel for you. I've been lucky with having Olive and now Sadie to help me, but I can imagine if I was older I couldn't cope alone. Anyway, let me have a good look at her. Give her to me; let's get her out of the shawl so I can see her hands and feet. Oh, just look at you in your pretty little frock and tiny bootees! Did you make these, Mother? Oh you must have done. I had to pass on Johnny's clothes to Georgie this time." She lowered her voice in case her servants could hear her. "We'll have to talk alone later. Eddie has done something you might disapprove of, but at the time he couldn't think of anything else to do. You're staying, aren't you? I can have a bed made up for you in the back bedroom and Rosemary can sleep in one of the tallboy drawers. You'll notice we don't have much in the way of furniture; only bits and pieces that the Kennets left behind."

Maggie nodded. She had noticed the threadbare rugs on the cold stone floors, the moth-eaten curtains that hung at the windows, the sparsely furnished sitting room and nothing in the hall. She shuddered when she thought of what Hannah had got used to in her life at Selwyn Lodge.

"We've lots of land though, and an orchard, a paddock and lots of trees. There's a stable and a workshop that Eddie will make into a builder's yard. We have a quarry too, which will go someway to paying our bills."

"And two servants to pay wages to, Hannah. How on earth have you been managing since I've been away?"

"From my allowance, and of course Eddie's wages from Sheldon, but he finished there last week. Up to now Michael has not put a stop to my allowance, which is giving Eddie a fighting chance of setting up for himself."

There came a knock on the door as Maggie began to formulate some questions for her stepdaughter. Sadie put her head around it. "Dinner on the table in ten minutes, Missis. I take it your mother's staying so I've laid an extra place."

"Ten minutes to try to feed my baby, Hannah. Would yer leave us and I'll wake her, then I'll see if she'll have a go."

"She's in the front room, Eddie," said Hannah, as her husband walked in through the back door and took off his jacket.

"Who is?" asked Eddie, wondering who on earth could be in the sitting room. His heart sank into his boots when he thought it might be Alice or even Michael, then he quickly realised they didn't know where they'd moved to.

"Mother and her little girl, Rosemary. She's feeding her and naturally she wants a bit of privacy. Which reminds me, I'll be needing to feed Georgie in an hour or so. Are you rushing off after dinner, Eddie? I don't want to leave Mother on her own."

"I'll look after Johnny fer yer, if yer want," broke in Sadie. "He can come with me after I've fed him his dinner, then he'll be out of the road."

"Oh, thank you," answered Hannah, pleased that her maid had offered her help though it was really her half day off. That's what she liked about both her servants; nothing was too much trouble and they didn't ask for extra pay.

"How's she looking?" asked Eddie, as the couple walked into the orchard while they waited for their meal to be served. Neither had got their servants' measure and didn't want to be overheard.

"A lot plumper, but her face looks older and haggard. That sparkle she used to have has gone and her eyes look full of misery."

"Has she said anything about Sheldon, what her plans are, what she'll do with Michael? Is she in any position, now she has the baby, to carry on?"

"Oh, hang on, Eddie, she's only just got here. Give her a chance. I'll suggest I take care of Rosemary this afternoon, while she has a sleep in her bedroom. Yes, she's staying, Eddie. Then perhaps this evening we can all sit round and discuss it."

"As long as she doesn't get on at me for anything. I did the best that I could fer her and I do deserve that loan."

Chapter 22

"Have yer seen any sight of your Uncle, Eddie?" Maggie asked, as the three of them settled in front of the fire in the sitting room, that evening. "I wondered if he had called in to see your parents at Christmas time. He has in the past, hasn't he?"

Eddie shook his head, regretfully. "No, no one's seen him since yer came over together that time from Liverpool, but me Dad did say he was thinking of giving the sea up and starting a business somewhere."

"Aye, that's what I thought, but he didn't tell him where?"

Eddie shook his head again and wondered when they were going to get round to discussing the business. He felt unsure and very nervous at what Maggie's reaction would be to him taking the loan. Hannah also felt tense on her husband's behalf; he shouldn't have done it without consulting her mother. Maggie could get very angry if she thought someone was trying to pull the wool over her eyes.

"So what do yer think of Rosemary, then?" This was Maggie trying to lull the conversation. She knew the couple had a lot to say, but wasn't ready to hear it yet.

"She's beautiful, a little poppet," Hannah cried. "I hope I have one just like her next time."

"She looks like Georgie, both have the hair colour and dark eyes. Don't yer think so, Maggie?"

"Probably because they're both Dockertys, Eddie. I'm sure that Hannah has already told yer the tale."

Eddie coloured slightly and looked at Hannah. "Yes, but it's up to you what yer do with yer life."

"Shocking behaviour, though. A woman of my age gallivanting off and having an affair with your uncle. Not the done thing, eh, Eddie?"

"Well, it seems to have caused a lot of complications."

"Exactly, and that's why I've come back, and you're here, and me baby is sleeping upstairs with your two."

"Mmm," said Eddie.

"So who wants to start first? Shall I?" The couple nodded. "Well, I want to know what happened from the very beginning. I trusted yer both to get on with things while I got on with what I had to do in Ireland. Everything was legal; you had all the authorisation, Eddie. You, Hannah, only had to continue taking care of Selwyn Lodge. Then I get a letter. Michael's come back from the Army. So, had I left him in charge, made him my manager? No, it was you, Eddie and now you've let me down."

"But what could we have done, Mother?" Hannah cried, seeing the hurt in Maggie's eyes. "I'm not your legal daughter, am I? I had Grandmama on my back pointing her fingers, Michael threatening to see a solicitor and Mr. Arlington poking his nose in. We were worried at what they could do to us, because Eddie had borrowed a substantial loan. We were treading on egg shells. Like I said, we didn't know what they were up to, so we panicked and here we are telling you the tale."

"Nothing changes, Hannah," Maggie said sadly. "Alice has had it in fer me since your father went off to work fer Lord Belsham. She hated the fact that I stood on me own two feet and made a success of my business. This would be her chance to create my downfall. By putting Michael into Sheldon, she knows the place will fail."

"So what can we do then?" Eddie said "I don't want to go back there, Maggie. I've a chance here of building up a good business for meself. There's a quarry included with the property and I can sell the stone on to local tradesmen and there's a place at the back, which I can turn into a builders' yard. Hannah loves it here, don't yer darlin'? And there's space when they're older, fer the kids to run and play."

"I suppose I'll have to sort it out meself then, though I'm loathe to go just yet, as you can see. I'm tired and Rosemary takes a lot of energy. It could wait another week, don't yer think?"

"Oh, yes," Hannah said eagerly, relieved that Eddie and she had got off so lightly. "You're very welcome to stay, that's if you don't mind the austerity. But, Mother, you've made no mention of this loan from Sheldon. Richard Clegg is not to blame; he did ask for collateral."

"You're frightening me now, Hannah. How much was the loan for? Eddie did have authorisation, after all."

"Five hundred and thirty pounds," Eddie mumbled, waiting for his mother-in-law to erupt in flames.

"Oh, is that all? I thought you'd gone and bankrupted me. Though I suppose a letter to let me know would have saved you both from going to Hell and back, as it were."

-

381

The next morning was as bright and spring like as the day before and Maggie, having lain in bed most of the night worrying about the future, suggested that Hannah take her for a guided tour of the surrounding area.

"It will take me mind off me troubles, Hannah and I'm sure the walk will do us all good." They stood at the side of the narrow country lane, deciding on their direction. Redstone House was near a crossroads, so they had four different ways in which they could go.

"If we go down that way, it leads to Frankby," Hannah said. "There's a village, a church and an old manor house. If we go to the left, it eventually leads to Caldy shore; to the right lies the village of Greasby – that's at the bottom of Arrowe Brook lane. Then up there is Irby, with a village, a tavern and another manorial hall."

"What do you feel up to then? We've got the babies to consider and little Johnny too. Which do yer think is the shortest way for us?"

"I think we'll go up this way. There's a duck pond by the windmill that Johnny will be interested in, then we'll cut through the lane to a tea shack and we can have a little rest. Are you sure you don't want Rosemary opposite Georgie in the perambulator? Johnny can walk very well now, you know."

"No, I like her here next to me, Hannah, tucked up in my nice warm shawl. Yer know in Ireland they don't have these fancy prams that we have. All the mothers that I saw carried their babies under their shawls."

The two women walked companionably along, taking in the fresh air and cooing to Georgie and Rosemary. Johnny gabbled unintelligibly, pointing out 'birdies' as they flew in and out of the hedgerows intent on making their nests, mooing as he heard the cows lowing in the pastures nearby and clapping his hands excitedly when he saw the plump white ducklings as they swam around the pond.

"He loves coming along here, Mother. Watch. Now here's the windmill, Johnny. What do the sails on the windmill do? Whoooooooooosh!"

Both of them laughed as the little boy made circling movements with his arms. It was a time of contentment for Maggie and she felt all her tension begin to drain away.

Later, when they sat having their drinks in the friendly woman's garden, Maggie asked the questions that had begun to niggle her. "Yer know, Hannah, I find it puzzling that you and Eddie gave in to Michael so easily. Is there something yer hiding; something yer not telling me? It's hard to understand, especially when I know that as a child you would never give in to your brother. He was always coming 'telling' when he couldn't get his way."

"Jeremy Adshead, Mother!" Hannah replied, blushing as she said the name, but knowing that Maggie would understand.

"Well, the little so and so. How did he find out about it? What did he say? Oh no, he never tried to blackmail you?"

"I faced him out and told him I'd sue for defamation; that Johnny is my husband's child. But I couldn't let even a whisper get to Eddie's ears."

"Of course not," Maggie soothed. "Well, now he's made me mind up. I'll sell the company from under him; then he'll get what he deserves."

"No, Mother! You can't do that. You've been building Sheldon up for over twenty years. He's right, it's his inheritance, not mine nor Eddie's or the children's. What you have is his."

"Yes, but not until I'm dead, Hannah, and I'm not willing to hand over the reins to him just yet. Then there's Rosemary. How am I going to explain her existence? You see, I had my life planned out until I got your letter. I'd bought a small cottage in Killala and I was going to live there with Rosemary."

"Then Eddie and I threw the towel in and we've left you high and dry."

"Something like that. I thought that Michael was safely with his regiment, that I wouldn't have to face the problem fer many years to come."

"Another cup, ladies?" The woman who ran the tea shack came to their table with a teapot in her hand. "And we've some freshly made biscuits, if the little boy would like one to eat with his lemon drink."

"Thank you, but we're just going," Maggie replied. "Can I pay yer what we owe? A nice cup of tea by the way, Missis, and we'll buy a few of your biscuits for little Johnny to be munching on."

"I was just saying to my daughter," the woman said to Hannah. "You're the lady who bought the Kennet's house down at the crossroads, aren't you? Are these all your little babies too?"

Maggie looked at Hannah helplessly. She was going to have to get used to this. People asking, people being curious, even if it was kindly meant. So she was shocked when Hannah took the problem from her and smilingly gestured at the little ones.

"This one is Johnny, he's my eldest and a little monster. Then the baby in the pram is Georgie and over here is Georgie's twin. Her name is Rosemary."

"Oh, they're all little darlings, aren't they? And Rosemary, what a pretty name. Well, I'd better let yer get on then. You must be so proud to be their granny."

The woman smiled at them happily, then went back to the tea shack to get the biscuits that Maggie had said she would take with her.

"What was that all about, Hannah?" said Maggie tersely, as they walked up the hill to the village. "Did yer have to show me up like that? I could have explained meself, yer know."

"Well yes, you could have, Mother, but what would you have said? I'm a mum again at forty-two?"

"Women do have babies at my age, Hannah and I'll have yer know I'm not forty-two until August."

"Yes and what if it was mentioned to someone who knows you? Hannah Dockerty's mother has a baby too, you know!"

"You've an answer fer everything, you have. Pity yer couldn't have thought of something better than leaving me to face all these problems you've created; then I could be hiding meself in Killala and not being such an embarrassment."

"Natter natter. Natter natter," Hannah covered her ears with her hands, pretending she couldn't hear what Maggie said.

"Oh, you," Maggie said laughing. "You never change, do yer? I remember that's what yer used to do when you were just a child yerself."

"Now here we are in Irby, Mother. To your right, you'll see the Anchor Inn. Eddie's been in there and he said they do a good drop of porter. To my left is Manor Farm, which has been on that site for nearly a hundred years. Over in the trees is the manor house. A black and white half–timbered dwelling that is now in use as a farmhouse. In the village is a blacksmith, a wheelwright, a shoemakers and a general store. How's that, Mother? A potted version of what there is to see in Irby. In modulated tones, copied from Miss Buckley, my old teacher, when she showed us round the Chester walls!"

Maggie started to laugh again. Her spirits were beginning to lighten by the minute. "I knew that expensive education would stand yer in good stead one day, Hannah."

"So what do you think?"

"Think about what?"

"You know, me looking after Rosemary while you go and sort out this empire of yours?"

"Oh, I don't know, Hannah, she's my responsibility. Let me give it a few more days, then I'll let yer know how I feel."

—

It was drizzling with rain on the day that Maggie returned to Selwyn Lodge, having borrowed the carriage and horses from Eddie. With his mother-in-law's encouragement, he was seeing a local inhabitant, who had applied for the position of quarry foreman. Her clothes were dripping as she stabled the horses, rubbed them down, gave them a bucket of feed, then let herself in by way of the conservatory.

The house was silent, other than a wooden clock ticking away on the mantelpiece. The kitchen range stared at her blankly as she took off her travelling coat and hung it over the wooden clothes maid that someone had left unfolded there. It was chilly and the place smelt damp.

There was a kind of dreary sadness in the room, as if it knew it had been abandoned. Joan had gone, Olive had gone. Never to come back and work in her kitchen again.

Maggie shivered and started to make up the fire with what was left of the kindling. She checked there was coal in the scuttle; at least she was able to make herself a cup of tea. She wandered while the fire took hold in the range, checking windows and doors, taking stock of the furniture, opening curtains that someone had left closed. She nibbled on a piece of cheese that Hannah had wrapped in a cloth for her, along with a twist of tea and a half loaf of bread, waiting with impatience for the kettle to sing.

Her eyes met the hands of the clock; it was twenty-five past two. She thought about her little girl and wondered what she had done. Was the child already missing her, knowing that the breasts that suckled her weren't the one's she'd got used to? Was she being lovingly cuddled or was Hannah too busy with Georgie, her little son?

Maggie cradled her head in her hands, trying not to let the tears start flowing. This was something she had to do; a sacrifice she felt was necessary. So sitting there moping wasn't helping anyone. She made her drink, ate her food, then got changed into her finery.

-

"Good afternoon, can I help you?" Another new girl on the office desk, thought Maggie, as she entered the Sheldon rooms.

"I'm Maggie Haines, the owner of this place. Kindly tell the manager I would like a word."

"Oh," said the young woman in a startled tone.

"Do you want to see Mr. Clegg or Mr. Arlington, Mrs. Haines?"

"I think both of them will do, don't you?"

"Would you like to go on up then, Mrs. Haines? Both are in the Loan Department, going through some papers there."

"I'd like that, thank you." Maggie walked quietly up the carpeted stairs.

"Good afternoon, Mr. Arlington, Richard," Maggie said, as she opened the door of the office. Why should she knock anyway? The place belonged to her.

She could see the men had got a shock when they both spun around upon hearing her voice. They seemed to be having a serious conversation, standing by the filing cabinets at the far end of the room.

"Maggie!"

"Mrs. Haines!"

Both men spoke at the same time when they saw her. Both men came towards her, and both outstretched a hand.

It was Mr. Arlington who got to Maggie first, greeting her in a solicitous manner while inquiring of her health, pulling out a chair for her and asking how long she had been back.

"Richard, would you get Mrs. Haines a coffee? Two sugars wasn't it, my dear? And Richard, would you bring me one as well?" Arlington was trying to put the young man in his place.

"Why, thank you, Mr. Arlington, and Richard, perhaps you would like to get yourself a coffee too. I have quite a lot to say, so I'll wait until you come back."

"Something amiss, dear lady?" Arlington asked, while they sat facing each other across the office desk, him trying to ascertain the reason for her visit before his protégé returned.

"And may I say that it looks as if your holiday has done you a power of good. You'll be surprised to see me here as well as Mr. Clegg, won't you? Did you know your son-in-law left him in the lurch and I felt it my duty to assist him?"

"I had heard, and that's why I'm here today, Mr. Arlington. I need to sort out what's happening and see what I can do."

Mr. Arlington went quiet then and she observed him under lowered lashes, until the silence became uncomfortable and she began to fiddle with her hem. He tapped a foot and shifted about, then walked to a cabinet and then came back. In his hand he carried a paper wallet and placed it on the desk before her without an explanation of what was within.

"Ah, yer back then, Richard. Shall I be Mother or shall I let you pour?"

Richard smiled at her attempt to lighten the mood; perhaps now they could get back to normal again. "Now then, Maggie, before we make a start I'd like you to have a look at that file I've just placed before you. You will notice that your son-in-law has taken out a substantial loan without your permission. Mr. Clegg here did ask him for collateral, but he refused to give it. Am I to take it that Eddie Dockerty is a thief?"

"Strong words, Mr. Arlington," replied Maggie, as in the background she heard Richard gasp at the man's affront. He would have adopted a more subtle approach if the matter had been left to him.

"In fact I gave him my authorisation, but it was held up, as I remember, in the post."

"Oh." Arlington looked rather agitated. "I wish I'd known that earlier; we were thinking of taking court proceedings against the man."

"In whose name, Mr. Arlington? Mine or Sheldon's? Surely yer didn't think that I'd be suing one of me own?"

"I don't know what to think," he began, looking helplessly at Richard. "It was your mother-in-law who suggested that I oversee the business until such time your son returned."

"Ah, Michael. I wondered when we would get on to him. Have I missed something? When was my funeral? Did yer send me a floral wreath? Was there a mention of it in the Chester broadsheet? Because I seemed to have missed it all, yer know."

"Oh, come now, Maggie, you can see our point of view. Michael had come home from India and you had disappeared off the face of the earth. It was natural that his grandmama would want him to be restored to his rightful place as your inheritor."

"This company was doing fine under the steward-ship of my son-in-law. As far as I'm aware, Richard was running the Loan Department just as well. Because of your wife's interference, Mr. Arlington, I have lost a very good Works Manager and the company of my family in our home at Selwyn Lodge. I am reliably informed that Michael still has three years to do in his regiment. What am I to do meantime, run the place meself?"

"Well, yes. If you're not requiring my help and from the tone of your voice it seems you won't be wanting me to, it appears you will have to run Sheldon, until such times that your son is able to take over. But remember, my dear lady, that you are running your business in a man's world. Men don't take kindly to women proprietors, as you already know."

"Yes, you've always made that very clear, a woman's place is in the home. But what do *you* say about it, Richard? Are you still willing to work for me?"

The young man nodded and smiled at Maggie gratefully.

"Good, I'm glad to hear that, because now I'm going to tell yer of me plan. I've decided to sell Sheldon, both the loans and the property. You may look alarmed, Mr. Arlington, but it's a decision that I'll not be thwarted from."

"But my dear… Surely this needs some thinking through? What about Michael? Alice will be so angry…"

"Good day, Mr. Arlington, and thank you fer what you've done."

—

Maggie sat on the sofa in the drawing room later, still trembling a little from her 'run in' with Mr. Arlington. She sipped at a warming brandy while she thought on what Mr. Arlington would call 'her audacity'. Well, she'd seen him off, hadn't she? No more interference; no more snide remarks from Alice. Once she had sold the business she could do just as she pleased. She thought for a moment of Rosemary. Soon, she'd be able to claim her back and take her to their cottage in Killala. Though she'd miss the view of the Welsh hills from her bedroom window; it was little enough sacrifice to be with her child.

The place was warm now and the boiler hot, so after checking on the horses, Maggie soaked herself for a while in a scented bath. There was thinking to do and plans to make. An early night would see her right.

The first shafts of sunlight poked their way through the chink in Maggie's bedroom curtains next morning. She awoke slowly, surprisingly refreshed in her mind, considering all the thoughts that had been churning around her head the night before. It was time to put her plans into action. First she'd feed the horses, visit the butcher and grocer, then catch the midday train to Chester to see her solicitor. She wandered into the bathroom wearing her morning gown, then heard the postman knocking on the front door. The knocking grew louder; more impatient. So annoyed was Maggie that she ran in anger down the stairs. She would tell that Alec to stop his noise in no uncertain terms!

"What do yer thinking you're doing, Alec?" she shouted through the door, as she fumbled with the locks and bolts and cursed as she scraped her hand. But it wasn't the postman standing there; it was an entirely different man.

"Johnny!" Maggie gaped. He'd come back again after all this time. There he was on her doorstep, looking haggard, wild and bleary-eyed.

"I've come to see me daughter, Maggie."

"How did yer get to know?"

"From Fred Ellery, then the Heaneys... I heard from the solicitor that you had bought my house. Maggie, why didn't you tell me? Why give birth to our baby without the slightest hint?"

She opened the front door wider, feeling her spirits rising as she looked upon his face. "I've got a lot to tell yer, Johnny. I think you'd best come in."